RING

OF

DESTINY

RING

OF

DESTINY

RONALD J. RAYMOND, JR.
NANCY MAXWELL

MILL CITY PRESS *Minneapolis*

Mill City Press, Inc.
212 3rd Avenue North, Suite 290
Minneapolis, MN 55401
612.455.2294
www.millcitypublishing.com

ISBN-13: 978-1-937600-95-2
LCCN: 2012933496

Book design by Kristeen Ott

Printed in the United States of America

ACKNOWLEDGMENTS

We are thankful to our family and friends
who supported and encouraged us through
the many hours devoted to writing this book.
We deeply appreciate those who edited this work
and provided invaluable suggestions.

CHAPTER ONE

Eleonore ascended the staircase of the Pavillon de Flore and swept through the enfilade of rooms that led to the private apartment, nodding distractedly to the stone-faced ushers who silently opened each door before her. The antechamber was almost empty at this time of night, and Eleonore noticed only three pages, on hand to run errands should there be such a need, leaning casually against the dark red wall. In the service salon a handful of officers, dramatic in their gold braid epaulets, richly colored capes, and feathered tricorn hats, clustered in earnest conversation, oblivious to any but those of their own rank. The tall paneled doors of the topographical room closed silently behind her as she crossed the threshold.

Frowning in concentration and absent-mindedly massaging his stomach, the emperor sat hunched at his desk, scanning documents and scratching hasty comments in the margins. Eleonore had but a moment to take in the now familiar surroundings, the straight-backed, mono-grammed chairs, the grand desk with the golden lion pedestals, and the map of Egypt permanently opened on a side table, before he sprang up to greet her. As usual, he was courteous and faintly affectionate, but perfunctory.

"At last, something far more compelling to look at than letters from my officers. That general Menou is an ass! But you, Madame, are pleasing to my eye, and, if the past can be trusted, pleasing in other ways as well." He gazed at her intently, touched her cheek and then tweaked her chin a little too roughly.

Eleonore bowed her head and replied, "Sire, I am honored if my company is pleasing to you."

"Come, sit, and speak to me of your light hearted life." Grasping her elbow, he guided her to the bedroom.

Eleonore knew that the emperor was not in love with her, nor she with him, although, like so many, she was fascinated by the power of his personality and position. His lovemaking fulfilled a physical need, just like hunger or thirst, and he satisfied it with the same urgency and haste.

Afterward, he kissed her affectionately, teased her about being a seductress, and then moved to his dressing room. Eleonore knew that he would bathe, dress, and return to his work immediately. Normally she would have left as quickly, but this time she lingered on the bed for a few moments, taking in the simple but luxurious furnishings of the room, the green damask drapery, the highly polished parquet floors, and the glittering chandelier. Something was different this time, and she knew with a women's intuitive certainty that she had just conceived. She would be carrying the emperor's child. Turning her head to the side, she noticed, on a nearby table, a porcelain box with its top left carelessly off to the side and a tangle of gold chain spilling over its edges. The gold letters of the Empress Josephine's initials were clearly visible on the front of the box. Sighing, Eleonore rose and dressed, taking time to rearrange her hair and smooth her gown. Moving toward the door, she paused to look at the contents of the box again, idly sorting the pieces with her index finger. There was a wide, gold, delicately engraved bangle, a number of single earrings, their mates probably lost at some state ball, a few loose pearls, and some rings, none of them with diamonds. Eleonore clicked her tongue with a touch of disappointment. She turned over one of the rings, observed its unusual yellow and orange stone which seemed to flicker like a candle, and, on impulse, slipped it onto her own finger before departing from the palace.

"Well, if nothing else I can give this ring to my child to prove his heritage," Elenore whispered to herself.

CHAPTER TWO

The only access to the Eden-like haven was via a narrow, unmarked dirt road, which snaked through woodland to arrive at a pristine, clear blue lake. The setting offered a sanctuary to many different birds. Yellow-bellied Sapsuckers with their bright red crowns sent nasal mewing and squealing sounds across the lake celebrating their freedom. Then, as if orchestrated, their beautiful voices ceased for a few moments and they began their character-istic fast drumming into tree bark. Flitting across the surface of the water the olive colored Acadian Flycatchers, emitting their plaintive sound like a rising *per-wee,* looked like trapeze artists swinging from their perches. The swallows seemed content to sit peacefully in the trees, calling to each other with a series of buzzy, short, *dzrrt* notes. Under all of this activity Wood Ducks and American Black Ducks glided across the lake, interested only in feeding on the life under the water. Squirrels scurried about, busily attending to the myriad pinecones littering the woodland floor.

Alice Hawkins had succeeded brilliantly. She had raised sufficient money from the members of the SELF group and had purchased this magnificent property for their meeting place and headquarters. The surroundings, tranquil, quiet, and conducive to meditation, were perfect for the new headquarters. Tucked in a small copse on the property stood the original estate house. An 1830 colonial, it had classic proportions and fine details that had been grand in their day. Four graceful Corinthian columns balanced the long front porch, and a handsomely carved wooden door opened into the fourteen-room interior. The tread of countless feet had worn the paint to the bare wood on the airy porch, and, like a trusted confidante, the house seemed to have nurtured its many inhabitants. The main room on the ground floor was wide and expansive, having once been used as the meeting place for a local church congregation. A battered pump organ, long past its prime, sat abandoned in a corner. On the north side the house was surrounded by stately pine trees whose towering peaks seemed to merge with the sky, while to the south a field of sweet smelling wild alfalfa interspersed with echinacea offered a peaceful vista. The house faced east, where an abundance of shrubs, wild flowers, and live oak trees separated it from the lake. Gentle breezes blew across the water, carrying the mingling fragrances of the field and refreshing the house with clean, calming air. Remote and obscured by the wilderness around it, the house was impossible to find unless one was specifically directed there.

In the morning room, Adam and Monica sat frozen, struck mute by what they had just read in the newspaper lying before them on the wrought iron table.

"Monica, listen to this!" Adam began reading aloud.

"This self-proclaimed spiritual guru appears to have brainwashed hundreds of people into joining his cult, SELF, and represents himself as a god, demanding blind obedience from his followers. He is suspected of using psychedelics to manipulate people. Reportedly an anarchist, he has been under investigation by the CIA for plotting subversive activities. The FBI and local police are looking for this doctor in connection with drug trafficking and the death of a woman earlier this year. His whereabouts are unknown and he is to be considered dangerous. Is this Jonestown all over again?"

Monica stared emptily at the stylized lion's paw of the table leg, unable to pull her gaze away. Her face had turned ashen, and she trembled with fear as she mindlessly twisted the opal ring on her right index finger. Unable to control her panic Monica cried, "I can't believe this! What on earth is going on? Adam, what does this mean?"

The other members of SELF, busy setting up Adam's equipment, were unaware of the article and went about their tasks with a contagious air of quiet joy and tranquility, confident that they were building the perfect setting to advance the purpose of their group. The stereo system had been installed and several Mozart disks were set to play. The familiar strains of *Eine Kleine Nacht-musik* drifted through the rooms, and several members hummed along, content to be in each other's company and happy to be contributing to the project. Chloe Belmon, who had a live-in maid and probably hadn't touched a cleaning implement in her own house for years, was on her hands and knees scrubbing the kitchen floor. She and Susan Atkins had already washed all the old white wooden cabinets. Men were moving furniture around, getting ample advice from the women about the placement of each piece. Jack Theabold and Perry Salacito, two of the computer geniuses in the group, were wiring the instruments.

In the midst of all the activity, Adam and

Monica sat immobilized, overcome by the implications of the newspaper article. Instinctively they grasped each other's hands and squeezed in silent communication. Adam was aware of Monica's opal ring digging into the flesh of his palm. It felt strangely hot. Their bewildered silence was broken by the scream of an electronic megaphone.

"Everyone out of the house with your hands in the air!" There was no identification of the speaker, but the loud metallic voice screeched again.

"Everyone out of the house! Immediately, with your hands in the air!" Panic quickly spread among the people in the house, and despite their training and work on internal control, they screamed hysterically. Everyone automatically turned to Adam in search of explanation. He ran to the window and cautiously parted the translucent curtains to peek outside.

"For God's sake!" he yelled, "It looks like a swat team out there! They've got guns! Looks like automatic weapons. I can't see them clearly. They're all in black and hiding in the bushes. God! There are more behind the trees!"

He could feel the veins in his temples swelling and pulsing and every muscle in his body tightening. His blood raced, his neck throbbed, and his heart felt like a pounding bass drum. Sweat dripped from his forehead into his eyes and began to blur his vision. He glanced at Monica. Her face was pale. Her eyes were wide with alarm and her mouth formed an "o" of fear. The commanding voice barked again.

"This is the last warning, everyone out of the house, single file, hands over your heads." Paralyzed by confusion and fear, the group stared at Adam.

Adam released the curtain to face his frightened group. "I have no idea who those guys are or what they want. They haven't identified themselves. I have to figure this out and decide what we'll do."

At that moment a barrage of terrifyingly loud shots rang out. Glass shattered into thousands of tiny pieces, flying through the room in a lightening explosion. It happened so unexpectedly and quickly that no one had a chance to take cover. Tiny shards of glass and splinters of wood struck randomly. The deadly debris wounded people, and blood splattered the newly painted walls.

Eunice screamed, "John's been hit! Oh my Lord, he's hurt bad! God help us! Adam, what is going on?"

Adam thought quickly. "It must be me they're after. I'll leave. Then if the rest of you walk out as they ordered, you'll be okay."

He dashed for the back door. "Monica, you walk out with the rest."

Monica hesitated and then turned to Adam. "No way, I am coming with you."

"No, it's not safe, it's me they want. You read the newspaper. I have to figure out what to do."

"Adam, I said I'm coming with you."

Adam grabbed her hand and they fled out the back door. Crouching to conceal themselves, they worked their way into the underbrush behind the house and headed for the relative protection of the woods. In an instant they realized that the men in black were pursuing them. Thorns and branches scratched and clutched at Adam and Monica, as if in league with their pursuers. Blood seeped through their clothing, but they were too frightened to notice either the bleeding or the pain inflicted by the bushes. Monica's light cotton blouse tore open, exposing her skin to the ripping thorns. They dove behind a boulder, and Adam peered over the top.

"We seem to be gaining on them a bit," Adam whispered breathlessly. "Don't move in a straight line. Follow me! This way! Just keep moving. We'll shake these guys."

"Why this way? How would you know which way to go?"

"I just know, that's all. Just stay with me."

Eventually they reached a wide stream that fed the lake below.

"We'll cross here. We'll lose those bastards

- whoever they are." Grabbing Monica's hand Adam charged into the water. Monica stiffened, reluctant to jump into the dark unknown depths.

"It isn't that deep, Monica. Just keep going. We can't slow down. When we get to the other side we should separate."

"No! We stay together."

Adam glanced over his shoulder. "I can still see them. I think they're gaining on us."

The chilling water of the stream dulled the pain of their bruises and scratches, but was also cold enough to make them aware of the numbness that wrapped itself around their ankles and legs.

"Faster, faster!" Adam yelled. "We have to reach a road and try to hitch a ride. Then I'll figure out what to do."

"Adam, don't forget that your picture was in the paper. It could be dangerous for us to be picked up."

"I'll cross that bridge when I get to it."

Several shots rang out but the bullets fell wide.

"This is crazy! Who are these guys? They're gonna kill us! Move faster Monica!"

Monica, panting and crying, collapsed to her knees. "I can't go any further. Maybe you should stop and try to talk to them. Find out who they are and what they want."

"Are you crazy? We can't stop. They don't want to talk. They want to kill us! Don't you realize they've been shooting at us? Those aren't cap guns you're hearing! That's live ammo! And you want to talk to them? Get up! We gotta get outa here now!"

"Adam! Who are these guys? What haven't you told me?"

CHAPTER THREE

Dr. Peterson had just finished his session with Donna and not a moment too soon. Fifty minutes of listening to her myriad grievances about her husband was about all he could take. Lamentations that he didn't spend enough time with her, didn't pay attention to her, didn't listen to her, and did nothing to help with the three children had led her to conclude that she was not important to him. Donna wanted to be the most important person in the world to someone; it wasn't working with her husband, and Dr. Peterson knew he would be the next target for the fulfillment of her needs. Years of experience warned him that it would not be long before she began to test him with some form of acting out. Calls at all hours of the night, reports to others that her analyst had made advances, and late night emergencies would soon begin. Donna had already begun to ask him about his marriage. She had confided to Dr. Peterson that she was sexually deprived and in the last moments of the session had asked, "Am I way off? How often do you have sex with your wife?"

With a coy look she crossed her legs, revealing a good portion of her upper thigh and the edge of blue lace underwear.

"Maybe this is a problem area for you also, Adam."

He was worn out by the number of women who had projected onto him those qualities that they felt were lacking in their husbands.

To the non-psychologist, the job of listening to someone like Donna, might seem like an easy one, but Adam Peterson had listened to thousands of Donnas, thousands of wives and husbands complaining over the years, and the task of responding to their multitude of depressions, fears, obsessions, and delusions was exhausting. Each of his responses throughout the day had to be a calculated one. There was no room for informal conversation. There is no water cooler talk for a psychologist.

Donna being his last appointment of the day, Adam allowed himself to collapse into his comfortable leather reclining chair. He was a moderate size man, about five-feet-ten-inches tall, but thought that twelve hours of sitting each day had compressed his spine and made him shorter, and he was reminded of this as he massaged the knotted muscles of his back. Broad shoulders and a mesomorphic physique revealed his dedication to daily exercise and Tae Kwon Do. His angular jaw line and well-defined cheekbones suggested determination and courage. A horseshoe of gray hair circled his otherwise baldhead. His hazel eyes were an asset, communicating sincerity and openness. People meeting Adam read into his naturally empathic expression a permission to share their worries and problems in the most inappropriate places. It was one of the reasons he loathed cocktail parties. He also found the nonsensical chatter of suburban lawns, the one-upmanship of the last exotic vacation, and insider talk from the political people in the Washington, DC area intolerable. It amazed him that so many people seemed to feel that they could use a social gathering to ask him about family, children, and sexual matters. Perhaps most annoying were their innuendoes that he had gleaned classified information from the wide array of political dignitaries who saw him in therapy or whose spouses he was treating. He could never get away from work.

As Adam reclined, he mused about his office. Anyone walking in would admire and see it as a pleasant, comfortable, and relaxing place. The Capital area was full of affluent clients with varied and interesting backgrounds, and it was important for him to maintain an office that matched the expectations of his client population. In the center of a generously proportioned room sat four rich dark brown leather recliners facing each other to form a smaller square. Adam's formal redwood desk sat in the corner, adjacent to a window, but he used it only for paper work, believing that sitting behind a desk created a barrier to a relationship. With its elaborately carved borders and seven-foot length, the desk was imposing, but, although beautiful and grand, it was far too pretentious for his personality. It was there because his wife, Ellen, had found it at an antique store and thought it perfect to convey the image she believed he should project. The Persian rug that anchored the configuration of leather recliner chairs was another one of her purchases. She had insisted that he have this particular rug, at the cost of twelve thousand dollars. Every so often, as he gazed at it, the scene at the rug dealer returned and he recalled Ellen's deprecating words, as she insisted on the purchase. "It's time you left the middle class dear, and recognize who we are. You moved up from motel modern when you married me. Your patients will judge you by your office. Class attracts class."

The walls of the room were finished with warm mahogany paneling and heavy, carved molding around the ceiling. A small oval redwood table stood next to each chair, with the requisite tissue box on each one, for the tears that so often flowed from his patients. Adam had selected several pictures to remind him of what really mattered to him in life. One was of his fishing boat where he cherished hours of solitude and silence. To the left of his own chair were autographed photographs of two of his idols from his baseball playing days, Jackie Robinson and Duke Snider. He had so idolized Jackie Robinson that his team buddies had dubbed him "Robbie", a name he proudly wore on his baseball jacket. Sometimes, when a client was droning on, Adam would glance inconspicuously at the photographs and mentally escape the tedium emanating from the chair across from him. He would regress into a fantasy of his wonderful, carefree high school and college days on the baseball field. A mental replay of his heroic moments at shortstop was a luxury he occasionally afforded himself. The far wall held a large oil painting of an ocean beach scene, which also permitted a mental retreat to his summer house at the seashore. Adam often marveled at his ability to escape into these fantasy states without missing a beat in the session.

The wall of bookshelves behind his desk held hundreds of volumes representing his research, interests, and experience. At the end of one shelf stood his two favorite books, Hemmingway's *The Old Man and the Sea* and a book about Wile E. Coyote. At parties, when Adam explained that he most identified with the character of Wile E. Coyote, people would laugh and insist that he was spoofing them, trying to be funny, or in someway using psychology to gain insight into them. He found it impossible to convince people that he identified with the cartoon character simply because, just as the coyote was haplessly chasing that damn bird, he too felt like he had been symbolically chasing a roadrunner all his life, coming close but just missing it a thousand times. From childhood he had carried a sense that he was destined to discover something, but the "something" remained elusive.

Adam realized that the same room that offered tranquility, security and a sense of freedom to his patients often felt like a prison to him. However, that feeling of captivity vanished the moment he turned toward the bay window and looked onto a small lake and a gradually ascending landscape of trees. Gazing at this scene, Adam would find himself inhaling deeply, taking in the beauty and invigorating energy of nature. He believed this energy enabled people to transcend the enslavement of aggressive, competitive materialism, a force that disrupted human harmony. Adam felt that energy and beauty were on the same continuum. The majesty of mountains, lakes, oceans, and wildlife gave him a caffeine-like surge. It was an unconscious process, but one he thought revealed a great deal about a human's need to return to natural roots and the land. It annoyed him that when he tried to share this exuberance with Ellen, she could never relate to the intensity of his feelings.

As his attention returned to the room, Adam gazed at the bookcase where each book sat perfectly aligned, set back a precise inch from the edge. His office manager, Cathy, was obsessed with the organization of his books. For some reason this irritated Adam, and he frequently removed a book from the shelf, deliberately returning it a little out of line. He enjoyed betting with himself as to how long Cathy would take to discover it and feel compelled to re-align the books.

Just then Cathy gave a perfunctory knock at the door, and, as always, entered before Adam had a chance to respond. Cathy had been with Adam for twelve years. Despite raising three children, maintaining an impeccable home, and keeping the accounts for her husband's landscape business, she always came to work fashionably dressed for her administrative position. Although her features were generally unremarkable, the cut of her highlighted hair emphasized her beautiful brown eyes. Cathy had an organized approach to life, and it was often difficult to distinguish between her roles of mother and office manager. There was no question that she was very intelligent, and had she been born into a more affluent family, she would undoubtedly have gone to college and perhaps further in her education. She often surprised Adam by the intellectual level of her reading.

Adam felt a synergy with Cathy and believed that if she ever left him, he might have to close the practice. He was amazed at her efficiency and how orderly she kept the office, as she continuously tried to clean up the disorder he created. She knew the billing and filing system, computer codes, insurance procedures, essential phone numbers, suppliers of office equipment, and every practical and necessary aspect of running the office. Most importantly, she knew him and seemed to be accurately tuned into his moods, worries, and overall emotional needs.

"You have a lot of calls to make before you leave tonight, Adam. Here's a disk with the report outlines you need to work on for tomorrow."

"I can't bear the idea of making any calls or writing reports tonight. Remember, I'm presenting a paper at the APA conference tomorrow afternoon. I need to review my notes and prepare for the criticism that will undoubtedly come from such a conservative, skeptical audience. My research is going to rock their world."

CHAPTER FOUR

The domes and spires of the Eternal City glistened in the bright sun that shone upon the masses of people below. A young man descended the Spanish steps, carefully making his way through the thousands of milling tourists slavishly clicking their cameras. His suave demeanor, golden tan, designer sun glasses, black silk shirt open from the neck to the third button, and rows of gold chains turned the heads of many of the young women as he made his way toward the Piazza Navona. The look was perfect and unquestionably identified him as a young native Italian who knew his way around Rome. There was an easy confidence in his walk and he handled the raging stampede of Roman traffic with aplomb.

The Piazza was crowded and he walked straight past the magnificent fountains without a glance, immune to their splendor. As he approached an outdoor café, a middle-aged man seated at a small round table waved to him. Clean-shaven and dark haired, he had even features of unidentifiable origin. He sat with his legs crossed as if to display his stylish Gucci leather shoes to the young Italian women seated at the surrounding tables. He wore immaculately pressed chinos and a fine linen shirt with the sleeves rolled casually up. He rose to greet the younger man.

"Buon Giorno, Senor Michel, come stai?"

"Molto bene, e lei?"

"Bene, grazie."

They motioned to the waiter and without any hint of an accent to betray that Italian was not their mother tongue; each ordered a large cappuccino with a shot of Strega. Their table was far enough from others that their conversation could not be overheard, and they proceeded to speak softly in English, but switched into mundane chatter in Italian whenever the waiter or other patrons passed by.

"Have you been in touch with headquarters lately?"

Michel responded briskly, "Yesterday! Jack wanted to be sure that I review the mission and assignment with you. He also wanted us to agree on a meeting time in Washington. I met with the Moose in Egypt last week. I'm sure glad it's him and not me traipsing through that Godforsaken land. Man, he went into some cave with his guide and found himself in the middle of hundreds of snakes. Somehow, he got out okay. He showed me his boots. There must have been twenty or more snake fang strikes, but none penetrated. You know him. He just shrugged it off. The chief has the three of us and Doc set to meet in France. He wouldn't go into any further detail except to say we'll receive more info within the week, via the usual code."

"You know Michel, I get pissed at his attitude toward me. What the hell does he mean that you have to review our mission with me? We've been hunting this damn myth or whatever the hell it is, for two years now. I understand damn well what we're going after and the implications of the whole thing. What I don't understand is how you became the golden boy! My family has been involved in the Middle East for four generations. Christ, my great great grandfather was one of the Egyptians who fought against Napoleon. At one point, as the story goes, my great grandfather was packed off to safety on a Mameluke's horse to escape the French. He grew up as a Mameluke. I've got generations of experience in my blood. What do you have?"

"Hey man, don't put your fist down my throat. Don't shoot the messenger. Like you, I just carry out orders, that's all. I've always covered your back in tough spots."

"Sorry, you know after awhile you get tired of being treated like the new kid on the block. It's been two years now and I've earned an equal place with the rest of you, except for Doc, he's different."

Michel steered the conversation to the main issue. "Okay, just let that be. I might be on to something else that may narrow our search. Jack was in Cairo at the same time I was last week. We had a few drinks together and he told me about his wife Eunice and her experience with some shrink guy. Apparently this guy has developed a way of moving people's minds in and out of the past and maybe even into the future. Jack thinks that this guy could be useful to us. We were both getting pretty drunk but he went on about it for more than an hour. I bought most of what he was saying because this shrink is talking about electrical and magnetic energy. This is all stuff I can believe in. That's what my academic background is. We played around with this stuff at the University of Chicago and the Franck Institute. If this shrink can get people into the past, maybe way back, we can use him or his method to find the damn thing. Even if it doesn't get us whatever the hell it is we're looking for, the ability to control people's minds would sure make our asses shine at the agency."

"You're a little over my head. Are you talking about magic or supernatural stuff? You know I don't believe in that crap."

"No man it's not supernatural, this is science."

"Does this guy also saw women in half and pull rabbits out of a hat?"

"I should have known better than to think a P.E. major would be able to understand it. I'm trying to tell you, idiot, this is scientific. This shrink may be onto something. I think we should look into it, but they've got me scheduled to meet with Senor Pancho, in Madrid. You're going home tomorrow so I leave it up to you to follow up on this guy and find out what he's doing. By the way, how is your son, Emir, doing?"

"Thanks for asking. He's still struggling with fears and we have a hell of a time getting him to go to sleep at night. Okay, I'll figure out some way to find out more about this guy and his magnetic brain stuff. What bothers me most about what you said is that Jack was drunk and opened his mouth about stuff that should be confidential. That scares me. What else does he spill when he's had too much? You know, we're the ones who face Berettas ready to blow our heads off, not him.

What the hell does he care if too much is leaked, he's sitting behind a two ton carved walnut desk, with dinner waiting on the table at home."

"Let's pay for the coffee. I've got a young lady waiting for dinner. I'll see you at three tomorrow, at the entrance to the Vatican. I have our passes for the Papal library."

"You bastard! What does your wife think of your dinner engagements when you're away?"

"Same thing your wife thinks."

"Not me, man. I'm a faithful husband."

"Yeah, sure. Don't forget who you're talking to. What about Naples last month, Hong Kong before that, and the week when we couldn't even find you in Israel?"

"The terrorists had me in Israel. I told you guys but you wouldn't believe me. Anyway, you can reach me anytime tonight at my hotel. It's a bottle of Tuscan vino and a good book for me tonight. See you tomorrow."

The bill paid, the two men melted into the crowd and disappeared.

CHAPTER FIVE

Adam rushed across the street balancing his steaming hot black coffee from his favorite Deli. Cathy had already placed his list of appointments on his desk and greeted him with the air of aloof professionalism she always brought to the job. They reviewed the day's schedule.

"Ah, Eunice is my first appointment. She's a good one to start the patient parade. Eunice is interesting, and I like working with her. She's getting a lot out of therapy and talks without me having to think of questions. That always makes it easier."

Eunice, a very attractive thirty-eight year old married woman with two young children, had initially consulted Adam because she had been experiencing increasing depression, morbid thoughts, and chronic undefined muscular aches and pains. The pain was often so intense that she was unable to perform her daily tasks or engage in enjoyable activities with her family. After the usual preliminary greetings, Eunice settled into the reclining chair and relaxed herself with a few abdominal breaths.

"I had a really powerful dream last night. I woke up with a start, sweating from head to toe. I guess you want me to tell you about it."

"Eunice, you've been in therapy with me long enough to know that I only want to hear about it if you feel you want to talk about it."

"Well of course I want to talk about it otherwise I wouldn't have mentioned it to you. There was a woman. She was dressed in a smock, with a blue and white checked kerchief tied around her head, and wore odd-looking shoes that seemed to be boots laced up well above her ankles." Eunice paused for a minute and her face contorted with confusion.

"I was really frightened. I don't know why. It's really strange, Adam, because even though this woman frightened me, I was also drawn to her. I walked toward her and she held out her hand. Whoever she was, I remember I wanted to avoid any physical contact with her, but she eventually touched me."

Eunice stopped talking. After a time, Adam decided to break the silence.

"This is very interesting Eunice. Something is going on in your thoughts. Will you share that or tell us more about the woman in the dream?"

"I stopped talking because I really can't figure out how old the woman is."

There was another long pause. "I'm embarrassed to say this, but the woman became naked and then walked toward me. As soon as she touched me, her limbs stiffened, and they turned to metal, frozen in place. I woke up from the dream with every part of my body aching, and Adam, I was very, very frightened. I was sweating and shaking."

Adam responded, "Every dream is unique to the individual. Try to think of what it means to you and what thoughts come to you about its content."

Eunice seemed unable to make sense of the dream other than realizing that it might have something to do with the muscular aches she had been experiencing for the last five years. Adam suggested that they try a hypnotic trance using transcranial magnetic stimulation. Eunice's voice was soft and somewhat shaky as she spoke in the trance.

"The woman from the dream is here. She's crying and talking to a little girl. She just discovered something bad about herself and is telling the little girl. I don't

recognize the little girl. I'm trying, but I don't know who she is. Oh how horrible, that woman's arms and legs turned into hard steel." Eunice's own arms shot out in a rigid form as she spoke.

"She can't move. That poor little girl is so scared. Her face is pure fright. It's, it's, no, no, yes! It's my mother's face! The little girl is my mother! It's my mother!" Adam didn't have to bring Eunice out of the trance. She snapped out of it on her own. Appealing to him with her eyes, she asked, "Do you know what just happened? Can you explain it?"

Adam looked at her with a smile, and said, "No, but you seem to have had an epiphany. If it's comfortable for you to share it with me, I would certainly feel privileged to be part of it."

Eunice rose from the chair and walked briskly to the window. "My grandmother died when my mother was ten years old. She had Lou Gehrig's disease. That's what she was telling my mother. My mother was terrified."

Eunice whirled from the window to look at Adam. "I never knew this. My mother never told me anything about my grandmother and certainly nothing about any illness or reason for her early death. I don't even know what Lou Gehrig's disease is. I don't think I've ever heard of it. Could we go back into trance? I need to know more."

Eunice returned to her chair with tears flowing down her cheeks but with a simultaneous expression of joy. Adam was not sure that another immediate trance was advisable. He checked his schedule and saw that he was free at two o'clock.

"You've been through a very insightful experience and used a great deal of psychic energy to get there. I don't think it would be good to go right back into trance. But we're in luck. I can see you again at two o'clock, if you can make it."

"Adam, I was just in my mother's presence when she was a little girl! I'll come back anytime you say."

Eunice returned punctually that afternoon. Her trance was easily established, and afterward she believed she had gained the insight of her life. She got up from the therapy chair and attempted to hug Adam. He quickly signaled that this was inappropriate in a therapeutic relationship and she reluctantly stepped back saying, "I just wanted to thank you. I think you just changed my life."

Eunice moved toward the door and then turned back. "Dr. Peterson, can you help me understand what happened? I want to tell others." Adam invited her to return to her chair. Always willing to parade his superior knowledge, he began to pontificate.

"We turn to Karl Jung's concept of the collective unconscious for understanding this. Freud thought of the unconscious as a storehouse of forgotten experiences. The critical aspect of his definition of the unconscious is that it is a personal entity, unique to each individual, which develops out of that person's experiences from birth to death. The unconscious is the mainstay of most therapeutic approaches. But this idea of the individual unconscious alone has never satisfied me. Jung took a broader view of the unconscious. He called Freud's notion of the unconscious the "personal unconscious". For Jung the broader unconscious was made up of not only experiences from the individual's life but also from material and modes of behavior common to all humanity. Jung labeled this the collective unconscious.

Eunice nodded her understanding.

"The point is that all people everywhere from the beginning of time have carried with them the material of their collective unconscious. Jung's concept of the collective unconscious offers us the possibility of fulfilling our deepest need to find our connection to the cosmos. This is the framework I use to understand both the adaptive and maladaptive behavior of people, and this was my guide for opening new doors of experience for you. Through my special hypnosis you tapped into your personal collective unconscious."

Eunice beamed with delight and left the room smiling radiantly. As with so many of Adam's patients, she stopped at the reception area to share some of her experience with Cathy.

As Adam was making notes about the session, Cathy walked in and proclaimed, "Eunice thinks a miracle just occurred. She said she's free of pain and for the first time in years felt bouncy and light. She said that she learned from the hypnosis that her grandmother had Lou Gehrig's disease."

Cathy's voice was animated as she related the story. "Eunice said she now understands why any little normal ache or pain was terrifying for her. She believes that she saw her grandmother in the trance, telling her mother about the disease and that she was going to die from it. Eunice inherited the fear of muscular pain from her mother even though no one in the family ever told her about the disease. Boy, what an experience! Is this an example of the collective memory you've been working on?"

Adam did not want to discuss the matter with Cathy, but then thought that it was time to acknowledge what he had been doing. With a smile he nodded. "Right, she got in touch with a genetic memory that was at the root of her problems."

Cathy moved to the bookcase to straighten a row of periodicals. "I can understand why you've been so preoccupied over the last few months. You know, I've been typing your reports and patient and research notes for a long time, and I've been listening to you talk about this collective or genetic unconscious. It really interests me. Every time I type one of those notes about it, I'm intrigued. I'd love to find some of my memories. Would you be willing to explain it to me in layman's language?"

"Sure, I've sort of kept the whole area to myself. I've been reluctant to tell anyone about it. I think you know, from typing so many of my lectures, that most people assume that whatever they see, hear, taste, smell, or feel, is exactly what exists. The assumption is that perception is reality. But every sensory perception is interpreted from our previous experiences. The combination of the perception of the raw stimuli and the person's interpretation of it makes up the final experience. The interpretation is based on experiences, attitudes, needs, and overall emotional structure. I know you're a faithful reader of the Bible, so you'll know that the apostle Paul wrote, "That you see doth not come from what you see."

"I think I understand. You're saying that objective reality itself does not create harsh or soothing, pleasant or foul, beautiful or ugly. The most beautiful sunset or beautiful rainbow is in our mind, not just in the sky."

Adam was pleased by Cathy's quick comprehension. He continued, "I've developed a formula that enables me to find the exact place in the cortex of the brain to focus the magnetic stimulation, the exact EEG frequencies to be generated, and the exact placement of electrodes to enable a person to access his collective unconscious. It's different for each person. What's new about all this is that now we can understand that the way we interpret everything is based not only on what we bring from this life's experience, but also on what we bring from the collective unconscious."

"My gosh! What are we going to do with you when you topple Freud from his pedestal?"

Adam knew that his reputation was growing. People were starting to seek him out just for the experience of a regressive hypnosis.

Still musing on his project he responded to the message light on the phone as it rang. It was Susan Atkins. Adam had treated her for various obsessive-compulsive behaviors, and she had been delighted that all her symptoms had been alleviated after regressive trances. Adam took her call thinking that she wanted another appointment.

"Dr. Peterson, I just want to tell you again that you changed my life. My family is eternally grateful to you and so am I. Your discovery cannot remain unheralded or confined to just the few who see you. The world needs to know about you. Alice Hawkins and I have contacted many of your patients who also had wonderful experiences, and we are forming a group to promote your technique. Would you honor us by coming to our first meeting next Thursday? I think you'll be surprised by what you'll see."

CHAPTER SIX

Like ants following an instinctive trail home, men scurried about, some bent almost double by the weight on their shoulders, others teaming together to haul large bundled loads. Shouted orders and counter orders, grunts of effort, curses of exasperation, and an almost palpable urgency filled the hot, dusty air. Tri-color cockades identified the French soldiers among the throngs of Egyptian workers. Wooden carts, wobbly under their heavy cargos, lined the cobbled street outside the French Historical institute, while the harnessed donkeys, alone indifferent to the pressure of time, waited patiently for the signal to pull forward. Stone slabs, rough wooden crates packed with smaller collections, statues hastily bundled in burlap, and yet more crates were carried from the interior of the building out to the sun parched streets.

Inside, the rooms were almost empty. General Menou, the last French commander in Egypt after Napoleon's surreptitious departure, was seated at a table stacked with the records of the contents of the crates, his heavy body overflowing the small straight-backed chair. A few remaining un-catalogued relics, small figurines, fragments of stone, and a copper funeral collar lay among the papers. The General signaled to a porter to collect the remaining pieces. He was fuming with impotent rage as he watched the caravan of ancient treasures pull away toward the British ships in the harbor.

"How could I, a General in the Grande Army, be so humiliated? Damn the English! We fight the Mamelukes, we bring the savants, we do the digging, we do the documenting, and they take the artifacts away on their ships."

He had delayed the handover as long as possible, but in the end the defeated French army had to forsake their treasures of antiquity. Menou wiped the perspiration from his brow with a cotton cloth and shrugged as he rose to leave. Gathering his papers together, he stuffed them into a saddlebag and glanced at the few relics that had been overlooked. He grabbed a fragment of greenish stone and tossed it into the bag.

"That's one piece that's not going to England", he smirked to himself as the train of donkeys began to move to the port of Alexandria.

CHAPTER SEVEN

Adam strode into the enormous ostentatiously ornate lobby of the conference hotel and thought to himself that the soaring Dorian columns, gleaming Venetian marble floor, and dazzling crystal chandeliers set an appropriately grand tone for the words he was about to deliver to the world. Hundreds of psychologists milled around the registration desk discussing the various sessions and their individual selections. Adam moved to the wide curving staircase, its sides flanked by two stately bronze Anubis-like dogs, and, reaching the second ballroom floor, confidently proceeded to the sign on the door that read, *"Past life or Genetic Memory:* Presenter: Adam Peterson, Ph.D., FAClinP." Adam approached the presenter's platform and was greeted by the president of the clinical psychology division of the American Psychological Association.

"Hello Adam, we're looking forward to your presentation. How have you been and how is your family?"

Adam soothed the uneasiness in his stomach with gentle pressure from his right hand, an unconscious movement he often adopted when anxious.

"We're all fine Alex, thanks for asking. Are we expecting a large crowd for my paper?"

"You're going to be surprised. I checked last night and we have about eighty members set to attend. There would have been more but your talk is scheduled for the same time as Dr. Agee's, 'How to Beat Managed Care Insurance.'"

Adam smiled, "It's hard to compete with managed care. Maybe I should go to that instead of giving my paper."

Alex put his hand on Adam's shoulder, "There's more to life than managed care. I'll be back in a few minutes. I'm presiding over your session."

Alex returned, stepped to the podium and introduced Adam, citing his dual degree in clinical psychology and genetic engineering and his work as a researcher, professor, practicing clinical psychologist, and now as an innovator in hypnotic work.

Adam scanned his audience. Recognizing several eminent psychologists seated in the first row intensified his anxiety, but he assumed a self-confident posture and successfully camouflaged his growling stomach, sweaty brow, and trembling hands. His trained relaxation took effect as he began his lecture.

"Welcome, I'm flattered and honored to have so many of you here today."

The concept of a collective unconscious has wide acceptance but little research has been designed to investigate ways of accessing that elusive entity. Today I will present my discovery of how to easily access the personal collective unconscious, showing you the results of an experimental population of sixty adults. The methodology involves the unique formula I developed consisting of a specific number and directionality of bilateral stimulation through Eye Movement Desensitization Reprocessing techniques. The formula further involves Ericsonian hypnotic techniques and the application of transcranial magnetic stimulation to create specific EEG frequencies at very micro-specific cortical sites.

There is a plethora of literature documenting the validity of regressive hypnosis and numerous reports of subjects experiencing past lives. The unique amalgam of my techniques created particular patterns of EEG activity, which are the pathway to discovering one's personal collective unconscious.

Something new emerged from the application of this unique combination of techniques on subjects. They formed new patterns of energy within the patients' brains that permitted them to enter the realm of the collective unconscious, escape the limitations of time, and choose new and different realities. These realities already existed, of course. They were simply waiting to be perceived. Just as Michelangelo explained how he created David, 'David already existed in the marble, it was only necessary to chisel out that which was not David.' We too have all within us, the past, present, and future! We just have to learn how to chisel out that which prevents us from allowing the David within us to emerge."

Adam moved to his Power Point presentation. "The data you are about to see demonstrate that it is possible to uncover genetic memories and relive them in the present. It illustrates that the past exists in the present because it has been encoded and carried from generation to generation."

Adam explained how his findings proved that incongruity and emotional suffering were often a product of material from ancestral experiences seeping into the present life through genetic memory. The material troubling a particular person was often from past generations and represented turmoil that had not been resolved at that time. Adam moved to the next PowerPoint slide.

"Here is an example. The left column of the chart contains the content of regressions. On the right are the patients' presenting conflicts. You can see that the subject matter of the two columns is related, which leads to the hypothesis that the patients were responding to unresolved ancestral experiences, as if they were present day issues."

Adam abandoned his formal presentation style, to communicate his emotional investment in his work. Stepping from behind the podium and descending from the stage, he walked up and down the main aisle, engaging his audience in a personal way.

"It's as if a person's psyche was being haunted by the past through promptings from a genetic code. While this may not be a new idea to some of you, what is new is that by combining psychological and genetic research I have established that there is a biological substrate to the transmission of the past. Genetic memory is actually material that is physiologically encoded in the DNA and transmitted genetically from one generation to another. My research also clearly demonstrates that individuals can make contact with their genetic memories and thereby resolve present conflicts and find their true destinies. They can become the Michelanglos of their destinies."

Adam paused for a moment and then continued.

"The concept of a genetic memory becomes more believable when we consider the basic tenets of quantum physics which deal with matter, including that of human beings, of course, at the subatomic level. At this level, unimaginably tiny particles are all connected by energy. Think about it this way. The universe was once the size of a pea. Even though it may have expanded through whatever means one chooses to believe – the big bang theory or other ideas - all the stuff of which the pea size universe was composed is still the same and still here, no less, no more. In this respect we are all a part of that original universe. I remind you of the famous remark of Madame de Sevigny when she learned that a witch had been burned. 'So we're all breathing her now.' That was over 300 years ago. We now know how correct she was.

I find my theory to be an essential approach in my work with patients. Think of the potential of this tool as a conceptual framework for therapeutic strategies. What are the implications of considering each individual patient, in fact all humanity, actually, as being connected in critical ways with everything else in the universe? The connections are, of course, usually obscured or hidden from our perception, but to believe in, search for, and to experience these connections can open new doors and windows beyond anything we have ever known. My proposal to each of you today is that the role of therapy, in fact the mission for all of us, is to search for these connections and find the way to open new doors in our lives. The DNA memory to which I refer provides the matrix that connects all of us."

The raised hands in the audience signaled to Adam that his renowned colleagues had questions and comments, but he instructed them to hold their reactions until the end of the presentation.

"I have always been impressed by the many patients who believe that they have relived a past life during their regressive trances. For years I tried to reconcile my disbelief in reincarnation with the experience my patients were relating. As a result of my work with genetic engineering I formulated the hypothesis that the experience my patients reported was a result of their having accessed information that was stored in their DNA.

I will now show you a video of a session that illustrates my point. Before we view it, I'll tell you a bit about the patient.

Jane is thirty-six years old and married to a prominent political figure. She had suffered for several years, constantly feeling frightened by a premonition that something "awful" was about to occur. The fears and anxiety had begun to interfere with sleeping, eating, and her ability to enjoy what she thought should be a very comfortable life. Let's begin the video."

A woman's distraught face filled the screen. Crystal like tears slowly rolled toward her quivering lips. Her eyes were downcast.

"Doctor Peterson, I've come to see you because I'm overwhelmed by fear. I have no idea what's causing it, but it's consuming my life. I can never let go, I'm on guard all the time and driving my kids, my husband, and my friends mad. I'm sure they all think I'm crazy. I imagine something will happen to the children as they get on the school bus. Each night I check, at least fifteen times, that I've turned off the stove. Every time the furnace goes on I worry that it might blow up. I see a disaster on the news and feel that it's going to happen to us. I know this doesn't make any sense but I can't stop it."

Adam paused the video.

"Notice that Jane's words are coming out in a rapid-fire, frenzied manner. She's sitting tensely on the edge of the chair, gesturing nervously with her hands. Watch how she collapses back, as if drained by what she has just said. This patient was in significant emotional pain and clearly highly anxious. Observe also how she now continues in a subdued voice."

The video continued.

"It's reached the point where I cook dinner an hour before we eat. I have to taste everything before serving it to be sure that it's not tainted or poisoned. I'm miserable, Doctor. I can't go on like this."

Adam interrupted the video.

"I spent seven more sessions of talk therapy with Jane but we were unable to isolate or define the cause of the fears. She had good recollection of most of her life and couldn't remember any traumas or significant events that might have spawned this terrible sense of dread. The patient related that her marriage was quite good and her two children where doing well. There were no financial difficulties and the family was in good health. Her husband's political position was not a stressful one and she could not identify any current or past stressors in her life. We will pick up at the ninth session."

Jane's face filled the screen again with Adam's voice in the background.

"Jane, I'm aware that you don't feel we're making any progress. I've been thinking about your therapy sessions and would like to try regressive hypnosis."

"Doctor Peterson, I trust you. That's why I came to you. As I told you before, I did my research and everyone I spoke to told me you were the guy to see. I'm willing to try anything you suggest as long as it's not medication."

Adam stopped the video.

"Using my formula, I conducted a neuro-assessment to determine the exact placement of transcranial magnetic electrodes. The video continues with Jane in her trance state. The amazing part is that she begins to speak in a strange language. My own confusion and incredulity is apparent. I could not understand one word and had no idea how to proceed. I had never experienced anything like this and wondered if I had moved her into a psychotic state. As she emerged from the trance Jane cried profusely and reported being exhausted."

The video resumed with Adam's response.

"Would you feel comfortable sharing your experience with me?"

"Absolutely! Wow, that was something. I saw myself as a young girl, maybe ten years old. I know it was me, but I didn't look like me. Does that make sense?"

"Yes, just let yourself go and say whatever comes to mind about the experience."

Jane began to speak as if the experience was ongoing.

"I'm on the top of a hill. The countryside is beautiful and peaceful with rolling green hills all around. I can't tell if it's farmland, but it sort of looks like it. There are no people and no other houses."

"As you look at the young girl you think is you, how are you dressed?"

"I have a plain dress with straps. Very simple but pretty. Nothing like anything I every remember having. I can even tell you the color of the dress. It's a blue and yellow pattern. Wait! Wait! The shoes are wooden! I am sure they're wooden!"

"Very good, you seem to be able to recall a good deal of detail about your experience. Relax and continue."

"The girl is watching a thatched roof cottage burning. She reminds me of pictures I've seen of people in olden times. Now I'm beginning to feel really nervous. Wait; wait, wow, I know. Oh my God! Oh no! That poor girl is watching it burn and her parents are inside! That poor little girl is watching her parents die. She has no one. She's completely alone. There is no one to turn to. I don't know if I can go on. This is horrible."

Adam instructed Jane to take a deep abdominal breadth. "I understand, but it's most important that you continue to talk about what you are thinking and feeling. To help with the anxiety, just keep in mind, that was then and this is now."

Jane sighed.

"I know you're right. The thing is, the cottage was burning because the young girl, who I think is me, neglected her chore of keeping an eye on the fire in the hearth. I know what happened. She was distracted by a wooden toy and failed to notice that the fire got out of control."

Adam paused the video and looked for audience reactions

"I hypothesized that the incident she described was an event from her collective unconscious that was now traumatizing her. That traumatic event was recorded in her DNA and transmitted just as strongly as a phenotypic characteristic. Just as surely as she knows that her eyes are blue, she knows she has experienced this fire. And by the technique I developed she has experienced it, not recalled it. By using the EMDR procedure, I enabled her to realize that the girl she met in the trance was not guilty of causing her parents' death. This experience was liberating for Jane, and extremely significant to me. As soon as I felt that she had resolved her guilt through the EMDR technique, I played the audiotape of the hypnotic portion of this session for her. As she heard it, she actually accused me of playing some type of trick on her.

"I sent the session tape to the linguistics department at Columbia University for a language identification. I thought you would be interested in their response."

A scanned letter appeared on the screen.

Dear Doctor Peterson,

I am writing in reference to the tape you sent for review. The faculty of the Department of Linguistics and two language specialists from the Department of Archeology listened to the recording. The consensus opinion is that the speaker on the tape was using a Gaelic tongue that has been dormant for over two hundred years. I must stress that this is our opinion, as we cannot identify the language with absolute certainty. If we are correct, the speaker seems to be describing a fire and a house burning. In order to pin it down further, which can be done, we would have to do a significant amount of research at a considerable cost to you. Let us know what you think. We were excited to hear your tape and are interested to know how this recording came about.

Adam returned to the podium.

"The following slides contain the data gathered from simultaneous PET scans recorded during the regressive hypnoses. On this first slide you will see that the ventromedial prefrontal cortex, an area with robust connections to the Posterior cingulated cortex, amygdala and hippo-campus, lights up during the regression. As you probably know, this is the area that is activated by recognition of familiar people. Obviously then, in the trance state, Jane's brain recognized the people she saw. The next slide shows what happened when Jane saw the little girl view the fire and realize that her parents had died. We know that in people suffering from PTSD, that area of the brain shuts down when they encounter triggers of the traumatic event. And look, in Jane at this point in the trance, we find a distinctly diminished level of activity in the ventromedial prefrontal cortex, suggesting that she is carrying the memory of the traumatic event. This is in marked contrast, as you can see in this next slide, to the activity level shown when Jane, in another trance, was exposed to traumatic stimuli that had no personal connection to her.

What you have observed is a person accessing a genetic memory. This is only one subject in my study of 60 subjects, all of whom accessed a genetic memory by means of my formula. These people have found, through memories recorded in their DNA, experiences from the past, which continue to exert influence on their present lives. Let's return to the chart that demonstrates the connection between the subject's behavioral complaints and the content of their regressive hypnoses."

At the back of the room, in the right corner

next to the entrance door, a man stood up with his hand raised. He did not wait to be acknowledged by Adam.

"Dr. Peterson, would you describe this procedure in greater depth and give us the formula so that we can better evaluate your findings and rather bold assumptions?"

The bright spotlights illuminating the stage made it impossible for Adam to discern the identity of the figure.

"I understand your questioning the research. However, I am not ready to release the formula. I'm in the early stages of developing this theory which will ultimately provide a new way of looking at the symptoms of our patients, and in fact, maybe a new way of viewing life."

The anonymous man, who had now moved to the center of the back of the room, challenged.

"Why the secrecy? Is there more that you haven't shared with us? I've never attended an APA presentation where the data that would permit us to replicate research was withheld. I doubt anyone here would disagree with me. This is unheard of."

Adam squinted and strained to see his adversarial colleague.

"I understand your frustration, but I'm not ready to present my formula. Let me continue with my presentation. As you know, brain function is based on electrical activity and principles. The formula I developed provides an individualized protocol, to force theta electrical frequencies to cross over into alpha electrical frequencies. Any of you who practice neurofeedback or hypnosis know that alpha is associated with quiet thoughts and the process of reflecting on inner feelings. Alpha is the dominant frequency operating when we are deep into imagination and fantasy. Dominant alpha silences mind chatter.

Some of you may be familiar with a new procedure called transcranial magnetic stimulation. This involves producing magnetic currents in the brain. I've developed a unique magnetic coil that enables me to stimulate minute specific neural pathways with magnetic forces and to produce certain EEG patterns. When this is combined with a simultaneous hypnotic technique, my patients experienced past events. What I am emphasizing is not that they were recalling past events, but that they all reported that the events from the past were being experienced as if they were occurring at the present moment. These events were unavailable to the person's conscious awareness until the exact moment of this particular EEG configuration. I am asking you to consider my hypothesis that with my technique these subjects contacted the wealth of universal genetic material that was encoded in their DNA. Ladies and Gentlemen, we have found and touched the collective unconscious."

The same man interrupted Adam for a third time. "I admit that you have caught my attention and I would like to do further research in this area. I don't understand why you won't share the formula with us, but perhaps we can talk privately."

Although the man's features were still obscured by the darkness, Adam could see that he was pointing aggressively at the podium. The rest of the room was silent. Alex rose quickly to thank Adam for his thought provoking presentation and the audience applauded appreciatively. Adam noticed that the man at the back was moving rapidly toward the door and he soon disappeared in the crowd.

He spent a few minutes fielding questions, but was puzzled that his challenger had not remained.

Adam rubbed his stomach again. "I wonder who that guy is."

CHAPTER EIGHT

The following morning Adam was back in his office by eight, invigorated by the success of the previous day's presentation. Cathy handed him a stack of papers to sign.

"Thanks Cathy." Adam quickly scrawled his signature everywhere Cathy had placed an X. "We made quick work of those damn insurance forms. I need a super latte from the deli. Would you like something?"

"No, thanks, but don't forget, you have a new patient coming in. No lingering there with the paper today."

"I'll be back in ten minutes."

Mr. and Mrs. Malvek arrived punctually for their first consultation. Adam found it impossible to identify Mr. Malvek's face by race or ethnic background. His dark complexion had an olive cast, and his features were regular and strong. He wore a light blue silk sport shirt, khaki pants, and, somewhat incongruously, expensive loafers without socks. Loafers without socks annoyed Adam. To him they suggested the over confidence of wealth and membership in the exclusive preppy society of which he felt he could never be a part. Adam stared at the man. He was certain that he had seen him before but couldn't place him. He turned his attention to Mrs. Malvek. She was clearly a member of the conservative upper class. Mrs. Malvek wore no makeup except a dusting of powder, and her hair was cut in a neutral bob that revealed simple pearl earrings. Her pleated navy skirt easily covered her knees as she sat erect in the chair opposite Adam, her ankles neatly crossed, and her hands relaxed in her lap. The Malveks' concern was their five-year-old son, Emir. The boy, their only child, was terrified of loud noises. He panicked at the sound of thunder, a motorcycle engine, fireworks, or even the dropping of a heavy object. Mrs. Malvek took responsibility for answering most of Adam's questions about Emir's development and described him as a very bright boy with a good deal of sensitivity and a loving personality. He was their biological child and there had been nothing unusual in his early development. He slept well and his eating habits were normal for his age. While Mrs. Malvek was clearly very concerned about her son, her husband seemed detached from the conversation. His eyes wandered about the office, and he seemed more interested in the décor than in his son. His face was expressionless. Adam couldn't tell what Mr. Malvek felt about Emir's issue. In fact, he couldn't read him at all.

"This guy's strange," Adam thought. "He doesn't want the world to know anything about him. He's not wearing any rings, not even a wedding band. And not even a watch."

On the intake sheet that they had filled out as new clients, Mr. Malvek identified himself as a tennis instructor at a local health and recreation club. Mrs. Malvek reported that she had worked for the State Department of Health and Education before having Emir and that she was presently staying home to care for him.

Adam had treated several other young children with similar symptoms and had found that play therapy and talk therapy were relatively useless in freeing a child of these fears. However, they did respond very well to hypnosis.

"Mr. and Mrs. Malvek, in my experience with this kind of fear in a child, I have found that hypnosis is the best approach. If this is okay with you, I will have you remain in the room so you can observe what I do."

Clearly skeptical, Mr. Malvek asked a lot of questions, but at length he consented to hypnosis.

"Okay, Dr. Peterson, if you say it worked in the past we're ready to give it a try. Can you assure me he will come out of it? I want to be sure that you're not going to put any false ideas in his head."

Adam concealed his irritation at the remark and assured them that the only purpose of the hypnosis was to gather information about the cause of the problem.

"I'm not in the business of putting ideas into people's heads," he replied.

Using a special technique he had developed for young children, Adam easily hypnotized Emir. As he led the boy back through his early years, slowly regressing him to a time prior to his current life, Emir suddenly began to talk in the labored voice common to the hypnotic state.

"There's black smoke all over, no sky, big things like where smoke comes out of with fire."

"Are you there with the smoke?"

"Yeah."

"What do you see around you?"

"A lot of red, a lot of fire. Boom, boom, boom! Three things boom, on fire, loud boom, people all on the ground, ghosts." Emir's face registered terror. He fell silent.

Adam decided to break the silence and asked, "What is happening? How did this boom happen?"

"Daddy lit the fire cracker. Daddy said you can get hurt bad, burned bad, with firecrackers. Don't go near any. Don't play with matches."

"Where are you when the boom, boom, boom, happens?"

"Lots of buildings, tents too, all burning. The people are all running away. Daddy grabs me on the horse and mommy is on the ground. Daddy put my head down and we rode really fast. But all the guns are making a lot of noise and Daddy yelled really loud. More big booms."

Emir went silent again. Adam asked him, "How are you dressed?"

My pants are tied on me. No shirt. No shoes. My skin is very dark. Why is Daddy leaving me here?"

Where is he leaving you?"

With this lady. It's way far away in the sand. I see horses and another little boy. I want to stay with you, Daddy. Daddy! Don't leave me here! The dust from the horse is all in my eyes. I don't see Daddy any more."

At that point Emir stopped talking again and seemed to drift into a place where Adam could not reach him. Although the boy's lips were moving, Adam could not decipher the low mumbled sounds. He brought Emir out of the hypnosis slowly, and the boy easily returned from the trance in a relaxed mood. Adam immediately followed with the technique of helping Emir understand that the boy's father loved him and rather than thinking he had abandoned him he had actually arranged a safe haven for him. Emir seemed to understand and appeared relieved.

"There is another important part of this that you must allow your mind to understand. You saw something from the past when you were under hypnosis. So be sure you know that was then and this is now. That event is over. It is not you today."

Before Adam could continue the session and further respond to the material with Emir or his parents, Mr. Malvek said, "Well, what do you think Doc? I guess it doesn't always work, your hypnosis. That was useless, just the fantasies of a little child. You're not going to try to tell me any of that means anything, are you?"

"Yes! It did mean something. Emir has begun to tell us something about a fantasy or some genetic memory that is creating his fear, without his knowing what it is on a conscious level." Before he could say more, Mr. Malvek cut Adam off.

"Well we really have to be going, I have an appointment and we can talk about it next time." The two parents stood up, Mr. Malvek took Emir by the hand, and Mrs. Malvek, without saying a word, followed dutifully behind.

The abrupt termination discomfited Adam.

"Mr. Malvek, there is nothing to be frightened about, this was actually an excellent session for a child of Emir's age, and we really are very close to discovering the core of the fear."

"Thanks Doc, we'll make another appointment." Malvek's tone was polite but clearly communicated that the session was over.

Cathy came into the room a few minutes later.

"That must have been some session. Those two acted as if they had seen a ghost and couldn't get out of here fast enough. Mr. Malvek paid in cash and didn't want a bill or receipt. And, I've never had this happen before, he asked for the intake information sheet. I didn't know what to do, but I figured it was theirs and I had to give it to them. He practically grabbed it from me. Frankly, he scared me, so I gave it to him. What a paranoid guy, right?"

"Hmm! Do we have any record at all of them being here, an address or phone number?"

"No! Sorry! We don't have any information on them. It was all on the intake sheet."

"I guess we have to let it go, then. Of course you had to give him the form. I'll just dictate a note about the session. As you so often say, Cathy, people sure can be strange. Oh, one other thing. Did that guy look familiar to you? Maybe like some actor or some other patient we've seen in the past?"

Cathy put her hand to her chin, thought for a moment with a furrowed brow, and said, "Hmm, no, not that I can think of. Why? Did he remind you of someone?"

"I'm not sure. I thought I had seen him before. Oh well, it doesn't matter."

Adam was still troubled by the session, puzzled by both the boy's account and Mr. Malvek's hasty departure. He was curious as to what Emir was experiencing. What material was he trying to process, and most of all why did Mr. Malvek react that way? It was as if something Emir said had alarmed his father.

CHAPTER NINE

A grand wooden armchair upholstered in red fabric threaded with gold sat on a raised dais in the center of a large, torch-lit room. Other smaller chairs were ranged on a low rise that ran along the sides of the room. The walls were hung with richly colored tapestries depicting the life of Christ, and the wide, dark floorboards were uniformly joined with hand-forged nails. A middle-aged man dressed in dark, tight fitting pants and a full red shirt with large cuffs and a ruffled front panel, sat in the main chair. He had European features and fair skin. Thin threads of dark brown hair were plastered against his skull as if glued in place, and several large rings adorned his soft hands. Suddenly he clutched his chest. As the man slumped over a young child ran to him.

"Papa, Papa, is you well? Why are you making

that sound? Sit up Papa, sit up!"

The man uttered in a strained whisper. "Too soon, my son, I fear you will be called upon to be a man."

"Papa, I am sorry I made you run so hard. I didn't mean to make you sick. I'll get the healer, the ointment, I will help you. I wish I'd never made you play that game."

"You did nothing wrong. This is not your fault my son. Stay by my side and listen. Let God and the saints be your guides. Remember always, if you were meant to look to the past with regret or guilt God would have put eyes in the back of your head. You are a fine lad and I know you will make good decisions and lead well." With that, the man fell to the floor, limp.

The young boy cried and knelt by his father. Finally he rose, and straightening his clothes, stood tall. His face broadcast a sudden, new maturity.

Adam, in the full power of his regressive trance, could feel, as he witnessed the scene, that the loss of his father was not going to scar the boy and that he would overcome the trauma. Adam saw the boy as a man, seated at a large table conducting a meeting. He looked pleased as he signed papers with the evident approval of those around him. Laying down his plumed pen he announced to the group that he was impressed with all the work they had done to accomplish their goals. Adam felt reassured that the young man understood his father's death, did not blame himself, and had gone on to lead a normal life.

The trance was broken by the faint ringing of the office telephone.

"Wow, what have I come upon? That was the most vivid and exciting experience I have ever had."

Adam was intuitively certain that in his self-hypnotic trance he had relived a time from his own past, a genetic recording of some ancestor whose experience resided in his DNA. He wondered if perhaps this ancestral event lay at the root of his anxiety about dying and leaving his sons with more pain than they could handle. Puzzled but incomparably curious about the experience, Adam recorded it in his journal and to his surprise realized that the entire trance had lasted no longer than fifteen minutes.

His drive home was uneventful, but as always, involved sitting stationary in several traffic snarl-ups, which were routine for the beltway. Everyone he knew complained about his or her frustrating nightly commute. The traffic didn't bother Adam and he simply enjoyed listening to music as he waited for the cars to move. Since the children had gone away to boarding school he never felt a need to get home at any particular time and was content and sometimes even happy to arrive late.

Ellen had prepared one of his favorite chicken dinners. As usual he and the boys, Kevin and William, who this week were home from school for a few days, had their plates loaded with far more food than they could eat. Also as usual, Ellen had served herself a half-dollar sized portion. Adam thought about confronting the disparate portions as he had unproductively done on so many previous occasions, but since the boys were present he controlled his impulse and decided to let it go. However, keeping quiet did nothing to reduce his growing anger and annoyance with Ellen.

Adam sat at the table pushing his food around, only snapping into consciousness when his oldest son, Kevin, loudly said, "Dad, would you listen to me please, I've been trying to talk to you about getting back to school a day early next week. Are you just being your weird usual self, or is there something wrong?"

Ellen chimed in. "Are you okay Adam, are you feeling well? Dad probably had a tough day at work."

Adam realized that musing about the afternoon's trance, he had been oblivious to his family. Although he was embarrassed, he was also annoyed by Ellen's patronizing voice and the "are you okay question."

"Yes I'm fine. I had a really troubling experience with a patient this afternoon, and I'm trying to decide if I should arrange for her to go to a hospital tonight."

Kevin looked at his father with irritation. "You're always thinking about your patients. I think you use that as an excuse. Are you sure you're not frying your brain with that idiotic transparent magnetic brain stimulation machine of yours?"

"It a transcranial magnetic stimulation coil and it is not idiotic, and it's not frying my brain."

"It's important to me! Could you please pay attention to what I'm asking you? I need to be back to school next Friday instead of Saturday, can you drive me or will you take me, Mom? All I want is an answer; I don't care about your patients or that stupid machine. Mom! Will you take me?"

"Just stop Kevin. There's no need to get hysterical."

Kevin barked back at his father. "You don't have to make everything psychological. We learned about hysterical personality in my behavioral science course. I am not hysterical. If you would just listen to us once in awhile maybe we wouldn't get so mad at you."

"I heard everything, Kevin, and I always pay attention to you. I'll arrange my schedule to take you back Friday and if Mom can go we'll all go together. We can have dinner with you at that restaurant you love and you can ask any of your friends to join us."

"Yeah, so you can grill us on what we're

studying and show how interested you are in economics, earth science, calculus, and our English literature classes.– I didn't mean for us to have a party Dad. I just need a ride back on Friday."

"Your father is just trying to be nice, Kevin. You can rest easy, We will take you back. If you don't want to have dinner, that's okay too." Ellen chimed in using her perfected patronizing and placating voice that conveyed her attitude that the family should always be loving, considerate, and respectful. Adam lost his temper with Ellen.

"I'm sick and tired of you always intervening to try to smooth everything over. Maybe it's not okay Ellen! If I want to take Kevin out to dinner he needs to go. Why can't I ever have a private disagreement with either of my children? Is it really so terrible if we have an argument, or I make a decision, or set some limits and consequences, even if it upsets them?"

Both boys left the table and turned on the TV to avoid the potential family squabble. However, deep down, they knew that it would never happen because their mother never argued with their father. She was always right and he was always wrong. Kevin wondered why they had ever married.

William, who had just turned twelve, grabbed the TV remote and began to surf the channels. He glanced at Kevin and said, "You know Kev, I'm glad we're at boarding school. At least we don't have to listen to them all the time. Why doesn't Mom ever let Dad talk to us without butting in? Does she even like Dad? Last night I heard her telling grandpa that Dad can't make good decisions and that she has to tell him what to do. I don't think Dad's happy with Mom."

"Just let it go William. You can never figure out why people get married."

"Kevin, I have to tell you something. Promise you won't tell?"

"Knock it off, William, you know I won't rat on you. I bet I know what it is. Can I guess? You got a detention for not doing your homework?"

"I always get my work done."

"You got some girl pregnant?"

"No dude, nothing like that. Don't be stupid, this is serious."

"What? I know! I bet you kissed a girl."

"Just stop, you're such a jerk. No, what I want to tell you is that I told the kids to call me Bill. You know how Mom is, always insisting that my name is William and that she hates nicknames or shortened names. But I felt like such a geek being called William, I told them my name is Bill."

"Good job, Bill. Wow, I like it, I always wanted to call you Will or Bill, but the few times I tried Mom had a hissy fit. No fear man, I ain't telling nobody."

Both boys sat back to watch professional wrestling. Kevin interrupted his intense focus on the match to say to his brother, "Now you have the remote so you're on guard. It's up to you to change the channel if Mom comes in. Don't let her catch us watching this or we'll never hear the end of it."

"Yeah, the lecture on how we have a responsibility to our minds and how it's a sin to clutter them with this garbage."

Adam helped clear the table and told Ellen that he would be in his office writing a psychological report. His home office was a small room next to the family room, and like his professional office, was decorated with sport pictures. Ellen always complained about Adam working in the evening. He was not sure why it bothered her, because she never wanted to play a game or even engage in interesting conversation. Of course, she was always willing to discuss decorating the house, her father's work, or something about one of her friends. Adam found all of this extremely boring and was happy to have a reason to avoid it. He also loathed sitting in front of sitcoms, hospital dramas or detective TV shows hour after hour, which was what Ellen enjoyed in the evenings.

Sitting in his cordovan leather chair, Adam automatically began gliding his hand across his chest to sooth the chronic ache. He suddenly realized that there was no pain for the first time in years. Then it struck him. The pain had ceased as a result of the regression. He marveled at the profound effect that experience had had on him. The man in the chair had been experiencing a fatal heart attack. Adam himself had been worried about his own chronic chest pain. He hadn't told Ellen because he never shared anything with her that might increase her annoying penchant for lecturing and over-protecting him. Several visits to his cardiologist, along with stress tests that showed no pathology, had done little to assuage his worry or to relieve the recurring pain. The content of the regression must have been triggered by his concern about the pain and his repression of intense emotion. The emotion was fear, but it was not for himself, but rather for his children, should something happen to him. Now he thought he understood the reason for the partic-ular content of the regression. Adam believed he must have accessed an experience of an ancestor who had witnessed his own father's death, and that event had been recorded in his own DNA. His mind had accessed that content in order to resolve a current struggle and to help him heal an area of potentially immobilizing anxiety. Adam realized that he had experienced the pain in his chest up to the point that the man in the trance died. When that man's pain stopped upon death, Adam's pain had ceased as well.

CHAPTER TEN

Mr. Brooksen arrived promptly for his weekly appointment with Adam. He had undergone ten traditional psychoanalytic sessions for his guilt issues, but since neither of them felt any progress had been made, Adam decided to induce a regressive trance in his patient. The results were extraordinary. Successfully contacting his collective unconscious, Mr. Brooksen found material stemming from unresolved events in the life of his great-grandfather Samuel that explained his own current guilt feelings. Mr. Brooksen's guilt originated from his great-grandfather's murderous deeds. The man had run a smuggling operation during the Peninsular war and had been responsible for the death of several innocent people. He had escaped justice and amassed a huge fortune from which his heirs continued to benefit. At the time Samuel had felt nothing about his cold-blooded arrangement for the murders, yet as he aged and confronted his own mortality, he became consumed by guilt. In search of solace, he turned to the teachings of the Roman Catholic Church and then became terrified for the fate of his soul. On his deathbed Samuel confessed his deeds to his priest, fearful that his sins would carry on and be repeated by his heirs. This was such a powerful, unresolved conflict for him that it had been stored in his DNA and transmitted, unresolved, to Adam's patient.

Adam's day passed quickly, and he remained at the office after reviewing the schedule and dictating the day's notes to Cathy. Usually he processed his own hypnotic experience each night in addition to reviewing his patient's psychotherapy sessions. However, as it grew dark, he decided to call it a night and headed home. Adam basked in the solitude of the drive and put in his new Rachmaninoff CD. He had developed the habit of searching through his ridiculously large collection of discs each Monday morning to select what he wanted to put in the car for the week. His uncontrolled acquisition of music discs and his meticulous Monday morning ritual rivaled any of his patient's obsessive-compulsive behaviors.

When he walked in the house, Ellen was in the family room packing her briefcase, and they gave each other the customary dutiful, emotionless hug and perfunctory kiss. He could see that Ellen was her usual hyperactive self, moving quickly on her way to accomplish some task. She had her leather jacket on and he realized she was preparing to go out.

"You can wait for me to eat if you want, I'll be back in about two hours, or go ahead and eat. There's a lot of food in the refrigerator," she said briskly.

"Where are you going?" Adam asked.

"To the high school. I enrolled in an adult education course. It will meet every Tuesday night for the next five weeks,"

"What course?"

Ellen responded brusquely, "It's a course on Napoleon."

There was an odd note in her voice as she said it, but Adam couldn't figure out the meaning of her tone or what she was unconsciously communicating. He was taken by surprise at her announcement.

"A course on Napoleon? Why are you taking a course about Napoleon?" he asked in disbelief.

In a tone uncharacteristic of someone who usually tried to avoid confrontation at all cost,

Ellen snapped, "Why do you say it that way? Can't I be interested in learning something new?"

Without waiting for a response, she continued. "Miss Ryan, but now she's Mrs. Strove. You remember, she was William and Kevin's history teacher, is giving the course through the Adult Ed. Helen, you know the one from my bridge group took a course with her last year and told me she's really great. We really liked her and so did the kids. I'm sure you'd remember her. Monica Ryan? Helen said that she married Mike Strove, a real bright light in the CIA, one of those spy type guys. Helen's husband Kyle, who has been with the agency for years, says that Mike is being groomed for administrative material. Mrs. Strove is teaching the course and I just thought it would be fun and interesting to learn something about Napoleon."

"How come you didn't ask me if I wanted to join you in the class?"

"I didn't think you'd be interested. You never like to leave the house after you get home from the office and you claim you hate to be around strangers in social situations. Look, you can come with me if you want, it's only sixty dollars for the course, and when I called to enroll this morning, they said that there were only three other people registered and there was still plenty of space. Do you want to go with me? If so, let's go right now because I don't want to be late."

Adam had intended to prepare one of his college class lectures that evening but without hesitation decided to go with Ellen. He wasn't sure why. He was tired, hungry, and not the least bit interested in Napoleon. During the ten-minute drive to the school he found himself mute and unable to initiate conversation with Ellen. His silence was deeper than usual, and he couldn't get himself to respond, even inanely, to her chatter. After a bit of internal debate as to what was going on he attributed it to fatigue. However, as he later came to understand, his unconscious mind was at that moment embarking on a new journey.

CHAPTER ELEVEN

Stepping into the high school classroom, Adam felt depressed. It reminded him of the many bored hours he had spent in his own drab schools with hardly anything registering in his brain. It was true that he had eventually gone on to be a very successful graduate student, but he had never enjoyed his early school years. In fact, he had been very unhappy. He hadn't done well and thought that they were a waste of time. Adam identified with Gandhi's comment on his school experience, which he described as "the most miserable years," of his life because he had no aptitude for lessons and rarely appreciated his teachers. Gandhi's comment that he would have done better had he never been to school echoed in Adam's mind as he made his way to an impersonal metal student desk.

There were three other members in the class besides Adam and Ellen. Mrs. Strove was sitting behind the teacher's desk reviewing her lecture notes. Adam recognized her from his children's school conferences, but now saw her in a different light. She was a bit older looking than he recalled. He had remembered her as seeming much too young to be a reliable teacher and observer of his children. Now she seemed to have what he regarded as a very intelligent face and sophisticated appearance. The teacher who had previously reminded him of an adolescent was now an attractive, mature woman. He also noticed that her clothing was fashionable, not at all like the stodgy middle-class dress he associated with teachers. Unlike those of the instructors he remembered from high school, her face was bright and alive. Adam felt a strange sense of portent.

Suspended from the board in front of the class was a poster size picture of Napoleon Bonaparte. Adam had never paid any attention to an image of the man before, but now he became inexplicably focused on the portrait. A strange curiosity swept over him and he found himself scanning Napoleon's face in search of some detail that would reveal something of his psychological nature. He had no idea what type of detail he was looking for or what he was trying to discover, but there was some strange attraction, almost a magnetic force, mesmerizing Adam as he stared at the three by five poster of Napoleon.

As he waited for the class to begin Adam felt a strange sensation as if he was floating above himself.

"Is this just lightheadedness or what? Or is this what my patients talk about when they think they've had an out-of-body experience?"

His hand wandered to the inside of the metal desk and he withdrew a blank piece of paper left behind by the student occupant. Adam began to doodle absentmindedly, his eyes still drawn to the picture. The spell-like state broke and he glanced down at the paper to see that he had produced a series of arrows. Looking more closely, he realized that he had unconsciously sketched the word "Destiny."

"Hmm, look at that, I've spelled out a word!"

Monica Strove emerged from behind the desk and asked the students to share their names and reasons for attending the course. The other students were high school teachers from neighboring towns who wanted to improve their own knowledge and teaching skills. Mrs. Strove turned to Ellen, who offered her name pretentiously and added, "I read about the course in the town paper. I've always been fascinated by Napoleon and thought this would be a good opportunity to learn more about him. I've always been intrigued by his accomplishments and the charismatic force he generates. I think he was a truly great man, maybe a genius, a man of incredible courage and foresight, and I hope to learn more about him in this class."

Adam couldn't believe he was hearing his own wife fawn over Napoleon. He mumbled to himself, "Interested in Napoleon? Where did that come from? We've been married twenty years and I never heard one word about Napoleon."

He continued to gaze fixedly at the picture, aware of a growing feeling of jealousy. He knew it was unreasonable, but he was actually jealous of Napoleon and wondered what it was that Ellen saw in him.

"Was she comparing me to him?" he asked himself almost audibly. His rational, intellectual side told him that this was just crazy thinking, but the feeling persisted.

Adam was startled out of his reverie when Mrs. Strove called upon him. Without knowing why, he introduced himself as Dr. Adam Peterson, realizing as he said it that he had emphasized his doctor title.

"I'm not sure why I enrolled in this class. When I arrived home tonight, Ellen told me she was taking the course, and I decided to join her. I know absolutely nothing about Napoleon, and if you had asked me before this very moment, I would have said that I had no interest in learning anything about him. But here I am."

Then impulsively, Adam began expanding on what should have been a two-sentence reply.

"As I learn more about Napoleon, I might be able to provide new insights and interpretations of his motivation and general personality organization, or perhaps even a psychological diagnosis of his pathology."

No sooner had the words left his mouth then Adam felt ridiculous about the way he had introduced himself and the narcissistic and arrogant sound of his words. He was deeply embarrassed by his behavior. Nervously shifting in his seat and arranging the note pad Ellen had just handed him, he fell silent and stared at the desk. He wondered if he was trying to impress Mrs. Strove, the other people in the class, and most of all Ellen. Adam realized how defensive and pompous he was acting. He was relieved and happy to find that Mrs. Strove emerged as a more appropriate person than he had been when she simply added that she would be interested in any thoughts that anyone in the class might offer.

"Thank God she didn't challenge me on that idea that I could interpret a man as complex as Napoleon after just a few classes."

Ellen, always out to ensure that Adam

came across as the preeminent, brilliant, and most of all successful, Washington psychologist, ignored Adam during his diatribe in an effort to draw attention away from his faux pas.

Monica. Strove rose in front of the class, leaving the notes she had been reviewing on the desk. She enjoyed sharing her historical knowledge and interests with adult students and was always stimulated by the discussions that ensued. She began to talk about some of Napoleon's ancestors and the era into which he had been born, and then explained that an understanding of Napoleon's life had to begin with some knowledge of the French Revolution.

"It's fair to say that the ideas and attitudes that led to the French Revolution, and the social and political upheaval that it sparked, influenced not only Napoleon and all Frenchmen, but also people throughout all of Europe for generations."

Mrs. Strove described the era so vividly that Adam imagined he was viewing an opera and was pulled emotionally into the scenes she depicted. The other students seemed similarly entranced with the performance.

"The French Revolution began in 1789. The king, Louis the XVI, was married to the infamous Marie Antoinette. There were about thirty million French people at that time. The vast majority living in small villages, and it was a world of haves and have-nots. The nobility and the Catholic Church owned most of the land, and hundreds of thousands of peasants worked the land. Poor, shabbily dressed, wretched and down-trodden, they lived a hand to mouth existence, working either their own small patches of land or the farms of bigger landowners. Those who didn't farm were laborers desperate to find work as a means of securing a place to sleep and some food to eat. Bread was the staple diet of these peas-ants, and they were dependent on flour to feed themselves and their children. In season, there were some vegetables, but meat was a rare treat. Imagine being utterly vulnerable to the vagaries of the government, which could tax them at whim, or to the weather, which could wipe out their crops in one storm.

One of the other students, who had identi-fied himself as a history and modern government teacher, raised his hand.

"I was just smiling and thinking to myself. That's just what I said to my U.S. History class about what I think is the current feeling of the majority of people in the United States."

The rest of the class laughed. Mrs. Strove smiled saying, "interesting thought." She continued, "At their local bakeries the peasants immediately felt the effect of any increased prices in the grain market. The threat of starvation was ever present. Those who didn't farm were laborers desperate to find work as a means of securing a place to sleep and some food to eat. Historians have estimated that in these very lean years, about ninety percent of the peasants lived at or below the subsistence level, barely able to earn enough to feed their families."

Adam empathized with the misery and poverty, envisioning masses of people in tattered, dirty dark clothes, with not only the pain of hunger but also the emerging deeper sense of anger and resentment portrayed on their faces as they looked to a seemingly unresponsive government for help. He listened intently to the lecture.

"Now compare this existence to the extraordinary ease and wealth of some of the French nobility. A powerful nobleman might own a country chateau with thousands of acres of land including formal gardens, forests, and cultivated fields, in addition to a grand gilded townhouse in Paris, with ballrooms, grounds, and stables. While the peasants worked his land, the wealthy nobleman, or wealthy bourgeois, spent time in idle pursuits such as hunting and gaming. Furs, jewels, silks, gold, fine food, and pleasure, it was all part of a nobleman's life. Of course, the peasants were not ignorant of these extremes of wealth."

Mrs. Strove changed tone to an emphatic, instructional voice.

"Let me make clear that, while the misery and poverty of the peasants should not be under-estimated, it did not cause the Revolution. To understand the activating force behind it, we need to know that the writings of the enlightened thinkers like Rousseau, Voltaire, and Hume, were all very popular. Their philosophy influenced the educated, intellectual portion of the French popu-lation, nobility and commoner alike."

Adam recognized these philosophers and quickly reviewed what he knew about each. He rarely thought about it, but his grandparents on both sides had emigrated from France. His mind began to wander into various hypotheses about his sudden interest in Napoleon, and he had to pull himself back to listening to the lecture. Mrs. Strove, was explaining how the philosophers had contributed to a cauldron of political thinking, which simmered on the flames of social inequi-ties, corruption, and oppression.

"When the people learned that Louis XVI had been forced to summon a meeting of the Estates General, representatives from all of France, they believed the moment of change had arrived. Suddenly, up bubbled the notions of equality, prison reform, demystification of religion, rights of women, and free market economy. The people chosen to represent the general population at the meeting were educated professionals, just the kind of people who would have read about the enlightened ideas I just described. While the philosophers may have been content to muse, and write, the revolutionaries were determined to implement their ideas and create a new society and government. Also fueling the pressure for change was anger from those who felt exploited or ignored, greed from those who saw a danger to their positions or an opportunity for greater gain, and fear from those who stood to lose a great deal."

Mrs. Strove stirred empathy in her students as she described the conditions in France. Adam felt a wave of retaliatory anger toward those who abused the less fortunate or created class differences and his thoughts swung to Ellen, who was so concerned with class and status. It annoyed him that she tried to make him act in a superior manner to those less fortunate. He thought he could easily have been one of the peasants working for the nobility and constantly feeling a sense of oppression from those with more money and material wealth. He remembered his boyhood friends, Jimmy, Junior, Ivan, and Ashton, black children who had moved into his basically all white neighborhood. He had spent much of his youth defending these boys against the prejudice of his white neighbors. The class learned that few authorities in 1789 believed that violent revolution would occur, and for many there was a spirit of hope for a better world and optimism for the future.

"In an attempt to rectify the oppressive conditions the Estates General abolished privilege by birth and established equality before the law. They also confiscated and sold church lands and limited the autonomy of the French Catholic church. Had Louis XVI been a man of different, more decisive character," Mrs. Strove exclaimed with a mixture of frustration and regret, "he might have controlled the reforms. Had Marie Antoinette not been Austrian and youthfully extravagant, she might not have served as a lightening rod for resentment. Had some of the aristocracy not sought help abroad, had the Parisians not been inflamed by radicals, there might have been a smoother transition to an enlightened state. However, threatened by invasion, fearful of treachery, and vulnerable to the increased pressure from violent extremists, the new government was buffeted by different political factions and was obliged to respond to the immediate demands of the most forceful voices."

Adam raised his hand and asked, "And what of the average citizenry? What did they think as they saw the great looming Bastille, a symbol of royal oppression, assaulted and seized?"

"Well, the day they did that, July 14th, which we call Bastille Day, was the first day of violence and bloodshed in the French Revolution, and it was lead by angry mobs in Paris, not by the people in the Estates General who were writing the constitution. Perhaps because of this both the people themselves and the representatives to the meeting began to sense the power of the masses. Only a few weeks later, with the Declaration of the Rights of Man, centuries of feudal privilege were abolished in a matter of days. The Church, another symbol of wealth and power, was humbled and diminished, and all Frenchmen could now enjoy equality of opportunity and freedom of speech."

Looking around the class she asked rhetorically, "Can you imagine how they felt and their new sense of hope and optimism?" Without waiting for a response she continued. "But imagine how others must have felt as well. Members of the middle class who had worked hard to achieve their wealth now saw it threatened, and people born into the aristocracy saw their entire way of life jeopardized. Some of the nobility left the country feeling they had lost too much or would lose more. These émigrés were to remain a thorn in the side of France for years to come, as some of them worked from abroad to unravel the reforms."

Adam interrupted without raising his hand, "So, how did Napoleon react to these events? What was his position at the time?"

Mrs. Strove responded, "Napoleon was in Paris when mobs stormed the Tuileries palace, slaughtered the Swiss Guard protecting Louis XVI, and forced the royal family first to flee for their lives and then to relinquish the throne. We know that Napoleon was aghast at the bloodshed, but also that he later condemned the king for his lack of resolve and firm direction in an emergency."

Adam immediately thought that he saw bifurcation in Napoleon. "Mrs. Strove, are you saying that he claimed to be opposed to the bloodshed that took place and yet his solution would have been for King Louis, to open fire on his own people, the citizens of France?"

"Good question, Dr. Peterson. My sense is that Napoleon was always in favor of rational action. He was not opposed to bloodshed, but he objected to unstructured, rash and impulsive aggression. If the military had been in control of the aggression he would have approved, but he didn't condone mob action."

Mrs. Strove asked the class, "How do you think Napoleon, who was so well read, so persuaded by the ideas of the enlightenment, felt about the new reforms? We know that he had formed definite ideas of heroism, good leadership, and government. How did this man, raised as a Catholic, respond to the changes in the church? We know that he embraced the civil constitution of the church and defended it in front of others. How did he, as a young nobleman, feel about the abolition of privilege? Napoleon's family had enjoyed some social status in Corsica, and his father had worked to have the family's Corsican nobility recognized in France. Yet, Napoleon had suffered teasing and derision from his French school mates because of his poverty and foreign birth. How did he feel about the dramatic changes transpiring in a nation that had conquered his homeland but paid for his education? We know that Napoleon believed in the prospect of enlightened government and came to believe that Corsica was better off as a part of France than as an independent state. How did he as a French officer feel about the violence? We know that Napoleon was appalled at the idea of civil war and sickened by mindless bloodshed."

Adam thought that Napoleon's early experience with these events could provide a direction to the psychological understanding of the kind of man he later became. He listened to Mrs. Strove with a growing interest and attraction.

Mrs. Strove began to discuss Napoleon's parents, Letizia and Carlo. As she talked about them Adam began to form a mental image of their appearance. Just then Mrs. Strove projected a picture of the couple. Adam was shocked at the sight of them. The faces he had imagined were exactly what he now saw before him.

"How could this be?" he asked himself. "I've never seen pictures of these people before. Maybe my mind is playing some kind of trick, but this is uncanny and almost mystical. I know these people!"

Adam mentally ran through a number of different psychological theories to explain this troubling feeling, but none of them provided a rational interpretation of the experience.

"I'm sure I never saw any pictures of these two people before. In fact I've never even heard of them. This is definitely not déjà vu. Wow! Could this be something from my collective unconscious?"

Mrs. Strove stretched her arms above her head slightly arching her back in a relaxing pose and suggested a ten-minute break.

The other students made their way to the water fountain, chatting about the class, but Adam was preoccupied with his recent recognition of Latizia and Carlo, and did not join in the conversation. A few minutes later, Monica Strove, who had remained at her desk called out, summoning the class to return.

The students filed back to the classroom. Adam, the last to enter, stood incognizant in the doorway, gazing at Monica. Their eyes riveted as she looked up and each seemed incapable of breaking the visual hold. The other students noticed Monica and Adam's peculiar behavior but said nothing. Finally, Ellen spoke.

"Adam, are you okay? Come sit so Mrs. Strove can continue our class."

CHAPTER TWELVE

Wheezing with exhaustion, their muscles spasming, and overcome by terror, they collapsed face down in the slimy bog. The odor of centuries of decaying vegetation and animal matter invaded their nostrils, and instantly an army of mosquitoes arrived to banquet on their exposed flesh.

"Enough rest Monica. I hear them coming again."

They crawled forward along the wet ground careful to move silently through the vegetation, which finally gave way to an uneven rocky terrain. Climbing over fallen scrub trees they reached the edge of a pond. Small animals that had never set eye on a human in this isolated place scattered in haste, startling Adam and

Monica as they made their way along the water. They wound back into thick woodland where the dense growth hindered their progress. The land seemed to belong to a prehistoric age. As they made their way up an incline they encountered large, jagged outcroppings of rock, striated with layers of different sediment that revealed their ancient heritage. They stopped for a few moments to survey the area. There were no houses or roads in sight, only a few birds that fortunately did not take flight and alert the pursuers to their position. Adam spotted a crevice between two boulders.

"Look there's a small opening. Maybe it's a cave! If they don't follow us in here we can probably sit it out long enough for them to give up."

Crouching and squeezing, they contorted their bodies to fit through the unyielding opening. The razor sharp edges of the rocks tore through their clothing, further scraping and ripping their skin as they made their way into the dark damp cave. Moving deeper into the dark abyss Adam urged Monica to follow. Hundreds of startled bats took flight, screeching, circling, and slamming into various parts of their bodies. As Monica and Adam cringed in horror, they were pelted by splats of guano. Monica choked and spat in disgust.

"Now what?"

"I got bat feces in my mouth, Adam!"

"Just keep moving! We have to get further

in so they can't trace us. There's an exit from this cave to another part of the mountain."

"How the hell would you know that Adam? Have you been in this cave before?"

"Of course not. I've never been in any cave before."

"It's too dark. We can't see. How do you know we won't fall into a pit? Adam we'll never get out of here!"

Monica held his hand, trembling.

"Don't be afraid. I'm not sure how, but I can see where we're going, and I know what's ahead. This cave will eventually come out into the woods about a mile from here. I can see every turn, rise and dip ahead of us."

"Adam, it's pitch black in here. How could you know where we're going? Don't make things up to try to help me feel better, that won't work with me. I can't believe this is happening."

"I'm not making things up. And I wouldn't do that to you."

"I'm not sure I believe that. I don't want to go any deeper. Can't we just stay right here and hide?"

"It's incredible, Monica. I tell you, I can see where we're going. Look out for this next ledge. It's not stable."

They were standing before a large flat circle of rock surrounded by swirling water. The slab itself seemed to move up and down as the water splashed against its edges. Adam was afraid that if they tried to walk across the rock it would tilt and pitch them into the turbulent water beneath.

"Take my other hand, Monica. We need to climb onto this ledge that goes around the slab. There's a torrent of water running under us and we don't want to fall in."

"I don't hear anything but my knees knocking and my teeth chattering."

Adam ignored her fear and tried to keep her moving.

"Keep your body flat against this wall. See the tiny lights of the crystals imbedded in the rock? Keep them on you right side. Hold my hand with your left hand and run your right hand along the wall for balance."

"For balance or to have it eaten by some huge snake? It feels like my hand is in seaweed."

Slowly they made their way through the cave, climbing up and down precipices, crossing narrow streams, and pushing through small fissures. Monica, unable to see, was squeamish about stepping into the sloshy, dank smelling ground. Suddenly a strong suction pulled her shoe off and she screamed at Adam to stop.

"Adam! Adam! Stop, stop, something grabbed my shoe. I can't go on without a shoe."

Adam stopped and turned to her. She was

balancing on her left leg, holding her right shoe-less foot in the air. She gripped his shoulder with one hand and gingerly propped herself against the slimy mass of the wall with the other."

"It's right there by your left foot. Just reach down and get it."

"No! I won't put my hand in that stuff, whatever it is. And how can you see it? It's totally dark in here. If you can really see it then, get it for me."

Adam laughed a little. He had no idea how he was able to see the shoe. He was aware that there was absolutely no light in the cave and yet he could see. Reaching directly to the shoe he slipped it back onto Monica's raised foot. Real-izing how frightened and sickened she must feel, he suggested that they sit for a few minutes and positioned her on a ledge free of slime and the grasping reach of roots growing down through the ceiling of the cavern. Monica, anticipating the warmth of his body next to her, panicked when she did not sense him at all. Adam spoke to let her know he was sitting nearby. Reaching to check that the pouch was still hanging around his neck, he felt the reassuring warmth of the artifact and removed it to hold it directly in his hand. Clutching it, he looked over at Monica.

"Adam, I just want to get out of here."

Monica reached out to reassure herself by

touching Adam. Unable to see in the black void, she reached out, and her outstretched hand met the artifact in Adam's hand. She felt the "clunk" of her opal ring as it made contact with the stone.

"Adam, look at my ring. It's like a flash-light."

CHAPTER THIRTEEN

The bright sunshine falling on the deep red awnings cast the scene below in a fiery light. The spring warmth had brought people out, and the Parisian café was busy, with waiters in their black pants and white aprons moving quickly among the packed round tables. The clinking of glasses and cutlery mingled with the sound of chatter and nearby traffic. Many patrons were smoking. At one of the tables a young man in a dark turtleneck sweater greeted another as he approached.

"Hello Brother Hiram."

"Hail Brother Hiram. How was your flight?"

"The flight from Cairo was late as usual, and also crowded and bumpy. And predictably, the movie was third rate and boring. Ah! Look there is our other brother"

Dressed in traditional clergyman's garb, a third man emerged from a grey Renault cab and made his way to the table. His black pants and white collar failed to conceal an understructure of bulging arm muscles and powerful chest. His face was square with a hardened jaw and a nose and ears that would have been more at home in a boxing ring.

"Hail Brethren. For a while I wasn't sure this meeting was within the length of my cable tow, but I made it. Is our Grand Exalted Commander coming?"

The man in the black sweater responded in the affirmative. "In fact, as we speak, I see him crossing the street."

Now four, the men sat at the table, speaking English except when ordering their lunch, which they did in fluent French.

With the arrival of their food, the Exalted Commander, in a suit and tie, took control of the meeting.

"There is increased pressure on us to show some progress. We need to be sure we know what information we want you to gather at lodge tonight. I'm sure the elders, and specifically the secretary, Marcel, have some knowledge of the ancient documents Napoleon stole from the

Vatican and sequestered in the bibliotheca. Some place, buried in that information, is the key to what we're looking for."

The youngest member of the group looked at the Exalted Commander challengingly.

"How can you be so sure that the information lies within this lodge?"

"Much research has been done to lead us here. I myself have not been told all the details, but after years of investigation the agency believes that this lodge, here in Paris, had a direct link to Napoleon. They believe that Napoleon involved the brothers of the lodge in his quest to find the connection between the Templars and some great treasure."

The priest, with an impatient air, leaned over to the youngest man. "God knows who came up with this notion! Whoever it was has been watching too many Davinci Code movies, but if it be the will of the agency, let's get on with it." He turned back to the Commander. "So what's the plan?"

"The lodge will open on the master mason degree and will be held under the stars. The communication made it clear that it was an unscheduled meeting for the purpose of dealing with business that is not to be shared with the whole of the brethren. This is what the intelligence report from the agency says. The brothers who know certain secrets of the lodge from the time of

Napoleon are very old, and they don't feel it would be safe for the younger master masons to know of this history. Remember that in France there is still a lot of suspicion about the Masonic order and its connection to the Knights Templar. They still fear being accused of heresy and devil worship. Let's not forget our brother Jacques DeMoley. It was in this very place that he was seized and taken to the Vatican and tortured."

The priest ordered a bottle of Napoleon Brandy to be brought to the table. Pouring for each of them, he turned toward the senior member of the group. "I thought this would be appropriate in light of the mission."

The men raised their glasses and savored the fine brandy.

"Let's get to the most important thing. What about the women?"

The older man smiled and said, "I've made the arrangements, as usual. Just call the concierge after you check in and ask for your champagne to be sent up."

The other three men chuckled in approval. The youngest lit a cigarette and said, "One of the perks of the job to make up for the crap we have to do."

CHAPTER FOURTEEN

Driving home after the class Adam was animated and tried to discuss Napoleon with Ellen. She showed interest as they exchanged ideas, but as usual, failed to share Adam's enthusiasm or excitement. Once home, they both headed for the refrigerator. Adam was famished and ready to consume the first thing his hands could grab. When he was really hungry he would wolf down anything, making haphazard concoctions without bothering to heat them. Ellen watched bemused, as he heaped several forkfuls of spaghetti onto his plate, mounded spinach on top, and stacked cold baked beans around the side. This mindless type of eating annoyed her, and she never missed an opportunity to label it as animalistic and primitive.

"How can you eat cold spaghetti?" She snapped. "At least heat it up. Anyway, have you even bothered to taste it before swallowing? I'm pretty sure it's at least seven or eight days old. You're impossible. I can just imagine what your house was like when you were growing up. Didn't Isabel even try to teach you decent eating habits?"

Ellen's words set Adam off on an inner tirade that would have been heard a mile away had he let it out.

"It's Mom, not Isabel. We have Daddy and Mommy on your side, but when it comes to my mother or father its Isabel and Lawrence. And why do you always have to bring my mother into your annoyances with me? You know how I feel about my mother and the difficulties I've had with her."

Ellen, eternally on a diet, glared at him and said nothing. She took some low fat cottage cheese and went into the family room to read her novel. Adam knew she had an eating disorder and that he had been neglectful by ignoring it and her strange diets. As she faded out of the kitchen Adam decided to have some fun for himself and asked her, "Do you want any fried chicken? I'm going to put a few pieces in the microwave for myself."

"No thanks, I have some cottage cheese. I don't want any fried chicken. It's a little too fattening for me. Actually, all the research says we should stay away from all fried foods."

"So why the hell do you make it for me? Especially since I've told you at least two hundred times that I don't like it. Hoping to collect the life insurance at an early age?"

As Adam sat eating at the kitchen table he mused about the Latizia and Carlo experience. The sense of familiarity and recognition of the couple haunted him. He had not shared the incident with Ellen, but wanted to, and several times rose from his chair to join her only to sit back down, fearing she would dismiss his remarks and diminish his experience. This feeling was not new to him. Ellen was such a pragmatist and so concrete in her thinking that Adam never felt safe telling her about his fantasies or feelings. Although they had been married for twenty years, each time he hid his true self by not expressing his feelings to Ellen, he wondered exactly what had motivated him to marry her in the first place. Deep down he knew that it had been for the wrong reasons. Her affluent family had offered a ready-made upper social class world for him, and he was not in love with anyone else at the time. He was about to finish graduate school, wanted to start a practice in the area, and to teach at Georgetown University. Marrying Ellen gave automatic *entree* into all of that. Her father, a professor at George-town, was the head of the faculty hiring and standards committee. Her mother had inherited an enormous fortune, and they were, in Adam's eyes, wealthy beyond anything he had ever imagined. He remembered his first visit to Ellen's home and his awe at finding himself in such a grand mansion. The original Rembrandts, Goyas, and Van Goghs on the walls left him speechless. Reminiscing, he realized that it was the trappings of wealth, not Ellen herself that had attracted him. He should have known that something was not right when he met her father. He was clearly wound as tight as the E string on a guitar. Ellen's parents had entered the room together; both dressed in what seemed to Adam semiformal attire. And that was his first mistake. As they introduced themselves as Doctor and Mrs. Patrick, he responded by saying, "Very nice to meet you. It looks as if you're about to go out. I don't want to detain you."

Ellen's mother had smiled wanly. "Oh, we're not going anywhere, just settling down for a quiet evening at home. You two have a good time."

As Adam left his reverie and returned to his bewilderment about Latizia and Carlo, a feeling of diffuse fear swept over him, and he wondered if he had somehow rearranged his neural structure with his brain experiments. The fear intensified as he compared himself to Timothy Leary and his use of LSD in the 60's. The brilliant Harvard psychology professor had eventually become psychotic as a result of his mind-expanding experiments with LSD. The thoughts scared Adam, but he nevertheless felt compelled to pursue his quest for the collective unconscious, and he ran through his following day's schedule to see if he had any free time to hook himself up to the equipment.

Adam stayed late at the office every night that week, placing himself in a regressive hypnotic state, now certain that he was perfecting the technique for contacting his collective unconscious. His earlier experience of the dying man confirmed that he had relived an event in his personal collective unconscious that had direct effect on his current life. His chest pain really was gone.

CHAPTER FIFTEEN

Over the next weeks Adam induced numerous self-regressions, always ending by sitting quietly, gazing out the window at the forest, and savoring the euphoria of the experience. Psychically energized by the contact with his ancestral memory Adam felt a deep spiritual connection to the earth. As he surveyed the view he felt that he could see the veins of every leaf in every tree and realized that watching the gently swaying branches and the flight of a bird created not only visual perceptions but also physiological sensations. Space and time expanded to create awareness far beyond himself. The energy emanating from within was the energy left by millenniums of ancestors, not that created by a psychedelic drug.

His introspection was broken when Cathy entered the room.

"Are you ready to dictate your patient session notes?"

"Leave me alone, I can't take any more of your sanctimonious efficiency and pressure."

Cathy froze and stared at Adam.

"God, I don't know where that came from, I am truly sorry, Cathy. I don't know where my mind was."

Cathy sat and pulled her chair up to his. Leaning towards him, she said, "Adam I'm really worried about you. We're far behind in patient session notes, there are letters to be written, phone calls that should have been returned last week, and tons of insurance forms to complete. You cancelled four appointments this week. I've never known you to do this unless it was for an absolute emergency. Is there something bothering you? Can I do anything to help?" Cathy was solicitous, but once again she questioned which was the real Adam, the empathic, ever-understanding person or the quick-tempered, arrogant man she had just seen.

Adam was disconcerted by the intensity of Cathy's concern. "I'm fine, don't worry we'll catch up on the work next week." What's going on with Cathy, he wondered? She's never looked at me that way before. Oh well, transference is the curse of my lot, so why not again with my secretary?"

Their interchange played through his mind during the drive home, which on this occasion he made without the accompaniment of music. Adam found that he had never noticed how attractive Cathy was and for that brief moment in the office he had actually been aroused.

Ellen greeted him from the kitchen. "I have a great bottle of red wine, would you like a glass before dinner?"

Adam, still struggling with the ambivalent feelings from the ride home, tried to be cordial.

"Thanks, Ellen, I think I'll run up and change clothes and then have the wine with the meal."

Comfortable in what he liked to call his leisure clothes, he joined Ellen at the table. She had prepared the meal as if for a special occasion, which made him suspicious, although he could not figure why.

"So how was your day today?" Ellen inquired cheerily.

"Well, I feel like I'm making progress. I'm finally nailing down the regressive hypnotic techniques I've been working on for the last few years. I'm close to being able to calibrate the transcranial magnetic stimulation coil to hit a very specific cortical site. When it does this, it elicits specific regressive memories or zeros in on certain historical times for the person."

Ellen's face showed interest, deceiving Adam as it had hundreds of times before. She responded, "Oh, I meant to tell you that Jean Underhill called today. She asked me to head up a committee to develop the youth section at the library. It would mean a lot of work, but I think it's a worthwhile endeavor. I talked to mother about it, because she did the same thing in Maryland several years ago. She thinks I should do it. It can't hurt your career to get our name out there every chance I get. Daddy said that he could arrange to have graduate students assigned to do research for me."

Adam continued to work at the mountain of food. Once again Ellen had dismissed his attempt to share his success with her. There was nothing new in this. He wondered why it bothered him, and why he would expect anything different.

"I think that's wonderful. Of course let's get our name out there. Who knows, some day I may be appointed as the secretary of Health and Education."

Adam proceeded to deliberately cut his meat with his fork, mix the potatoes with the peas, and smack his lips as he chewed.

"I'm sure that was one of the possibilities Daddy and Mommy had in mind when they approved our marriage."

Looking miffed, Ellen said in a soft

controlled voice, "I never know how to take you. I can never figure out whether you're being sarcastic or genuine."

There was a long period of silence. Ellen rose to clear the table while Adam was still eating and then finally spoke.

"I saw Mary Beth today and she told me Jim was unexpectedly made senior vice-president. Boy, was she excited. She's invited us to join them, to celebrate, Saturday night at Le Chateau Vert. You and Jim seemed to like it so much last time we were there together; she thought it would be a great choice. We had nothing scheduled and I knew you would probably like to be with them on this special occasion, so I arranged for us to pick them up at seven o'clock."

Adam put his fork down abruptly, glared at her furiously, and snapped, "For God's sake Ellen, can't I ever have a free evening? Do we have to be booked every single moment?" His voice was harsh, his look was cruel, and his posture was aggressive.

Ellen fled from the room, knocking her chair over in her haste to run upstairs. Tears flowed down her cheeks. Adam was shocked at himself. He didn't know how to interpret his reaction but felt ashamed and frightened because he had lost control for a second time within a few hours. He followed her upstairs to their bedroom and found her lying across the bed sobbing. He sat next to her and put his hand on her shoulders. She allowed his caress, but with her usual stiffness sat up and returned an "A" frame hug, ensuring no real body contact.

"My mind must have been preoccupied with work, and I certainly didn't mean what I said. Of course we can go on Saturday."

Ellen gave him a slightly warmer hug, and patting his back said, "I care for you, I care about you too much not to know that something is going on with you. Adam, you must tell me what it is. You can talk to me about anything, I'm sure you know that. I know now is not the time, but we really have to get into whatever is bothering you and talk."

Adam wished he felt free to tell her the truth that he had never felt safe talking about personal matters with her.

CHAPTER SIXTEEN

Chief B. J. Kelly of unit 786, sat with his legs propped on his large oak desk, with a picture window spanning the entire wall behind him. The window offered a view of Washington's famous cherry trees in full bloom. His office was unadorned, as were most of the unit chief's offices at the Pentagon. B. J. had been with the agency for over twenty-five years and was nearing his fifty-fifth birthday. He stood about six feet four but with his lean body build, appeared much younger than his age.

"Come on in, gentlemen," he barked in a voice like an ill-played tuba. "How are you hood-lums doing? Oh, of course you know, Doctor, that I don't include you in the same category as these three."

"Beej, I'm not sure being excluded from that title is a compliment, or a suggestion that I'm getting too old to engage in life's amusements. I trust you've been well. I don't want to be a pain in the butt, but I should tell you I need to be out of here in half an hour. My presence has been requested, if you know what I mean, at the meeting in unit 49."

B.J. reached into his drawer and pulled out a thick tattered manila folder. "Okay gentlemen, I'm getting pressure from above to show some progress on our mission. I don't know how much you know about what the guys at the Advanced Research Projects Agency are up to, but at last week's meeting it sounded to me like they are right on our tails and starting to step on our heels. ARPA has some really bright stars. It seems to me they speak in code even at their meetings, but I sensed that they might have gotten into our area. I have to file a report from our group and meet with the budget committee about funding. So, let's first hear from our duo in France."

Another of the four men spoke. "Okay, this is from the French team. We think we're on to something, Beej. Doc found out about an old Masonic lodge that may have information in their archives about the Templars and their treasure. It's a Masonic lodge now, but it may have grown out of either the Prion or Golden Fleece. Elio and I managed to get very friendly with the wives of two of the younger members. The two women arrange the catering for the lodge. This lodge has hundreds of years of history behind it, and all the members have heard rumors about ancient secrets that the older brothers have been concealing. The lodge is located deep in the woods on the grounds of an old private school. We made contact with the secretary, presenting ourselves as Masonic historians from the U.S. and Great Britain. And I've got to give you credit, Doc. You've taught Elio enough that he was able to convince the lodge secretary that he was really a Masonic historian. And by the way, the secretary must be 90 years old."

B.J.'s encouraging nods conveyed his approval. "What do you think, Doc.? Is this worth pursuing?"

"Definitely, Beej. Did you guys get more detail on the exact location?"

"No, the wives have never actually been to the building, because they use a room in a restaurant for the social gatherings. It was obvious that the secretary was evasive about the exact location. All we could come up with is that it is either on or next to the campus of an old school. In fact, the meeting we're going to attend may not take place at the lodge itself because it's an unscheduled meeting restricted to the older brothers. Frankly, we both felt like we were in the middle of a James Bond film with this secretary. He kept glancing around furtively while he was talking. I tell you guys, it was weird. So we really don't know anything further about it Doc, but we're working on it."

"I hope you can pinpoint the location. I wonder where in France it is, because I'm starting to put some pieces together. Right now I don't have enough to go on."

The fourth agent broke his silence.

"I can report on my trip to Egypt which has also been fruitful. I found a guide who's an expert on Biblical and other ancient texts. He served for three years with the agency translating the Dead Sea Scrolls. This guy is a real find. He worked on the copper scroll and probably knows more about it than anyone else. He took me on an excursion into the dessert and we came up with some artifacts that I think will be revealing, but I have yet to analyze them. The last thing I will add is that my family and my parishioners are becoming suspicious of my trips, and we had better be careful that we don't blow my cover."

Elio spoke again. Hey guys, there's something else I want to bring up with you."

"Go ahead, tell us what's on you mind." B.J. shrugged with a sign of impatience.

"Well, I've followed up on a psychologist Mike asked me to check on. This guy has developed a trance technique. His patients regress to a previous time and know exactly what was going on at that period in history. I think this might prove to be something we could use. He talks about using magnetic forces in the brain to go back in time."

"That's interesting," B.J. responded. "I'm not sure what it's all about, but it sounds like some of the things I heard at the ARPA meeting. They were talking about using magnetic implants in the brain to create cyborg soldiers who could control weapon systems via these brain chips. So you're not the only one interested in this. I think it's another thread to follow. Keep looking into that one. Any danger in it?"

"No, none at all. He's a scientist and an easy mark."

CHAPTER SEVENTEEN

Adam had decided to accept Alice's invitation to the first meeting of his collective unconscious disciples. Intending to put himself in a trance beforehand, he knew he wouldn't make it home for dinner and asked Cathy to get Ellen on the phone. Cathy wondered to herself, as she had many times, what kept Adam and Ellen together. As efficient as ever, she immediately made the call.

"Hi, it's me. I won't be home for dinner tonight. I have some work to catch up on, and then I'm going to a meeting and probably won't be home until ten or so."

Ellen replied with annoyance. "You didn't say anything about a meeting. It's Friday night, and I asked Susan and Peter to stop by for dessert.

What meeting is this?"

Adam realized he was trapped. He hadn't told Ellen about the group.

"It's actually a group meeting that some of my patients arranged. They want to review some of the hypnotic work they've been doing."

"Typical you, Adam. You never tell my anything, and now I have to look like a fool and change our arrangements."

Cathy poked her head in once more to ask if he needed anything else, and then said good night. As Adam attached the electrodes to his cranium, he again worried that no one really knew the long-term effects of repeated magnetic stimulation to the brain.

"I'm really playing with fire. What if at some point they find that all of this is detrimental to the brain? Oh my God, and all the poor people I dragged into this. My God, I could get sued for everything I have and maybe even be liable for criminal action."

The drive to continue his research won over the anxiety. The classes on Napoleon had spurred his interest in the man, and Adam decided to try to experience him as a living person via a trance. After reviewing notes from the class, Adam began the induction by presenting subliminal pictures of the young Napoleon to himself.

A stone-clad school stood surrounded by gravel walkways. To the side of the main building was a little fenced garden separated from the rest of the school grounds. A young boy sprang from the stone bench on which he had been reading to chase away two other boys who were trying to hide from the schoolmaster after playing with fireworks. The boy resumed his seat on the bench. Adam knew immediately that he was in the presence of young Napoleon. He couldn't see himself and had no physical form, but he could perceive the situation with all his senses. It was France, and the school at Autun.

One of the boys uttered in a suppressed voice, "The young one is made of granite but we all know there's a volcano inside." Adam was aware of Napoleon's ardent need for independence, and the detachment, coldness and social isolation that set him apart from the other boys at the school.

A bell signaled the end of recess and Napoleon left the garden and entered his dormitory room. It was simple and unadorned but contained many books, including several by Rousseau and Voltaire. A letter lay squarely on the small dark, single drawer desk, and Adam could see that it was addressed to Napoleon's father, Carlo. The only light in the room entered from a small solitary window high above, and the darkness and Spartan furnishings lent a dismal air to the surroundings. Somehow able to absorb the Corsican words of the boy's letter, Adam sensed the depth of Napoleon's emotional turmoil. Napoleon had written of his loathing for the *school and his yearning to go home.*

The scene shifted, and as Napoleon walked out of his math class, several students commented about his ridiculous name. They mocked his clothes, his small stature, and his appearance. Then they teased him about his poor French and Corsican accent. The boys continued to poke fun at Napoleon, declaring that his coat was too long and that his clothes fit him like a peasant. As he turned away from them, one boy challenged Napoleon about his claim to nobility. Knowing that he was still within earshot, another boy taunted, "If you Corsicans are such brave fellows, why did you let yourselves be beaten by our unconquerable troops?" For the first time in this ongoing harassment, Napoleon turned to face his tormenters. He stood erect; chest puffed out, face rigid with anger, and jaw jutting in defiance. With his right hand fisted waist high, he answered in a slow, deliberate, and caustic voice, "We were one to ten." The power of his words and the penetrating tone immobilized the boys into mute stone-like statues. They stared in shock, as Napoleon, his face white with rage and his teeth clenched, continued, "You just wait till I'm grown up, and I will pay you Frenchmen out."

The scene switched in an instant. Napoleon was seated, talking to another man, and from the paunch of his belly and his thinning hair Adam perceived that he was now with the middle aged emperor. Napoleon was dictating his memoirs and his face betrayed an intensity of emotion.

"One of the interesting and I am sure important effects on my growth was something my father said to me one day while we were walking together in Villefranche. I remember telling my trusted friend General Bertrand how I thought this influenced me. My dear father said, "How stupid we are to be so proud of our own country. We speak grandly about the Main Street of Ajaccio yet here in one French town alone there is a street every bit as fine." Napoleon continued. "You see, I had always admired the commitment and faithfulness of my father to Corsica, and had determined to carry out his wishes for Corsican strength and independence, as well as letting those Frenchmen who teased and ridiculed me at Autun and Brienne pay dearly. I felt as if he was a traitor saying that, even though in my heart I did not believe it. You know that I was sent to Autun and then Brienne when I was only nine. I had to leave my home and most of all my beloved Corsica. I went with Joseph but it was still a very significant separation for me. I had been granted a bursary and a place in the military school at Brienne as a Royal Parbel, all expenses paid by the King. My father had arranged that. I found Autun and Brienne to be intolerable at first. I wrote home from Autun describing the ridicule I was given by French children who treated me as inferior to them because of their wealth and nobility. I asked to come home but my father refused. I wrote another letter from Brienne in my first year there. I can tell you exactly what I said. I wrote to my father and mother saying, If you or my patrons can't *let me have sufficient funds to keep up a more respectable appearance at this college, then please write and ask for me to be sent home and as quickly as possible. I told them that I was tired of looking like a beggar and being jeered at by impertinent schoolboys whose one claim to be my superior is a rich background. I received a letter from my mother, I am not sure where my father was at the time, but she answered. Her answer led me to feel completely misunderstood and abandoned. She wrote, 'if you ever write such a letter again to us we will have nothing ever again to do with you.' He looked at the other man in the room and asked, "Can you imagine how a young boy who is living with constant embarrassment and ridicule feels when getting that kind of response from his mother? This was especially difficult for me because we had been raised with a very strong allegiance to family. My father had us all to believe that we live to give to our family."*

The trance ended abruptly. Adam emerged jubilant, knowing that he had been with Napoleon. His knowledge of him went far beyond the content of Mrs. Strove's presentation. She hadn't mentioned anything about his experiences at his first school in France and Adam was absolutely certain that he had never read or heard anything about that part of Napoleon's life.

"My God! I felt exactly what Napoleon was feeling. I felt it just as sure as if it was me!"

CHAPTER EIGHTEEN

Adam parked his Jaguar in neat parallel in front of Alice Hawkins's house. He had mixed feelings about attending this meeting, thinking he might be violating the patient-therapist relationship ethic he valued, but he rationalized that these were no longer his patients, just human beings reaching for new dimensions of knowledge. As he approached the double width front door of the brick mansion, he reassured himself aloud, "Right, it's ok, these are no longer my patients, they're my students."

Alice greeted him with a hug and an elated smile. Controlling the impulse to brush her away, he followed her into the living room, discretely taking in the grandeur of the area; from the high ceilings and multiple crown moldings to the clearly priceless art collection. He noticed a few personal photographs clustered on the ormolu chest near the plush, cut velvet sofa. Glancing about the room, Adam sorted through the crowd and recognized that they were all his former or present patients. Alice gestured toward the buffet table set up in the dinning room and invited him to help himself. Adam declined, falsely stating that he had eaten earlier.

Taking him by the arm, Alice led Adam to John Ormsby, who was going to introduce the meeting. John's hypnotic work with Adam about a year earlier had been extremely enlightening and healing, and he was convinced, as was everyone else at the meeting, that Adam's technique had freed him from the burden of the past and enabled him to resolve his present emotional issues. John, a charismatic speaker with a smooth, persuasive voice, stood up and began to portray the group as pilgrims on a journey to create a new world order. In the new world he described, people would no longer be held under the sway of religion, living in fear of facing heaven or hell as a consequence of their behavior on earth.

"We are on the verge of proving that eternal life lies in the collective unconscious. Once Doctor Peterson perfects the technique, all people will be able to access it, and it will change the world."

Adam listened with smug satisfaction. Overnight he had become the key figure in a developing transcendental movement. He felt energized and inspired.

Looking at Adam, John said, "As our leader, Doctor Peterson, will you share some of your thoughts about how our group should proceed? More people will want to join us, but we have to be careful who we permit in."

Adam nodded, realizing that the group understood the brilliance of his research and could bring him the recognition he deserved. He chose his next words carefully, recognizing that they would serve as a guiding light for the direction of the group.

With gravitas and imposing dignity he began. "I have some thoughts that will help with the general tone and path you'll want to take with your group."

Many voices chimed, "You mean *our* group."

"One process that occurs in psychotherapy is that the patient seeks energy and power to compensate for, and to replenish his own drained energy and sense of weakness. Not to offend any of you but this is ultimately an attempt by the patient to gain control. The result of every interaction we experience is that we feel either strong or weak. People try to say whatever will enable them to feel strong or gain a feeling of control. We gain energy when we feel strong. We will manipulate in any way we can to get energy from others or from a situation. Even leaders of governments and institutions may present a public goal as altruistic, when in fact their motivation can be understood as a need to create a situation that will psychologically energize them. The motivation to control others is not conscious. People only sense the outcome; namely, when they control others they feel strong and better. The war our nation is fighting may on the surface be explained as a need to protect national interests, but, in fact, it can be attributed to an individual's, such as the President's, need to engage in conflict in order to produce an experience of control that brings psychic energy.

It behooves us to be aware of just how much effort we expend trying to control others to gain psychic energy. You, who have each experienced your genetic past, will understand what I am about say. We have a new, better source of energy. The energy derived from control is a poor substitute for the true enlightened energy that lies in the collective unconscious. The collective unconscious offers an unending source of unpolluted energy. Using my method, people will be able to tap into their own collective unconscious, their own personal wells of pure energy and use them to create a new World. There would be no need for global conflicts or the individual struggles that arise out of the old need to gain energy through dominance. Instead, everyone will draw upon energy from within.

Freud taught us that it is through knowledge of our own unconscious that we learn who we are and grow capable of finding peace. Freud's notion of the unconscious is that its contents are confined to the events of one lifetime. Carl Jung added that in addition we carry what he termed the collective unconscious. This contains the memories of all of humanity through the ages. My research shows that there's more than just what Freud and Jung proposed. We have within us Freud's unconscious, Jung's collective unconscious, and now, what I term the personal collective unconscious. This is the storehouse of personal genetic memories passed on through our unique genetic heritage. When I learned how to access my personal collective unconscious I knew that I had touched my immortal soul. With access to my collective unconscious I have become aware of the powerful energy that is generated by my ancestors and the effect that it has on who I am and how I feel. Yes, I have been emphasizing that genetic memories are carried in the DNA, a new and revolutionary idea. But we must take this finding to an even higher level of understanding. My friends, what I'm telling you is that the soul exists after the death of the physical body and returns time and again to other bodies through the transmission of genetic material. That's right, your soul is encoded in your DNA."

The group stared at Adam in stunned silence and awe. Finally Alice spoke. "Adam, your words are profound. I can envision huge ramifications to this concept."

Adam smiled beatifically and continued. "The dimension we presently live in is not the only dimension and therefore not the only place souls dwell. As my patients recalled traumatic events in their genetic memories, their current problems were cured. Eastern religions have long professed past life existence, and many people have reported experiencing previous lives. Until the Romans censored it, the New Testament contained references to reincarnation. Jesus himself may have believed in it. Remember, he asked the apostles if they recognized John the Baptist as Elijah returned. Elijah had lived over nine hundred years prior to Jesus.

Many of you have traditional beliefs about the soul, but explanation of it is always vague. In most religions the soul assumes a mystical, amorphous form that is somehow within us but then floating somewhere out in space when we die. My research proves that the soul is a body of energy that blends with universal energy and is transferred from one being to another through the DNA. Therefore it has a physical as well as a mystical entity. The soul registers its experiences. It feels the appreciation and gratitude of everyone you have helped and loved. It also feels the power, anger, and despair of everyone you and all who have gone before you, have hurt."

Adam was confident that he had made his point and gathered his sheep. He turned the floor over to John.

"Thank you Dr. Peterson, your presentation was indeed powerfully enlightening. It's clear to me that we have a very important common purpose. So, I think the first step is for our group to come up with a name. Any suggestions?"

There was an instant murmur of discussion and John raised his hand to quiet the group.

A middle-aged woman took the floor. "I agree that coming up with a name is important but I think first we need to discuss a meeting place. It is certainly gracious of Alice to offer her home but I think we ought to consider finding a regular venue. It should be someplace where we could permanently set up the equipment Adam needs to continue his work and where we could gather at times other than for formal meetings."

As if orchestrated, the groups expressed a hearty vote of agreement.

Susan Atkins raised her hand to speak. "I know the perfect place. It's an old house in a secluded spot, and would fit our needs perfectly. My friend Rosalie is a realtor who showed it to me about a week ago. It's been on the market for a long time so we can probably get a good deal. I'll get more information and report at our next meeting."

Eunice nearly leapt out of her cordovan leather chair, exclaiming, "I've been thinking about a name from the moment Alice suggested we form a group. Based on my experience with Dr. Peterson, and the experiences of most of you here tonight, I propose this name: Society for Eternal Life and Freedom. Think of its acronym, SELF. The SELF-group for short. Doesn't it just say it all? A new vision of eternal life has been revealed to us and we have been set free."

CHAPTER NINETEEN

The business of the meeting over, the people gathered at the buffet table to nibble and socialize. Adam could hear the talk centering on his words and thought it best to slip out unseen. He found Alice, thanked her for hosting the evening, and took his leave.

Ellen was reading in the family room when he arrived home.

"Well, how was your meeting? Did you have to give a speech? What was it all about anyway?"

"You know Ellen, we don't often talk about what I'm doing. Every time I try, something seems to interfere and we get onto another subject.

"Well I know what you do. But what does this group have to do with it?"

"This is a group of people I've treated, who see the implications of finding and using the collective unconscious in a way that goes far beyond psychotherapeutic application. They see it as a spiritual connection to everything and everyone who has ever existed. They see it as having found the human soul. They believe it is the way to a new world of peace."

"Oh come on Adam! Do you really believe that stuff?"

"Yes, of course I do! Why does it bother you?"

"Can you hear yourself talk? It's fanatical. It sounds like Timothy Leary all over again."

"Don't say that. He was crazy and I'm not. It's late and I have an early appointment in the morning and have to be up at five. Good night, I'll try not to wake you." Adam leaned over and gave Ellen a perfunctory kiss on the cheek, which went unreciprocated, and turned to go upstairs.

Adam's early morning appointment was with himself. He wanted to make detailed notes in his research journal and then put himself into a regressive trance. In his barely legible scrawl, he began to write.

"One of the major challenges for neurology has been that even with the use of microelectrodes it has proven difficult to record the activation of specific brain cells.

Previous researchers have reported that the smallest microelectrodes are apt to pick up signals from the surrounding neural cells, as well as the target cell, and this can confuse the data gathered. I have overcome this problem. I have developed a nano electrode and a process that permits me to isolate the specific cells that are responsible for the storage of the collective unconscious. The critical part of this work has been the creation of a program that mathematically separates and unravels overlapping pulses and information coming from the surrounding cells."

Just as he was about to write the formula down on paper for the first time, he stopped abruptly. He mused on the magnitude of his discoveries and techniques and their potential political implications. If misused they could actually be put to evil purpose.

"No," he thought. "This formula is the basic core of my research and the result of over fifteen years of work. I'm not about to give it away or take the chance of it falling into the wrong hands. I'll have to store it in a safe place. I know where I can put it. From now on I'll refer to it as Jung's Code, in anything I write in this journal."

He closed the book and proceeded to put himself in a trance. He had discovered that by introducing specific stimuli in an unconscious form he could guide the regression to a particular place and time. Adam began the transcranial magnetic stimulation by flashing pictures of Carlo and Latizia at subliminal speed

As if at military attention, Carlo Buonaparte of Ajaccio stood waiting. He was tall and slender but clearly muscular, and his overall appearance portrayed Mediterranean descent. He had thick eyebrows, a coarse but weak mouth, and a generally amiable face. About to make his marriage vows to Latizia, his expression left no doubt that he was committed to the marriage through love and intended to dedicate himself to Latizia Ramolino, also of Ajaccio. The ceremony concluded, the fashionably dressed crowd gathered under the high arches of the gothic cathedral to congratulate the newlyweds. Carlo, holding Latizia's hand, responded to one of the guests. "We will be living on the ground floor of my mother's house, along with Uncle Lucciano." He gestured to the man in Archdeacon's regalia seated nearby."

Latizia was a beauty, with huge flashing black eyes, and a pleasant countenance. Her raven hair was pulled back and glistened in the sun shining through the stained glass windows of the cathedral. Her beauty was heightened by a strange light reflecting off the statue of the Virgin Mary behind her. Speaking in her native Corsican, Latizia thanked everyone for coming.

Adam emerged from the trance with a magnificent insight. As in his other regressive trances, he had experienced the strange sensation of being identity-less, of being a non-physical entity observing an event.

"That's why I recognized those pictures Mrs. Strove put up in the classroom! I did know them! They're a part of my collective unconscious! Somewhere in my ancestral history, someone knew Latizia and Carlo." Adam was elated. "I can't wait to tell Mrs. Strove."

Completely preoccupied by this experience Adam arrived home that evening and without greeting or kissing Ellen he immediately asked if she had Mrs. Strove's phone number. Ellen regarded him quizzically and asked, "Why do you want to get in touch with Mrs. Strove? Did you hear any changes about the class on Tuesday?"

"I've had some insights into Napoleon's psychological development that I want to share with her. I want to hear what she thinks about my ideas."

Ellen thought this was strange and answered caustically. "Her home number is in the adult education directory, which I think is in the left hand drawer of the hall table. Do you really want to call her at home? She might think it's inappropriate and an intrusion. You'll see her next Tuesday. Can't it wait?"

"Ellen, it's ok, I'm excited about my thoughts and I'll be very polite. If she feels it's inappropriate to discuss it outside of class I'm sure she'll tell me."

Adam retrieved the directory and easily

found the number. With some trepidation, he dialed. What troubled him most was the possibility that if Mrs. Strove was not interested, he would have to concede to Ellen that she had been right.

"Hello, this is Monica," a pleasant voice answered the phone on the second ring.

"Hi, I don't know if you remember me, but this is Adam Peterson, from your Napoleon class. I've gotten deeply involved in the whole Napoleon saga and I have some thoughts about his psychological development that could lead to an interesting biographical profile. I wondered if you were at all interested in discussing it."

Monica responded without hesitation. She was delighted to hear someone speak about Napoleon with her level of enthusiasm. "Of course I know who you are, and I would be most interested in your thoughts. You may not know that hundreds of volumes have been written about Napoleon, but in my opinion there is not one good piece of work on the psychology of this critical figure in history."

Adam's pulse rate and blood pressure shot up and he felt an excitement and physical rush. "Great, when would be a good day for us to meet?"

Monica didn't hesitate. "Id like to do it as soon as possible. Let's see. My problem is that for the next two nights we have parent teacher meetings at school. Mike is out of town, as usual, for the next five or six days. I never really know when he will return from a trip. I have my college room-mate and her husband coming from New Jersey to spend the weekend. After that I'm free any evening, except Tuesday." Their simultaneous laughter signaled a shared sense of humor. Why don't we make it the Wednesday after our next class?"

Adam pushed the issue and asked if Monday night would be possible, but Monica declined.

"I guess it will have to wait until next Wednesday then. How about meeting at my office at seven?"

Monica agreed.

Adam returned to the kitchen for dinner. Ellen, sitting at the table, looked at him questioningly. "So, did you reach her? I bet you were just the interruption she was looking for at home during dinner time."

"I reached her and she was interested in working with me on a psychobiography of Napoleon. We arranged to get together to talk about it next Wednesday night."

Ellen was surprised and puzzled but showed no emotion as she replied, "Oh okay, I'll have some cake and coffee ready for us. Hmm, a psychobiography, that'll be interesting for us. We're really getting into this guy, aren't we?"

"Oh! I figured it would be best to keep the meeting with Mrs. Strove at a professional level, so I scheduled it at the office for seven Wednesday night."

Ellen blanched. "Oh, that's probably best. In fact I just realized that next Wednesday night is the photography club meeting, and I haven't been to one for the last three months. I really should go this time, so it will work out just fine. You can tell me about your meeting with Strove when we both get home."

Adam was relieved.

CHAPTER TWENTY

On Tuesday afternoon Ellen called Adam to remind him of their second Napoleon class that evening.

"You did remember that we had class tonight, didn't you? I wondered if you wanted to meet at the diner and have a quick bite to eat before class."

"I finish my last appointment at 5:30, and the diner sounds great. I can get there by six, I hope, but if I'm late go ahead and order for me."

"You want your usual or something healthy tonight?"

Adam bit his lip and clenched his right fist unconsciously. "Oh, by all means, something healthy. I'll have a double cheeseburger, French fries, onion rings, and regular coffee. Oh yeah, and I'll have a piece of their Italian Cheese Cake with my coffee."

"Don't be silly. What do you really want?"

Adam laughed to overcome the hostility he was feeling. He wanted to say, "That's what I really want" but instead he answered, "No, I'll have their broiled salmon dinner and unsweetened ice tea."

He had wanted to share his enthusiasm about the class with Ellen, but her comment about his choice of food killed any desire to relate to her. Anticipating the class, Adam had thought about Napoleon a good deal during the day. In fact, Napoleon had begun to supplant Duke Snider, Jackie Robinson, and the boat, in his fantasy world.

As he walked into class that evening, Adam's eyes were drawn to Mrs. Strove. She was wearing a form-fitting blue dress that he found particularly provocative. Her feminine curves filled the dress in all the right places. "Wow, she looks good."

"Welcome. I'm happy to see that you all returned. We have a lot of new material to cover."

Adam was flooded with thoughts and questions, but he seemed to be physically frozen and mute. He realized he was afraid to ask anything, something he had never experienced before. He searched within to discover the reason. What was he afraid of and why? He sensed that there was something fateful about his presence in this course. Acting as his own analyst, he wondered if the fear might be arising from a past event in his personal collective unconscious. This thought intrigued him and opened a new door to his thinking about Mrs. Strove and Napoleon.

Mrs. Strove began.

"I'll be talking about Napoleon's early years in Corsica, where political tensions were running high. We'll follow this with a look at Napoleon's school years on the French mainland. Then we'll cover his early military experience, including his witnessing of mob violence and civil war. We'll look at his struggle to win an appropriate position in the French army, his successful dispersal of an anti-government demonstration - the famous *whiff of grape shot* - and finally we will explore his rise to military power. I think this will help you to see the sequential threads of his life and lead to a more comprehensive understanding of our hero."

Adam, engrossed in the presentation, reached into his briefcase and drew out a notepad.

"Napoleon was born in Ajaccio, on the island of Corsica. His birth on this island, and not in France itself, had major effects on the development of his character. Unlike most of the landed aristocracy of the time whose marriages were arranged to maintain and consolidate property,

Napoleon's parents, Carlo and Letizia, probably married for love. She had a strong, disciplined character, like her mother. Carlo, in contrast, seems to have been a bit dissolute and opportunistic. As a nobleman, he felt he had a role to play in the tumultuous politics of the island.

The Corsicans were fiercely nationalistic and deeply resented the fact that their island had been sold by the Genovese to the French. The Corsicans were also notoriously proud and readily engaged in vendettas and revenge. A man named Paoli was leading the independence movement against France. Carlo joined the rebellion, serving as Paoli's secretary. Letizia, pregnant with Napoleon, accompanied her husband into the mountainous interior of the island, the stronghold of the patriots."

Mrs. Strove turned to the chalkboard and wrote Napoleon Buonoparte and his birth date.

"Napoleon Buonaparte, the Corsicans spelled it with an "e," was born into this world of simmering rebellion. The young Napoleon was feisty, often scrapping with other children. He started school at the age of five, and we know that he was teased for wearing droopy stockings and for having been seen holding hands with Giacominetta, a little girl in his class. Imagine how being teased might have affected a small boy's development. Also Letizia frequently ordered the young

Napoleon to spy on his father and report to her on his gambling and drinking. Napoleon deeply resented this. You can imagine how having to spy on your own father would affect a child.

Adam was ready to respond and raised his hand. Mrs. Strove looked at him and said, "I can see you're eager to dissect him. Let's hold it for a little later."

Adam acknowledged this comment with a smile and slight nod of his head.

"Napoleon next attended a Jesuit school, where, although he continued to bristle at perceived wrongs, he learned self-discipline. His mother also stressed self-discipline at home. Letizia believed in showing a good face to the public no matter what, and sometimes sent her children to bed without supper so that they would learn to do without and not complain. During this time Carlo was selected to go to France to pay the Corsicans' respects to Louis XVI, the king of France, and it was in this period of time that, Marbeuf, the French Governor of Corsica, fell in love with Letizia. He took an interest in her family and apprised them of the educational opportunities for impoverished French nobles. It was decided that Napoleon's older brother would be prepared for the priesthood, and Napoleon himself for the military. Both boys were to be sent to the French mainland, but of course, they had to learn French first. Marbeuf arranged for them to stay with his nephew, the bishop of the French town of Autun, to study French and continue their education. From there, Napoleon was sent on to the boarding school at Brienne."

Without raising her hand, one of the students asked how old Napoleon was when he was sent away from home.

"He was probably about eight."

The student groaned. "That's young for a kid to leave mom and home. That must have affected him. I can tell you, I would have felt abandoned. "

For the first time, Ellen commented. "You have to realize that in some societies it's still customary to send a young child away to boarding school. Our children went to boarding school in seventh grade."

Adam mumbled under his breath, not caring if Ellen heard and almost hoping that Mrs. Strove would. "It wasn't my idea. I wanted my boys at home." He continued to think in silence. "But we're upper class, so off they went. After all, Daddy insisted, and he's paying the bill. I didn't stand a chance. Daddy said it's the sure route to the Ivy League. And to the Ivies they must go." Disgruntled, Adam turned his attention back to the class.

"Most of the students at Brienne were wealthier and felt superior to Napoleon. Once again he was teased, this time for his accent, clothing, and social position. Napoleon did not excel at his studies, but his teachers saw that he was quick witted. Imagine what this boy, with a naturally fiery temperament and a learned Corsican pride, must have felt, to be alone in a foreign place, scorned by his peers. He must have suffered, but it didn't quell his spirit. He was impatient if a teacher repeated anything, claiming he had gotten it the first time. At the end of five and a half years the school inspector recommended that Napoleon be sent to military school in Paris. Napoleon completed his military training a year sooner than his classmates and received an officer's commission.

His rise to military prominence was not straightforward. First he tried to support the French revolution within Corsica, but Napoleon and his entire family were forced to flee the Island when conservative voices turned against them. They settled, impoverished, in Marseilles, where Napoleon, never idle, wrote articles defending the constitution. He had read widely, thought carefully and concluded that constitutional government, not absolute monarchy, was the right path. When Napoleon's regiment was ordered to help suppress a royalist uprising in Toulon, he won recognition for his ability to see the route to victory where others could not. Napoleon's strategic vision told him that if the pro-royalist English ships in the harbor could be repelled, the town would collapse. Having tried and failed with other tactics, Napoleon's superior officer finally took his advice. They won and Napoleon was promoted to the rank of general. He now stood proudly with a general's insignia on his chest, commended and rewarded by the political deputy for the south, who just happened to be the brother of the all powerful Maximilian Robespierre. Robespierre was the dominant figure in the revolutionary government, and Napoleon felt his star was on the rise. He figured that with his new connection to the most powerful man in France, he had it made. But, alas, things backfired. Within months, Robespierre had been overthrown, and Napoleon was cast into prison simply for being associated with the name. Luckily, friends secured his release and Napoleon traveled to Paris in search of his next command. He was assigned to an infantry division. For an artilleryman this was an insult and he declined the command. Proud, quick, fiery, and ambitious, he sought another appointment. But when nothing materialized Napoleon concluded that his career was finished, and grew discouraged and depressed. Nevertheless, his ingenious thinking flourished as ever."

The young man across the room from Adam raised his hand. "Dr. Peterson, do you think that depression may have played a significant role in his life?"

Adam's face flushed and he raised his hands in surrender. "Please, I know less about Napoleon than the rest of you in this class. And I don't analyze for free. Back to Mrs. Strove."

"My, this class is getting exciting. It's great to see all of you getting so involved. Anyway, Napoleon settled on the idea of helping the Sultan reorganize the Turkish army. Here we begin to see his early fascination with the East. But just as he was making plans to leave, there was another revolt in Paris, and Napoleon was assigned to control the situation. In accepting the assignment he replied, "I accept, but I warn you that once my sword is out of its scabbard I shall not replace it till I have established order."

"Mrs. Strove, would you repeat that quote please? It's revealing about Napoleon's character structure."

Mrs. Strove was happy to oblige. "I believe these words really reflect the general's approach to life. With brilliance and lightning speed, Napoleon ordered guns positioned around the palace and released a short, deadly, decisive fire on the insurrection. This was the *whiff of grape shot* to which I referred earlier, that signaled Napoleon's rise to power. Saved, the government promoted Napoleon to General in chief of the

Army of the Interior. His next assignment was to launch a campaign into the Italian peninsula, the soft underbelly of the Austrian Empire. At this time, you see, France was at war with the European powers. They were afraid of the changes the revolution brought and wanted to prevent it from contaminating their political systems.

Think of it. This small, thin, young man is not yet thirty years old, and is now in command of the French army with its much older, experienced, and well known officers, who, you can be sure, were most cynical about his appointment. Yet, to a man, these officers fell under Napoleon's unswerving leadership and authority. They came into his presence expecting to influence and control him and left in speechless awe. Napoleon inherited a poor, ragged army. The men were ill clothed and tired, but mostly they were restless and undisciplined because previous commanders had done nothing to change the situation in the Italian peninsula. Within days Napoleon transformed the army and launched his assault. Out-marching and outwitting the Austrians, he succeeded in splitting the enemy army and preventing its reinforcement. Then he picked off the fragments in almost daily, victorious battles. In ten days he defeated two armies. By his victory at Lodi he pushed the Austrians completely out of Piedmont. But more important, in the deadly cannon fire of the battle,

Napoleon learned that he led not just by tactical brilliance but by physical courage as well, for he was at the front of the charge, and fearlessly led his men in battle. Then, Napoleon the victor became Napoleon the diplomat, as he secured the peace treaty. Just as had occurred in France, the impoverished common people of Piedmont welcomed the French army, because it brought the reforms and civil rights of the revolution, but the nobility and clergy, who stood to lose property and power, resisted. It is in this duality that Napoleon finds his true diplomatic side and brings about a peaceful and agreeable resolution."

Mrs. Strove glanced at the clock. "It's 9.00 o'clock. This is probably a good place to stop for the night."

"Just before we stop Mrs. Strove, where was Josephine in all of this? Has she come into the picture yet?"

"Good question, Ellen. Throughout this, Napoleon was a man in love. He wrote to Josephine daily, passionate, honest, open letters that revealed his heart. With pride he related his successes on the battlefield. With unusual vulnerability he described his anguish at not hearing from her. He chided her for not writing, he avowed his love for her. What a pity she was betraying him."

CHAPTER TWNETY-ONE

There was a tentative knock at the door of the outer office. Guessing it was Mrs. Strove, Adam opened the door and greeted her warmly. Mrs. Strove was dressed in a light blue skirt and a loose fitting maroon cashmere cardigan. She appeared quite different to him than the way he had seen her in class. Her dark blonde hair was in a ponytail and she wore no make-up. Adam, formal and a bit stilted, welcomed her into the room.

"Good evening Mrs. Strove, thanks for coming. I've really become absorbed with Napoleon, and your course has stimulated me to think about the possibility of writing his psychobiography. I'm impressed with your knowledge and the passion you seem to have for the subject, and I think we could collaborate successfully."

Mrs. Strove interrupted. "I'm uncomfortable with you calling me Mrs. Strove. I think if we're to work on a book together it's going to require me to be Monica and you Adam. What do you think?"

Adam relaxed and responded in an accepting and genuine manner. They looked at each other and laughed.

"Of course Monica, that's much better isn't it?"

Both realized that they felt an instant chemistry. Monica was attracted to Adam's warmth, the empathy he exuded, and the feeling of unconditional positive regard that he communicated. She felt an immediate sense of intimacy and trust, and could not resist comparing Adam to Mike. She thought, "What a difference. He seems so open and genuine. Mike is all fact and it's like pulling teeth to get feeling from him. He never shares feelings or shows any vulnerability." She started to question what had attracted her to him in the first place and what had possessed her to marry him. By almost physically grabbing herself she shifted her thoughts back to Adam and the room.

Adam had his own internal dialogue going on. "She's incredibly soft and warm. Boy, what a contrast to Ellen. I bet she has everything I'm missing in my marriage. Sure, to the outside world

Ellen looks like the perfect, totally dedicated wife. It's her distorted idea of dedication that's killing me. Her obsessive organization, damn healthy meals, dictating what I wear, cramming those damn ridiculous vitamins down my throat, and spending a fortune on furniture! And oh yes, keeping us connected to all the right people."

Adam felt an emptiness as he was reminded of the many times he had yearned for emotional intimacy and passion from Ellen, and the oneness of a soul mate. His eyes were drawn to Monica's legs. They were discretely crossed but nevertheless revealed enough to stimulate him. He thought how much more attractive she was than Ellen. A woman with a little flesh aroused a much more erotic and tender feeling than he got from Ellen and her bony, anorexic legs. Adam jolted himself out of his reverie and returned to Napoleon, but the feeling of unity and congruence with Monica remained.

Monica relaxed back in her chair. Adam said invitingly, "that chair reclines by pulling on the lever on the side, if you'd like."

Monica smiled. "Oh no, thanks, I'm quite comfortable. Do many of your patients recline while talking with you?"

"It all depends on the person, some do and others don't. Some are actually afraid to get that relaxed." He waited for her to settle in a new position in the chair and continued.

"Monica, I don't mean to come across as if I'm the teacher and you the pupil, but I'm eager to tell you about the premise I think we could use for this book."

"Yes, go ahead, I want to hear your thoughts."

Reassured by Monica's response Adam began.

"Each person, based on his own unique experiences, creates mental models of the world that differ in various ways from the actual world. Because each person's apperceptive mass and history of events is different, no two models are the same, no matter how close any two individuals may believe or feel they are to each other. The models that we create delete those parts of our experiences that are too threatening or anxiety producing. As Sigmund Freud explained, the repression of some material can be regarded as a necessary component of healthy existence. However, the deletion of events, feelings, or beliefs can also be an impoverishing aspect of a person's modeling process. When we think about the sources we use for the book, that is, the authors who have written about Napoleon, we have to remember that they were all writing through the filter of their own worldviews. All historical writing is apperceptive and interpretive. The reporting of any past event reveals the biases, character structure, and individual beliefs of the writer. In class you mentioned Gourgaud, who actually accompanied Napoleon into exile and recorded history through his conversations with Napoleon. The reader of those conversations must realize that Gourgaud's own inner turmoil and jealousy of Napoleon colored and guided his interpretations. When reading Gourgaud's account we not only learn about Napoleon, but we also gain insights into Gourgaud and his model of the world."

Monica smiled in complete understanding and agreement.

"I know just what you mean Adam, because in my reading I've come across so many different accounts of Napoleon that I'm never sure which one really captures him. One historian portrays him in one way and another depicts him differently. I feel like saying, will the real Napoleon please stand up! It's frustrating because the biographers talk about him and use direct quotations, but often I feel as if they may be telling me more about themselves than Napoleon. I also know that whichever aspect I choose to believe it's a function of my own worldview. Now, with your explanation, I see that what I'm missing is an understanding of Napoleon's own worldview. I wish I could find the true man, so exploring him through the eyes of a psychologist and writing a psychobiography intrigues me. You have to understand, Adam, that just as you have probably experienced some life passion for yourself, mine has become a search for the real Napoleon."

"When I found myself growing so interested in this man, Monica, I realized that something greater than just writing a psychobiography was driving me. You're right, I do have a passion. I've been deeply involved in a process of living history, and we're going to integrate this process into our collaboration. You'll see, we'll be breaking new ground and embarking on a momentous journey."

Monica frowned, puzzled.

"Most of the time people are unaware of what they delete from memory. Many psychologists believe that some of what we delete may include our intuitive strengths and an awareness of paranormal processes. It's hard for most people to believe this, but all children have the ability to see into the past, predict the future, and to sense what others think or feel. I believe we are influenced by our conformist and pragmatic society to think that we are weird or peculiar if we have these abilities. Most people are encouraged to believe that everyone thinks alike and to build a mental model that is similar to everyone else's. This lets them feel safe and healthy. But Monica, I've spent many years opposing and defying the conformist approach. If I have these abilities as an adult, if they make me strange, so be it. It is precisely the ability to sense beyond mainstream thought that has brought us together. I feel we have a mutual destiny and I knew it the moment I saw you. I believe we are at the dawn of a new era of understanding life and our connection to the universe."

Monica had been listening carefully and not only understood Adam's words but could also relate them to her own life.

"You know, I can't believe you're talking about this. I've always felt that I too had those intuitions, the ability to know the past and future. But, just as you said, I left them in my childhood because my parents and everyone I knew made me believe I was crazy to have them. I don't know if those are the right words to describe what I feel, but I know exactly what you mean. I wonder if my passion for history is somehow connected to this."

Adam was gratified by Monica's response and further assured that he had found the right person.

"Should I continue?"

"Absolutely!"

"Well, I don't know if I could listen to me all night. But let me just continue a bit. We will present Napoleon to our readers as we have experienced him from actually being in his presence. Our writing won't be a product of our personal worldviews that, as I just said, by definition consist of deletions, inclusions and distortions.

It won't be easy to convince people that I was actually in the presence of Napoleon. In order for them to accept this, they'll have to abandon many of the generalizations upon which their sense of reality is based. If people are able to do this, you can see that our book will have ramifications far beyond those of a mere psychobiography. If successful, we will demonstrate the possibility that anyone from the past can be accessed, and we can join these people while in our present experience. Writing about Napoleon is important, but I believe he will be a vehicle to communicating a much broader piece of knowledge that could change the world."

Monica felt a queasy turning in her stomach. "What are you saying? In the presence of Napoleon? What are you talking about?"

"Sorry, I got ahead of myself. I need to explain a critical detail." Adam proceeded to explain his theory of the personal unconscious and genetic memories and told her about his hypnotic regression work that had brought him into contact with Napoleon.

"Monica, I've been with him. And not just once."

I'm sure you had no way of knowing, but I've always been interested in the paranormal and I believe that what you said is possible. This is really exciting. Is the regressive hypnosis the same as a past life regression? Does it involve reincarnation?"

Adam sat for several moments in his own introspective world. "Have I finally found a soul mate?" He wondered.

"I'm delighted with your interest and enthusiasm. But Monica, this is not science fiction. It's not paranormal. It's based on scientific research."

Adam realized that his voice was different as he spoke to Monica He felt something long dormant awakening in him.

"I've always felt a tumultuous force driving me to identify, capture, and follow my destiny, which I believe is to show the validity of the collective unconscious and its power to change the world. I believe that if we can persuade people that we have been in the actual presence of Napoleon we will finally demonstrate that the past, present, and future are one. There's a personal side to this. I think you and I were destined to discover each other. Our meeting was not a chance happening. I don't believe in coincidence. I'm sure we'll find our personal connectedness."

Adam pulled his chair closer to Monica and leaned toward her.

"You see, the more we search and the

deeper we introspect, the more we realize that all truth lies within ourselves. And that truth, Monica, is that all lives are an entanglement of the present and all that preceded us in the past."

Monica held Adam's stare. "My thoughts are racing. Everything is coming together. I always knew I was destined for something of importance, and now, all of a sudden, here's the path. My magnetic fascination with Napoleon has always been a mystery to me. I have a feeling I'm going to find out why."

"Of course, neither of us knows where this effort will take us, but intuitively I bet we both know that we have to make the journey."

The shrill ring of the private phone line startled them. Adam quickly picked it up, thinking it might be one of the boys. Hello!

Hi, I just got home from my photography club and wondered how the authors were doing. Making progress?"

Adam's fury at being checked up on exploded. He struck his arm across the desk, inadvertently knocking a stack of papers to the floor. A pyramid paperweight tumbled and rolled towards Monica's feet.

"Oh, we're just about finished. See you in a little while." About to slam the phone down, he glanced at Monica and quickly restrained himself.

"Sorry about that. Let's continue. Another

area we need to cover is quantum physics."

"Oh no, I was afraid of this."

"Quantum physics teaches us that at the subatomic level, the particles that make up the substance of matter, which of course includes human beings, are unimaginably tiny and are all connected by energy. The universe was once the size of a pea and even though it may have expanded, through whatever means one chooses to believe, such as the big bang theory, all the stuff of which the pea size universe was comprised is still the same, and we are made up of that stuff. Modern physics teaches us that the universe is made up of energy fields and that everything within an energy field is connected in a state of vibration.

OK, now let me give you still another piece of the whole picture. Within recent years, the use of holograms has helped us see the relationship of these energy fields. A hologram is a three dimensional projection of an object into empty space. It's an amazing experience to see something such as the figure of a person projected this way, so that one can walk 360 degrees around it and view it from all sides. A hologram appears solid but matter can pass right through the image. Arranging laser beams so that they collide with each other after reflecting off the object to be projected creates holograms. Each small fragment of the holographic "film" contains all the information recorded in the whole. This is very different from a regular photographic image. If you tear a regular photograph, the image is also torn apart and only the separate pieces can be discerned. A holographic film can be torn into a hundred pieces and every tiny piece is able to reproduce the whole image. Every part contains the whole. I believe that this is a model for the content of the human brain and explains many aspects of memory, information retrieval, experiences, and the unconscious. Much like the hologram, every event that ever occurred in a person's life, as well as every event that may have been stored in a genetic warehouse, is interconnected in the neural hardwiring of the brain. It takes no greater leap of faith to believe this than it does to accept that one DNA cell can produce or clone the entire sheep. Every characteristic of the sheep is contained in the one cell. Perhaps every characteristic of human existence is also contained in DNA cells and is a part of us at birth. Our DNA cells may be just like a hologram, with the entirety of all-previous human experience encoded in each cell.

For centuries many philosophers subscribed to the *tabula rasa* theory, which maintains that we come into the world empty, like a blank slate, and that only our present existence writes itself upon our tablet, containing our chronology from birth to death. The *tabula rasa* construct of a person's development doesn't fit with modern genetics or new understanding of neurology and psychology. We enter the world with over a hundred billion cortical neural cells with many specialized systems already encoded. We're talking about as many cells as there are stars in the Milky Way galaxy. Our brains come into this world loaded with information."

"I think I see where you're going with all of this. There are two threads. One is that people carry genetic memories of the past, and the other is that through your regressions you've actually been able to be in the presence of the past. And we're going to put these two threads together for our psychobiography."

"Exactly. Think of it this way. Freeing ourselves from the limiting notion of a *tabula rasa* theory permits the acceptance of an alternate view. We may enter this world with the encoded history not only of our own souls, but with that of the souls of others as well. Opening the mind to that possibility creates the opportunity to contact that cauldron of genetic experience."

They sat and gazed at each other for a few moments. There eyes unable to break contact. "Well what do you think? Are you interested? Shall we meet again?"

"Absolutely! This is even better than I

expected. Let's do some scheduling. I'm sure this will be easier for me than for you. Mike is away most of the time." She paused but seemed compelled to continue. "Not only is he away a lot, I don't even know where he is. He always tells me that it's best that I not know or that it's a secret government assignment that he can't tell me about. It's nerve racking and disorienting for me. Lots of wives have husbands who travel, but they know where they are, they're able to call each other and know when they'll be back. Sorry, I just unloaded on you didn't I? I didn't mean to, it just poured out."

"Sounds like a frustrating situation. Let's decide where and when we will meet again." Both were aware that this suddenly became a loaded question. Adam wondered if staying late two more nights a week would upset Ellen and debated whether it would be better to have Monica come to the house. His next thought was that Ellen was going to feel threatened no matter what he did. He felt overwhelmed with what should have been a simple decision. The long period of silence alerted Monica to Adam's struggle.

"It doesn't matter to me where we meet, anywhere is fine."

"Okay, let's plan to meet here next week

Just then the phone rang again. Monica offered to go to the waiting room but Adam signaled her to stay.

"Hi, I just wondered if you were still there. Have you eaten?"

It was classic Ellen.

Exhilarated by the meeting and permitting himself the luxury of fantasy about Monica, Adam decided that going home to Ellen would dampen his pleasurable arousal. An unusual urge directed him to the Blue Lagoon Pub instead where he sat at the bar, sipping five orders of a single malt scotch on the rocks and engaging in baseball talk with the bartender.

CHAPTER TWENTY-TWO

Toying with the ice in his glass, ostensibly bantering about baseball, Adam, frequently went inside himself to review the meeting with Monica. He realized that his attraction to her was growing on an intellectual, physical and emotional level.

It was midnight when he arrived home. Ellen was already asleep, and he crept silently into bed without putting on any light, lest she waken and chastise him like a naughty schoolboy. He lay on his back and quickly fell into a deep sleep.

He awakened in a panic from a vivid dream. The red LED clock next to his bed was flashing exactly 3:00 a.m. Sweating, and with heart pounding, he began to record his recollections of the dream on the notepad he kept on the night table. Adam was certain he had heard Monica's voice calling to him.

"I know it was a French village and it was Napoleon and Josephine having an intimate conversation. Napoleon was sharing some type of secret with Josephine but having difficulty getting her to believe or accept it. Ah! I have it! It was Napoleon and Josephine all right. But what woke me was that their faces transformed into Monica's and mine."

In a voice loud enough to stir Ellen, he blurted, "That's it! One of us is genetically related to those people! Maybe we both are! We must be unconsciously processing a genetic memory trace.

It hit him like an electric shock. "My God! It's been in front of me all the time. That's why I'm intrigued with Napoleon and why I'm falling in love with Monica. I bet we're genetically related in some way and fulfilling some destiny. Fate has brought us together."

Ellen had not been roused by Adam's exclamation, and he crawled gingerly out of bed and went to the family room where he began to pace. He circled the desk six times, each time reaching for the phone and then withdrawing his hand.

"I know it's 3:45 in the morning, but I have to tell her. Please Ellen, don't wake up."

He dialed Monica's number. She answered on the first ring, sounding wide awake.

"Monica, I've just had an epiphany and had to share it with you. Sorry for waking you."

"Adam, something very strange is going on."

"What do you mean, are you all right?"

"Adam, I'm sitting here, wide awake, because I woke up hearing your voice calling me. I heard it. 'Monica, Monica!' Just as if you were at the foot of my bed. It was a telepathic communication, I'm sure. This is so weird. What on earth is going on?"

"I don't know but we better find out. Let's meet at the office now."

There was a hesitation. "Uh, I really don't want to go out by myself at this time of night."

"Of course, I should have thought of that. What if I come there?"

Monica hesitated again. "I don't think we should do that either. What time do you finish your appointments today?"

"If you can make it, I'll get someone to cover my class tonight and we can meet at the office at five."

"I'll be there."

Adam quickly showered and dressed. The realization that he and Monica might have a relationship based in genetic memories was powerful, and he wanted to see what might emerge in a trance.

Ellen sat up in bed just as Adam was tiptoeing down the hall towards the door.

"Where are you going? Are you ok? It's 4:15, where are you going?"

"I couldn't sleep. My mind is on the paper work I have to get done at the office. I figured instead of just tossing and turning in bed I would get to the office early and get a head start on the mess. I'm sorry I woke you."

"Adam, I'm worried about you. You haven't been yourself for weeks. You seem so unsettled and irritable. What's going on?"

"It's nothing. I'm overwhelmed at the office. It's really been crazy there. I'll call you later. Go back to sleep."

At the office Adam immediately began a regressive hypnotic trance. He activated the transcranial electromagnetic stimulation and could feel the usual strange sensation that he and all his clients always reported. It seemed as if the right and left sides of his brain were being separated. He turned on the self-hypnosis audiotape, activated the neurofeedback program, and focused on following the pinpoint of light as it wove a rhombic pattern on the EMDR screen.

Two soaring Doric columns flanked the entrance to the room. Over the lintel an elaborate image of Ra, the Egyptian sun god, was superimposed on a sun that radiated six large, undulating, golden snakes. The highly polished dark marble floor reflected the candles eerily. Benches lined two sides of the room while a large throne-

like chair sat in the center of the third wall. Men in elaborate aprons and bejeweled sashes signifying their authority occupied large chairs. Other men filled the benches. All wore white robes with a red cross on the chest and an apron emblazoned with a square and compass and a radiant sun with a large seeing eye above it. The man seated on the east wall wore a black fez. An air of solemnity and reverence permeated throughout. In the back corner, before a closed door, stood a figure, lance and sword in hand. A slight gaunt man with his chest bared knelt before the altar in the center of the room. On the altar lay an open Bible with some metal instruments atop. The deafening silence of the dark tomb-like setting was suddenly broken as a pump organ began a mournful dirge.

The man with the fez left the throne and moved toward the altar. The other men rose from their chairs and benches, placed their right hands over their heart and took two steps forward toward the center of the room, chanting in unison, "We meet on the level, we meet on the level."

The man with the fez stopped at the altar.

"Fellow craft brother, Napoleon Bonaparte, you are about to receive the light of a master mason. Do you solemnly swear to keep the vows you have sworn to on this Bible and should you betray any to willingly accept the penalties? If so, place your right hand over your left hand on the sacred tools upon the Bible and so again solemnly swear."

Napoleon placed his hands on the Bible as instructed, looked to the dark blue ceiling with painted *stars surrounded by snakes, and so vowed. At that moment the mood changed and the rest of the lodge began to chant ominously. "Baphomet. Baphomet. Baphomet." The rasping sound created a fearful atmosphere. The pump organ moaned synchronously with the chant. The leader at the altar placed his hand on Napoleon's head and spoke. "You will never admit to having heard this word, you will to death deny you know it's meaning, and you will forever defend that as brothers we have no allegiance to any figure other than the Great Architect of the Universe. Do you solemnly swear this under penalty of having your tongue torn from your throat should you violate your vow?"*

The leader thrust a silver tray in front of Napoleon's face. A strange bloodied mass covered the tray. It was a human tongue. "Again, Napoleon Bonaparte, do you so swear on this Holiest of books, sworn upon by our ancient brothers from the days of King Solomon?"

"I do, Worshipful Master."

"You, Napoleon Bonaparte are now a master mason entitled to the secret grip of a master mason and the secret word."

In rhythm with the dirge, Napoleon's conductor and guide throughout the three degrees stepped from the rear of the room to stand at his side. He handed Napoleon an upside down human skull with images of Isis etched on both sides. The skull contained a dark liquid. Three candles were snuffed out, further darkening the room. The conductor began to speak.

"Master Mason Napoleon Bonaparte, you will drink of this wine and repeat after me. "May this wine I now drink become a deadly poison to me, as deadly as the Hemlock juice drunk by Socrates, should I ever knowingly or willfully violate the solemn oaths I have sworn to on this Holy Book."

Napoleon drank the wine and repeated as instructed. One of the brothers, dressed as a skeleton, stepped out of the shadow, threw his arms around Napoleon, and whispered in his ear, "And may these cold arms forever encircle you should you ever knowingly or willfully violate the same."

There was no gradual emergence from the trance this time. Adam, terrified, was startled into wakeful awareness.

"God! That was awful! I've never seen anything like it. That word, what was it? Bar... no, Baph, Baph, Baphomet! What the hell does that mean? Christ! Look at me. I'm shaking like a leaf. I need to calm down and make some sense of this."

Adam leaned back and tried to recreate the pictures of the experience. He was sure he had witnessed Napoleon being inducted into the fraternity of masonry.

"I bet I was in an ancient lodge, in Egypt, where Napoleon must have become a mason. I wonder if that word, *Baphomet,* has some meaning in Masonic history. I sure wish Dad or Granddad

176

was alive so I could ask them. They both knew a lot about the early history of masonry and the Templars."

"Good Morning, Adam." Adam had no idea of the time when Cathy entered the office with her greeting.

"I came in early to get some paper work done but it looks like you beat me here. There's a message on the answering machine from Ellen. She asked if you were okay and said she couldn't get back to sleep after you left. She said she was going to be out running and then at the exercise club, so you won't be able to reach her until after eleven.

Adam mumbled, "Go run off another two pounds, get even more boney. God! I'm married to a real anorexic."

He looked up and in a more audible voice replied, "Thanks Cathy. How are you?"

"I'm fine Adam. Do you want your schedule and the phone calls that have to be made today?"

Adam was well aware that Cathy had emphasized the word today. He knew he had been neglecting essential phone calls and paper work.

Cathy continued, "Mrs. Perez left a message reminding you to call her insurance company for pre-authorization. You're not in her network. I've told her that at least six times."

"Cathy, I can't be bothered with that

nonsense any longer. Tell her to work with her company for whatever benefits she can get. You take care of it."

Visibly upset, Cathy left the room. Adam didn't care. He returned to his preoccupation.

"If I'm right, I accessed some genetic memory. But where was I? Where was this in history?"

Ellen called three more times, but Adam convinced himself that he didn't have time to get back to her.

"She has no idea of what it's like to see one patient after another all day, fit in phone calls, deal with insurance companies, and listen to Cathy tell me I have several hundred more things to do. Oh boy, I didn't tell her that I'd be working on the book tonight and be home late."

He finally forced himself to call. "Hi, it's me. How was your day?"

"Great, I exercised this morning, paid all the bills, went to the monthly meeting and lunch for University Women, and came home to make supper. I called you but you didn't get back to me. I'm sure Cathy told you. I was worried about you all day; not sleeping and leaving for work so early. Will you be home soon?"

In a hesitant, cautious voice Adam responded. "I'm working on the Napoleon book with Strove tonight and probably won't get home until nine or so. Just keep the supper warm and I'll eat then."

"Adam this is getting ridiculous. There's another thing I haven't had a chance to tell you, because you're never around and don't even return my calls. For several weeks I've been getting strange calls. This same woman calls and says hello, is this Mrs. Peterson, Dr. Peterson's wife? I say yes, and she hangs up. You need to do something about this. Do you have any idea who it could be?"

"No! But I'll have Cathy follow-up on it

"I talked to my father about how concerned I am about you. You're scattered, doing too many things. Daddy suggested that we spend some time with them this Sunday and maybe the two of you can talk. I just know something is bothering you and I thought that perhaps Daddy could help."

His anger slowly swelling, Adam wanted to terminate the call by disconnecting the line. He thought, "Daddy, of course, always turn to the old boy. I can't think of anyone I would less want to talk to than him."

He composed himself to answer Ellen.

"We can visit Mommy and Daddy Sunday. I'm sure the brunch on the patio will be super and the manhattans just right with three and not four drops of that special vermouth. Sure it will be fine. Tell them we'll be there."

CHAPTER
TWENTY-THREE

Adam had not been to a Masonic Lodge meeting
for several years and felt awkward as he entered
the outer room where the brothers were milling
around in lighthearted conversation. He didn't
recognize anyone and feared that he might have to
go through the usual examination to prove he was
a mason. He doubted he would be able to recall all
the signs and answers of the exam and was relieved
to finally notice several older brothers who could
vouch for him. Alex Roberts, the secretary and
historian of the lodge, walked toward the outer
room and warmly welcomed him, assuring the
junior warden that Adam was not only a master
mason but also a member of their lodge.

The Master of the Lodge greeted Adam

during the opening ceremony. "It's very good to see you, Brother Adam. You have been a traveling man for a long time, welcome home."

Rising from the bench, placing his right hand over his heart, and bowing slightly, Adam responded. "Thank you Worshipful Master. It is indeed a pleasure to be here this evening. Attending meetings has been impossible because I teach a course at Georgetown medical college on Monday evenings."

Adam muddled through the opening rituals, giving the correct signs about ninety percent of the time and effectively concealing his forgetfulness for the other ten percent. He had joined the masons to please his father, an ardent mason, and recalled his father's pride on the night he had raised Adam to the third degree of masonry. He reminisced, thinking of the great honor it was for a father to be Master of a lodge and raise his own son to be a master mason.

The rituals over and the business finished, the Worshipful Master invited the brothers to the recreation room for refreshments. Adam joined the group, sitting next to Alex, a Masonic historian with fifty years of accumulated knowledge. While most of the brothers were engaged in talk about one or another sporting event, Adam took the opportunity to quietly inquire if Alex knew anything about the connection between Napoleon and Freemasonry.

"I've been reading about Napoleon and there is some suggestion in the literature that he may have been a Mason. Do you know anything about this?"

"Just a little," Alex replied. "I've researched this subject myself, since, as you must remember from when you were attending lodge more often, one of my goals has been to identify well-known historic figures who were masons. I believe that Napoleon became a mason during his Egyptian campaign. We are sure his brothers were Freemasons. Many historians write that Napoleon appointed his brothers to positions in the lodge. You know as well as I do that no one other than a duly-qualified degreed mason in a position of authority has the ability or right to appoint anyone to a place in the lodge. Throughout Masonic literature there are many intimations that Napoleon appointed his three brothers Louis, Jerome, and Lucien to the positions of Deputy and Grand Master of regions in France. There is unquestionable documentation that Lucien was a member of the Grand Orient of France. We are also certain that Napoleon's other brother Joseph became a Freemason at the Tuilleries in April of 1805 and was later appointed Grand Master of the Grand Orient of France. Some historians believe that Napoleon used the Craft to befriend the people of

Egypt, intending to convey respect for their religion and to gain acceptance by mixing with them socially through our international brotherhood."

"That's the information I've been seeking. I'd like to learn more about this but I have another question. It's too complicated for me to go into why I'm asking this, but I have some suspicion that it may have to do with Napoleon and Masonry. Do you know a word that sounds like Baphomet?"

Alex's eyes widened and he looked away.

"I don't know what that word means. You should consult Leopold Robsen, the Grand Historian for the Grand Lodge, if you want to know more about the connection of Napoleon to Masonry. Dr. Robsen's office is in the Masonic Museum in Arlington. You know, the George Washington Masonic Museum. He probably knows more than anyone else about the history of Masonry. It's very difficult to get an appointment with him, but I know him well, and I think the fact that your father was the Grand Master of the State of New Jersey and your grandfather the Grand District Deputy, will carry enough weight to get you in to see him. I should warn you. He's always pressed for time, and he can be very abrupt. In fact, sometimes he's downright rude. He'll respond best if you're well prepared with a list of questions and ask them in as concise a manner as possible."

"I would really appreciate it, Alex, if you

would contact him for me. Tell him I will see him whenever it's convenient for him. He can call my office and leave a message with my secretary, Cathy."

"I'll try to reach him tomorrow. Perhaps sometime you will give us a little talk about what you've discovered about Napoleon and Masonry."

"Thanks Alex, I really appreciate this, and of course I'd be happy to give a talk. I'm going to try to be more active in the future."

Adam had no interest in engaging in the surface conversations going on around him or getting involved in the poker or pool games. He slipped quietly out of the lodge, choosing to take the long route home to give himself time to process his thoughts. The lights from oncoming cars were blinding as torrential rain pelted the windshield. His mental absorption diverted his attention from the road and his driving grew shockingly reckless. As soon as Adam closed the front door Ellen was in front of him like a wrestler ready to pounce.

"Where have you been, it's twelve o'clock! I've been pacing the floor worried about you, thinking that you had an accident driving home in this rain. The weather channel kept broadcasting the floods around the city and warnings about accidents. Where were you?"

As usual, despite the words, Ellen's delivery was an attack rather than an expression of concern. He wanted to ignore her and go upstairs to bed but realized he was guilty of not having told her of his whereabouts.

"Ellen, I'm sorry."

Before he could explain, Ellen charged at him again verbally.

"Forget the sorry, that's all I've been hearing lately. You've been spending too much time with Monica Strove. This thing is getting out of hand. You don't even bother to have Cathy call to let me know what's happening. I've had it, Adam. You're obsessed with this transcranial magnetic stuff, Napoleon, and Strove, to the point of neglecting work, home, the boys, and me."

"Damn it Ellen, back off! I was not with Monica tonight. I went to a lodge meeting and I'm sorry I didn't tell you or Cathy. Why did you say I've been neglecting work? What fictive creation are you weaving now? "

"Don't try to pull that psychology shit on me by trying to distract me from the real issue. You're lost in another world. You're acting as if you don't have a wife, a home or a family. Where were you really tonight? You haven't been to a Masonic meeting in years, so how come all of a sudden you decide to go? Am I supposed to believe that? You were with Strove, weren't you?"

"Monica," he caught himself in one of the worst Freudian slips imaginable. He quickly covered himself by saying, "Monica, Ellen, is nothing more than a co-author. It takes time together to write a book. I'm sure we have the makings of a good book. Who knows, it might even become a best seller. But I was not with Strove tonight. I was at a lodge meeting because I wanted to ask Alex about the connection between Napoleon and Masonry."

"I don't know what to believe anymore, Adam. I was just very scared."

Adam began to soften towards Ellen, realizing that maybe she was worried about him driving in the monsoon, but then she ruined it.

"I even called Daddy to see if he had heard from you. He tried to calm me down, reminding me of how absent minded you are."

Adam's momentary compassion evaporated, transforming into rage. An inner voice boomed in his ear. "Why did you call Daddy? Won't you ever grow up?" Stifling his urge to attack, he simply said with exhaustion, "Ellen, I'm very tired and I bet you are too after the anxiety I put you through tonight, so let's get some sleep."

Adam was too tired to do anything other than undress and collapse into bed. He grew increasingly irate listening to Ellen floss and brush her teeth, massage her gums and then perform a final brushing. Predictably, she closed the bathroom door to ensure he did not see her undress. As always she folded each item of clothing, building them into a tidy stack to place neatly in the hamper. Then she began her ritual of breathing exercises, which sounded like seals barking, followed by twenty minutes of stretching exercises. These completed, Ellen moved to the bed and obsessively positioned her three pillows in a precise stair-like formation.

Adam thought, "You uptight, asexual bitch. The rituals are going to drive me crazy." He turned away from Ellen in disgust, shifted his thoughts, and fell asleep.

A few hours later he awoke feeling wretched and unsettled. Knowing that sleep would be impossible, he decided to go the office to put himself in a regressive trance.

A large canopied bed curtained by dark green damask sat in the center of the room, which was brightly lit by chandeliers. Heavy velvet drapes covered the windows, blocking the interior view to outsiders. Two candelabras on a grand mahogany desk provided additional light. Cafarelli sat dutiful and attentive in a straight-backed armchair. Napoleon, dressed in his general's uniform but without a jacket, stood directly in front of Cafarelli and began to speak in a subdued but authoritative voice.

"Cafarelli my friend, I dare to tell you something that I would tell no one other than you, because it is only you I trust unequivocally."

"*My dearest general and trusted friend, you need say no more. I am honored to be your confidante.*"

"*Sleep did not come easily last night. Major decisions were weighing on my mind and I watched the flickering candles on my desk. I thought the rhythmical activity of shifting my eyes back and forth from one candle to the other might quell my restless thoughts. I am certain that I did not drift asleep but instead fell under some spell and a strange scene opened before me. I was in an underground stable with a man who was a Templar. You must trust my perception of this. I tell you I was there last night just as I am with you at this very moment.*"

Cafarelli remained calmly attentive.

"*The Templar spoke to me. 'We have for centuries protected the most important information the world will ever have. It has been by ancient and divine command entrusted to our order of Knights Templar, to be protected and harbored with the utmost secrecy, until the world has the methods and knowledge to use it properly. This will not happen until the chosen individual arrives. When the destined one discovers this treasure he will not simply rule a country or a religion, but will join all peoples under one kingdom, one God, and will in fact, rule the world. The secret that was given to our ancient brothers is a knowledge that would unify all races and religions, for a oneness of Islamic, Christian, and Judaic. However, the man destined to find this supremacy will meet with great resistance and will be seen as the enemy of many.*"

Napoleon paced rapidly back and forth with

nervous energy, never taking his eyes off Cafarelli.

"What I tell you is real my friend. You know I'm not a frivolous man. There's more. I asked the Templar why he was telling me this. I have never forgotten his words. He said." "You have come upon this information from a time ahead, a time to be. It is your destiny I speak of. Yes your destiny, as you learned from Alexander. Yours, but beware of your enemies. The Pope, the kings, England, the Eastern world, trusted friends, and your own drives.' "What do you make of this, Cafarelli?"

CHAPTER
TWENTY-FOUR

Adam approached the reception desk at the Masonic museum in Arlington and asked for Leopold Robsen's office. As the receptionist ran her fingers through the appointment book, a very large, imposing guard approached Adam.

"Do you have an appointment with Doctor Robsen?"

"Yes, I'm Doctor Adam Peterson. I was notified by his office that he would see me at nine this morning."

The guard turned to the receptionist and spoke in a firm authoritarian voice that resonated throughout the marble lobby.

"Check with Pamela to confirm Doctor Peterson's appointment. Doctor, please have a seat while we contact Doctor Robsen's office"

Adam dutifully sat on the marble bench across from the reception desk.

"Damn, you'd think I was asking to see the president."

The receptionist nodded to the guard who then gestured to Adam.

"Take the elevator to the third floor, and Doctor Robsen's secretary, Pamela, will meet you there."

The elevator doors opened to a middle-aged woman in a dark blue skirt, white blouse and grey cashmere sweater.

"Good morning Doctor Peterson. I spoke with Alex from your lodge and arranged the appointment for you. Follow me. Doctor Robsen's office is at the end of this corridor. Did you have any difficulty parking?"

"No, there were plenty of spaces. Is Doctor Robsen ready for me?" Adam could not understand why he was feeling anxious about meeting this man. He thought, "Why am I nervous? This guy's just a civil servant. But there's something spooky about this setup."

"Oh Yes, Doctor Robsen is waiting for you. I'll let him know you're here."

As Pamela opened the door, Leopold Robsen, seated behind his desk, greeted Adam by motioning for him to enter. Adam walked in, and Robsen, still silent, pointed to the chair across from his large desk. Adam sat down. Robsen, a professorial, patriarchal looking man of about fifty, was dressed in a tan shirt and dark brown sweater. His face was intelligent and serious.

Adam glanced at the wall behind the desk and noticed a dense cluster of framed Masonic awards, along with a bachelor's degree from Georgetown University, a Master of Arts degree in religion from Columbia University, a second Master of Arts degree from the University of Egypt at Cairo, and a Ph.D. in Ancient History from Cambridge in England. The wall to the left of the desk held more awards and a high school Diploma from France.

Adam thought, "Hmm, this guy's impressive. No wonder it's so hard to get into see him. I never expected this, France, Egypt, Cambridge. Man, he's been around"

"So, what can I do for you Brother Adam?"

"I'm doing research for a psychobiography of Napoleon."

"Interesting! Hasn't that already been done many times?"

"Yes it has, but I'm doing something totally different."

"Okay, so what's so different?"

Adam decided to jump right in and explain that his book would be unique because he had the ability to regress in time and be present with Napoleon. To make this credible to a layperson, he would have to tell Robsen about regressive hypnotic trances and the genetic unconscious, and he questioned the advisability of this. But then looking into Leopold's eyes and recalling the Masonic vows of brotherly loyalty he chose to ignore his personal disquiet and trust the man.

"I'm a clinical psychologist. Are you familiar with Jung's ideas of the collective unconscious?"

"Of course."

"I have refined Jung's notion of a collective unconscious into a theory of a personal unconscious that contains all the events that ever occurred in the genetic history of an individual. All events are recorded in the genetic memory, which is encoded in the DNA."

"That's an interesting idea, but just an idea, right?" Robsen's voice was contemptuous.

"No! I've developed a method, a very complicated one that permits me to access this genetic memory. This is why I'm here."

"What do you mean? I am a historian, not a psychologist. I'm not into this psychic stuff. I can't imagine how I can be helpful to you." Robson's face registered his impatience and skepticism. Undeterred, Adam held Robsen's eye and continued.

"Well, in my regressions I have been in the presence of Napoleon and other figures from that period. I know this is hard to believe. But I have experienced history by actually being there as it happened. It's very complicated. Recently I've experienced regressions that lead me to believe that Napoleon had an intimate and important connection to Masonry. In fact, Napoleon may have been connected to the Templars through his own genetic memory. So I thought you might be able to help me find out more about this. One regression was frightening and I heard the word *Baphomet*. I've never heard it before, but in my trance it seemed to be related to the Templars or Masons."

"I won't pretend to understand the psychological part of what you're saying, but maybe I can help by answering your questions about the Templars. How much do you know about them?"

"Absolutely nothing. I know that may seem strange to you, but my life has been devoted to psychological theory and practice, and all of my reading has been related to my profession. I suppose I could be accused of being a one dimensional person."

"We're not here to discuss you. I can direct you to a number of books about the Knights Templar."

Adam was not to be dismissed and replied assertively. "Alex led me to believe that you would have insights not published in books."

"Okay," Robson sighed. "Let's talk. The earliest account we have of the Templars, which most historians believe is accurate, was written between 1175 and 1185 by a Frankish historian Guillaume de Tyre. Be aware, we are dealing with medieval history so accuracy and validity must always be questioned. According to de Tyre, a fraternity called the Order of the Poor Knights of Christ was founded around 1118. Hugues de Payen is credited as the founder of this order, which evolved into the order of the Knights Templar. Pilgrimages to the Holy Land were, of course, a major activity in those days. But, as you can imagine traveling was fraught with danger from thieves and murderers. The stated purpose of the Templars was to ensure the safety of the pilgrims by protecting the roads. What is of special interest to us as Freemasons is that it is pretty well documented that the Templars were housed within the remains of King Solomon's Temple, in Jerusalem, which of course was built by the first members of our fraternity."

Intrigued by the information Robsen was providing, Adam inquired, "Do we know why they were housed there?"

"Well Brother, that's still a mystery to us. As a third degree brother you are fully aware that most of our rituals are based on the building of King Solomon's temple. Over time a great deal of suspicion developed around the Templars. People began to believe that they were keeping and protecting great treasures and secrets. Treasures and secrets of unparalleled value. Secrets of the universe. A knowledge that could disrupt all political and religious systems."

"Wow! I had no idea of this history. Please continue."

"Ah yes! It's interesting, isn't it? But of course I've spent a lifetime immersed in history, so for me, it has special attraction. The Templars became a great political and economic power. They acquired large land holdings in France, Scotland, England, Italy, Spain, Austria, Flanders, Portugal, Hungary, and deep into the Holy Land.

"As protectors of the pilgrims, were they only allied with Christendom?"

"No absolutely not, which is very important. They had very close ties with the Muslim world and were held in the highest respect by the Saracens."

Adam, normally the quintessential example of a great listener, peppered Robsen with questions, preventing him from completing his sentences.

"What happened to all the power and wealth?"

"The Templars were prospering in Europe but disaster hit the Holy Land."

"What was the disaster? What happened in the Holy Land?"

Robsen showed irritation with the rapid fire questioning.

"This is too much to go into. It would take hours for me to explain the situation in the Holy Land and what happened to the Templars. Suffice it to say that a significant conflict developed between Gerard de Ridefort, the Grand Master of the Temple, and others seeking to rule Jerusalem. Several issues brought Palestine to the edge of civil war. The Templars fought at Halten along with all the Christian forces and they were almost wiped out. Jerusalem fell under the rule of the Saracens and the Holy Land fell under Muslim control."

"This is so interesting, Leopold. I know nothing about any of this, nothing at all, so it's all new and fascinating to me."

"You said that before. There are volumes written about this period of history. Far too much for me to do it justice in a brief synopsis of centuries of intriguing tales. I can direct you to the best accounts of the time."

"I understand, but what about the word *baphomet*? It sure seemed important in my regression. The fear it aroused in me is in some way significant to my research."

Robsen exhaled deeply. "The Templars

were rounded up and arrested in France under the direction of King Philippe and with the strong urging and support of Pope Clement V. One of the tactics they used to gather popular support was to accuse the Templars of devil worship. This was the reason given to the people to explain why the Templars were seized, tortured, and eventually put to death. But many historians, including myself, believe the real purpose was to extract from the Templars the location of the mysterious treasure to which I alluded earlier. While the authorities confiscated a good deal of material wealth, their extraordinary efforts of torture and execution failed to extract any secrets. The Templars apparently kept their vows to protect their special knowledge. Now to your word, *baphomet*. That word refers to the symbol that the Templars were accused of worshipping as the devil. The Pope encouraged the propaganda that the Templars prostrated themselves before this devil, *baphomet,* as a way of ritualistically denying Christ. All of this, of course, was totally unfounded. As you know, when you took the vows of a master mason, you too committed yourself to denying this false accusation."

Adam glanced at his watch and realized he had been with Doctor Robsen for over an hour.

"This has all been most informative Doctor Robsen. I've taken enough of your precious time.

Thank you for seeing me."

Adam rose from his chair with the intent of offering Leopold the secret handshake of third degree masons, when Leopold said, "Brother Adam, I'm intrigued with what you told me about your regressive trances to relive history as if you are actually there, and especially your interest in Napoleon. I too have been interested in Napoleon and the role that Masonry might have played in his life. I'm convinced that he was a Mason and that our order was a motivating force in many of his decisions. I wonder if you would give me a few minutes of *your* time to tell me what you've discovered."

Feeling victorious for having whetted the proud historian's appetite, Adam resumed his seat to expound on his regressive encounters with Napoleon.

"In one of my regressive trances I was present when Napoleon told Cafarelli about a dream he had as a young man."

"Cafarelli? What do you know of Cafarelli? He is hardly mentioned in the historical literature. I've been intrigued with the relationship between the two men and the influence he had on Napoleon. Tell me about this trance."

With great animation Adam related the regression about Napoleon's dream

Leopold absorbed every word.

"I don't know what to say about your regression stuff, but with regard to Napoleon and the Templars or Freemasonry, your story makes me think you're dealing with your own imagination and fantasy world. I can tell you that the legacy of the Templars in France has been a popular subject in the occult category for centuries. Mystics follow the Templars like other wackos follow the Yeti in this country or the Loch Ness monster in Great Britain. There's no question that during Napoleon's lifetime, the French people were interested in the Templars and Freemasonry. There were many powerful Masonic lodges throughout France and Egypt and many believed that the Templars were guarding ancient secrets concerning the origins of Christianity, Christ's life, or other divine secrets. This, of course, has been the inspiration behind the many stories about the Holy Grail, the De Vinci symbolism, and so on. Once you can free yourself from the narrow minded attitude that the Holy Grail deals with Christ, and recall that the Templars were involved with not only Christian but also Judaic, and Islamic nations, then the notion of the nature of this hidden secret can be expanded."

"So, do you believe the Templars were protecting some secret of enormous value?"

"Brother Adam, I am a purist, a traditional historian. I cannot indulge in these forays into speculation and fantasy. Is there an Ark of the Covenant? Is there a Holy Grail? Was Christ married? Did Moses part the Red Sea? These nonsensical questions are beneath me. But you are clearly interested."

"Don't misunderstand me. I'm not in pursuit of answers to any of those questions either. I just wanted to get your thoughts on Napoleon's connection to Masonry."

"Well, on that you have my opinion. There is ample evidence to support that Napoleon was degreed. And now I really must go. I wish you luck in your research."

Leopold moved from behind his mammoth mahogany desk, shook Adam's hand using the secret third degree handshake, and ushered him to the door.

As Adam was walking through the waiting room, he thought of one more question. He turned on his heel back toward Leopold's office. The door was locked. Adam could hear Leopold on the phone but could detect only a few words. He put his ear to the door, instinctively watching for the secretary. Then he quickly pulled away, "That would be embarrassing."

"Psychologist, bunch of questions, we need to have a meeting." Adam tried to make sense of the few words he heard and left the building with a vague uneasiness. He unconsciously rubbed his stomach.

CHAPTER
TWENTY-FIVE

It seemed like an eternity to Adam until the next class. When Tuesday finally arrived, he was impatient to go and encouraged Ellen to hurry.

"Let's go Ellen, I don't want to be late. I can't believe how this course has sparked my interest in Napoleon and that period of history. It's strange for me. I never had any interest before and always found reading historical accounts boring."

Ellen looked at him quizzically. "I too have wondered about your new found interest. But lately you've been somewhat strange in a lot of ways."

"What the hell does that mean?"

"Oh, just drop it Adam. This is not the time to talk about it. Let's just go and enjoy the class."

Mrs. Strove greeted the class cheerfully. She explained that she was going to cover the Egyptian campaign which illustrated the richness of Napoleon's talents as well as the many facets of his fascinating personality. As she spoke, Adam recalled their discussion in his office and was convinced that her relationship with Napoleon was indeed more than simply a historical fascination. It was as if she really knew this man on a personal level, perhaps even loved him, or was having an imaginary affair with him.

Mrs. Strove moved from the military campaign to Napoleon's blind love for his wife Josephine. Adam was surprised at this seemingly strange juxtaposition of topics. For him it was a non sequitur to move from the Egyptian campaign to the love affair between Napoleon and Josephine.

Mrs. Strove returned to the Egyptian campaign and described the many aspects of Napoleon's invasion of Egypt, from the mapping of the land and the recording of the flora and fauna, to the precise measuring of the ancient monuments. She stressed that Napoleon used the time in Egypt not only for military ventures but also for gathering information of every possible kind about the natural and man-made aspects of the area. He was extremely interested in any ancient artifacts that might be discovered. Mrs. Strove moved from behind her desk to stand in the middle of the classroom among the students and continued her lecture.

"Most historians focus on the military exploits of Napoleon's time in Egypt, but I want to make you aware of another feature of the campaign, because it helps us to see another side of Napoleon. As well as his army, he brought many savants with him. The term savant in those days referred to scientists, intellectual explorers, and experts in various fields. Napoleon wanted to enrich the world with exploration and the discovery of ancient relics and perhaps things that would create new meaning for old assumptions. He sent regular reports of the savants' findings back to France, and these were published, providing information and knowledge about this mysterious ancient land for the French people. These publications can still be found in the French archives. This is important because it shows the depth of Napoleon's thinking, and that his interests went far beyond military victories and territorial conquest."

Adam and another student simultaneously asked if the savants had discovered anything important.

"Ah yes! Perhaps one of the most important discoveries of all time. Have you heard of the Rosetta stone? Well, the savants found that. If you're not familiar with the Rosetta stone, it is an ancient tablet that eventually permitted a trans-

lation of ancient hieroglyphics, Demotic hieroglyphics, and the Greek language. The Rosetta
stone is key to our current understanding of
ancient history."

Adam was about to join the other students
as they left the room for a ten minute break, but
as he began to corkscrew himself out from the
student desk, he realized Ellen was not getting up.
She had begun to talk with Mrs. Strove.

"I have to tell you that you have really
sparked my interest and I read two biographies of
Napoleon this week."

Mrs. Strove smiled with pleasure. "I guess
that's one of the most gratifying things any teacher
can hear. Did you enjoy them?"

Adam sat back down to listen to their
discussion, his eyes wide with astonishment. It
was as if he was listening to one of his patients
enamored with some man or two adolescent girls
gushing about their new boyfriends.

"Your lectures and these two books have
shown me what a truly great man Napoleon was.
I'm so impressed by his extreme courage and intellectual genius. Both books emphasized his intense
love for Josephine, which I found interesting in the
light of how their relationship seemed to wind up."

Mrs. Strove nodded in agreement. Adam
looked at Ellen in amazement, and in an incredulous, attacking voice snapped, "You read two

books about Napoleon this week? How come you didn't say anything to me? When did you get the time to do that? How come you read two books about Napoleon?"

Ellen stared at him. Mrs. Strove, sensing a domestic spat, excused herself. "I think I'll get some water before we start again." She was somewhat taken aback by Adam's flash of temper.

Alone in the room, Ellen said, "What's the matter with you? Where did all of that come from?"

Adam knew he had sounded foolish and felt ridiculous. "I don't know. I was just surprised that you read so much about Napoleon."

He left the room trying to understand his reaction. He was aware that he had felt somehow betrayed.

When the class resumed Adam was still distracted by his over-reaction to Ellen and had trouble concentrating. He heard Mrs. Strove say that Napoleon's attempt to exert influence over Egypt was because of economics and a political need to weaken Britain, but he wondered if something else had driven the General to Egypt. He thought that Mrs. Strove seemed to very conveniently omit any possible narcissistic motivation in this man. Mrs. Strove continued the class.

"The French, at war with the British, wanted Napoleon to invade England. Napoleon judged that a direct invasion was not feasible, and determined instead that the situation and time was right to invade Egypt. His intention was to expel the ruling Mamelukes and establish a modern style of government friendly towards French ways, as this would threaten English trade and influence in the region. But Napoleon had another goal as well. He was deeply intrigued by the history, archeology, and religion of this ancient land, and wanted to reveal and document the wealth of antiquity that lay in the sands of the timeless Egyptian desert. Within three months, the young general had raised and outfitted an expeditionary force of some 40,000 men, including scientists, engineers and veteran troops under his command. On the way to Egypt, the French seized Malta and its considerable treasury. Under Napoleon's command they proceeded towards Alexandria and the city fell within hours of the French fleet's arrival. It must have been a powerful feeling for Napoleon to take Alexandria, the city that one of his heroes had established so many centuries ago, and open the path for its return to the progressive civilized form that Alexander had intended. The first major engagement against the Mamelukes occurred at El Rahmaniya where victory was achieved as a result of Napoleon's clever and brilliant use of modern European military tactics and weapons. Following that skirmish, although his troops were exhausted and suffering the trials of battle, Napoleon, with his own fierce conviction and enthusiasm, marched his men up the Nile towards Cairo."

One of the students asked, "You refer to Napoleon's enthusiasm and conviction. Do we have any idea about the attitudes of the troops? I ask this because in the history course on the Second World War I'm teaching this semester my students have been focusing on the morale and emotions of the fighting men."

Mrs. Strove smiled and acknowledged the question.

"You're right. I was referring to Napoleon's enthusiasm. Picture what it must have been like being on the battle field and marching in the Egyptian climate. Napoleon kept strict discipline, but his soldiers were unaccustomed to the relentless heat and arid land of Egypt. As they marched towards Cairo, parched, exhausted, and fully conscious of being in an alien land, their morale wavered. The sun was so intense that every exposed part of their bodies burned as they marched, led by their determined leader who did not seem to acknowledge their agony. The glare of the sun against the parched land was painfully blinding. Men flung off their shirts in an attempt to get some relief from the oven-like temperatures."

Adam raised his hand. "That's a vivid

picture you drew of a group of demoralized soldiers. Was there a different attitude or reaction among the officers?"

"No! This extreme reaction was not limited to the foot soldiers, and in a most unusual manner Napoleon's officers also shed their heavy garments in search of some relief from the burning heat. They too were exhausted by the march forward. The promise of good pay now seemed hollow, as they continued struggling across the empty, dry, deserted sands. Worn first by the battle at Alexandria, and further worn by even more difficult fighting against the Mamelukes, these men were now plodding toward an unknown and unsure goal. Napoleon stayed with his men but presented a marked contrast in demeanor and appearance. In defiance of the grueling situation and harsh climate, he remained in full dress uniform, with an added sash of brightly striped native weave."

As Adam listened to this stirring description of the march, he felt he was gaining insight into Napoleon's character structure and methods of motivating his men. He raised his hand again.

"The picture you present tells us a bit about Napoleon. It's an interesting strategy. He presents himself in a superior manner, contrasting the difference between him, the great invincible general, and them, the common mortal men. In this way, he gives them something to strive for. I think he presents himself as a superior being. Of course I can tell you from a psychological point of view, that to be effective at this motivational technique he had to believe it himself."

Mrs. Strove agreed that Adam probably had a good picture of the situation and that his comments were thought provoking. She continued to describe what were probably the thoughts and internal experiences of the army as they marched forward.

"Cairo seemed always to be another march away, and if and when the army reached it, the ferocious, relentless Mamelukes under Murad Bey would be waiting for them."

Adam began to feel the pain and apprehension these men must have been experiencing. He appreciated Mrs. Strove's talents as a story-teller. He admired this aspect of a person because story-telling was a critical part of his therapeutic technique and especially useful in hypnosis. It had fascinated him from his early work with Native Americans where he had learned the value of a story as a way of relating connectedness and commonality. Adam began to wonder just how Mrs. Strove's unique ability to create such strong images for others could be capitalized on instead of being wasted on high school kids and evening classes. He grew even more excited about their collaboration on the book.

CHAPTER TWENTY-FIVE

Mrs. Strove continued with her lecture.

"In July of that year, 1798, the French army came within sight of the majestic pyramids and also within sight of some twenty thousand Mameluke soldiers under Murad Bey. There was an immediate confrontation. In the distance were thousands more Mamelukes under the command of Ibrahim Bey. Napoleon prepared for what portended to be a bloody battle."

Mrs. Strove struck a dramatic pose and quoted Napoleon. "Think of it, soldiers; from the summit of these pyramids, forty centuries look down upon you."

For a moment Adam no longer saw Mrs. Strove, but Napoleon standing before him, the charismatic General, talking to his troops. "Yes," Adam thought, "Napoleon was enthusiastic and impressive in his full uniform and pose, but what about the men he was addressing? I bet those guys didn't give a damn about the pyramids and forty centuries looking down upon them. I bet they would have rather been back in France with a nice cool drink under a shady tree."

Mrs. Strove asked if there were any further questions or comments. No one responded so she continued.

"At the Battle of the Pyramids the ordered and disciplined firing of the French guns proved superior to the wild raids of the Mamelukes, and

Cairo fell to Napoleon. However, the thrill of victory was curtailed by the news that Nelson, the English admiral, had sunk the French fleet off Aboukir, removing their means of transportation back to France and essentially trapping the French army in Egypt. Napoleon, a clear, levelheaded thinker under pressure, took the news of this defeat in stride. A pragmatic idealist, he saw the potential of using the extended time in Egypt to further his projects. Napoleon not only wanted to take from Egypt but also envisioned that he could bring to Egypt the reforms of the revolution as well as the benefits of European advances. Fired with the energy of accomplishment, he declared the Egyptians free of Turkish rule and embarked on a peaceful campaign of road works, sanitation, record keeping, and law making. Already familiar with the Koran, which he had read on the voyage to Egypt, he worked with the local leaders to create a modern state within the terms of the native culture. He kept his company of savants and experts at work on their research. He worked on plans to secure peace with Egypt and England. He also thought about how he could leave Egypt and evade the English, concluding that the only route out was through what is now Israel and into the territory of the hostile Turks. For this reason he decided to march the army toward Acre, the ancient fortress city on the Mediterranean coast."

Mrs. Strove reached for a glass of water and said "I know I've given you a lot of material tonight, and I'm sure you're as tired as I am. But before we end, I want to introduce one other thought for you. Something else of great importance in Napoleon's life occurred during the Egyptian campaign. Napoleon learned from his friend Junot that Josephine had been unfaithful to him. Rumors had circulated in the past; but this time the truth was out. France knew it, and Napoleon couldn't deny it. Napoleon's ideal image of Josephine was shattered, his honor tarnished, his pride wounded."

Adam felt a sense of indignation. He had not known this about Napoleon and Josephine and thought their love for each other was like a match made in heaven. He began an internal dialogue. "Here we have this great man of destiny with a world mission, bringing a new social order to oppressed peoples, and the woman he loves is cheating on him. Just like all women, trivial and demanding. Ellen sure fits that description. She doesn't appreciate the genius of my work. All she does is bitch about my not spending enough time with her. So I wonder what she's up to. Maybe all this time at the gym isn't really at the gym."

When the class ended Adam approached Mrs. Strove's desk to compliment her on the fascinating lecture. He was effusive in his praise and tried to engage her in deeper conversation, but Ellen seemed uncomfortable with the discussion and said, "Come Adam, it's late and I'm sure Mrs. Strove wants to get home."

Adam quickly agreed and Mrs. Strove answered, "Yes, it's late, and I am tired, but I want you to know that I thrive on Napoleon and am really looking forward to our meeting tomorrow night to work on the book. I'll see you then"

Ellen and Adam left the classroom as Mrs. Strove was packing up her material. As they walked down the hall Ellen challenged Adam in a caustic tone.

"For a guy who was so reluctant to come to the class in the first place you sure seem to have gotten interested in the subject of Napoleon. How come?"

Adam answered matter-of-factly. "I just find him to be an interesting character from a psychological point of view. I think it will be fun to do the psychobiography on him."

Ellen flushed a little as she answered, "Well, as long as it's motivated by Napoleon and not by Mrs. Strove."

Adam glanced at her condescendingly.

"Ellen, where did that come from? Don't be ridiculous."

Nothing more was said, but Ellen's face betrayed her anger and doubt.

Monica tossed her books onto the back seat of her Mustang convertible and drove home. She was feeling good.

"Whew! This is exciting. It will be fantastic if Adam Peterson and I can produce the ultimate book on Napoleon. And maybe it will finally help me understand this relentless thirst I've had for knowledge of the emperor. Teaming up with such an enlightened and famous psychologist could really propel me into my own fame. I've always felt destined for something great."

Her thoughts shifted to Mike and their unfulfilling relationship.

"Marriage is a contractual thing. I didn't sign on to marriage to lead a life of loneliness. I get no support from him and he takes no interest in my life. He doesn't appreciate my potential. He's away eighty percent of the time and ninety nine percent of that time I don't even know where he is. That damned CIA! If he had told me he was a CIA agent I never would have started this relationship. He's married to the Agency, not me."

CHAPTER TWENTY-SIX

Adam's trances had put him in the presence of Napoleon so often that he was growing more certain about an ancestral connection to the emperor. Since he and his sister Liz were both adopted, but from different birth parents, he thought it would be an interesting experiment to have her go through regressive trances to find if she accessed similar time periods or regressions to Napoleon's life. If she did, he reasoned, he would have to conclude that his own regressions to that time period were a result of a quirk in his methodology rather than a sign of a direct ancestral link.

Liz's husband, Philip Wesley Hunter, was the Lutheran minister of one of the most prominent churches in the Washington area. They had met in her final year of college while volunteering for a church Appalachian project, repairing houses for the less fortunate in central West Virginia. According to Liz it had been love at first sight, and they were married, much to Adam's surprise, within two months. Philip was in his second year of seminary and was ordained shortly after the marriage. His first assignment had been in a small church close to his home in Nebraska, but that had lasted only a year. The publication of his book, *God Is in Your Home*, made him an overnight celebrity, and he was invited to become pastor of his present church.

Shortly after taking over his new parish, Philip enrolled in a Ph.D. program in the department of theology at George Washington University and had been working on his dissertation for several years. Adam knew that the research had something to do with the Old Testament, but Philip was always somewhat evasive when describing it. Adam sensed that Philip didn't like him and probably didn't trust him. He figured Philip might be suffering from "dissertation paranoia," afraid that someone would steal his idea, and that Adam might be a likely culprit. Philip had made several trips to the Middle East to gather data for his dissertation but he avoided talking about these visits as well.

Adam usually called Liz at least once a week, but because of his hectic schedule there had been a lapse in their contact. He decided to call to see how she was doing, tell her about his work, and ask her to go through a regression. He pressed her speed dial number.

"Hi Liz, it's me."

"Well, hello brother. Are you okay? Long time no hear. I've left messages with Ellen. She said you've been incredibly busy."

"I'm sorry I didn't get back to you. Ellen must have forgotten to tell me you called. I'm fine, and it's true that I've been really busy. How are you and the girls?"

"Great! Ruth and Sara are both getting bigger by the minute. Sara is a little mischief maker and reminds me of you."

"Oh, come on, me a mischief maker? I was just more curious and a bigger risk taker than you. Listen, I'm excited about the research I've been doing. I haven't fully shared it with anyone yet, but I want to tell you about it. I've developed a technique that enables people to regress and to actually live the past in the present. When I do it on myself, I've been surprised to find that I repeatedly regress to the Napoleonic period. I wanted to see if it was something in my genetic background or the way we were raised. I thought if you would be willing to go through a regression, it would help clarify this, since our genetic backgrounds are totally different."

"I'm not sure I understand what you're talking about. Is it going to hurt? Are you going to electrocute me?"

"Don't be silly Liz. Would I ask you to do anything dangerous? There's absolutely no danger. I've done it many times myself. It's called transcranial magnetic stimulation and it permits us to experience the past in the present."

"Sounds like gibberish to me, but don't just slough off my worry about it being dangerous. I'll never forget the last time you promised me there was no danger. You made me hold the two wires to those stupid batteries connected to that machine you invented. I can't believe it, a machine that would tell you what I was thinking. I thought I was going to die, I had burns on my hands for a month."

"Liz! I was twelve years old and you were ten. And besides you're exaggerating again. It was a mild current and, to this day I still think you put Dad's shoe polish on your hands to make him think I had burned you. Anyway I got the usual beating from Mom."

"Yeah, and as usual you showed no emotion and never let her know that she hurt you."

"Precisely! Now, back to what I am asking. Believe me, there's no possibility of any shock or danger with my equipment."

"I'll think about it. It's been months since

I've seen you, Ellen, or the boys. Kevin e-mailed me to say they would both be home this coming weekend. Why don't all of you come here on Sunday for a cook out? Ruth and Sara would love to see their cousins and they can swim in the pool while we catch up on things."

"Sounds good! I'll check with Ellen. If we're free we'll be there."

Adam paused. "You know, Liz, this is not the time, but at some point I'm going to have to confront Philip about his attitude toward me and find out why he dislikes me. I don't want our family to be like this. One of the reasons I don't see you more often is that I feel uncomfortable around him, and I don't think he wants me there. I love you and wish we could go back to the close-ness we had before Goliath came into the picture. Is he still putting on mounds of muscle? God, last time I saw him he could easily pass for a profes-sional wrestler."

Adam felt the tense silence on the other end of the phone. Then he heard Philip's voice in the background.

"Hi honey, who's on the phone?"

"It's Adam, calling to see how we're doing."

"Say hello to the lunatic for me."

Liz made a disapproving face at Philip and turned back to the phone, hoping that Adam hadn't heard his remark."

CHAPTER TWENTY-SIX

"Philip just got home and says hello."

"I heard him. See, that's what I'm talking about."

Without missing a beat Liz changed the subject. "The girls will be home from tennis practice any moment. They'll be starving. I need to go and start dinner. Have Ellen call to let me know about Sunday."

Philip walked over and greeted Liz with a kiss on the cheek as she hung up the phone.

Liz began to prepare dinner, expertly creating a julienne of carrots as she chattered about Adam's work and his request that she undergo regressive hypnosis. "Liz, I'm telling you, your brother is crazy and if I were you I would be very careful of getting seduced by any of his mad ideas. He just wants to use you as a guinea pig. He could hurt you in some way and wouldn't ever admit it. He's dangerous Liz, stay away from him, there's a lot you are not aware of about him."

Liz was deeply in love with Philip and felt caught between her husband and her brother.

"I invited them here for Sunday afternoon. The boys will be home."

"Well that's okay. We don't have anything going on. There are no after church meetings scheduled this week. It should be easy for your brother to come Sunday, atheists don't go to church."

"Honey, just stop it. I've told you many

times Adam is not an atheist. He's just not religious. In fact, he's a very spiritual person."

"I don't buy that spirituality without religion stuff. It's just running away from commitment. Instead of all that time he devotes to his hypnosis he ought to spend his time praying and finding God for himself. I've listened to him and his quote spirituality. You know Liz, Christians, Muslims, and Jews, which make up over ninety percent of the world, all have a common source to fall back on, a book, but your spiritualists, like your brother, are pagans, they are not in any way united and have no common base. We live our life based on the scriptures, he doesn't, and that's the critical difference."

Liz's face reddened, and she clutched the frying pan handle as anger surged through her body. Throughout their marriage Philip had always overwhelmed her in any intellectual, especially religious discussion, so she swallowed her feelings and continued cooking.

Adam called Ellen as soon as he ended his conversation with Liz.

"I just talked with Liz. How come you didn't tell me she had called several times? You've done that before. I never fail to tell you when you get a call."

"I simply forgot. Don't go reading things

into this. Leave that for the office." Adam let the matter drop but remained annoyed.

CHAPTER
TWENTY-SEVEN

The barbeque was fired up and succulent aromas poured from the kitchen. Philip greeted Adam amicably. This time, once Adam began telling Philip about the book on Napoleon, the two men seemed to relate well together. Adam shared what he was doing with his regressive hypnosis, and this clearly sparked Philip's curiosity. They discussed Napoleon's Egyptian campaign, and Adam asked Philip if he would share something about his dissertation topic and his research trips to the Middle East. Uncharacteristically, Philip seemed relaxed and began to speak freely to Adam.

"In most theology programs the story of Moses is taught in a literal way, just as we find it in the Old Testament. The good book tells us that he was an Israelite and that God spoke to him in the form of a burning bush on Mt. Sinai. As a student I discovered a number of ancient writings that presented alternative stories of Moses. My dissertation is based on the hypothesis that Moses was not an Israelite, but rather that he was an Egyptian prince from Amenhotep's reign. My thesis proposes that his name was Tuthmose. There are several reliable historical accounts of Tuthmose, and his profile fits the Biblical description of Moses. Tuthmose commanded an army for Egypt during their campaign in Ethiopia. The Bible tells us that Moses was appointed by the pharaoh as commander of an army sent to wage war against the Ethiopians. I know, Adam, that you have done a lot of research in your field, but you have no idea of what it's like to trace history that far back. A Jewish historian, Josephus, in his book, *Jewish Antiquities,* provides what seems to be an accurate account of the similarities between Moses and Tuthmose. He points out that Tuthmose was at one time the high priest at the Temple of Ra in Heliopolis. Guess what, Josephus found that Moses was also at one time the Priest at that Temple. Both figures were driven into exile but I'm sure this is boring you."

"Not at all, in fact, I find this most interesting. It must be exciting research. You're right, far different from brain research."

Just then Liz swished opened the sliding glass doors to the patio and they could see the children playing and splashing in the pool.

"Why don't you two join us? The kids are having a ball and the food is almost ready."

"We'll be there in a moment. I've got a captive audience to talk about my research and Adam is really interested. Let me tell you a little more. I guess you can see it's become a passion for me."

"Believe me Phil, I totally understand. That's the only way anyone can get a dissertation done."

"Right! Well, an Italian archeologist, Giovanni Belzoni, discovered Tuthmose's tomb in the Valley of the Kings. But it was never used and I'm starting to conclude that this was because Tuthmose had been disgraced and exiled. How similar to Moses can you get? I've made trips to Egypt to gather data to support my hypothesis, and I have actually visited Tuthmose's tomb. I've talked to local guides who believe they know the real site of the encounter between God and Moses. Most of the authorities in the field are sure it isn't Mount Sinai, but Mebel Madhbah."

Adam was intrigued by Philip's hypothesis and felt that they were finally interacting in a closer way.

"Fascinating and provocative too! If you

can prove that Moses was an Egyptian, I would think it necessitates a significant retooling of religious thinking and raises all sorts of questions about the traditional Moses and the ten-commandment story in the Bible. What about the burning bush, the parting of the Red Sea, and the forty years of wandering in the wilderness?"

"Ah, all interesting questions. You've been through dissertation writing so I'm sure you know it's imperative to narrow the study as much as you can. I'm certainly interested in all of those questions and have collected some information on them, but I have to place limits on myself. If I don't restrict the study to manageable parameters, you can be sure my doctoral committee will."

Adam stroked his baldhead, a habit he had developed when thinking deeply. He wanted to hear more and hoped that Philip would continue, but at that moment Liz interrupted again, summoning Philip to rescue the chicken burning on the barbeque. Philip sprang to action, leaving Adam in the family room. While deftly removing the chicken he shouted, "Hey Adam, come and grab yourself a beer!"

Adam headed toward the patio, pausing for a moment to admire several statues of Egyptian origin on a table next to Philip's desk. He glanced at the top of the desk and noticed many pages of dissertation notes scattered across the surface. His attention was drawn to a folder with the letters MKULTRA printed in the upper right hand corner. There was something vaguely familiar about this unusual combination of letters. Philip called to him again.

"Adam, I've got your beer. Come and help me with this chicken."

The afternoon passed pleasantly. The two couples talked about the children and reminisced about the past. Adam was surprised that Philip paid a good deal of attention to him and brought up the topic of his regressive hypnosis several times, expressing particular interest in the transcranial magnetic stimulation coil. In his eagerness to strengthen their rapport, he shared details of his regressive technique and access to the collective unconscious. Philip was intrigued with the idea of living the past in the present moment and probed Adam for the potential this might have in predicting future events, even pushing Adam for his thoughts on the possibility of using it to change history. Adam avoided expressing his opinion in either area.

At home later, although he wasn't sure, the letters MKULTRA resurfaced in Adam's mind and he was driven to figure out why he had recognized them and what they represented. He thought they might refer to something he had studied in graduate school but couldn't place it. He was distracted from these thoughts when Kevin asked if he wanted to play Scrabble. Adam responded with enthusiasm. Despite Ellen's disapproving looks, he grabbed two bags of chips, a bowl of sour cream dip, a large bottle of coke, and a bowl of peanuts and placed them on the Scrabble table. For some reason, Ellen refrained from her usual verbal chastise about his proclivity for junk food and his bad influence on the boys. Adam felt relieved. However, she did caution them about bedtime, reminding them that they had to get up early for her to drive them back to school the next morning.

Hours later Adam awoke with a start. He glanced at the clock on his night table to see that it was 3:20 a.m.

"Got it! I have some notes on that work, MKULTRA, from my class with Doctor Bowen. It was the course on psychology and government."

Adam slipped quietly out of bed and went to his study. He searched frantically through old graduate school notes, scattering papers across the floor until he found what he was looking for. MKULTRA was a government project in the late 1950's. He began reading his notes aloud.

"1953 Allen W. Dulles, director of the CIA, maybe developed, but definitely approved, a project termed MKULTRA. Project was designed to find chemical, biological, psychological, and

radiological approaches to interrogation and behavior modification. Renowned psychologists-professor won't name them-exploring mental telepathy, hypnosis, and types of electrical stimulation for mind control. Government trying to explore mind control? Used LSD with subjects to try to penetrate minds. Bowen admits being part of this. Thinks we won't believe it. CIA into very risky experimentation with little concern for moral aspects. Prof. was part of a committee set up by ethics division of the APA and AMA to investigate these practices. Says his committee was abruptly shut down and each committee member was under IRS audit for the next five years."

Adam stopped reading. "Why in the world does Philip have a folder with the title of that organization? I remember being surprised that Bowen told us anything at all about it. He just used it to illustrate how the government might misuse the discipline of psychology. He charged us all to do whatever we could as psychologists to keep checks and balances within the government. What the hell could Philip have to do with MKULTRA? If it even still exists. It probably stands for something else. Maybe I misread it. Probably did. I need to get some sleep."

CHAPTER
TWENTY-EIGHT

The office was hectic the next day. Adam's mind was continuously pulling him toward his newfound passion of writing the book with Monica. However, a new patient presenting very significant suicidal ideation, forced him to focus on his work.

Janette was a twenty-one year old woman. She had gotten drunk at a college party and awakened the following morning to the horrible realization that she had had sex with at least four different fraternity members. She could not recall any of them, but did know that it had been unprotected sex. Janette sobbed uncontrollably throughout the session. Up to the night of that party she had been a virgin and had intended to remain so until marriage.

"This was random!" she screamed. "I don't even know who they were! All I remember is that they called the first one Robby. I can't believe this happened to me! I know I resisted a bit but probably not enough. I don't know! Either way, they're bastards! They knew I was drunk! They took advantage of me. People like that don't deserve to live. If I knew who they were I would kill them, especially that Robby guy. He started the whole thing and encouraged the others and he wasn't drunk. The others were. He's just a bastard. He needs to die. I can't face myself. All I can think of doing is killing myself. Do you understand? I'm no longer Janette, I'm someone I don't know and don't want to know. My God, how could I have done this? I know it's a mortal sin, but I'm doomed to hell anyway so why not kill myself? I know it's a mortal sin, but I don't care. My parents must never find out. Believe me, it's better that I die."

Adam asked her, "Why are you here, if you so much want to kill yourself? Why have you come to me?"

Janette sobbed and gasped for several minutes before she responded.

"I want to kill myself. But I want you to stop me."

Adam paused before asking why and permitted a further silence before continuing.

"Why do you want me to stop you? I

believe everyone has the right to kill herself if she wants to, and I also believe that if you really want to do it there's nothing I can do to stop you."

Janette looked up at him with some of the tears abating and almost whispered, "Please help me. I can't bear the idea of leaving the legacy of a suicide to my sisters, my little five- year old nephew, and my poor parents. Please help me."

Adam asked, "How close are you to doing it and how will you do it?" Janette took a jumble of pill bottles from her purse. Adam noticed the labels for aspirin, Valium, and Prozac. Janette placed them on the table next to his chair and said, "I swallow pills very easily. The aspirin I can buy at any drug store or supermarket, and my roommate has a storehouse of different tranquilizers in the bathroom."

This was enough for Adam. "We can talk about the guilt you feel and the reasons for that guilt another time. I know I can help you come to terms with your behavior and see it very differently from the way you do now. However, I always take it seriously when someone has an actual plan for suicide. So you need time to spend with this thought and time to acknowledge to yourself that there are alternatives to handling your feelings. Time will help you to forgive yourself. You will come to realize that your God forgives you. I think it's important that you allow me to get you into the hospital for a few days where you will be safe and have some time to think a little longer about such a serious decision, from which there is no return."

Janette answered, "Do you really believe that everyone has the choice to kill themselves and that it's their right to make that choice if they wish to?"

Adam very quickly responded. "Absolutely, it's your right to choose, not mine or anyone else's. It's your life to do with as you wish."

Janette looked relieved. She thanked Adam for being so understanding and acknowledged that it was a good idea for her to go to the hospital.

"But what about my parents? Will you be able see me while I'm in the hospital? I don't want this on my record, it could ruin my career."

Adam smiled understandingly. "Well, it won't ruin your career nearly as much as killing yourself will."

Janette actually laughed. "But what will we tell my parents?"

"You mean what will you, not me, tell your parents. I think it would be acceptable to tell them that school pressure reached a point where it was affecting you physically and your doctor suggested a total rest in the hospital for a few days. Where do they live?"

Janette perked up even more. "They live in Arizona, and right now my father is out of the country for two weeks on business. My mother watches my nephew all day so she can't get away. Now I know why you asked me where they live. No! There's no way my mother will be able to leave to come to see me."

Adam was perplexed by Janette's strange smile. He assured her that he would arrange for her to be in a regular hospital bed and her family would never know that she was on suicide watch. Adam breathed a long but imperceptible sigh of relief. He asked Cathy to come into the office and said in front of Janette, "Cathy, Janette is another one of our students who has become overwhelmed with the anxiety of school work, law school applications, and the plain old stress of Georgetown. She needs a few days to rehabilitate herself. Please call Dr. Winters and tell him I need a bed for Janette for the usual reasons."

Adam turned back to Janette. "I feel privileged that you shared your struggles with me, and you should feel you are a very strong person, taking the initiative to consult me. The strong enter through this door; the weak never make it. I'll stop by to see you very early in the morning, probably about seven o'clock. The nurses will know that I'm coming and have you awake and dressed. Sorry it has to be so early but I have appointments here beginning at nine. See you tomorrow, bright and early."

As Janette followed Cathy to the outer office, Adam hoped that Dr. Winters had a bed and that it would be easy to get her admitted. If not, he knew he was in for five or six lengthy phone calls to try another hospital or to pull some strings with Winters.

At the end of the day Cathy came into his office to say good night.

"I have an appointment at seven with my Napoleon teacher. Would you please call Ellen to remind her that I'll be home late tonight?"

Cathy seemed to linger. Finally she said, "You and this teacher are putting a lot of time in together, aren't you?" Her tone was accusing.

Adam wondered if Ellen had been questioning Cathy about his relationship with Monica. Cathy and Ellen had grown relatively close over the years and by now Cathy was complicit in helping Ellen keep tabs on him. Adam quickly replied, "Oh, we're working on a book. It's a break from the office work."

"One more thing on our plate, but I'm sure if you want to do it you'll find a way." Then she raised the subject of Allison, another patient, who had been telling her how regressive hypnosis had explained her fear of water. Adam smiled but did not respond verbally. He was eager to get himself into a trance and did not want a prolonged conversation. Cathy understood the signal.

CHAPTER TWENTY-EIGHT

"Good night Adam, see you in the morning."

In his impatience Adam neglected to respond. Sitting in his comfortable chair with only a dim floor lamp lighting the room, he prepared to go to work. As had occurred in previous regressions, he soon became aware of being in a previous time.

Soldiers in tattered uniforms drifted around an encampment. The uniforms were basically French, but some soldiers wore Arab garb, others wore a combination of the two, and still others were dressed in unidentifiable clothes. Walls of bone gray stone, pocked, chipped, and either partially or totally collapsed, could be seen throughout the camp. The weary walls blocked any view of the deep, sparkling blue sea beyond, where enemy ships were drawing near the periphery of the camp. On the right a group of soldiers sat around a campfire, which itself seemed to be fighting to stay alive. It was clear that exhaustion pervaded the camp. The small, scattered fires emitted a heavy, putrid smell. The air was still and the primary sound was of the crunching of leather boots on stony arid earth, which seemed to record the movement of this mass of bedraggled, pathetic soldiers. The sound was black and portended sadness. Many of the men appeared ill and there was talk that the plague had hit the camp. Those who seemed relatively healthy expressed fear that the plague would spread even further and that they would all be wiped out. Walls of bone gray stone, pocked, chipped, and in various states of collapse, could be seen throughout the camp. The weary walls blocked any view of the deep, sparkling blue sea beyond, where enemy ships were drawing near the periphery of the camp. There was a sense of doom and defeat among the men. Everyone was aware of the odor of sickness and the silent inner suffering of the men. And a cloud of despair laden with the fear of death and defeat hung over the camp. The many cannons lay silent as if their strength had been sapped, and there were no cannon balls stacked next to them and no storehouse of ammunition in sight.

Buried slightly to the left of the center of the camp was a bunker. Inside, a man lay on a cot. He bore horrific wounds and was clearly dying. The voice of someone reading aloud from Voltaire wafted through the air. Two soldiers stood outside the bunker, but seemed too tired and ill to guard anything should there be a real threat.

"Cafarelli was warned repeatedly to stay low and keep below the wall during the attack."

"I know! He just stood up there ignoring the warnings as if he was invincible."

"Well that should be a lesson to all of us. You see what reckless bravery gets you."

"I couldn't believe it. He could hear everyone cautioning him to get down, but he wouldn't listen. He stood up with his hand on his hip to balance himself. That exposed his elbow above the trench and he was struck by an Arab cannonball that exploded into a million fragments."

They both glanced into the bunker, looking at the disfigured form of Cafarelli, with his missing leg and bloody bandages covering the stump of his amputated arm.

"God, I can't look at him."

"I know. It makes me squirm to think of losing my arm or leg. I think I'd rather die."

"Yeah, I know. So maybe he's lucky. He won't have to face the horror of being a cripple. But of course we both know what the little corporal would say. Giving into that kind of fear is cowardly."

Suddenly all of the tortured sounds ceased, and an uncanny silence descended, except for the sound of a single set of boots crunching the dry and solid ground. Napoleon stood only a few feet away. Supreme confidence emanated from every pore of his body and he appeared to be oblivious to the dismal nature of their surroundings. His voice was clear, firm, and strong.

"If I had had the twenty-four pounders we would be tasting victory right now. But it is surely ahead of us. If Smith had not intercepted my supply ship and taken the guns, our enemy would not have stood a chance. It's not over. We will breach the walls and take Acre. Once we have done that, it is definite that we can hold off the Turks."

An officer stepped up and warned, "Sir, there is grave illness moving among the men. The symptoms are undeniable; there is fever and swelling. It's the plague, Mon General. It is moving rapidly through the camp. The men who are ill are hardly able to lift their heads, they're not eating and we're doing all we can to keep water in them. The water itself is turning vile, the troops are tired, battle worn, and disillusioned. They're saying that Smith's armada should have been predicted and was not."

Napoleon looked straight ahead and in a matter-of-fact voice, replied; "My men will do anything for me. One more assault on the walls before the ships reach Acre. I must do this for my friend Cafarelli. He understands the importance of this undertaking."

Napoleon stared at the dying Cafarelli. "We have mapped Egypt, recorded its history, made images of its flora and fauna, made engravings of its monuments, built roads and hospitals. We accomplished a great deal, and for you my dear friend, and for the secrets I have shared with you, I shall continue. My savants and my soldiers are uncovering the past and opening the path to the future. I will not let you down. This is my destiny and I will fulfill it."

Napoleon was obdurate. He was focused on what he thought was paramount and seemed confident that his men would show their allegiance to him under any conditions. His charisma was almost palpable and despite the dismal circumstances, those around him seemed to be ready to rally to the task.

No longer addressing Cafarelli but standing boldly and looking toward the sky, Napoleon announced in a loud, commanding voice, "The world is ready for one unifying leader. With your guidance from the past I will blend Muslim, Judaic, and European ideas. I will take the turban, drive the English out, and bring sound government to the region. You have taught me, as did my father, and all my mentors, that a man is only a man, but circumstances create his destiny."

Suddenly the young man who had been reading to Cafarelli said, "Sir I believe he is dead."

Napoleon raised his left arm and pronounced. "We will return to Cairo. Sinclair Smith has robbed me of my destiny just for now. Destiny is destiny and I know I will fulfill mine."

CHAPTER
TWENTY-NINE

Adam's half-hour on the treadmill, usually an effortless routine seemed like an impossible challenge. His legs felt leaden, and his heart pounded in rebellion. No amount of determination could coerce his body into obedience, and he stepped off the machine in disgust.

"Great, now I can't even exercise."

An hour later, still grumpy, he strode through the office door. Before he could put his briefcase down or remove his jacket, Cathy accosted him.

"You'll never guess this one! Dr. Winters wants you to call him immediately."

Adam cringed, "Oh, I forgot to visit Janette this morning. Is it bad news about her? Did he tell you anything?"

"I think you better talk to him yourself. I'll get him for you."

"Adam! I've got something interesting for you. The hospital social worker met with your patient for the routine intake. It turns out she's not enrolled in college at all. The name she gave us was different from the one on her insurance card so we had to try to contact a member of her family to get the correct information. Guess what! Everything she told us was false! And now, for the crowning blow. On physical examination she turned out to be a virgin. There were no signs, and I mean none, of any sexual contact ever having occurred. Lastly, she's gone! She left the hospital, AMA, sometime in the middle of the night. No one saw her and we have no idea where she is. We don't even know who she is. How about that?"

Adam exhaled audibly. "Bill, I don't know what to say. I guess I was taken in. I really thought she was relating a major traumatic experience. I believed it all. But why would she do this?"

"Hey man, I'm only a psychiatrist, not a soothsayer. That's for you to figure out. I've got a ward full of twenty-two legitimately crazy people. No time for this playacting stuff, I'll leave it to you guys getting rich in private practice. Maybe she has a thing for you and just used the story to see you. Who knows? If there's a real patient you need help with, call me. You know I'm just giving you a hard time. Let's have lunch soon. Bye."

Speechless, Adam hung up without saying good-bye. He called Cathy in to get her take on the story. She was as confused as he was, but reminded Adam that it was his job to deal with abnormal behavior. She also reminded him that his first patient was waiting, that they were booked straight through the day, and that he had to be sure to end on time to attend the SELF meeting that night.

"Thanks Cathy. Give me just five minutes before I see Mrs. Rudolph."

As Cathy closed the door Adam muttered to himself, "Damn! Why is this upsetting me so much? That girl touched my heart. I felt a lot for her. I felt immediate empathy and yet none of it was true. Odd that the one name she remembered was Robbie."

CHAPTER THIRTY

Adam parked his Jaguar near Alice's driveway for the second meeting of SELF. This time there were at least ten more cars at the house, and he noticed a number of unfamiliar faces, people who were neither patients nor friends. In the past he would have felt awkward in such a situation, but now to his surprise it was quite the opposite. He was excited and began to see this group, cultish as it might be, as a possible avenue to greater fame and influence. He was stirred with a growing sense of power and he began to think that he might have a calling. Perhaps he was to be God's messenger, to finally deliver the truth to the world without the self-serving distortions that ages of organized religion had created.

"Look at this. Ellen signs up for a class, I uncharacteristically jump at the opportunity to attend it, and my trance regressions lead me to Napoleon's life. This cannot be just coincidence or chance. Maybe it is divinely ordained. Yes, that could be it! Divinely arranged. I have a new message to communicate. Different from any other spiritual message. Mine is based on scientific research and tangible methods of investigation. Mine is not based on faith. I have to show the world that eternal life exists within each one of us through our genetic memory. This doesn't have to be accepted by blind faith. I can prove this."

Alice's voice abruptly interrupted his deep thoughts.

"Isn't this exciting, Doctor Peterson? We have ten new people who want to be members of our group and have you regress them to a genetic memory. They believe that something lies in their collective unconscious that will dramatically change their lives. My husband Jack is one of them. You must be thrilled by what's happening. Jack is so impressed with the changes he sees in me and what I've discovered, that it has made him a believer."

Adam smiled, nodded his head slightly, and was just about to comment when Alice manically continued.

"I had the caterers prepare a buffet for us. You'll love it. They're the same ones who did the party for the ambassador's gathering at Eunice's house. It's all in the dining room. Why don't you have something before we start the meeting?"

This time Adam did not feel awkward about getting something to eat. He was shocked at the elaborate array of food that extended over three large carved walnut tables. It seemed like overkill to him but he savored a number of exotic offerings, including raw oysters. He was surprised by the affluence and social-political status of the group and excited by the potential he imagined they could have. He began to envision the members of the group as his soldiers, those who would, in Napoleon's words, "do anything for me."

Carrying their plates of food, many of the guests approached Adam with complimentary words, talking about the future and the potential of the power he had discovered. Adam felt their excitement was sincere, intense, and certainly ego building for him. Some of the most encouraging remarks came from people who, having been through a regression, now saw themselves and the world in a totally different way. They now saw themselves as being at one with nature and of belonging to something far greater than their social worlds. They felt a heightened awareness and the inter-relatedness of all matter. Just as Adam was about to take his last bite of lobster Newberg, which he had saved for the end, Alice announced that it was time to start the meeting.

The group moved into the living room and John again opened the meeting by thanking everyone for attending.

"I know that many of you, as I do myself, feel that sharing our regressive hypnotic experiences will help us to bond as a group and to develop a deeper sense of the scope and potential of the process. Eunice has been through a unique experience with Dr. Peterson. She has experienced what he calls a progressive hypnosis. She is so elated and eager to share her experience that I'm surprised she hasn't already interrupted me. Her husband Jack is with us and he can attest to the fantastic results. Dr. Peterson, would you say a few words before we hear from Eunice?"

Adam graciously acknowledged the request and rose to address the group. He assumed an imposing stance, his sense of power growing deeper by the moment.

"I believe that you are all here tonight for the same basic reason. Each of you believes that human beings need a new way to think about the world if peace is ever to reign. Every day we face the horrors created by those of one religion or another trying to assert that theirs is the one true Way. Our experiences in regressive hypnosis may seem as if we are talking about going back in time. However, we must move beyond that view and grapple with the very difficult notion that time does not really exist. Ah! I see many of you are beginning to squirm. Understanding this concept requires a broad fund of knowledge that few of you possess. Pay attention and I will explain. We operate within the dimensions of height, width, and depth each day in order to negotiate the world. These three dimensions seem unquestionable. The dimension of time is different. We once thought that nothing could travel faster than the speed of light but physicists now tell us even that's not so. They have recently been able to accelerate light pulses up to three hundred times their normal limit of 186,000 miles per second. Think of that. It means that those light pulses arrived at their destination before they started their journey. Think about it this way. We all watch movies. A movie film is really just thousands of still frames. It you saw one frame at a time, as we do with slides, you would not perceive any motion and there would be no sensation of time passing in the content of the pictures. However, project those single frames at a rate of 15 or 16 per second, and suddenly you perceive motion and a passage of time. What has actually happened is that your brain has deceived you. Now what does this mean for us? If time is only a creation of our minds, then there really is never a beginning or end to anything, and we are indeed immortal. Of course, I'm not talking about the religious view of a heaven in the clouds where angels play harps. Nor am I promising eternal youth. I am saying that instead of life after death there is constant life alongside death. Think of a flowing river. As you watch the water it seems to move past, but at any given spot on which you focus, the river is the same. Each of us exists in many universes where nothing ever moves or ages, since time is not present in any of them. In one universe we are newly born, in another we are graduating from college, and in yet another we are catching our last glimpse of light in a hospital bed as we close our eyes to die. All of these universes exist simultaneously in a mass of unimaginable size and variety, so we are at once many different versions of ourselves. You see, there is immortality for each of those stages of existence because each exists permanently, side by side with the others."

Indifferent to audience reaction, Adam continued his diatribe.

"I know this is complex and probably too esoteric for many of you, but we are not in a fictional fantasy. I am talking to you about time, because I believe it is essential for each of you in our Society for Eternal Life and Freedom to fully accept that time is nothing but a measure, if we are going to bring our message to humanity. Time is only shorthand for representing the changing positions of objects. You must abandon the notion of time. This is the only way you'll understand what Eunice is going to say tonight about seeing into the future. Okay, enough said, now let's hear from Eunice."

The group stared at Adam with a mixture of confusion and admiration.

John stood up. "Thank you Dr. Peterson, truly inspirational. Your theory is provocative but difficult to grasp. It looks like Eunice is about to burst in her eagerness to tell you about her experience."

Eunice rose, smiling broadly, and walked to the front of the room.

"Two weeks ago Adam asked me if I wanted to try a progressive hypnosis in which we would attempt to see the future. I must admit that at first I thought he was going too far. However, because I completely trust him I agreed to do it. I can't say how long it took to get into trance, or, I guess I should use my newly acquired language and say that I was unaware of the process of moving from one position in psychic space to another."

Adam smiled patronizingly. "Very good Eunice."

Eunice blushed and continued. "Suddenly I was sitting in our present living room with my husband Jack, talking about how fortunate we were to have decided to sell our oil drilling stock ten years ago. Both of us seemed to be a bit older than we are now, but still looking fine I might add. Jack was reviewing what had happened, saying that many people had been seriously burned by that stock and that we had been lucky to get out at the right moment. He said, 'Do you realize we had over a million in it?' I was still smiling and just felt tremendously good. That was all there was to the progressive trance.

After the trance I went home and asked Jack about our investments. I learned that we had about a million dollars invested in an oil drilling company that was sure to make a fortune for us. The owners, friends of Jack's brother, predicted that within three months we would quadruple our money. I told him about my progressive trance and that we must sell the stock right away. He laughed and said that he wasn't going to follow any nutty trance and my imagination. He also asked what Dr. Peterson had to gain by putting this in my head. I won't go into the tears and battle that ensued, but I so trusted that I had seen the future that I persisted and had Jack sell the stock the next day. Well, one week later, last week, the stock collapsed over night. We would have lost everything. I know this is hard to believe, but it happened and Jack is here tonight, a true convert."

There ensued a hearty round of applause and a lot of low level talking. Adam immediately stood before the group.

"I think Eunice's experience is wonderful, but I really have to caution all of you that we are in new territory with the progressive trance. Don't start thinking that we're all going to become billionaires overnight."

Amanda, in line for a cabinet position if there was a party change in the next election, asked to say a few words.

"We mustn't lose sight of the greater whole, the fact that we are beginning to learn how to be a unit, one people together, all part of one universe, gathering lost knowledge from our ancestors. The greatest part of this for me is that we can now truly understand how history happened. By being with the people who actually lived it and created it, we may be able to make totally different decisions about how we manage the world. As a former advisor to the president I can tell you this is going to change the world. Talk about power!"

A young woman, hunched over with her head down, caught Adam's eye as she hurried across the back of the room. Adam whirled around to find Alice standing beside him.

"Alice, who is that girl back there? Do you know her?"

"Hmm, no! I've never seen her before. I had everyone sign in when they arrived, but I don't recall seeing her. Why, is there some problem?"

"I just thought I recognized her, that's all"

With the swiftness of a panther Adam reached the rear of the room as the young woman opened a door that led to a patio beside the pool. He followed her.

"Wait a minute! Janette! I just want to talk to you for a minute. Please stop!"

The young woman, quick and agile, reached the three-foot boxwood hedge, leapt over without breaking her stride, and headed for her car. Adam's hurdle was less successful and he landed a-straddle the bushes.

"Janette! Please wait. I need to know what's going on. I want to help you."

The young woman hurried down the lane and jumped into a foreign vehicle that had seen better days. Adam chased after the car, but was brought to his knees, choking; by a belch of oily black exhaust fumes. As the car sped away, the driver threw a crumpled paper out the window. It blew to the center of the lane.

Adam picked himself up and retrieved the paper. He smoothed it enough to read: "Hi Robby! The day of reckoning is near. Don't worry you will see me again."

CHAPTER THIRTY-ONE

The SELF-meeting had fed Adam's growing sense of power and destiny. Throughout his talk he had had the sporadic sense that Napoleon was hovering near him. Now, on the ride home, ruminative thoughts about his adoption and his ignorance about his own heritage dominated. As he felt the emptiness of his rootlessness, Adam's elation shifted to despair. He screamed to the heavens through his open window, "Who am I? Where did I come from? Who made me?"

Impulsively he swung the steering wheel sharply to the right and swerved into the exit lane. Luck was on his side. There were no other cars. Accelerating dangerously, in seconds he sped off the beltway, drove through the red light at the end of the ramp, made a U turn, and re-entered the highway headed in the opposite direction.

Minutes later he screeched into the parking lot, raced up the stairs, fumbled impatiently for the keys, and burst into his office. Rummaging through his personal papers, he finally put his hands on his birth certificate.

"Christ! What the hell use is this birth certificate? Father unknown! Mother, Ramona Smith, age 19, race-Caucasian. Smith, couldn't she have come up with something better than that? August fifteenth, well, I guess I can assume the birth date is right. Nothing I didn't already know. Why am I surprised? I have no idea who I came from. I wonder if Liz knows more about it. She was always talking to Mom. I bet Mom told her more about me than I know."

Adam pressed the speed dial and called his sister.

"Adam! What's wrong? I was asleep, what's happened?"

"Nothing! Why does there always have to be something wrong?"

"Adam it's after midnight! People don't call at this time of night unless something is wrong."

"Liz, I have to find out about my birth parents. Maybe you know something I don't. Did Mom ever tell you anything? What do you know?"

"Sometimes Adam, I think Phil is right

about you. You are nuts? I don't know anything more than you do. Mom never spoke of either of our birth parents. All I know, which I'm sure you heard too, is that your mother was very young and that she probably got pregnant in another country, but came here to have you. I don't know anything else. Can I go back to sleep now?"

"Liz, think carefully. Didn't Mom tell you anything about my father?"

"I never heard anything about your biological father. Thank God, we're not genetically connected in any way. You're the sole heir to your family line of craziness. Now, say goodbye so I can get back to sleep. Crazy as you may be, I love you, good night."

Adam smiled as he hung up. The next step was clear. To the regression room to get into a trance to see what he could learn. Using the birth certificate and a baby picture of himself on the day his parents adopted him, he induced a transcranial magnetic regressive trance.

In a dimly lit room a young girl sat slumped on a bed. She held her head in her hands as tears trickled down her cheeks. A picture of a young soldier lay on her lap. Standing in the corner was an older man in military uniform, his face battle weary and worn, and his cap respectfully in his hand. The explosions in the distance didn't seem to bother the girl, but she flinched at the bursts of gunfire close by.

"He was a brave young man, Ramona. This damned accursed war has taken many of our best. France will never be the same. Your man gave his life for his country as well as for yours. He wanted you to have all of his possessions and wants you to give this letter to his parents in the United States. I was his commanding officer. I held his hand as he died. He asked me to find you and tell you how much he loved you. He had intended to send this letter to his parents to tell them that you were carrying his child. He also wrote this letter to you.

The Captain gently placed the letters and a dented ammunition box in the girl's hands. With tentative, tear soaked fingers she tore open the envelope, and then wiping her eyes, she looked beseechingly at the Captain. "I speak English but I can't read it. This letter is in English. Please, will you read it to me?"

"It would be an honor. I deeply respected your young man. He was brave beyond the call of duty. I am sure your child is destined to be great, I know his father was. If only we had not been ambushed. I want you to know that he received his wounds trying to save three soldiers who had been hit and were lying in the path of enemy fire."

The Captain asked if he could use the chair on the other side of the room and pulled it next to the girl. She seemed frozen but gave a barely perceptible affirmative nod. The Captain began to read.

"My dearest Mona, it is with great sadness that I write this, because I fear that death is very close. I *will not see you again, and I will not see our child born. You will be alone to raise him (I feel sure it will be a boy), and there are things you must know which I have never revealed to anyone. You will be bearing a child from a most aristocratic line. My grandfather, Matthew Mesnard married my grandmother Charlotte, the daughter of Charles, Count de Leon. I'm sure this name will mean nothing to you, but our child should know his heritage. Charles, Count de Leon was the son of Eleonore Denouelle. Again another name whose significance you will wonder about. Eleonore was Napoleon Bonaparte's mistress. Napoleon was unable to have a child with his wife, Josephine, and for a time there was uncertainty as to whose fault this was. It was not Napoleon's fault. He was not sterile. He had a child with my great-grandmother. You must understand the importance of this. I am a direct descendent of Napoleon. Our son will also be a direct descendent of Napoleon. Truly, he also will be destined to greatness. I want you to have my great-grandmother's ring. I had intended to give it to you in person when we wed."*

The Captain stood still, in silent awe. Ramona, overcome with grief and astonishment, was unable to look up, but she reached into the box and removed the ring. She turned it between her fingers, staring at the fiery yellow and orange stone. Then she brushed the ring with her lips, held it to her heart, and placed it on the fourth finger of her left hand. The Captain left the room to return with a glass of water which she slowly sipped *as she began to calm herself.*

"Shall I read the other letter?"

At first Ramona shook her head in refusal but then looked at the Captain and said, "Oui, s'il vous plait."

"Dear Mother and Father, I have given this letter to my love, Ramona, with instructions. I also want to introduce her to you. We were to be married but as you will have learned before reading this, God had other plans for me. Do not mourn for me. I will be awaiting our meeting in eternal life. Ramona is my wife. We became husband and wife in the eyes of God. My friends here will be sure she makes it to the United States where I would like her to have our child. Please take care of her and accept your new grandchild. Your loving son."

The trance ended abruptly, and Adam was overcome with sadness. Slapping his palms to his temples, he bellowed, "What does all of this mean? Was that about me? Who am I?"

CHAPTER THIRTY-TWO

"Hi Monica. Are you ready to go to work? Cathy is going to be staying late this evening to catch up on insurance forms, so I would rather not work here tonight. With the way things are between Ellen and me right now I don't think it would be a good idea to work at home either. What do you think?" Adam cradled the phone against his shoulder.

"I'm sorry to hear there's tension between the two of you. Would you like to come here, to my house? Mike is away. I have no idea where he is, but he called last night and said that he would be gone for at least three weeks, so I'm free."

"Great! I'll be there in about thirty minutes. I'm looking forward to it."

Adam dashed around the office gathering up his material and strode briskly to his car. Thrilled to be getting to work on the book and also distinctly excited about being alone with Monica, he made full use of the Jaguar's power.

"I feel like a teenage boy driving to his first date."

The Strove house was set back from the road, and as he pulled into the drive Adam had a pleasing impression of an unpretentious, welcoming home. The cobblestone walkway from the driveway to the door was lined with rows of brightly colored marigolds, petunias, and impatiens, artistically clustered amidst evergreen bushes. The house was painted ochre yellow with darker toned shutters. Flower boxes under the three front windows overflowed with blossoms. Adam thought, "How simple and yet warmly inviting this house looks."

Just as he was about to ring the doorbell Monica appeared, greeting him with a happy smile. "I'm glad to see you. How are you doing, okay?"

"Hi, it's good to see you also. This is a great house and a nice neighborhood."

"Why, thank you. I like the house, but I haven't gotten to know any of my neighbors. Most of them have children and are very family oriented. Mike is never here, so we don't socialize with anyone. I get invited to the gatherings, but I don't feel comfortable going by myself. Come in. We can work in the living room, there's a table where we can put our laptops. Make yourself at home while I go and put on my "real" work clothes."

Adam caught Monica's emphasis and smiled appreciatively at her meaning.

A few minutes later she emerged from her bedroom dressed in blue jeans, sneakers, and a loose fitting sweatshirt with a discreet college insignia on the front. Monica liked to wear it when she was doing research, just as she had in college. She had released her hair from its bun, and it flowed smoothly over her shoulders. For and instant, as she entered the living room, she was framed by a sunbeam and the light seemed to shine from her.

"My God, she's vibrant and alive!" Adam said to himself.

"Okay doctor, let's get to work."

Adam moved away from the table and sat on the couch.

"I believe we should try to understand Napoleon's personality organization within Jungian theory. After all, it's the expansion of his theory that has enabled me to actually be with Napoleon in regressions. To start with, we must realize that every thought, feeing, and behavior results from all that has been placed in our unconscious minds from the time of conception."

Monica interrupted.

"Adam, we have to remember that this book will be for the layman, so we have to cut the jargon. I bet seventy-five percent of our readers, and I certainly hope we have thousands of them, have never even heard of Carl Jung."

"Of course, but we have to teach our readers, don't we?"

Monica smiled, "Yes I'm sure we do, but you're not teaching one of your graduate classes. So KISS, keep it short and simple, as I often say to my students."

"You're right, so I'll rely on you to keep me in check as we go along. Perhaps we should describe the idea of the collective unconscious and then the new dimension of the personal collective unconscious."

"That makes sense to me, but I'll leave that part to you. Go ahead. I'll listen and let you know how it sounds."

Adam continued, "Okay, it is traditionally assumed that we have a personal conscious and a personal unconscious. The conscious level, of course, is everything an individual is aware of. The personal unconscious consists of all of a person's experiences since birth, experiences which have lost their intensity, lost their usefulness, or been too threatening to the ego state to be available for immediate recall. There is a third psychic level that is not so commonly accepted. This is the collective unconscious. It contains the entire history of human existence, that is, all ancestral experiences, that have been passed on to each of us. According to Jung, the collective unconscious is common to all humankind and is the true basis of the individual's psyche. The depth of Jung's conviction about the collective unconscious and primordial images is made wonderfully clear in his last released writings and drawings, *The Red Book*. For Jung the collective unconscious is the source of instinctual forces and of the forms that regulate them, namely what he called the archetypes."

Monica looked up. "I don't understand what an archetype is."

"Explain archetype? Ah! This is important for you to understand and for us to describe in the book. The collective unconscious is a storehouse of all humanity's instincts, urges, and memories, which have been inherited from the beginning of time. Carl Jung called these inherited universal memories archetypes. They reflect the common experiences of everyone who has ever lived. The archetypical elements in the personality are innate dispositions to act, interact, and create behaviors in certain typical and predictable ways. They are similar to the innate release mechanisms of animals. Understand! They are inherited, not learned. The archetypes belong to every human being because of DNA. Each human being unconsciously shapes his or her life into a certain archetype, which provides a sense of self. All shamanic traditions believe there are four primary archetypes, the warrior, the healer, the visionary, and the teacher. In order to live in harmony and balance with our environment and with our own inner nature, we must identify which of the four is our personal dominant archetype. Once this is done we can draw on the power of that archetype. When we learn to accept these archetypes within ourselves, we will begin to heal ourselves and our fragmented world. For example, Gandhi may have had a predominant archetype of the healer, which was translated into a Christ-like figure. Jung, of course, did not talk of DNA. That's my twist on what has created the archetypes. We will need to define what archetypical elements Napoleon brought forward in his particular inherited DNA line that motivated and directed his life."

"What a great idea! We'll describe Napoleon's archetype. This offers a whole new dimension for understanding the key figures that have shaped the course of history."

"Precisely."

"Just a minute," Monica interrupted again. "Just to be sure I have it clearly in my notes, you're saying that Napoleon is made up of his conscious, his personal unconscious, which are things that were probably at one time conscious but have disappeared from awareness, and the content of his collective unconscious, primarily his archetypes, which were never acquired through his own individual experience."

"Right! Then we have to introduce the new dimension that will explain how I have been in the presence of Napoleon himself. I have seen what he has seen and felt. From my regressions I know that I have Napoleon's life encoded in my DNA. This is how we are able to understand Napoleon differently from previous historians and psychologists."

Monica proposed a break. "It's about dinner time. Are you hungry?

"You bet I am. What do you want to do for dinner?"

"I made a beef stew last night and the pot is still full. All I have to do is heat it up. It's not fancy, but it's good. Would you like that?"

"Great. I love stew. Are you sure it's not too much trouble?"

"Absolutely not. I also have some of my delicious cornbread to go with it, if I do say so myself. It's an old family recipe, handed down for several generations. However, I must warn you it has pounds of butter in it."

"Sounds great. In fact, just my style."

"Wonderful, just give me a chance to

change this sweatshirt, I don't want to splash gravy on it. If we're going to have dinner here, let's be comfortable."

Adam followed Monica with his eyes as she returned to her bedroom to change. He watched through the open door as she sat on the edge of her bed reaching for her slippers. He walked to the bedroom and sat down next to her.

"I don't know how to tell you this, Monica. We hardly know one another, but I've never felt about anyone the way I feel about you." He reached over and gently grasped her hand looking deeply into her eyes.

Monica returned his gaze. "Adam I'm frightened. I think I have the same feelings."

Without further words they embraced. There was no hesitation or doubt for Adam, and he delighted in the inviting softness of Monica's body. His movements were reciprocated and as he held her closer and caressed her form, their bodies became as one. There was no thinking, just pure, joyous, abandoned passion.

CHAPTER
THIRTY-THREE

As if by cosmic design they awoke at the same moment and gazed with love and wonder into each other's eyes. The morning embrace only heightened the experience of the previous night. Their lovemaking had easily substituted for the stew, but now they felt the pangs of hunger. They were both famished.

"I don't have any breakfast food, Adam. I could go to the supermarket to get bagels, if you'd like."

"No need to do that for me. What about the stew we were supposed to have last night?"

"I can't believe you said that. You'd eat stew for breakfast?"

"I know I'm probably strange, but I eat

anything for breakfast, left-over pizza, spaghetti, fish, whatever. You name it and I'll eat it."

"You're the only person I know, other than my father, who does that. I'm the same way. I enjoy anything for breakfast, whatever I feel like. Mike always criticizes me about it."

"Welcome to my world. Ellen calls me crude and crass for eating this way."

Adam took the lead and asked Monica to let him heat the stew and serve her breakfast. Sated by two bowls of the savory meat with thick slices of buttery cornbread, Monica said, "Adam, last night was wonderful. I hope you can understand that right now I'm very confused. I need some time away from you to think about my marriage and myself. I've never cheated on Mike before, and I never thought I'd break my marriage vows. I feel guilty, and yet I don't regret it."

Adam put his arm around her.

"Of course I know that. I hope you know this is not usual for me either. In fact this is the first time I've made love to anyone other than Ellen. Monica, you've shown me what true lovemaking should be, so now I know what I've been missing all these years. Of course I understand that you need some time to think. I'm in a similar place. But believe me, last night was a love communion like I've never experienced before. It's the first time I've ever felt a oneness of sex and love. They were truly the same for me last night."

Monica blushed and hugged him warmly.

"So you understand why I need to get away and think, to be sure of what I feel. I'll be back Thursday or Friday, probably late afternoon, and will call you as soon as I arrive. Will it be okay to call at home?"

"Absolutely!" Adam was about to say 'love you' as Monica accompanied him to his car, but he held back, thinking that it might frighten her. As he pulled out of the drive his cell phone rang.

Ellen screeched. "Where the hell have you been? This is new, staying out all night!"

Adam didn't miss a beat. "Oh, Ellen! You just woke me up. I must have fallen asleep at my desk. I'm here at the office."

"Oh come on Adam! What do you take me for? I'm not that naïve." Ellen ended the call.

Monica packed an overnight bag, locked up the house, and headed straight to her parents' home in North Carolina. It was a beautifully clear day, a bright autumn morning with a cloudless sky and sunshine that intensified the colors of the foliage. Preoccupied with thoughts about Adam and her marriage, she frequently realized that minutes had gone by without her having been aware of time or place. The traffic through Virginia was exceptionally heavy, but the slow creep didn't bother her, as it gave her more time to think and plan how to present the situation to her mother. As she pulled into her parents' driveway, she felt a wave of comfort and security. Her mother, Grace, dressed in her usual combination of bright slacks and coordinating pullover, hurried eagerly from the front door to greet her daughter. With a big hug and tears in her eyes Grace softly said, "Oh dear, it's been too long, it's so good to see you. How are you?"

Monica reciprocated with a strong hug, "I'm fine. How are you and Dad?"

"We're fine, we always miss you, and are so glad you decided to drive down. We'd get up there more often, but you know, Dad has to take it easy after his surgery. He's doing pretty well, but the doctors want him to rest a lot and avoid traveling any distance. We thank God everyday that we got him to the hospital in time and that Dr. Wyatt was available. I still see him clutching his chest and collapsing to the floor right before my eyes. Even now I can't get the picture out of my mind. I thought I had lost him. The cardiac surgical team at UNC is the greatest. They told me, it's a miracle he's alive. Praise the Lord."

"I'm just so glad."

"So how are you and how's Mike? All you ever say to us in your email is that he's traveling."

"I guess he's ok. I don't get to see him much. When you work for the government your life is not your own, they say. But I'm fine."

"Come on in, Dad has been pacing anxiously since you called this morning. He's asked me if you were here yet at least ten times."

Monica laughed. "Some things never change."

She enjoyed sitting and chatting with her parents in the old living room, on a chair that brought back memories of the hours of study when she was at North Carolina University. After a nostalgic dinner of her favorite corned beef, cabbage, and boiled potatoes, her father excused himself, kissed her on the cheek, and said good night.

"I wish I could stay up longer and talk with you, but I better not push it. Mornings are good times for me, so I'll get up early and make your favorite breakfast, I'm sure you'll like that. I love you."

"Oh Dad, that sounds great, but I don't expect you to fuss. Remember, it's only me. I lived here for twenty years. I know where everything is and should be making breakfast for you."

Monica accompanied her father to the stairs and watched him begin the climb, clinging to the banister and laboring over each step. She could hear his heavy breathing and low grunts of pain. The sight of her formerly robust, energetic father struggling to make it upstairs saddened and troubled her. Her mother saw the look on Monica's face and tried to distract her from the same sorrow that she herself had been experiencing over the last six weeks, as she had watched her husband recuperating.

"Come Monica, let's sit in the living room and have a cup of tea."

After catching up with the local news, hearing about the church, the neighbors, the Eastern Star, and her mother's needlepoint group, Monica interrupted.

"Mom, I need to talk to you."

Grace looked at her daughter with a mother's intuition. She already suspected that Monica was struggling with something.

Monica began, "Things haven't been going well between Mike and me. He's never home, and when he is, he seems so distant and cold. We're just such different personalities. We're never on the same wavelength. Mom, this is hard for me to say, but I'm not happy. I've always looked at you and Dad as the model of what a marriage should be, and I wanted the same thing. But Mike is all work, and I'm just there for his convenience. It's gotten to the point where I don't know what the attraction was to begin with. I guess I was starry eyed about being married to a James Bond."

"Oh Monica, I'm so sorry to hear this. Have you tried talking to him about it?"

"Yes, but it always falls on deaf ears. He

always says the same thing. That I knew what I was getting into when I married him, that his job would involve a lot of travel. When I try to explain that it's not just the travel but the way he treats me when he is home, he dismisses me. He always accuses me of being too sensitive and demanding"

"Well sweetie, I have to tell you, I'm not surprised. Dad and I never thought you two were right for each other. You're such a warm, feeling person and he has always been mechanical and aloof. Remember, your closest friends, Betty and Lorie, tried to tell you that you and Mike were incompatible."

Monica shook her head and snapped, "Mom! Saying I told you so isn't going to help me now."

"That's not what I meant. You know that. The two of you haven't been married that long, and it takes a while to work through the rough patches."

"It's worse than that, Mom. It's not just a rough patch. I don't think I love Mike, and I don't feel he loves me."

Monica's mother stood up, walked over to her daughter, kneeled at her chair and put her arms around her.

"I've been so attuned to you from the first day you entered our lives. Is there someone else?"

Monica's eyes brimmed with tears and her

mouth quivered as she nervously rubbed the back of her hands.

"Oh mother!" Monica sobbed and let her mother hug her for several seconds. "I met a man through one of my adult education courses. He's a well-known psychologist. He approached me about the possibility of writing a psychobiography of Napoleon. The idea intrigued me and I agreed. We started meeting to talk about the project. He's a fascinating man who has developed a unique and world-changing technique of getting people to access their genetic memories. I've never felt this way about anyone before. Now I know what they mean by soul mate. I get vibes from him that makes me think he feels the same way. He's loving, caring, and we are definitely on the same wave length."

"Is he married?"

"Yes, but not happily."

Grace suppressed a cynical smirk.

"Children?"

"Two boys, away at school, in middle and high school. He seems attached to them."

"So, it's not so simple. I came pretty close to being in your situation myself once. I was within inches of marrying someone else when I met your father. The wedding plans had been made, the invitations printed, and both sets of parents supported the marriage. Three weeks before the wedding,

I met your father at a church retreat and fell in love with him within fifteen minutes. Sounds crazy, I know. But I was struck by the connection I felt with him, not that anything happened that night, if you know what I mean. I just knew I had met someone who made me feel very different than Paul, my fiancé did. Well, you can imagine what I had to deal with when I told Paul that the marriage was off! Then I had to tell granddad and grandma. It was awful. They couldn't understand, and I didn't get any support or understanding from anyone. But I'm lucky it happened before, rather than after the marriage. Because I know that had I met your Dad after being married to Paul, I would have been in your shoes and would have ended up leaving Paul."

"Mom, I had no idea. I guess I always fantasized that there was never anyone other than Dad for you. That makes me feel a bit better. From the time I was little I admired you and wanted to be just like you. Maybe we're more alike than I ever thought, even though you are not my birth mother. I love you."

"I gather you're still interested in Napoleon. When we adopted you the agency lady indicated that you might have a French background. Your interest in Napoleon always made us wonder about the French connection. Dad and I were so proud of you and all the awards you won for your

Master's thesis. Now, look at this. Napoleon seems to be the catalyst leading you to someone you think is your soul mate. Is it fate? I don't know. I don't believe in mere coincidence. I believe it was destiny that I couldn't have a child, because it led us to you. You are our pride and joy."

"What do you mean some French connection in my background? I never heard this. Why didn't you tell me before?"

"Monica, don't tell me you don't remember that every time I tried to talk to you about being adopted or anything to do with your birth parents, you tuned me out. You didn't want to know. Anyway, we never thought it would make any difference. Who knows what that old nun really knew about your genealogy? We really know very little about your biological parents. All we were told is that your mother was a university student, thought to be brilliant, and your father was a graduate student working on his Ph.D. They weren't married and thought it best to find a good home for you. The nun at the agency just threw in, as an aside, that she thought your birth grandparents on both sides were from France. That's all we knew."

Monica was amazed that her mother had been so sympathetic about her predicament. The confession and discussion about Mike and a new love left her exhausted, and she just wanted to go to sleep. At the same time she was intrigued with her possible French ancestry. She kissed her mother good night and went to her room, where her old, familiar, stuffed animals and various cherished childhood treasures rekindled a sense of snug wellbeing. With FooFoo, her tattered stuffed rabbit cuddled in her arms, she became a seven-year-old girl again. As she lay in bed hugging FooFoo, drifting toward sleep, her thoughts were filled with Adam, and there was no longer any doubt in her mind that, in him, she had found at least part of her destiny.

CHAPTER THIRTY-FOUR

The next morning seemed like a new beginning. The aroma of bacon signaled that her father was in the kitchen concocting his signature breakfast of blueberry pancakes, bacon, fried eggs on the side and real maple syrup. As they were eating, he indicated that he was aware of the previous night's conversation and offered his understanding and support for any decision she might make. Then he asked her to join him in the living room as he had something he wanted to show her.

Monica tucked her knees up on the sofa in excited anticipation, expecting that her father was about to show her pictures or something that had to do with her biological parents. Instead he placed a small, exquisitely hand carved wooden chest on the floor in front of her and opened it almost reverently.

"Many years ago a good friend of mine, Harry Basset, who was also a colleague and history teacher at the high school, was dying from intestinal cancer. His wife had passed away several years earlier and Harry didn't have any living relatives. He and I had been very close, so during his last days I served the same role as today's Hospice organization, looking after him in his home. This was before you were born. Harry knew he had only a few days left on this earth. The night before he died, I was sitting at his bedside, when he asked me to get this box from his closet. His voice was so frail that I could hardly hear him. He was struggling to speak but was determined to relate this story to me before he died. I put the box on the edge of his bed and opened it for him because the latch was stiff with age and Harry was too weak to pry it open. Inside were some papers and things that had been given to Harry's father by someone named George. I can't remember the first name, but I am sure that George was the last name. The contents of the box and what Harry needed to tell me was all about someone named Ney, a Peter Ney, whose real name might have been Michael Ney. Apparently this guy had something to do with Napoleon and escaped to the U.S. and changed his first name to Peter in order to hide his identity.

Have you ever heard of Michael Ney?"

"Oh yes! Michael Ney was one of Napoleon's Marshals. Marshal Ney, the bravest of the brave."

"Really? So there is such a guy?"

"There sure is! Do you want me to tell you about him?"

"Absolutely, I want to see what I got instead of a Lamborghini for my money," her father said with a big laugh.

Monica always loved her father's teasing and laughed with him.

"Okay, here's your Lamborghini. By 1806 Napoleon had brought a good deal of trouble upon himself. He had alienated most of the European monarchs with his empire building and his continental system, which attempted to control their trade. Most of the leaders were well aware of his intent and looked for ways to defy him. A coalition consisting of Great Britain, Prussia, Sweden, Saxony, and Russia was formed. I might get bogged down in details, so let me know if it's too much. King Friedrich Wilhelm of Prussia gave Napoleon an ultimatum. 'Get out of Germany or face war.' Napoleon wasn't the sort to respond to this kind of threat and proceeded with his own war plans. This is the first we hear of Marshal Ney. He was a career officer who fought through the French Revolution and came to prominence because of his fearless conduct. With the rise of Napoleon, Ney was appointed as the head of the sixth Corps to lead the Grand Army into Austria. Ney was amazingly successful in his campaign and contributed greatly to Napoleon's decimation of the Prussian army."

"I'm impressed that you can just spout this off. Continue teacher."

"Later as his allies deserted him, Napoleon made the decision to invade Russia, an act that most historians regard as his biggest military blunder. He lost over six hundred thousand men in the campaign and because the Russian army kept falling back, got sucked deeper and deeper into Russia. Winter arrived earlier than usual and the French were forced to attempt a retreat across the frozen tundra. Thousands of French soldiers froze to death, others starved, many were ambushed and slaughtered by the peasants, and many deserted. It was a major catastrophe for Napoleon. However, Marshal Ney saved what was left of his army. Napoleon referred to Ney as the bravest of the brave. How about it Dad, had enough yet?"

"Not at all, because when I show you what Harry gave me, some things may make sense."

Monica's mother sat nearby working on her needlepoint and listening to the conversation. "Don't forget Sweetie, Dad is a romantic and will create novels out of nothing. I've heard this Harry story many times. Would you two like some tea?"

Monica switched her attention to her mother, admiring the precision of the needlework. "I still think you should submit some of your work to art galleries instead of just hanging them on every wall in the house. Tea would be great."

Monica's father was eager to hear more of the Ney story.

"But not all went well between Ney and Napoleon. After Russia, Napoleon was on the defensive. The European powers saw that he was weakened and attacked France again. Despite his diminished army, Napoleon again fought well, but the enemy, a coalition of Prussia, Russia, Austria, and England, continued to move towards France. It was at this point that the Bourbons, led by King Louis XVIII saw their chance to over-throw Napoleon and restore the royal family to the throne. Remember that Louis XVIII's brother, Louis XVI, had been guillotined during the revo-lution. Some of Napoleon's officers and entourage were also starting to feel that Napoleon's power was waning and that his regime was detrimental to France. Ney was one of these men who demanded Napoleon's abdication. Defeated in battle and deserted by his former comrades, Napoleon's fate seemed to be sealed, and he did abdicate. With his departure, all the leaders of Europe gathered in Vienna to redraw the map of Europe for the post- Napoleonic era. France was deprived of all its territories east of the Rhine and relegated back to its boundaries of 1792. Napoleon was exiled to Elba, and that's a story in itself. Even in exile the improvement projects that he began on that island, roads, forts, governmental systems, were astonishing. Think of this, Dad, here's a man in exile who's still building empires. Napoleon was certainly not the type of man to accept anonymity however, and he began to plot a return to France. In less than a year Napoleon escaped from Elba and sailed for the mainland. When he landed he had no idea of how much support he would get from his old army, but as he moved toward Paris with the supporters who had followed him from Elba, he found hundreds of his old soldiers joining him along the road. When Louis XVIII heard the news of Napoleon's landing he failed to act decisively, but Marshal Ney, newly loyal to the king, assured him that he would bring Napoleon to him in a basket. Marshal Ney pursued his mission and met Napoleon face to face. Once again confronted with the contrast between this charismatic man and his ineffectual king, Ney changed loyalty. This same man who had forced the emperor to abdicate the year before was now to be Napoleon's leading general. Europe rushed to gather their armies to attack Napoleon and prevent his return to power. The forces converged in Belgium.

Napoleon gave Ney command of forty-five thousand men and ordered him to push the British back toward the Brussels Road and to occupy Quatre Bras, a strategic position. But Ney, who always had ambivalent feelings about Napoleon, vacillated and procrastinated in following the battle plan. This failure on Ney's part played a decisive role in Napoleon's defeat at Waterloo. Unfortunately, when Louis XVIII was back in power Ney was condemned to death."

Monica's father beamed with pride. "Wow, you really know your stuff. Well, see what you think of all of this." He opened the box and handed her several pieces of aging, brittle paper. This is the story that Harry told me.

"There was a high school teacher in a rural town in North Carolina whose name was Peter Ney. People suspected that wasn't really his name and that he was actually this guy we're talking about, Marshal Michael Ney. The story was that, after Waterloo, Marshal Ney escaped execution in France and made it to the U.S. According to the legend that developed, Ney formed a close mentor relationship with his most gifted student, Lucius Buttler. Lucius later became a teacher himself. Ney, who had no family and was an isolate except for his relationship with Lucius Buttler, left this chest to Buttler when he died. Lucius formed the type of relationship he had had with Ney with one of his own students, Wesley George and passed the chest on to him. Wesley George in turn gave this material to his grandson A. W. George. Harry told me that when Ney was on his deathbed, Lucius was at his side. Ney held Lucius's hand and pointed to a box in the corner of his closet. He asked Lucius to lean in close and assume the five points of Masonic fellowship. Then he whispered. 'In this trunk are papers and things that will shock and surprise the world. I managed to take them with me when I escaped. Now I am entrusting them to you. But I caution you. All is not what it seems.' Lucius was given this very box, Monica. Harry told me that the owners of Ney's home, the Foard family, said that the day Peter Ney died, two men claiming to be his relatives from Philadelphia came and turned his room upside down, searching for something. Harry was sure that they were looking for this box. They found nothing because Lucius had already taken it. Lucius reported Ney's last words to the Foard family. Just before dying he said, "I will not die with a lie on my lips. I am Marshal Michael Ney of France and of Napoleon's army."

Monica sat dumbstruck. "Marshal Ney not executed and in the U.S.? I never heard that story."

One by one Monica's father handed her the items from the box.

"This story has been investigated by local

historians, all of whom verified that Peter Ney's physical build was exactly the same as Michael Ney's. In addition to this, Peter had scars on his body that could only have been produced by battle wounds."

Her father handed Monica an old piece of paper, brown around the edges with tiny tears up the sides. Monica handled it reverently, like a sacred doctrine, aware that she might be holding a precious piece of history.

"Though I of the chosen the choicest
To fame gave her loftest tone
Though I 'mong the brave was the bravest
My plume and my baton are gone."

Next her father handed her a fragment of dark, broken stone. On it was a bit of strange engraving resembling some sort of ancient writing. Monica turned it over in her hand, gently feeling the uneven surface.

"Dad do you realize what we may have here? This is incredible! If Peter Ney was really Michael Ney, then this stuff must be from France, and maybe even connected with Napoleon. We need to get it to an archeologist who can analyze it."

"Years ago I talked to Brian, the historian at the lodge, about the possibility that Peter was really Michael Ney. Brian was familiar with the story and believed it. He told me that Michael Ney was a Mason and that our brothers in France had arranged his escape to America."

Monica couldn't wait to tell Adam and dialed his cell phone. "Adam, I've got to tell you something. I've come upon an astonishing thing at my parents' house. It could be that one of Napoleon's most famous marshals; Marshal Ney escaped to the U.S. and became a teacher in North Carolina. My father inherited this box with some of Ney's notes and some history books. There's writing and drawing in the margins. It's a long story as to how my father got this stuff, but he's giving it to me. I'm so excited about it that I can't wait to show you. I want to start back tonight."

"Wow, that's exciting. I'll be at your house waiting for you. I'll get the hidden key you showed me and just wait 'til you arrive. By the way, I've been thinking about this from the moment you left yesterday, and I'm sure I want to say it. I love you."

Monica had wondered whether if and when Adam said this, she would be frightened or feel panic. Instead, she felt calm, relieved, and happy.

CHAPTER THIRTY-FIVE

Replacing the receiver, Monica turned toward her mother who was once again nodding knowingly. Monica knew her face was a give away. Since childhood, a glowing blush had always broadcast her high emotions. It was apparent to both her parents that she was eager to share her exciting discovery with her new love. Before she could explain her haste to depart, Monica's father spoke for her, endorsing her decision to leave.

This time the five-hour drive to Virginia seemed interminable. Monica's thoughts were racing with ideas about the possibilities of the contents of the chest. Beating a happy refrain behind these thoughts was Adam's declaration of love.

True to his word he was waiting for Monica and opened the front door as she rushed from her car to the steps. They flung themselves into each other's arms and embraced silently, content just to feel each other's presence. Then they both began to speak at the same time.

Seated at the dining room table, Monica, beaming delight, offered the box to Adam, placing it in front of him. Drawing the box to him he allowed his fingers to linger on the lid, caressing the fine grain of the wood and feeling the aged texture of the carving.

"Monica, this box is really old. Look at the patina of the wood! Look at the style of the hinges! Not only is it old, but also it's obviously the work of a skilled craftsman. It's beautiful walnut wood. Let's look inside."

Together they examined each item in the box, taking care not to damage them. "Monica! I'm wondering. What's the connection? Here you are an expert on Napoleon and suddenly this box materializes. We now know you have French ancestry. You know there is no such thing as coincidence. You're family lives in North Carolina. Maybe there's a connection of some sort between you and Ney. Let's experiment with this. We could use some of this material as stimuli for a regression."

"I was thinking the same thing."

They decided that since the material had

been given to Monica she should be the one to enter the trance. Although Adam's heart was palpitating with anticipation, as was Monica's, he felt a scintilla of skepticism creeping in.

"Let's just see if there's anything written that supports your father's story, that Peter is Michael Ney. Let's look up Peter Ney and Michael Ney on the internet before we go to the office."

"Okay, let's see what we can learn about Ney actually being in North Carolina."

They both set to work on their laptops.

"Adam, listen to this. Here's a reference from Davidson College. Apparently Peter Ney, who is referred to in this literature as the alleged Marshall Michael Ney of Napoleon's army, designed the school motto for the college. The motto is, "Let learning be cherished where liberty has arisen."

"Neat! Wait, look what I've just found. This looks like an obituary or something published in a newspaper when Ney was executed. I'll read it to you. 'Marshall Michel Ney, Napoleon's right hand at Waterloo, was executed. He was called Le Rougeaud, the Redhead, because of his hair color that he inherited from his Scottish father. After Napoleon's army was defeated at Waterloo, the restored French royalty needed a scapegoat for whatever had enabled Napoleon, now regarded as a Corsican upstart, to retake France. Michel Ney was the scapegoat and was court-martialed. He was condemned to be executed by firing squad in the Luxembourg Gardens.'

Monica had turned away from her computer screen to listen to him. "So far that fits with what I've read in my studies."

"But here's the twist. Listen to this part. It says that Ney showed no repentance and no sign of fear. In fact, he even gave the 'Ready, Aim, Fire' command himself. However, many believe the execution was a sham arranged by Wellington, and that Ney was not really executed. This belief is supported by the fact that in a most uncommon manner, the public was kept away from the execution site, and the soldiers of the firing squad were handpicked from Ney's old veterans and steadfast followers. A dozen musket balls supposedly struck him. The force of such a barrage would naturally send the victim flying backwards. This account says that instead, Ney fell forward in a slumping movement. In addition to this, for reasons unknown, the customary coupe de grace pistol shot to the head was not administered. Instead of leaving the body for viewing, which was also customary, it was immediately bundled into a carriage and driven away. Although no one knows why, the royalist government arrested the officer in charge of the execution. Man, this is astonishing. I'm quickly becoming a believer."

"Adam, we may have one of the most important historical finds of the century in the contents of this box. Here's what I found. In 1837 a French immigrant schoolteacher named Peter Steward died in North Carolina. On his deathbed he swore to his confessor, "I swear before God that I am Michel Ney, Marshal of France." When his body was being embalmed, it was discovered that he was covered with scars from old musket and saber wounds, exactly the type that would have been sustained by a veteran soldier of the nineteenth century."

Adam flicked off his computer, sprang from his chair, and grabbed Monica's hand. "I've heard enough! Your father's story makes sense. Let's get to the office."

They rushed out with the chest. Monica was bubbling with excitement and impatience to have Adam hook her up to the apparatus. Adam photographed the notes that were purportedly written by Ney, including the poem describing him as the bravest of the brave that Monica had read earlier. He transferred them to the tachisto-scope, using them to stimulate and direct the trance process. It took a few minutes, but Monica's willingness enabled her to enter into a deep trance.

She sat silent for several minutes but as her forehead furrowed, her lips tightened, and her jaw clenched, Adam could tell she was experiencing something. She remained silent and Adam decided to let her experience the trance without verbalizing.

"Just let yourself be wherever you are and allow yourself to be in the moment."

Three crisply uniformed military officers stood over the prisoner, who was to be executed in his Marshall's uniform.

"You understand. Your last wish has been granted. You will give the order to fire. These packets that we're placing under your shirt are filled with pig's blood. At the crack of the rifles you drop. Once you hit the ground the wagon will pull-up in front of you, obscuring you from the squad captain's line of sight. Don't move a muscle! Remember, you are dead. What the devil is that ugly thing hanging around your neck? Should we remove it now?"

"No! It's my lucky charm. I had it all through Russia. If it got me through that hell it will get me through anything. I must keep it. No one will know I have it on."

The soldier in charge of the process was more than curious. "Where did you get it? It looks like a dirty old rock."

"My mother gave it to me for luck when I gradu-ated from the military academy. I have no idea where she got it or what it means. But I do believe it's gotten me out of many a tough spot. It's my courage. And Napoleon did call me the bravest of the brave. Now let's get back to important things."

The Marshal stood unrepentantly proud before the firing squad, facing the barrels of eleven rifles.

Soldiers, when I give the command to fire, fire straight at my heart. Wait for the order. It will be my last to you. I protest against my condemnation. I have fought a hundred battles for France, and not one against her. Soldiers, Fire!'

Monica slumped in her chair a breath of exhaustion escaped her lips. Adam eased her out of the trance and guided her into a mentally relaxed safe place.

"Are you ok? Do you recall the trance?"

"Recall it? I just lived it. I was there. I saw Ney! I'm sure it was Marshal Michael Ney! Shot dead and fall to the ground. But not really dead."

CHAPTER THIRTY-SIX

The regression left Monica exhausted but filled her with an anticipatory energy. She and Adam left the hypnotic room, made tea, and settled in the main office.

"Adam, I think what I saw under hypnosis was what my father gave me. I think the artifact we have was around Ney's neck. My Gosh! We may really have Marshal Ney's stuff. I wonder if Ney really believed this old stone was a lucky charm."

Adam's eyes gleamed. "It could also be worth a fortune. We could be rich."

Monica sat further back in her chair, pulled the recline lever, and looked at him coyly.

"Oh, the fortune is to be shared, is it? Wait a minute! This stone is mine! I mean, we can talk about some profit sharing, maybe a few hundred out of the fifty million I get. But I'll have to think about it."

Adam's face dropped and a wave of doubt and disappointment crept over him. Monica enjoyed letting let him squirm for a minute.

"Gotcha! I can't believe you took me seriously."

They laughed and embraced. Adam held the stone in the air.

"You know the couch does pull out into a bed. Choose, sweetheart, work or play."

Monica replied with exaggerated disappointment.

"Okay, we'll go back to work."

They directed their attention to the stone. Adam turned it over in his hand, running his fingers over the surface as if reading Braille.

"I can't make out what this raised part is, but it sure looks like some ancient writing. It's not hieroglyphics or cuneiform script. I'm pretty sure about that. I can't figure out what the material is either. It's not simple rock, whatever that means. I really don't know what I'm looking for or talking about. We have to take this to an expert of some kind that might be able to analyze it and tell us what it is."

"How do we find someone like that? It will have to be someone we can trust."

Adam thought for a while, gazing out the window into the black woods and moonless night. Finally, he spun around to face Monica and with raised eyebrows said,

"I wonder if Leopold, that guy I went to see at the Masonic Museum, might know who to take this to?"

Monica looked troubled. "Surely there must be a lab or some expert on artifacts someplace in the Smithsonian organization. I would think we might get a team of scientists or archeologists to examine it. We could certainly trust people from the Smithsonian."

"Good idea. I don't know how to start that process but I'll make some calls first thing tomorrow morning. Maybe Leopold Robsen has had some experience with this kind of thing, after all he does have a Ph.D. in archeology and he studied in Europe. And he is a brother Mason. I can start there."

"Adam, you seem intent on contacting this man. I can't tell you why, but I don't think that's a good idea. You don't really know him and how do you know you can trust him? I'm not sure why but I'm a little frightened about having this thing."

"Okay, let me think about it, and I'll see what we can do with the Smithsonian."

They decided to call it a night. Adam suggested that they stop for a drink at one of the college bars on their way home. Monica confessed that she had never done anything like that but was eager to go. Adam chose a bar with a rock band that played mostly sixties music, and once inside, selected a table that offered a more intimate setting than the bar. A rather scantily dressed college girl with the bar's logo printed on the seat of her short shorts took their order. Monica ordered a whisky sour and Adam ordered a single malt scotch.

"I was just wondering, Adam, how would Ellen or Mike feel about us doing this?"

"I don't know about Mike, but I sure know what Ellen would think. She'd be very upset and probably make a scene right here in front of everyone. It's interesting, I thought of that earlier, and I really don't care. I think it's time for me to tell her the marriage is over."

"That's a big step. I guess I too have to face that with Mike. For some reason, I imagine it will be easier for me than for you. Mike and I have been married a much shorter time and he must know I am not happy. Oh, here are the drinks."

Adam took a large swallow of his single malt scotch and gently reached for Monica's hand. He scanned her face and looked lovingly into her eyes.

"Monica, I confess this invitation for a drink was not entirely spontaneous. There is some-thing I want to say to you. I've never felt this way

about anyone before, and I want to give you this."
He opened his hand to reveal a small purple velvet
box, which he then placed in Monica's hand.

"Open it Monica. This is a part of me that
I've never shared with anyone, not even Ellen.
My parents told me this ring was hanging on a
chain around my neck when they took me from
the orphanage."

Monica opened the box and inhaled her
breath. "Oh, Adam! This is so beautiful. The
orange and yellow look like fire. Is it an opal?"
Monica closed her fingers around the ring and
clasped it to her heart before placing it on the ring
finger of her right hand.

Still breathless she whispered, "It fits
perfectly."

Monica leaned across and kissed Adam
tenderly on the cheek. They lingered a while
longer over their drinks before departing.

Adam arrived home after midnight and
to his surprise found Ellen in the family room,
reading in her favorite reclining chair.

"I hope you and Monica accomplished a
lot tonight." The words sounded considerate but
the tone was clearly sarcastic. "I know it's very
late but I thought I'd wait up for you. "

Adam felt like a teenager about to be inter-
rogated by a suspicious parent for coming home
late. Old patterns kicked in and he avoided the

confrontation, talking as he moved away from her toward the stairs. He also didn't want her to smell the alcohol on his breath.

"Thanks for waiting up. Yeah, we made good progress on the book tonight. My schedule begins at eight tomorrow, so I better get some sleep. I'm getting tired of this commute."

Ellen followed. As they readied for bed she told him that Kevin and William had called and given her a complete run down of their soccer games. The boys had made her promise to tell their dad the details, which Ellen dutifully related as best she could. Adam listened eagerly, enjoying hearing about his sons' athletic prowess.

Adam's sleep was restless. Giving Monica the ring had been a big step for him. He felt that it solidified a bond with her deeper than anything he ever experienced with Ellen. In addition to feeling exhilarated by the gesture of giving Monica the ring he was also deeply intrigued by the artifact and perseveratively reviewed all the alternatives for having it safely evaluated. He finally fell asleep just before his alarm went off, but his excitement about the artifact provided ample energy to substitute for the lack of sleep.

CHAPTER
THIRTY-SEVEN

Despite his earlier than usual start, bumper-to-bumper traffic on the beltway nevertheless held Adam at a tediously slow crawl for the entire trip. Just before his exit a garish yellow muscle car from the mid '50's swerved into the middle lane and smashed into a construction worker's pick-up truck, stopping all traffic. Adam could see his exit tantalizingly close but sat unable to move for over half an hour until the accident was cleared.

Snuggling among bolsters of pillows in her bed, Monica lay admiring the ring. She realized the significance of Adam giving it to her and felt closer to him than she ever felt to Mike. The unique orange and red colors created dancing flickers, as if coming from a candle. The rhythmic pattern of the flicker mesmerized her and the room seemed to darken. Fixating on the wall at the foot of her bed Monica's vision blurred, and she felt as if she was leaving her body, drifting further and further away from the reality of the room. The dark wall became a formless bright light, and she felt a gentle force pulling her through a tunnel toward the brightness. She was surrounded by a buzzing sound like that of large bundles of electrical power lines. Compelled to enter the scene on the other side of the tunnel she drifted toward it.

A woman stood in an ivory silk Empire style dress. Her dark ringlets were carefully arranged around her oval face, and strings of pearls emphasized the creamy skin of her neck. There was a knock at the door. As the poised woman turned, saying "entrez," the front of her dress moved gracefully with her.

"Welcome Monsieur Ragideau. I will dismiss my servants so that we may speak with assurance of confidentiality."

"I received your request to meet and assumed you required counsel with your lawyer and business agent. I arranged to come as soon as possible."

"The children have been told of their father's death and I was informed that they received the news with tears in their eyes; they complained loudly and sorrowfully when told that I intended to give up the name of their father, and change it for another. They feared that the memory of their father would soon disap-

pear from my heart. I'm sure you understand that I was distraught. However, that turmoil was erased when on the following day I visited their school, Madame de Campan's institution in St. Germain. General Bonaparte accompanied me and I had the greatest pleasure to find that he embraced both of them with tender affection, and with deep heart-felt emotion and sincerity, he solemnly promised to treat them as a father and a friend. The children returned in kind and offered their hands to their new father to be. One of the things I wanted to discuss with you is what my friends think of my pending marriage to the General, and in fact your own thoughts about this."

Monica recognized the woman as Josephine Bonaparte. Josephine turned toward Ragideau as he shrugged his shoulders and assumed a thoughtful attitude.

"Your friends, Madame, talk of this marriage with sorrow. Their opinion is that you are going to marry a soldier, younger than yourself, who is unable to provide for you the type of life you have become accustomed to with General Beauharnais. They fear that if he is killed in battle you and the children will be left with nothing, no inheritance at all. I have not encountered any of your friends who are ready to give their approbation to your marriage to this small, insignificant general."

"So the world does not approve of this marriage. Do you share the opinion of my friends, my dear Monsieur Ragideau?"

"I hope you understand that I only have your interest at heart. But, yes, I share these fears for you. I do not believe that you should contract such a marriage. You are rich, Madame; you possess a capital which secures you a yearly income of twenty-five thousand francs; with such an income you had claims to a brilliant marriage; and I feel conscientiously obliged, as your friend and business agent, in whom you have trusted, and who has for you the deepest interest, to earnestly remonstrate with you while there is yet time. Consider it well, Viscountess; it is a reckless step you are taking, and I entreat you not to do it. I speak to your own advantage. General Bonaparte may be a very good man, possibly quite a distinguished soldier, but certain it is he has only his hat and his sword to offer you."

Josephine broke into a joyous laugh, as her beaming eyes turned to a young man standing partially hidden by drapery in a dark corner of the room. Dressed in modest dark gray clothing, gazing out the window with his back to Ragideau and Josephine, he had heretofore gone unnoticed.

"General, have you heard what Monsieur Ragideau says?"

Napoleon Bonaparte turned slowly around, his flaming glance falling upon the little advocate. His eyes fixed on Ragideau's, he spoke gravely. Josephine watched the two men. Napoleon slowly morphed into Adam Peterson.

"Yes! I have heard all. I believe Monsieur Ragideau as your lawyer has spoken as an honest man, and every thing he has said fills me with respect for him. I *want him to continue as our agent after we marry. I feel inclined to give him full confidence."*

The flickering sensation in the ring suddenly ceased. Instantly, Monica was back in her bed. She reached for a pillow, hugged it to her heart, imagining it to be Adam. "What on earth just happened? I've never been through anything like that. I have no idea what it was. I'm exhausted." With the pillow held tightly to her chest, she drifted into a deep sleep.

Cathy greeted Adam as he entered the office. "Were you caught in the same mess on the beltway that I was?"

"Yeah, I'm really sick and tired of this whole area. I often think I would be much happier in some little rural town in North Carolina."

The moment his watch beeped nine o'clock, Adam dialed the Smithsonian. Navigating through the menu, pressing number after number to reach the research department was a frustrating task, but he finally managed to get a live person with a human voice. His first statement was to marvel at this small success, and then he proceeded to inquire about talking to an investigating archeologist. After answering a barrage of questions he was eventually connected to the research department.

"This is Doctor Arnopolis. How can I help you?"

"Good morning Doctor Arnopolis. This is Dr. Adam Peterson. I'm a clinical psychologist. Through my research I have discovered a piece of broken stone with some unidentifiable writing on it. It's a long story but I have good reason to believe that it's an ancient relic of some sort. I want to have it examined by an expert."

"Dr. Peterson, I appreciate your curiosity about this stone. Please understand that at this moment we have hundreds of such items waiting for evaluation. We have to take them in the order in which they come to the institution. I will gladly transfer you to Agatha, the office manager, and she'll help you with the paper work."

"Doctor Arnopolis, please don't hang up or transfer me so quickly. I believe I have a very important piece of ancient history and it's imperative that I act quickly to have it evaluated. I can't wait years for the answer. Please help me. Is there any private organization or individual that you would trust to do this? I fully expect to pay a fair price for the assessment."

"What kind of doctor did you say you are?"

"I'm a clinical psychologist and a neuro-psychologist. I have a private practice but I'm also a full professor at Georgetown. I've published eleven journal articles and written four books that received awards from the American Psychological Association and the American Medical Association. I'm working on a book, and this artifact is key to the main theme. I would really appreciate it if you would help me to find someone or to move the project to the top of your list."

Doctor Arnopolis showed more interest when he learned that they had Georgetown University in common, as he had been a professor in the archeology department before joining the Smithsonian. He surprised Adam by asking him if he knew Doctor Alexander Patrick.

"Know him? He's my father-in-law."

"This is indeed a coincidence. He and I were co-chairmen of the faculty advisory committee and I got to know him and Louise, his wife, very well. Great guy. He actually may be responsible for me getting this job. Look, you just gained credibility with me and I'd like to help you. There is nothing I can do with the order of jobs in our research department. That would be near treason here, and I don't think my colleagues would stand for it. We have a rigid code of ethics and cling to certain principles. As a government agency we can't risk any signs of favoritism. However, I know someone who may be able to guide you to the right person."

"Great, I really appreciate this. Who is it?"

The gentleman who I think is probably best suited to help you is Doctor Leopold Robsen."

Before Doctor Arnopolis could continue

Adam interrupted.

"I know him. In fact he was one of the people I thought of consulting."

"Good! Do you need his phone number?

"No thanks, I've got it. Thanks for taking the time to talk with me. I'll call him."

Adam immediately called Monica, who answered the phone in her classroom. He related his conversation with Doctor Arnopolis and asked her advice about calling Robsen. Monica, surrounded by chattering students, could only respond briefly, but agreed that if the people at the Smithsonian recommended Robsen he must be okay. She told Adam to call her again if there was any news. Leopold Robsen was not available when Adam called. His secretary took the message and assured Adam that Doctor Robsen would return the call some time after four that afternoon, but the phone rang within minutes.

"Hi Leopold, thanks for returning my call so quickly. Your secretary thought it would be after four o'clock before you could get back to me."

"You're very welcome, Doctor Peterson. What is this all about? Your message said that you had discovered an artifact that you wanted to have evaluated."

"I have a stone with some kind of inscription. I believe it's ancient and I need an expert's opinion as to what it might be and just how old it really is."

"For a start tell me where you obtained this supposed piece of antiquity."

"At this point, Doctor Robsen, I would like to keep that to myself. I will share that with the person who examines it."

"Well, Doctor Peterson, perhaps I should take a look at it for you. If I see it, I might be better able to steer you to the most appropriate person to do the evaluation, which can be quite complicated. Just as there are specialists in your field, so there are all sorts of specialists in evaluative archaeology. I would be willing to make time to see it this afternoon, either here or at your office."

CHAPTER
THIRTY-EIGHT

The smell of the disinfectant spray used by the cleaning people chocked Adam as he opened the office door. He hated the smell and had repeatedly instructed them not to use it.

"God damn them! I know this is intentional. They're doing it on purpose. I pay them well, but they must get a real kick out of tormenting me with this damned stench each morning. How the hell does this thermostat work? I must be able to turn an exhaust fan on to get rid of this smell, it's nauseating me."

Adam fiddled with the thermostat for several minutes before figuring out the system and getting the fan to turn on. He decided to recline in his chair for a few minutes until Cathy arrived.

CHAPTER THIRTY-EIGHT

Feeling unusually tired, he drifted into sleep.

Cathy was surprised to find him this way and awakened him with a gentle shake to his shoulder. "Wow! That's unusual for you. Burning the candle at both ends, are you?"

"No, it was that damn cleaning fluid smell that must be toxic. It made me drowsy and I fell asleep."

Cathy asked if he was okay. Getting a reassuring nod, she went to her desk and began the usual morning routine.

Three hours later, when Adam had finished seeing his third patient, Cathy walked in with the day's mail. She handed him an envelope that she had slit open. "I think you'd better read this one immediately," she said.

Instead of returning to her desk as usual while he sifted through the mail, she lingered in his office and sat across from him. Before removing the letter from the envelope, Adam stared at Cathy's face. Her countenance bore a look he had never seen. He could not read it and a wave of apprehension overtook him. Slowly he opened the letter and read it silently.

Dear Daddy:

Did you get the whole Janette story? Did you figure out who I am? Just in case you haven't let me tell you. I am your daughter. To refresh your memory, look at this picture of that teen-age girl. That's my mother. The girl you raped. Yes! Raped! Now look at the picture of her two years ago, just before she died. What a difference a life of hell can make. Mom told me the story. Just like the one I told you in your office a few weeks ago. Fooled you Huh? You were the first one in and raped her three times before cheering the other two monsters on. You were first so there was no question in my mother's mind or mine that you are my father. Her parents abandoned her when they found out she was pregnant. She raised me on her own and things were really tough. She had to leave school and work as a waitress. We lived in a one bedroom rented apartment in a four story walk-up tenement in the projects. We had to go to the charity food pantry to get something to eat. All this, while you totally shirked responsibility for us, went about your life, getting an education and earning a lot of money. Daddy, we were starving. So, after Mom died, I made up my mind that I would find you and make you pay and pay dearly. I will destroy you, your career, your marriage, and your life. You don't deserve to live. But, death will be too kind a way for you and I will devote my life to making yours a prison of hell. Get ready, Daddy, the game has just begun and you don't stand a chance.

Your Bastard Daughter,
Janette

Adam sat in shock. The letter had jolted his mind and lifted his repression of the event. He tried to remain composed but the quivering letter in his hand betrayed him. He looked up at Cathy to find her staring knowingly into his eyes. He knew immediately that she had read the letter.

"You know Cathy, I'm getting sick and tired of transference. Patients project just about everything on me. Have you read this? I knew that girl Janette was crazy. Winters should have had her on suicide watch. That way she never would have been able to run."

CHAPTER THIRTY-NINE

The emperor stood before his map table, legs planted firmly apart, his right index finger jabbing angrily at the etched coastline of Spain.

"Well what is it then?" He snapped. Consumed by the frustrations of the war, Napoleon was in no mood to be interrupted. His Continental System, a tactic he thought would sever trade between England and his allies, was not working. The British had landed in Spain, and to his surprise were pushing his army back. The Spanish themselves were defying French occupation and interrupting his supply lines. Marshal Ney, returned from the front to update the emperor, was positioned at the side of the table. His red hair was tousled, but his uniform was immaculate, with the gold braid glinting in the candlelight.

A young lieutenant, embarrassed and in awe,

bowed before the two men. "Sire, I have come from Venice. As you know, General Menou has died. I was charged with organizing and removing his effects. I regret to report that he left his affairs in a shambles, with a fortune in unpaid debts. We have done what we could to close things up, and this chest contains the last of the papers from General Menou's personal office."

The lieutenant stepped hesitantly forward, loosening the tied closure as he placed a tooled leather case on the desk. Aware that the emperor had little regard for Menou, he did not want to be perceived as the deceased man's ally. Stepping back in regimental form, he bowed to the emperor. "I didn't know General Menou but was chosen from the ranks for this assignment, Sire. He stood erect, watching as Napoleon looked through Menou's effects and wondering at the strange career of the deceased general. He mused on his own military career prospects. Menou had played a pivotal role in Egypt, first receiving the news of the discovery of the Rosetta stone and then being left in complete charge of the area after Napoleon's return to France and the assassination of General Kleber. Then his reputation had been tarnished by the surrender of all the French discoveries to the English at Alexandria. After that he had seen no more military action but instead had been appointed governor to Florence and then Venice, where his reputation had not improved.

"He made a mess in Egypt, another one in Venice." The emperor's voice did not conceal his evident distain for Menou. He snatched up a few of General

Menou's papers, scanning them quickly with a practiced eye. Satisfied that they were of no importance, he tossed them aside and reached to remove the few remaining objects at the bottom of the chest. In their small way, the items spoke of Menou's past: two of his medals from the Grande Armee, a small Venetian glass inkwell, pens, a brass snuff box with an Egyptian ankh etched on the surface, and a leather pouch containing an uneven, coarse surfaced stone.

"Look at this! The man was common as well. These are cheap souvenirs. Imagine this as the legacy of a man. Pathetic! Well lieutenant, you've done your job. Well done. Now take one of these pieces as a keepsake."

The lieutenant looked at Napoleon, unsure of how to respond.

"Yes, yes, I mean it. Take something for your troubles, and then leave us."

The lieutenant bowed once more, took up the inkwell, saluted, and turned on his heel to depart.

"Well Ney, that's it then. Egypt is gone, and the nugatory Menou is gone. If you'd been there we'd have taken Acre. Here!" The emperor tossed the leather pouch to Ney, who caught it in one hand.

CHAPTER FORTY

An evening at home with no planned activity was a rare occasion at the Peterson house. Adam's day had been especially exhausting and emotionally draining. Mr. and Mrs. Balducci had found their four-month old infant lying lifeless in her crib, a victim of SIDS. Adam had been deeply touched as they sobbed over their tragedy, and at times found himself crying with them. The Balducci's were blaming themselves for not checking the baby during the night. Adam did everything possible to relieve them of their feelings of guilt. He knew that there was go greater pain than loosing a child, and very few issues affected him so profoundly. On top of that, Cathy had shown her true colors, and his idealized illusion of her was shattered. She was trying to blackmail him. She had waved the letter from his daughter in his face, and flagrantly demanded a bonus.

Adam changed into his old worn jeans and poured a good size portion of single malt scotch before collapsing into his huge leather chair. With his drink in hand, a disk of opera arias playing loudly, and the evening paper open to the sports page, he began to relax. Then Ellen arrived home.

"Wow you're home early tonight, how come? That music is way too loud. Turn it down. The whole world doesn't need to hear your opera."

Adam took a long drink of his scotch and ignored Ellen's demand. "How are you dear? Where have you been? Did you have a good day?"

Ellen moved to the stereo amplifier and lowered the volume.

"I had a good day. I worked out and then went to mother's. We went to lunch at that soup and salad place on 27th Street and then did a bit of shopping. It's a nice place. You can get a salad and a cup of tea or coffee for only six dollars. Mother said that two lighter colored tables would look better in the family room instead of the two walnut tables we have now. So we went to that neat furniture store in Baltimore and bought two new tables. They're exactly what we needed."

"That's great, I too had thought, since the day you and your mother bought those two walnut tables, that we needed lighter colored ones. How is mother dear?"

"Adam why are you so negative about everything I say to you?" Without waiting for an answer Ellen continued, "Let's have supper. I have broiled salmon with boiled potatoes and asparagus for you."

They moved to the table and Adam poured himself another scotch *en route*. He was beginning to feel a little lightheaded and was hoping the second glass would anesthetize him. He thought that if he could share his painful experience of the Balducci's it might help him to ease his sadness.

"Ellen, I had a really tough time today. I saw a couple that lost their infant to SIDS. I feel so bad for them. I can't get it out of my mind. It's making me think of all sorts of horrible possibilities with our own children."

There was no immediate response and Adam began eating while staring at the hardboiled egg and apple on Ellen's dish.

Finally she responded, "That's why it's so important for us always to count our blessings. Which brings me to what I wanted to talk to you about tonight. Kevin and William have written at least ten emails to you in the past three weeks and you haven't answered one of them."

Adam gripped his fork until it almost bent and he bit down so hard on his salmon that he pierced his cheek. He pushed his chair away from the table violently.

"Careful Adam, you'll scratch the floor. You know scuff won't just buff out of this redwood floor."

"Damn it Ellen! I can't stand your superficial world any more. I'm talking about the death of an infant and you're talking about your God Damn redwood floors!"

He stormed out of the kitchen, and went to watch a football game in the family room. Ellen was silent and remained in the kitchen. Adam could hear her cleaning the table and running water in the sink.

"There she goes, rinsing every damn dish, fork, knife, and glass before she loads the dishwasher." He lowered the volume on the TV and dialed Kevin's number at school. "Hi Kevin, it's Dad. How are you?"

"Hi Dad, I was just thinking about you, wondering if you had the game on."

"I do, quite a game so far. Listen, I know you sent me some emails that I didn't answer. I've been very busy in the office and making a draconian effort to write this book on Napoleon."

"No problem Dad. I know you're always thinking of me and William. We both know that if it was anything important you'd get right back to us or drive here. Things are going great. My grades are really good."

"That's my boy, Kevin. You want to give me odds on the game tonight? There are still three quarters left and it's tied."

"No way, every time I bet with you I loose. I can't afford it. By the way, Dad, I'm spending more than we figured on snacks and late night food. Could you send me a little more each month?"

"Of course Kevin, I ate my way through high school and college too. The more greasy fries, hamburgers, and cokes, the better. That's my motto."

"Dad, I would appreciate it if you didn't tell Mom about me wanting more money. She thinks that the three meals in the residence hall should be enough."

"Consider the money on its way and there's no need for anyone else to know about the raise I'm giving you."

"Thanks Dad, I gotta go. I have a lot of homework tonight. This stupid Shakespeare is going to drive me nuts. I hope I can get a weekend home soon or that you can come up to visit. Anyway, bye for now, I love you Dad."

"I love you too Kevin. Sure you don't want to bet on the game? Packers just fumbled on their own three yard line."

"Forget it Dad. I've been burned too many times by the Redskins. My gambling days are over. Bye, love you."

Adam was pleased with the call and felt vindicated. Next he called William, and after an equally smooth conversation, sank back on the couch with another scotch and resumed watching the football game.

"Would you like to go out for a Latte and sit outside? It's a beautiful night. I'll buy."

Adam picked up the humor in Ellen's I'll buy.

"How could I pass up a free Latte? Can I get the really big size?" Ellen smiled and said, "I guess I can spring for that."

They strolled to the café in the cool autumn evening and sat on the outdoor patio. Adam wasn't sure what Ellen was feeling. He hoped she was trying to convey regret for ignoring his needs. That wish was shattered.

"Oh, the Watsons are remodeling their house by adding a solarium. I'll bet that's costing a pretty penny."

Adam listened dutifully as they walked back home to finish their coffees in their family room. He still felt a need for closeness and after a short time of sitting together, asked Ellen if she would join him in bed.

"I guess we can do that. I was going to work on the invitations for the juvenile diabetes charity ball. Being president of the society has been a lot of work. Well it's still early. I can get to it later."

Adam was about to say, 'thanks for fitting me in', but controlled the impulse, realizing it would be self-defeating. He showered and got into bed just as Ellen emerged from the closet where she always undressed. As usual she had her panties on beneath her high-necked flannel nightgown. Ellen never permitted herself to be naked during sex. As always it was up to Adam to initiate contact. Ellen lay still and Adam moved over to her side of the bed. He just wanted to be physically close before anything sexual began, but Ellen seemed anxious to start. Adam tried to engage in some foreplay but she moved the process along very quickly. He became aware of her body and all he could think of was that he was having sex with a skeleton. As his hands caressed her he found himself counting her ribs, and then he became aware that her bony knees and ankles were pointing into his flesh like horse spurs. He tried to focus on kissing Ellen, but the high collar on her nightgown prevented him from reaching her neck. There was just nothing soft about her and Adam lost all sense of arousal. Instead he was repulsed. After a few minutes of awkward unsuccessful efforts he found himself thinking of Monica and began to fantasize about sex with her as he continued with Ellen. The mental image of Monica excited him and he was able to get an erection and reach orgasm. Afterward, still trying to gain a feeling of closeness Adam put his arm around his wife but there was no reciprocation.

"I need to get up Adam, I really have to get those invitations done and mailed out."

Adam lay in bed musing on the irony of his relationship with Ellen. "Here I am a psychologist and I have never dealt with her coldness, her eating disorder, our lack of sexual intimacy, her obsessive compulsive character, or my anger toward her and her parents. Boy I guess it's easier to help others than yourself. But I think I always knew she would never change and I just didn't want to fight that battle. So here I am."

Deciding to read one of the nine books on Napoleon that he had purchased, Adam put his clothes back on and went into his study. He was browsing through the table of contents of a biography when the phone rang.

Ellen picked it up. It was Cathy.

I'm sorry to call so late, but I want to make sure that Adam mailed his neurofeedback re-credentialing material. I left it on his desk. He said he would post it when he left. I wanted to be sure he did, since he has seemed so distracted with all he's trying to do."

"I know what you mean Cathy. He's upstairs, I'll ask him." Ellen darted upstairs to relay the message.

"Oh no! I forgot it on my desk. Man, if it doesn't get postmarked by tonight I might have to take an exam to get recertified. I'll have to go get it and take it to the post office. Tell Cathy I'll take care of it."

Ellen rushed back downstairs to talk to Cathy and then ran back upstairs to relay the message to Adam.

"Cathy said that she had to go out to get milk anyway, so she would stop by the office and mail it for you. She really is a jewel. You're lucky to have her. I hope you treat her well."

"No, I treat her very poorly. She gets four weeks vacation, as many sick days as she needs, time off for her children's school events, and probably more salary than a full professor at the university."

Adam made himself comfortable in his reclining leather chair and began reading, but he was obsessed with worry that Cathy might have read the letter from Janette. As he switched that thought off, his fantasies of Monica returned. He didn't feel the least bit guilty about his mental betrayal of Ellen. The fantasy had given him a sexual satisfaction he had never experienced with her. The residual feeling was so relaxing and peaceful that he decided to abandon the book and take a drive in his Jaguar. He called down to Ellen, "I'm going out for a little bit. I thought I would take a ride along the water."

CHAPTER FORTY-ONE

Ellen was not sure how long Adam had been gone when the phone rang again.

"Hello, Mrs. Peterson, it's Peter, Cathy's husband. Have you heard from my wife? She said she was going to the store and the office and would be back in about thirty minutes. It's now been over two hours."

"Oh my, Peter. I haven't heard from her since she called to tell Adam she was going to the office."

"She's always returns when she says and would have called if something had come up. There really is nowhere for her to go at this time of night. Her mother and father are in Florida. I called my parents, but they haven't heard from her either, and she's not answering her cell phone."

"I'll call Adam on his cell phone and have him go to the office to check. I'll have him call you as soon as I reach him."

Ellen contacted Adam who immediately returned the call to Peter.

"I haven't heard from Cathy, but I'll try to find her. I'm about fifteen minutes from the office and will call you as soon as I get there."

Adam had tried to calm Peter with words of assurance, but he felt uneasy. When he reached the office, the hallway was dark and there seemed to be a dry heaviness in the air that made it difficult to breathe. His office door was ajar. The vague feeling of apprehension turned to panic and fear as he realized that there really was someone was in his office. Slowly Adam pushed the door. He could see through the open door to Cathy's office. It was dimly light by light emanating from his office beyond. Cathy was not at her desk.

CHAPTER FORTY-TWO

Adam grabbed the phone and dialed 911.

"This is Doctor Peterson, come to my office on K Street. My secretary has been beaten up and my office burgled."

Cathy was lying on the floor, her head in a pool of blood. A trickle of blood oozed from the side of her mouth. A large angry welt covered her right temple. Adam checked her pulse again to see if she was still alive. His eyes shifted to all the valuable equipment in the room. It was intact, but it was obvious that every computer had been turned on, and the open CD drives suggested someone had tried to download information. The room was a total wreck. Every cabinet drawer was open with files strewn over the entire floor. His desk drawers had been turned over and emptied.

His books had been swept from the shelves. The stereo speakers had been cut open and lay gaping by the bay window. Adam dashed to the room where all of his regressive trance and EEG equipment was located. It was untouched.

"Thank God I encoded my formula and put it in a file where no one would find it. Damn clever of me to call it Jung's Code. Nobody could ever figure out what that meant."

Confused and distraught, Adam was uncertain about what to do while waiting for the ambulance and police. He called Monica.

"Monica, it's Adam. Something terrible has happened. Someone has broken into my office and attacked Cathy. I'm waiting for the ambulance and police."

Monica gasped. "Oh Adam, I'll be right there."

In a few moments the EMT's arrived along with the police. The EMT's went about their work very efficiently and quickly had Cathy on a stretcher and into the ambulance. She had not regained consciousness. As they tended to her Adam asked, "Will she be all right?"

Monica arrived at the office and immediately hugged Adam consolingly. A plainclothes policeman approached them. He was short and wore a tweed jacket and open collared shirt with a loosened garish tie. There was no discernable emotion on his face.

"Doctor Peterson, I'm detective Mancini, Joseph Mancini. I have to get a statement from you as to what happened." He turned to Monica. "And who are you, Mrs. Peterson?" Adam answered the question for her.

"This is Monica Strove, a colleague of mine. I called her because she has some of her own files here."

"Mancini's inquisitive eyes pierced Adam with suspicion. With an amusing rehearsed type movement, he whirled to face Monica directly and said, "We'll need a statement from you too. I'm going to have both of you go to the station and sergeant DeMarco will take the information. Is your office manager married?

"Yes, her husband's name is Peter."

"If you'll give me her address and phone number, it's our responsibility to inform her husband. Officer O'Brien will drive you to the station."

CHAPTER FORTY-THREE

Monica and Adam sat silently in the back seat of the police car.

"Does Ellen know what happened?"

"Oh, no! I'd better call her."

Adam fumbled through his pants and then his jacket in search of his cell phone. As he moved his eyes made contact, through the rear view mirror, with the officer driving the car, and he realized that the policeman was watching him closely while pulling off to the side of the road. The car stopped and the policeman turned to fully face Adam.

"Sir, I am going to ask you to stop right there and not move your hands at all. Now, slowly take your jacket off and hand it to me."

Adam was indignant. "What's this all

about? I'm just getting my cell phone to call my wife. I'm not some criminal you picked up off the streets. I resent this. What did you think? That I was reaching for a gun?"

Monica put her hand on his thigh and whispered, "Easy Adam, I'm sure the officer is just doing what he's been trained to do."

Officer O'Brien was a young, fair skinned man with a square face and a block- like jaw. He took the jacket, reached in the pocket and handed Adam the phone.

"Sorry sir, the young lady is right. I'm just doing what I've been trained to do. You know, we can never be too careful. Go ahead, sir, and make your call. Both of you are free to make any calls you wish."

Adam looked at Monica. "Do you need to tell Mike where you are?"

"Hmm! That's interesting. That didn't even occur to me. I have no idea where he is or how to reach him even if I wanted to. No, I don't have anyone to call."

"I'd better call Ellen and let her know what happened."

Adam pressed the speed dial and quickly related what had occurred.

Ellen was truly upset. "Oh no! "How badly is she hurt? Does Peter know?"

"She's at the hospital. I called 911 and the

EMT's came along with the police."

In her solution-oriented voice Ellen asked questions and gave instructions.

"First of all, did they get the files of any of your politically prominent patients? This could mean trouble for us. What if they stole confidential information about one of them? I've always warned you to be careful what you write. Can we be sued? Where are you now? You need to find those files immediately. You need to remind the police of your privileged communication. Have they asked you any questions?"

"Ellen stop! For God's sake, stop firing questions at me. I can handle this. As for where I am now, I'm in a police cruiser on my way to the station to give a statement."

"Adam, listen to me. Don't say anything to anyone until we get Myron there."

"I don't need an attorney. I'm just going to tell them what happened."

Ellen grew more dictatorial. "Adam for once don't be so stupid and naïve. Wait until Myron gets there. I'll call him immediately. Don't screw this up. Our lives are at stake. We could lose everything. Don't say a word to anyone."

At the police station they were escorted to a large over lit room with several desks.

"I'm Sergeant Dan DeMarco. I'll be taking your statements. Detective Mancini called the case in and explained what was going on. I assume you're Mrs. Monica Strove, Doctor Peterson's colleague? Please have a seat on that bench, Mrs. Strove. I'll start with Doctor Peterson's information."

Adam was about to answer Sergeant Demarco's first question when Ellen, her father, and Myron appeared. Ellen strode directly over to Sergeant Demarco and imperiously said, "I'm Mrs. Ellen Peterson, the Doctor's wife. This is my father, Doctor Alexander Patrick, president of Georgetown University, and this our attorney, Myron Goldman."

Resentful of his wife's attitude, Adam tried to distance himself from the group.

Ellen happened to glance at the bench and spotted Monica. Her face reddened and her eyes glowered with fury as she pointed.

"What's she doing here? I can't believe this Adam. Why is Strove here?"

"I'll explain later."

Ellen's father moved toward Ellen and gently led her to a bench along the wall. "Let's sit over here. I think it would be best for us to just stay out of it and let Myron and Adam talk to the sergeant."

Ellen looked over to where her father was directing her and hissed; "I don't want to sit near her, let's go over there."

CHAPTER FORTY-THREE

At that moment Detective Mancini arrived and pulled a chair up next to Adam.

"Mrs. Finley was admitted to the critical care unit and was still unconscious when I left. The attending physician told me that she had received a significant blow to the head and suffered a skull fracture and possibly some damage to her brain. Mr. Finley has been told. He arranged for his mother to stay with the children so he could go to the hospital. I had a policewoman accompany him. Dr. Peterson, now I need to ask you some questions."

Myron Goldman sprang into action.

"Adam, don't answer anything until we've had a chance to talk."

Ellen chimed in from across the room. "Adam this is why Myron is here, to counsel you on how to answer any questions."

Adam rose up and faced both of them.

"Ellen! For once keep your mouth shut. I have nothing to hide. I don't need Myron to tell the detective and sergeant what I know about the situation."

"Adam don't be a fool, Myron is here to help. It's his profession. It's time for you to take advice from someone else and give up your absurd romantic view of life. I know you'd like to think you are, but you're not the world's expert on everything."

Adam turned his back on Ellen in defiance.

"Detective Mancini, I'm ready to answer any questions you have. Don't pay any attention to the paranoid contingent over there. What can I tell you?"

Detective Mancini ignored Adam's remark and dispassionately gestured for him to take the seat across from him.

"Let's start by you telling me what happened."

"Well, earlier this evening Cathy realized that I had not mailed a very important document. She called my home and told Ellen, my wife, that she was going to the store and would stop by the office and take it to the post office. I later went out for a drive and Ellen called to tell me that Peter was worried because Cathy had not returned home and it had been over two hours. I called Peter and told him I would check at the office. When I got there I saw that the outside door to my office was open. My files were all over the place. My papers were everywhere. You know I have a lot of highly confidential material in there and years worth of research. To lose that! What a tragedy! Cathy was lying on the floor."

Myron interrupted. "Cathy has been Doctor Peterson's office manager for many years and the Petersons are very attached to her."

"I understand Attorney Goldman. I won't take much longer but I must ask some other questions in order to complete my file. Did you see anyone else at the time?"

"No."

"Did you move Mrs. Finley after you found her on the floor?"

"Move her? No! I don't think so, but I did reach down to take her pulse."

Detective Mancini looked at him quizzically. "I'm puzzled. If you didn't try to move her, then how did you get blood all over the outside of your left hand? There was no blood on Mrs. Finley's neck, just on her right temple and on the floor. Can you explain that to me?"

Myron practically threw himself between Adam and Mancini.

"Adam, don't say another word. Officer, my client must have legal counsel before this accusatory examination continues."

"Stop Myron, I have nothing to hide."

Mancini continued. "Doctor, I'm sure you understand. We have to ask these questions. We know that you are trained in the martial arts. You are perfectly capable of delivering the type of blow that fractured Mrs. Finley's skull."

Adam looked indignant. "I can't believe you're saying this. What are you thinking? Why would I have any reason to hurt Cathy? She knew everything about my practice and my life."

"Exactly my point, Doctor Peterson. Now,

do you know if any of your files have been taken?"

"No. How would I know? I didn't have time to search through that mess. The computers had been turned on so it's very possible they took information from those files."

"We'll need a list of all of your patients as soon as you can get it to us."

Myron cut him off. "I'm sure you're aware of confidentiality laws, and I believe you will need a court order to request that type of information."

Mancini, well aware that he could get any information he needed, regardless of confidentiality laws, ignored the lawyer and turned to Adam.

"You've been through enough tonight. You're free to go. I suggest you get a good night's sleep and we'll talk more tomorrow. I'm sure I don't have to tell you not to leave town."

Mancini turned to Ellen and Monica. "We haven't had a chance to talk yet, but I need to caution both of you in the same way. Don't leave town."

Adam, rose, faced Mancini squarely and looked him directly in the eye.

"Detective Mancini, I want to get to the bottom of this more than anyone. I can't believe that you might suspect me of having anything to do with it. I'll be in my office tomorrow and you can reach me there."

Adam walked over to Ellen, her father,

and Myron. He looked at Monica who was still sitting alone on the bench.

"The police drove Monica and me here so we'll both need a ride back to the office to get our cars."

Ellen glared at Monica. "Actually, I came separately. Myron met me here so he has his own car. I drove the BMW convertible, which doesn't have a back seat. Myron, would you be good enough to drive Mrs. Strove to the office to get her car?"

CHAPTER FORTY-FOUR

The next day, eager to get the analysis of the artifact as soon as possible, Adam put Cathy out of his mind and seized on Leopold Robsen's offer to inspect the stone. They made arrangements to meet at Adam's office that evening. Leopold arrived a few minutes early and helped himself to coffee while he waited for Adam to conclude with his last patient.

"Hi Leopold. Thanks for coming over to see my treasure."

Leopold sauntered into the office with an air of detachment.

"We shall see. What is it they say? One man's treasure is another man's junk. Let's see what you have."

Adam reached into the bottom drawer of his desk and very carefully removed the artifact from its pouch. As if holding a fragile, precious jewel, he handed it to Leopold.

Leopold turned it over in his hand, held it up to the light, and ran his fingers over the raised inscription. He tapped it, put it to his nose as if to test for an odor, and actually put it to his ear as if to test for sound.

"Well what do you think? How old do you think it is? Where do you think it's from?"

Leopold stopped him with a disapproving look and said, "Easy Brother Adam, easy. I've had this object in my hands for only a minute. Surely you don't think I could determine anything in that short a time."

Adam smiled and sat watching Leopold as he went through more machinations. He placed the artifact under the light on Adam's desk, tilting it in different directions. He took a large magnifying glass from his briefcase and carefully examined the object, lingering over the raised portions. With his head bent close and his eyes fixed, he mumbled something Adam could not quite hear. Finally, still staring at the artifact, he began to speak.

"It would be most helpful if you could tell me something about this mystery of yours. Frankly, Brother, I don't think it's anything of importance. I wouldn't be surprised if it wasn't anything more than a rock with some kid's nonsense chiseled on it. The one thing of interest is that there appears to be a small raised oval spot at the top edge. Have you noticed that? It's as if it's not part of the stone itself but has been imbedded there artificially. Or it could be there naturally, rocks often fuse together in the ground. Where did you get this and what makes you think it's ancient and important?"

"Someone gave it to me. He found it in his backyard while digging a hole for a fence post."

"Where was this? Here in Virginia?"

"Well actually, the person who gave it to me was not the one who first found it. I'm not sure exactly where it was found. I never thought to inquire about that. In fact I really don't know anything more. My friend just asked me to have it looked into. He thought it might be valuable."

"I doubt that it is ancient. Of course, I'm sure you are aware that any rock can go back thousands of years, perhaps even millions, but that doesn't make it unique in any way. As for the raised lines, well, it's a bit too far fetched for me to regard this as writing. It could be stress fractures in the stone. The one thing I'm sure of is that it would be quite costly to have an investigative archeologist go through a full evaluation. Truthfully, I don't see anything that would make me think it's worth the effort and expense, but if you want another opinion, you need to take it to someone who will be honest with you and tell you up front if there's enough about it to warrant a thorough evaluation. Dr. Shultz, Gus Shultz, might be just the right person to consult. I know Gus very well. He trained in Germany in one of the finest metallurgical programs in the world. He worked on the Utah excavation project for the government and has been a key figure in analyzing the mineral deposits found in the La Brea tar pits in Los Angeles. I can get in touch with him if you'd like."

"Thanks, Leopold, I guess after your appraisal of the stone I'm not sure I want to spend the money if it's going to turn out to be a piece of worthless rock. So, give me some time to think about it and I'll let you know what I decide."

"That's fine Adam. If there is anything else you think I might do to help you let me know."

"Well, thanks for coming over. I guess I had lapsed into a kind of fantasy. Sort of like winning the lottery. I'll keep in touch with you if I go any further with it."

Leopold left and Adam sat in his recliner, experiencing a multitude of feelings ranging from disappointment to anger toward Leopold for his summary dismissal of the object. As he held the rock, pensively viewing it from all angles, he suddenly became aware of a sensation in his hands. The artifact was growing unnaturally hot as he clutched it. The light in the room seemed to change, and Adam blinked to clear his vision. Transfixed he found himself staring at a barren mountain dessert scene. He was engulfed by the heat and desolation of the land and his gaze was drawn to a spot about half way up a steep mountain, where there appeared to be a cave. He was able to see the area in great detail.

The increasing heat of the stone pulled Adam's attention away from the scene, and he quickly placed it on the floor. He was utterly bewildered and disconcerted by what had just occurred. In the past, after some of his regressions, Adam had wondered if he had rearranged too many neural connections with his experimentation and had begun to hallucinate. This time there was no such thought. He was certain that this had been a supernatural occurrence somehow connected to the rock. He believed the vision was a guiding experience and he was convinced, through some sixth sense, that the scene before him had been Egypt. He became even more determined to discover the significance of the rock. Then he caught himself.

"What is happening to my head? God, am I going mad? I know I've never been to Egypt!"

CHAPTER FORTY-FIVE

Monica was eager to learn what Adam had discovered from his meeting with Leopold Robsen and called his office as soon as she arrived home from school. There was no answer. She hesitated about calling his house but could not resist.

"Hi Ellen, this is Monica Strove."

Ellen's voice was detached and clipped. Is there some change in the class schedule?"

"No, I just had an interesting idea about our book and I wanted to bounce it off Adam before I invested a lot of effort writing about something he may not feel is pertinent. Is he home yet?"

"No he's not home. Is the book almost finished? You two have been spending a lot of time together lately. Is it eating into your family time like it is ours?"

"It certainly is taking a good deal of our time, I know. It's probably a little different for me than for Adam and you, because I don't have children or family around here, but of course I do have a full time job." Monica tried to keep her voice pleasantly neutral, but there was clear tension in the air.

"Oh, I've been through four books with Adam. He worked hard on them but never put in this much time, particularly away from the house. Of course, this is the first time he has collaborated with anyone. You know, maybe the two of you ought to think about working here. Oh, here he comes. I'll get him and he can discuss it with you for a bit before we have dinner. Here he is."

Ellen shoved the phone at Adam and hissed, "It's you know who."

"Hi Adam, sorry to call you at home, but I just couldn't wait to hear about your meeting with Robsen."

"It's fine Monica, don't worry about it. I was going to call you later. I didn't like his attitude, and I don't know if he knows what he's talking about. He basically dismissed the stone as worthless. He didn't even think it was old. But after he left something happened. I had a very strange experience. I was holding the stone in my hand and it began to get hot, just like it did before, remember? Then I had a vision of a dessert mountain and caves, and I know, I don't know how I know, but I know, it was someplace in Egypt."

"Wow! That's extraordinary! We have to figure this out. I think I have just the person to help us. I called Dr. Wolfgang Taber, one of my professors at UNC. I took some physics courses with him. He's renowned for dating and evaluating ancient artifacts. He was the head of the honors curriculum committee and I was the student representative, so I got to know him quite well. I think he's a great guy. I told him about the stone and where I got it, and he was willing to discuss an analysis with us. He's an academician, but has participated in many archeological expeditions and is an expert on carbon dating. I think he's the right person because he also has an expertise in metallurgy. What do you think?"

"Sounds good. Did he say when he could start the analysis and how long it would take? Did he mention cost?"

"He said he had just finished a project and could begin immediately. He didn't know how to estimate cost until he looked at the object and spoke to us about exactly what we were interested in finding out."

"That's fine. What's the next step?"

"I told him we could meet with him this weekend. Is that okay?"

"Hmm, it's going to cause some problems for me here. I don't expect Ellen to be thrilled if I go away for the weekend. She was planning on us going to see the boys at school. They both have soccer games and I've only been to one this year. Do you think there's any chance we could fly down Thursday and return by Friday evening? That way I would be able to spend the weekend with the boys. It's not Ellen I'm worried about, it's disappointing the boys that would bother me."

"I understand. I guess I could take two professional days off at school. I have five coming to me and I haven't used any yet. You know we'll only be about thirty miles from my parents. I'd love to have them meet you."

Adam was speechless. Monica waited for his response with a sickening sense of dread that his silence implied uncertainty about the relationship. Finally she asked. "Adam, are you okay? I didn't mean to push you or make you nervous. Maybe it's too soon."

"I'm fine. It's just that we haven't talked about that at all, and I don't know what you've told your parents. Give me some time to think about it. There's no question that I want to meet them but it might be premature right now."

Monica felt a wave of relief. "You may be right. I didn't realize that I hadn't told you that they already know about us. I told them when I visited. Let's just focus on the stone."

Adam was pleased to learn this. "I hope you understand. There's no doubt in my mind that it's over with Ellen and that you and I will be together, but I don't think this is the right time for me to meet your parents. I'll feel better when I can say that I am no longer married. I'll book plane flights and a motel reservation. I'm going to tell Ellen the truth. That we're both going to UNC to consult with an expert about an aspect of our research. I'll anticipate the questions and assure Ellen that we have separate motel rooms. I'll book two rooms in case she decides to check up on us."

"Great! Just because we have two rooms doesn't mean we have to use them."

CHAPTER FORTY-SIX

Doctor Taber greeted Monica and Adam in a warm but professional manner. Monica introduced Adam in laudatory terms, explaining that they were collaborating on a book about Napoleon. Dr. Taber did not respond to the long list of credentials Monica used to introduce Adam, but he shook his hand and quickly summarized his student-teacher relationship with Monica. He was a short man who clearly enjoyed his food. His necktie was tied short with the underside trailing well below the front. His white beard was meticulously trimmed, but his hair, which consisted of only a few strands, flopped in an unkempt manner across his balding head. His face and posture showed him to be at least seventy years old. Monica and Doctor Taber reminisced and laughed over anecdotes about their work together. Adam, failing to see the humor in these recalled episodes, laughed politely along with them. Doctor Taber moved behind one of the lab tables and assumed his lecture pose, his straight arms gripping the front edge of the slate top.

"So let's see what you kids have. Whatever it is Monica, you sure sounded fascinated by it. It sounded to me like you think you hit the lottery."

Adam took the stone, which was in its leather pouch, out of his briefcase and handed it to Doctor Taber. Before he could say anything Doctor Taber grabbed a pair of goggles from a hook beside him, and placing the stone under an ultraviolet light, began to inspect it with a fixed magnifying glass. He viewed it in silence for at least ten minutes, examining it from every possible angle. Adam grew a little nervous when the professor reached for a small scraping tool.

"Oh, Doctor Taber, please be careful. We don't want to mar the stone in any way."

"Have no fear Doctor Peterson. I shall not harm your treasure. This is a brush of the finest fibers and will not scratch even the softest of materials, which is far from what you have here."

Doctor Taber continued his meticulous analysis of the stone. Finally he turned to Monica and Adam.

"Why don't you two go to the coffee shop

and I'll come and get you when I'm ready. I'm sure you remember the way to the coffee shop, Monica."

The stone hadn't left their possession since Monica's father had given it to her, and now they were being asked to entrust their child to someone else. They glanced questioningly at each other. Monica's body language told Adam she thought it was safe and they left the room.

Half an hour later a student in a lab coat came to inform Monica and Adam that the professor was ready for them. As they entered the lab he motioned them to sit along side his desk and carefully handed the stone back to Adam.

"I can't be sure what we have. I feel certain that you are right and that it's a piece of antiquity. What you need is an in-depth evaluation of the stone. Frankly, I am intrigued by this object and have a number of thoughts about its origin, so I might be willing to do it for you. I have access to the most comprehensive database of gems from all over the world. I also have available to me through the university and my affiliation with the Smithsonian, laboratories where I can perform a metallurgical examination and whatever kind of dating test proves appropriate after we discover the physical composition of the stone."

Again Monica and Adam looked at each other for confirmation of their thoughts and almost in unison gave their consent to Doctor Taber's proposal.

"Good! I will conduct a number of tests using a magnetometer, which will tell us about any special properties any portion of the stone might have. I will also put it through spectrometer readings. Subjecting it to the different wavelengths of ultraviolet light should also provide some data for us. If I find any signs of carbon residues I'll do a carbon dating on it. I will have to pay to use some of this equipment but I really can't estimate what that will cost. As for my fee, I will treat you fairly."

"When can you begin, Doctor Taber?"

"Immediately. It will take me about two weeks to complete the analysis."

"Fine! Here are office and cell phone numbers for both of us. Please call one of us as soon as you know something. It's an easy flight so we can get here quickly. I know that I can speak for Monica in telling you how much we appreciate your interest in this project."

Doctor Taber ignored the appreciative comment and simply shook their hands, assuring them that he would call as soon as he had anything to report. He also admonished them to be patient, as the investigation might take longer than anticipated.

Monica and Adam caught their scheduled flight home on Friday night. Adam dropped

Monica off at her house and arrived home to find Ellen waiting up for him.

"How was the meeting? Why exactly did the two of you need to go to North Carolina? What is there in North Carolina that has anything to do with a book on Napoleon?"

"Hi, Ellen, how's everything? I tried to call you last night but the phone was busy each time. Who were you talking to for so long?" Adam reversed the interrogation.

"Oh, both boys called, Mom called, and then your sister called and seemed to want to chat for hours. I finally had to cut it short by telling her I had things to do. So, why did you have to go to North Carolina?"

"It's very interesting but very involved. In our research we have come upon information that suggests that one of Napoleon's trusted marshals may have escaped execution in France, when Napoleon was in exile, and made his way to the United States. It seems that he may have settled in North Carolina and become a schoolteacher there. We wanted to check it out with one of the history professors at UNC. He's a professor that Monica studied with for several courses and she thought that if anyone could authenticate the story and tell us more about it, it would be this man."

"And, what did you find out?"

"He didn't have the information at his

finger tips, but he volunteered to do some research to verify the Marshal Ney story and said he would get back to me as soon as he finds anything."

"I recall from one of our classes that Mrs. Strove mentioned that her parents were still alive and living close to the university. Did the two of you go see her parents?"

"No Ellen, this was strictly business."

"You mean she didn't go see them at all?"

"No, Ellen, I told you this was a quick turn around trip, for one purpose only."

"Oh, by the way Adam. Something strange has been happening. Two nights in a row a woman with an unrecognizable voice called for you. She claimed to be from a magazine and wanted to interview you, but she wouldn't give her name and was really pushy about trying to get me to say when you'd be home. She also said she wanted to interview the boys to get a story about what it's like to be the children of a famous psychologist. She wanted to know what school they attended and wanted me to give her their phone numbers. Naturally I refused and told Miss. Strange Voice to call you at work tomorrow."

CHAPTER FORTY-SEVEN

Cathy remained in a coma, and Detective Mancini had continued to hover near Adam ever since the incident, appearing unannounced at his office and home, and calling him daily. As Adam sat at his desk that evening, trying to concentrate on necessary office work, the doorbell rang.

"Doctor, I know I must be intruding on your free time, which I am sure is precious to someone like you, but the situation is getting more serious. It appears that Mrs. Finley is not going to make it, and now I have not just an assault case on my hands, but maybe the big M, murder. My captain will be pressuring me to solve this case. I have to be honest with you. I feel that you are withholding information that would be helpful, and I'm puzzled as to why."

"Let's not stand in the doorway, Detective Mancini. Come in, take off your coat and have a seat."

Detective Mancini entered, his manner bold and assured. He smiled, handed Adam his coat, and remarked that it was very gracious of Adam to invite him in.

"Now, Detective Mancini, let's get right to your questions. What makes you think I'm withholding information?"

"Well Doctor, there are too many pieces that don't fit. For one, I can't figure out what the person or persons that broke in were looking for, and I think you may have an idea, but for some reason won't share it. I'm gonna be straight with you. I think you know what they were after and may even have an idea of who it was."

"If I am hiding information it's not consciously so."

Mancini was blunt. "Look Doc, I'm not in your league when it comes to conscious or unconscious. All I know is that my intuition tells me you know a hell of a lot more than you're telling me."

"The guy is right," Adam thought to himself. "It's my office, I'm the only one who really knows what's in there. Maybe I'll set him on a path by mentioning my formula. Or maybe not."

He turned to Mancini. "I can speculate,

Detective, if that's what you want. I would say that whoever broke into the office may have been looking for me. Perhaps they wanted me to reveal some information about one of my patients, some celebrity or someone in a government office. I think they were surprised to find Cathy rather than me at that time of night, and unfortunately she either recognized them or they were afraid she would be able to identify them."

Mancini watched Adam with skepticism and then fixed his eyes on Adam. "I can go along with that idea. I'll follow up on that if you will give me the names of the celebrities or governmental people who are or were your patients."

Adam looked at Mancini incredulously. "Oh come on Detective. You know I can't do that."

"Well, what are we going to do Doc.? You also know that I can hold you at the station for days on various charges. I can make it so that even Perry Mason couldn't get you released. And I can tell you that lawyer guy your wife brought to the station that first night is no Perry Mason, and her old man, king or emperor of the university, holds no clout with me. So think about it. It will be easier in the long run if you come clean with what you know. I don't want to drag you in and put you through the third degree. Think about it and give me a call. Is Mrs. Peterson home? I'd like to have a talk with her too."

"No she's at her mother's house. Look Mancini, I have a lot of work to do. I don't want to be impolite but if you're finished with your accusations and threats, I would like to get back to it."

"Of course, Doc. I'll catch the wife another time. Thanks for the talk tonight, see you soon. But think about being honest with me, it may make life a lot easier for you down the line. I've been at this job for a long time and when I smell a suspect not leveling with me, I can usually trust this old Italian nose." Mancini tapped his Roman nose in the classic gesture.

He took his coat from the hall closet and gave Adam a civilian type salute as he walked out the door. Adam did not acknowledge his departure. He was disturbed by Mancini's visit, and was thinking about Cathy. He knew that having been in a coma for so long, even if she survived, she would remain in a vegetative state. He felt a mixture of dread and relief. He could not negate the many years of their close relationship but neither could he overlook her recent betrayal. With Cathy gone he wouldn't have to deal with the threat. Then his face drained of color. Was it possible she had told Peter about Janette?

Ellen arrived home shortly after Detective Mancini had left. "Did you get a lot of work accomplished? I noticed when I left you were working on the book. Almost finished? Mother said to say hello. I arranged to go away with her and Dad next weekend to see Aunt Kristin. She's going in for surgery next week and Mom would like to see her. She asked me if I would go with them. It's about a seven-hour trip and Mom thought it would be good for me to help Dad with the driving. I just guessed you are too busy to join us, but if you want to you are certainly welcome."

Adam ignored his anger at the bombardment of superficiality.

"Thanks for thinking of me, but you're right I have a ton of work. What type of surgery? What's wrong with her?"

"I'm not sure exactly what's wrong but they are removing her spleen."

"That's not too serious a procedure. I always liked Kristin. She is so much more genuine and sincere than her sister."

Adam immediately regretted his remark. Ellen's eyes turned red as she glared at him. "Why? Why do you always have to be negative about my mother? This is not the time, but it's coming. I have a lot to say to you and you're not going to like it. I've been talking to Mother and Daddy and I'm gradually getting to the point of letting you know exactly what I know and how I feel. No more tonight. I'm going to bed."

Adam was unfazed by this tirade. He felt relieved that Ellen might be ready for a show down and it would be easier for him if she brought it up.

The next morning Adam arrived at his office and greeted, Carla Munez, the new secretary. It was particularly hard for him because he dreaded the task of breaking in a new person. She told him that there had been a call from a Doctor Taber who said he would be available for the next hour. Adam rushed to return the call.

"Doctor Taber here." The voice at the other end of the phone was gruff. As soon as Adam identified himself Doctor Taber continued. "Ah yes, glad you called back. I have something to report to you, but I think we should do it in person. Can you get here today with Monica?"

"I can certainly make it by this afternoon. I'll get in touch with Monica and get right back to you. Have you found something interesting?"

"We'll talk about it when you get here. Call me back within the hour because I have two lab classes and will be unavailable after that."

Adam called Monica immediately. She was excited and agreed to meet him at the airport for the five o'clock commuter plane to Raleigh. He instructed Carla to cancel his afternoon appointments and to reschedule them for later in the week. By the look on her face Adam knew she had no idea of what to do. He felt annoyed, thinking he had lost one of his limbs, and here was Carla, a prosthetic device to replace Cathy. She seemed to be trying however, and he knew he would have to adjust to her.

Doctor Taber was waiting for them in his office that evening and neither Adam nor Monica was surprised to see that he was wearing the same shirt and tie as before. The hair on the sides of his head stood out as if attracted by a magnet, cracker crumbs mingled in his beard, and his trousers were stained with drops of tea. He got up from his reading chair and with his characteristic mincing steps walked to the desk. Shuffling through piles of papers and books he pointed his left index finger to his temple, indicating the sudden recall of the location and, reaching into the bottom drawer pulled out a file. He spread several pieces of paper across the disarray of the desktop.

"I'll go over what I've found. Perhaps we could all go over to Mama Mia's restaurant and have some dinner after I'm done explaining the findings. I'm very hungry and would love to have you join me for dinner. It's a treat to have company for dinner, since Alice died." He addressed Monica mournfully. "I don't know if you knew that Alice died three years ago. Cancer. It was tough for both of us. I'm sure you remember the teas she used to hold for the students when you were here. In fact, I recall you helped her a number of times. Well, let's get to the results of the examination of the artifact."

CHAPTER FORTY-SEVEN

Monica sighed in sympathy and reached for Adam's hand.

"Let me start by explaining that certain gems are found only in particular geographical areas, and sometimes within a very specific and narrow place. Gems have a quality that is termed texture. The specific texture, which is measurable, along with the banding on a stone, provides information about the place in which it was mined. To our surprise, but exciting pleasure, we were able to carefully clean the raised area in the artifact and identify it as beryl."

Doctor Taber held the artifact toward Monica and Adam. They moved forward in their chairs and leaned over the desk, their eyes growing wide with anticipation.

He continued. "See, this is a beautiful beryl gem embedded in the artifact. It is truly a rare find. The fascinating part about this is that this particular gem can only be found in North Africa"

Monica lifted her eyes from the stone and looked at Doctor Taber.

"Are you sure of that? How can you be sure it's from North Africa?"

Doctor Taber smiled. "I'm sure. How can I be sure? It's a matter of sixty years of study and experience, the best testing equipment available, and my expertise. You could get another opinion, but I am sure any reputable person would consult me to be sure of their assessment."

"You see, Doctor Taber," Monica responded with a radiant smile, "This is a fantastic discovery for us. I haven't told you how I acquired the stone, but I have good reason to believe that it is an artifact that was unearthed in one of Napoleon's archeological expeditions during his Egyptian campaign. So is it possible that this gem came from Egypt?"

Adam couldn't contain his exuberance. "Doctor Taber, I'm amazed at your ability to zero in on not only the type of stone but also its provenance."

Doctor Taber chuckled, uttering something in German which neither Monica nor Adam understood. He rose from behind his desk and began to pace in a circle, moving in his tiny marionette manner.

"Yes, yes, yes, this part of the analysis is certain. But, unfortunately that is all the gem tells us at this point. It's an unusual beryl with a unique shape. Nothing like I have ever seen. If it was cut, then it was done by a tool unknown to me, which would surprise me. I know every type of gem cutting and modifying instrument, even those used centuries ago, as far back as the Roman and Egyptian periods. This cut doesn't match any known tool. In fact it's possible that this was never cut at all, but then I don't think this shape could occur naturally either. It's a perfect oval, a half-egg form with a taper on the under edge. The other strange thing is that it is set into the artifact without a bezel and no binding substance, as far as I could detect, has been used. It's as if a magnetic or an electro chemical force is holding it to the artifact."

Adam stood up with Doctor Taber and joined him in a pensive pace. "What about the artifact itself? Have you discovered anything about it?"

Doctor Taber halted in his circle, looked toward the ceiling, and tapped the side of his head with his forefinger as if accessing some processing portion of his brain. "Ah yes! I think you are aware that there is a place on the outer edge of the artifact itself, suggesting that it was broken off from a larger mass. I found a microscopic piece of another gem on the upper right corner of the edge where this portion of the artifact broke away from the larger piece. The gem itself must have remained with the larger piece, which unfortunately we do not have. However, I was able to use that tiny sample to identify the mother gem from which it broke. It is an unusual form of opal. I can't be sure of its geographical origin, but it has been reportedly found around the Dead Sea."

Monica now joined the two men standing in the middle of the room.

"This is extraordinary! It's beginning to

sound as if we really have an artifact that may have been unearthed in Egypt during Napoleon's campaign there. But what is it? What is its significance?" What can we do next to find out more about it?"

Doctor Taber again muttered in German, shaking his head questioningly. "Look folks, this is all interesting, but the one thing I cannot establish is the date of this object. Just because the gems are unusual and from that part of the world does not mean that this is a really old relic. I should clarify old. I think, although the two of you have not said this, that you are ready to believe that it is an ancient stone perhaps dating from the beginning of time. I'm not sure what you have in mind but we certainly need to investigate further."

Adam nodded in agreement. "Okay, what's next?"

Monica sat down again. "Is there any way to check what might be peculiar about the artifact itself? How is it different? I guess I don't even know what I'm asking."

Adam looked as if he had just experienced an epiphany. "I just recalled something I didn't even think to tell you. On two occasions, while holding the stone, it grew so hot in my hands that I actually dropped it. What could that mean?"

Doctor Taber looked quizzically at Adam. "Hot? The stone heated up in your hand? Very interesting. It never did that while I held it. Very interesting. Well, it's clear we have to do some more testing. Right now I'm hungry. What would you two say to dinner? Actually I made a reservation at Mama Mia's for seven, we'll just make it."

CHAPTER 48

Adam arrived back in Virginia late that night from the visit to Doctor Taber. The lights were on in the house but there was no sign of Ellen. He walked into the kitchen and found a note on the black glossy granite counter top. He read it aloud.

"I'm at the Finley's. Call when you get in, no matter what time."

Adam knew what the message meant.

"Finley residence, Ellen Peterson speaking."

"Ellen it's me. I just got home and found your note."

"Adam, Cathy's gone. It happened about ten o'clock. Peter called to tell us and I came right over. It's not good. He's in shock and the children are crying uncontrollably."

Adam knew he would be expected to exhibit shock and sadness, but other than the disturbance of losing a most efficient office manager, no other emotion came. Adept at projecting the appropriate image, he responded in a concerned voice.

"I'll be right there. Have her parents been told?"

"Peter couldn't bring himself to call them. He asked me to do it, but I just couldn't break the news to them."

"Okay, I'll be right there and I'll make the call. Make sure you keep your eye on Manny, the eleven year old. Cathy told me he has a habit of running away when he gets upset."

"Right now he's hiding under the dining room table."

The scene at the Finley house was chaotic. Adam sat with his arm around Peter and tried to console him wordlessly, holding his hand and offering gentle comforting sounds. Eventually Peter looked up, hugged Adam, and said, "I still can't believe it. Evil has befallen us. Why did this happen? Cathy was such a good person and I've lived a good Christian life. She always told me to try to see God's will in everything that happens. Well, you tell me where God's will is in this. She was a saint. Adam, I don't know what to do. I guess

Cathy's parents will make the arrangements. Will you help them?"

"Of course, Peter. Right now it's four in the morning. I don't see any point in waking them at this time but I'll call them about six. It will be easier for them to get over here when it's light. That will give the children some time to calm down."

Adam watched with a mixture of sympathy and distance. He found it difficult to get started with the arrangements and for once, Ellen's obsessive qualities were useful. She contacted the funeral home, organized someone to watch the children, and made the requisite calls to friends and family. When Cathy's parents arrived at the house there was even more anguish. Adam thought that keeping them busy with the funeral plans would be a distraction and suggested that Ellen accompany them to the funeral home to select the casket. It was fortunate that Ellen was with them, because they broke down and finally asked her to make all the decisions.

The last person Adam expected to appear that morning was detective Mancini. The bulldog didn't let up and was at the door at nine o'clock sharp.

"Well doctor I'm deeply sorry you lost your office manager."

Adam snapped back, "You mean a dear friend, don't you Mancini?"

'I'm sure you're very upset, but I need to talk to you and the family now."

Adam looked at Mancini as if he had two heads.

"How insensitive can you be? My God, this family just lost its mother and wife, and you want to ask questions!"

"I understand how you feel. But now the case has moved from a break-in and assault, to murder. Actually I have some information that I want you to hear. I thought you might be able to fill in some of the gaps. A cleaning lady from the building opposite yours came to the station last night with her brother. She couldn't speak English, so she had waited until her brother returned from some trip, so that he could accompany her to the station and translate. She said she saw a bald headed man running to a car and then driving off with the tires squealing. The car was a sports car, probably gray, an expensive type car."

Adam's curiosity was peaked. He wondered if Mancini was on to something. "I'm going to get a cup of coffee, want one?" Mancini accepted.

"So Doctor, does our witness's report mean anything to you?"

"No, it doesn't mean anything to me, but I'm not the detective. It sounds like a good clue for you to follow."

"Look Doctor, I don't believe in beating around the bush. I'm still not sure that you aren't involved in this crime. I know, before you say anything that my thinking infuriates you, but there are too many unanswered questions for me to leave you off the list of suspects. The woman's description of the car fits your Jaguar and there is the added piece of the man being bald."

"Yeah, well just who else is on that list besides me? There better be others because you couldn't be more wrong about me."

Mancini sat at the table, scribbling notes on his pad. Adam had a vision of the time the school principal had accused him of tripping Billy Kahn, a mean kid, down the stairs causing him to break his leg. The scene was still as vivid as the day it occurred.

"I didn't do it. I was nowhere near him. He's lying. He just wants to get me in trouble because he wants me to sell him the ball I caught at the Philly's game and no way would I let that creep get it. I hate that kid but I didn't trip him. He fell. Why are you taking his word over mine, Mr. Phelps? It's not fair. You can't kick me off the baseball team. My father will get you fired."

Then Mr. Phelps' voice sounded in his head.

"Mr. Peterson, you are suspended from school for two weeks and you will have to see a psychiatrist before you can return. I have to know that you will not do anything this violent again. You should be ashamed of yourself."

Adam grew teary as he recalled the scene of his mother scolding him and refusing to believe his innocence. He thought, "If only she would have believed me, instead of that bum Billy Kahn. I'll never forgive her. She convinced my father I was lying. I hate her too, maybe as much as Billy Kahn." As quickly as he had seen himself as a boy he saw the boy Napoleon and felt the sting of Latizia's rejection as she wrote to her son chastising him for his complaints.

Unable to decipher Adams incoherent sounds, and interpreting his tears as grief over Cathy, Detective Mancini paused, and moved toward Peter, who was sitting staring emptily out the bay window. Adam snapped back to the present and quickly put himself between the two men.

"Oh no, you wouldn't dare. This man is in far too much pain for your small-minded garbage. None of us had anything to do with Cathy's murder. Go get the real guys. I've had it with you and your insensitivity Detective Phelps. Get your facts straight, before you start jumping to conclusions. I had nothing to do with Cathy's death. If you can't read people better than to think I had something to do with this, you should be in some other line of work."

"It's Mancini Doctor. Mancini. You know Doctor Peterson, I've been nothing but polite to you, and I think it's inappropriate for you to talk to me that way. I don't mean to cause anyone distress here, but I've got a murder to solve and you must understand that you are in the middle of the entire affair."

With that, Mancini walked toward the door, indicating that he would not pursue Peter. He announced that he was going to give everyone some time to deal with Cathy's death but that he couldn't let too much time go by before he had to talk to the family. He also warned in a stern dictatorial voice that no one was to leave the vicinity. The door slammed as he left the house. Adam noticed three policemen outside who remained after Mancini drove away.

Adam joined Ellen in the family room, where now everyone sat silent, lost in his or her individual grief. Ellen had graciously assumed the responsibility for making arrangements, and to Adam's surprise, put her arms around him and kissed him on the cheek.

"I'm sorry Adam, I know what Cathy meant to your practice. I'll stay here until this evening and then I intend to stay at Mother's for a while. I'll talk to you by phone sometime tomorrow. I'll help Cathy's parents with the funeral and burial."

Adam was taken aback by Ellen's

announcement. "Staying at her mother's?" He struggled for a moment trying to decide whether or not to respond. Finally, he realized that he had no choice. "What's this about, staying at Mother's?"

Ellen's face grew more ashen than usual and she turned slightly away before answering.

"Not now, Adam. You know I've been very unhappy with our relationship for quite a while. Now I find out that I don't know you at all. Are you Adam or are you Robby? Who are you? What are you? I just can't take any more lies. I need some space, and want you to think about what you're doing. My parents think you need some time on your own to come to your senses.

A mixture of relief and apprehension swept over Adam. He thought, "This could make my life much easier, if Ellen realizes the marriage is over and just goes quietly. But really what chance is there of that? I know her well enough to predict she'll try to get every ounce of flesh from me and to make life as miserable as possible. Good Grief! I need to tell Monica about Cathy and let her know that Ellen is leaving."

Then another thought struck him. "How the hell does she know about the Robby thing? Oh no! I hope Cathy didn't tell her or Peter! Hell, this is getting out of control. That God damned girl could really screw me. I've got to get her off my back. Maybe money. Maybe she wants me to beg for forgiveness. No way. Hell can freeze over before I'd do that. Money, or whatever it takes. I'm not going to meet my Waterloo over this one!"

Adam slipped out of the house unobtrusively and called Monica from his car. She wanted to see him immediately, and they decided to meet in front of her school before classes started. They embraced tightly, holding each other for comfort. Monica's support needed no words.

"Monica, there's something else. Ellen has gone to stay with her parents. I think she has figured out that there's something serious between us."

"There's something sad about a relationship ending," Monica sighed, "even though I want us to be together."

"Yes, I guess so. It's the boys I worry about. You haven't had to live with unhappiness for as long as I have and fortunately you don't have children. Sad, yes, but the relief will outweigh the sadness. As far as the boys go, sometimes divorce is the most therapeutic thing that can happen in a family."

Adam's cell phone rang. "Hell, it's Mancini again. I'd better take it."

"Sorry to bother you at this time Doctor."

"Just get to it Mancini, I don't believe for one moment you're sorry to bother me."

"Doctor, I need you to come to the station.

You know that witness who saw a man leaving the office building? Well she just identified your picture as the man in the car. I could have one of the officers pick you up, but I thought I would extend to you the courtesy of letting you come down here yourself. Since you're so close to the station you could be here in a few minutes and we can see what this is about. I'm sure you'll be able to shed some light on this and maybe clear things up. Oh, by the way, since you're with Mrs. Strove, we need to speak to her as well, so have her come with you."

"Who is this witness, a blind Alzheimer's resident of the old age home on the corner? I'll be right there with Mrs. Strove."

Adam clicked the phone closed, took Monica by the hand, and walked toward the car.

"How the hell did he know you were with me and where we are?"

CHAPTER FORTY-NINE

The lobby of the police station was small and dimly lit. On the other side of a thick dark glass window sat the silhouette of the desk Sergeant.

"I'm Doctor Peterson and this is Mrs. Strove. We're here for Detective Mancini."

"Yes, he's expecting you. Just have a seat and someone will be right with you."

A buzzing sound opened the door beside the glass window. "I'm officer Tullio. Right through here."

The officer positioned himself between Monica and Adam and led them down a hallway crowded with policemen and odd-looking people. He motioned to Monica to enter a room on the right and then roughly took Adam by the upper arm and walked him into the interrogation room on the left, sitting him at a blue-topped rectangular table. Detective Mancini sat directly across with his shirtsleeves rolled up to just below the elbow and his shoulder holster displaying an ominous looking pistol.

Mancini leaned forward in his chair, authoritatively placing his elbows and clenched fists on the table, focusing fixedly into Adam's eyes.

"The polite dance is over Peterson. The game has swung in my favor. I have a witness. She's identified you as the person she saw attacking the victim in your office and then speeding away from the scene in a car that unquestionably matches your grey Jaguar."

Adam slapped the table with the flat of his hand, and arose from his chair to look down at Mancini. "What are you trying to pull, cop? What do you have? Some ignorant cleaning woman who had nothing better to do than spy out of the office windows across from me in the middle of the night when she should have been cleaning? All they're good for anyway, is spraying that damn stinky toxic stuff around offices. It gives them brain damage, I'm sure. That's what you have, Mancini, a brain damaged, illegal alien, who can't speak English. It's her word against mine. What halfway intelligent person would believe her? But I'm not dealing with even half-way intelligence, am I?"

Mancini pointed his finger at Adam's face and told him to sit down. He motioned to the officer at the window of the interrogation room to come in and stand behind Adam. Without saying a word, but with a cold steely stare, Mancini stood up and walked across the hall to the room where Monica was sitting across from a female police officer. He paced back and forth, occasionally glancing suspiciously at Monica. Then he stopped, leaned on the table along side the policewoman and began an accusatory monologue peppered with sexual innuendos about Monica and Adam. Monica maintained a cool attitude and mostly listened to the detective, determined to hide any emotional reaction to his subtle accusations. At the same time every organ in her body was gripped by fear. She realized that Mancini probably had a good deal of evidence that pointed to Adam. "What is going on? she wondered to herself. Years of using her defense system of denial kicked in and she successfully suppressed the fear.

A half-hour later, back together, Adam and Monica were accompanied to a small cluttered office and told to wait for Detective Mancini. It seemed to them as if hours passed while they sat, occasionally sharing their annoyance at having to waste all this time.

Adam's anger and impatience began to mount and he started to pace in front of Monica.

"You realize, Monica, that this is part of that bastard's game. He knows that by sitting us here our anxiety will grow and he thinks we'll crack. Well, he's dealing with someone far better at psychological strategy than him. I'm gonna get this guy. You'll see the real Adam. No one treats me this way. That ignorant cop doesn't have a chance against me!"

Mancini opened the door slowly, took an unusual amount of time to walk behind his desk, and stared out the window with his back to Adam and Monica.

"Look you two! I'm not going to hold you now, but you need to know that you are both under constant surveillance. There's a reason that I have the nickname "bull dog" around here. Once I have a bone in my mouth, no one, and I mean no one, can make me drop it. You're free to go. Of course, don't leave town. Now get out of here."

Adam stood defiantly. "Your tactics are so transparent. You don't realize who you're dealing with, Mancini. Before you know it you will be surrounded by my forces and you could very easily find yourself walking a beat, in downtown D.C. Don't be totally stupid. Back off while you can!"

Mancini smiled to show a complete dismissal of Adam's threats and pointed toward the door, signaling them to leave.

The next week in the office was awful. Adam had to fire Carla Muniz because she wasn't catching on to the office routine. He replaced her with Amelia Birmingham. Amelia, in her thirties was about five feet nine inches tall with a muscular but feminine build. Her hair was short and neatly cut and she dressed in a chic expensive knit dress. Amelia had been an office manager in a small, up-state New York psychiatric practice and had told Adam that she wanted to relocate to a warmer location where it snowed less. She had heard through a friend of a friend, whose name she could not recall, that Adam was looking for an office manager. Adam hired her because of her background, hoping she would have a fast learning curve. Since he needed someone immediately, he hadn't bothered to check her references, and her confident responses to his questions assured him that she would fit right in.

His expectation proved correct. By the third day Amelia had impressed him with her efficiency and quick adaptation to his office style. It was not until Friday that he finally found the time to call her previous employer to document her experience. An answering machine from the Main Street Psychiatric Practice greeted him with the common message that no one was available to take the call, but that it would be returned as soon as possible.

Amelia seemed eager to learn everything about the office, and Adam was pleased when she asked to look at old files in order to match his preferred format for recording patient notes. He liked her initiative and desire to understand the details of the practice.

Two hours later Doctor Martin from the Main Street Psychiatric Practice returned Adam's call with a glowing recommendation for Amelia. As they engaged in conversation about his background and orientation to treatment, Dr. Martin related that he had graduated from Harvard Medical School the same year that Adam finished at Georgetown Medical School. Curious about treatment approaches in other areas of the country, Adam engaged Doctor Martin in a discussion and was surprised at the simplistic level of the man's description of his therapeutic orientation and at an apparently weak understanding of psychopharmacology. However, he felt that he had learned what he needed to know about Amelia and attributed Dr. Martin's professional naiveté to the fact that he had spent his career in a small rural town.

Amelia opened the door to announce the arrival of his patient. It suddenly occurred to him that the boys didn't know that Ellen had gone to stay with her parents, and he wondered what, if anything, he should tell them. He decided to drive up to see them within the next few days and discuss the situation in person. As he imagined the conversation, he recalled the hundreds of times he had heard his own parents arguing and his mother's repeated threats to leave. He could still hear her saying to his father, "You'll appreciate me when I'm gone. Then you'll know all I do for you and your son. Don't be surprised when you come home some night and I'm gone."

Adam remembered his chest tightening with fear, the lump building in his throat, and his knees growing weak as he wondered if she would really leave or if they would divorce. But even more than that, he remembered how much he hated her when she was arguing with his father and referring to him as "your son". Then, for the first time, he recognized other feelings. He realized that for all those years he had really wished that his mother *would* leave so that he and his father could live happily together without her.

CHAPTER FIFTY

Two weeks had passed since Cathy's death, and Adam had become increasingly annoyed by detective Mancini's repeated intrusions into his life. His frustration tolerance for the man reached its lowest level that morning when he arrived at the office to find Mancini sitting behind his desk.

"How the hell did you get in here? How dare you come into my office like this and sit at my desk! This is breaking and entering even for a cop. Ever hear of a search warrant?"

"Take it easy, Doctor. The office door was open. I figured you were here."

"Bull shit! That door is always locked at night. Only my office manager and I have the key. You picked the lock, you bastard! You have a hell of a nerve breaking into my office. You're way off base cop. That's it. Just get out of here. Now!"

"Easy Doctor! Relax! You're a suspect in a murder case and I have a job to do."

"Out! Out! Before I call the police and have you arrested for breaking and entering."

Mancini slowly rose from the chair, looking at Adam in his special way that intimated he had accomplished what he had come to do, which was to make Adam nervous. At a snail's pace he moved toward the door, deliberately demonstrating his authority by glancing at the papers on Adam's desk.

As Mancini left the office Adam reached for his cell phone.

"Good morning, I need to speak with the Chief of Police."

He was immediately connected to a secretary. "Chief Belmon's office. Miss Young speaking. Can I help you?"

"This is Doctor Peterson. I want to speak with Chief Belmon."

"I'll see if he's available. May I tell him what this is in reference to?"

"It's a personal call. We're friends."

"Just a moment, I'll see if he's free."

Adam heard an extension pick up and spoke immediately. "Bill! Adam Peterson here."

"Well hi Adam, how've you been? It's

great to hear from you. I've been fine since seeing you in therapy. No more depression. I'm forever indebted to you Doc. The black cloud in my head is gone. Chloe thinks you're a miracle worker. Life has been so much better for both of us. I don't know if you saw her, but she attended two of the meetings of your new group."

"That's great Bill. You're probably wondering why I'm calling you. This time I'm the one who needs help. I don't know if you heard about the tragedy in my office."

"Sure did! I didn't call you because it's now an official murder case and as chief I have to maintain the highest level of confidentiality and ethics in this investigation. I'm sure you under-stand. I can't let my previous relationship with you appear to influence the investigation. But now that you called, let me express my sympathy about Cathy. She was always so nice to me when I came for my sessions."

"Well, Bill, here's why I'm calling. Your detective Mancini is really on my back. I think he has me under constant surveillance. I know he's already made up his mind and thinks I'm guilty. You know I could never do anything like that. So I was hoping you would speak to him and let him know he's on the wrong track."

"Damn it Adam! You're putting me in a tough place. Of course I'd like to help, but Mancini has an eyewitness that has identified you as the attacker. I shouldn't say this, but she has also identified your car. She saw it speeding away moments after the attack. I guess you've heard from Mancini that she identified your license plate?"

"That's totally crazy. Can you at least tell me her name? Maybe she's one of my former patients, or a present patient who has a negative transference and is using me to get even with her own father."

"Adam, I shouldn't even be talking to you about this. Look, I can't say anything further. I have an appointment at the courthouse. I hope all turns out well for you."

Adam picked up on the hint. Bill felt it was unsafe for him to say anything further on the phone. Adam ran out of the office, jumped in his Jaguar, and sped to the courthouse, hoping to catch Bill before he went in. Luck was on his side and he slid into the adjacent space just as the chief was getting out of his car.

"I hope I read you correctly and that you just couldn't take any chances on the phone."

"Adam, I will deny this conversation ever took place, but the girl's name is Janette Robby. I can't tell you anything else except that she consistently picked your picture out of hundreds, five out of five times. Good luck, I have to get to court. I don't think we should talk again until this whole thing is over."

Adam slumped over the fender of his Jaguar, his face reddening with anger, until his scream burst out. "You bitch!"

Realizing his voice had drawn the attention of several people in the parking area, he jumped into his car and pealed away as only a straight eight-cylinder Jaguar could do.

"Bitch! Bitch! Whore! She'll pay for this. She has no idea who she's dealing with. She'll wish she had never found me when I get through with her."

CHAPTER FIFTY-ONE

Each bolt of lightening struck frighteningly closer to the house, rattling the windows and threatening to shatter them. The lights blinked on and off, warning of the impending blackness that would come with the loss of electrical power. Monica was used to heavy thunderstorms from her childhood in North Carolina, but this was the worst she had ever experienced. She wished she had some companionship to dilute her sense of possible danger. The TV was out, the flickering lights interfered with reading, and her IPod had not been charged. She thought, "This is what alone really means." The sudden ring of the phone startled her but it was a welcome break from fearful thoughts.

"Hi Monica, it's Mike. My flight was

cancelled because of the storm and I'm coming home. The airport is closed down, but I should be able to get a cab. I have no idea when I'll get there but I'm on my way."

Despite not having been home or in touch with her for three weeks, he did not inquire how she was, how she was faring in the storm, or even say goodbye at the end of the conversation.

Monica thought, "Well there's one benefit to the storm. It will give us at least one night together to talk about us."

Mike burst in with a bang, as the wind caught the screen door and slammed it against the metal rail on the entrance steps. His drenched raincoat dripped a puddle on the foyer rug, and his face showed the battle he had fought to get through the storm. Monica met him at the door and they brushed together with a glancing cheek kiss.

"Wow! You're soaked to the bone. I'll make a cup of tea for you while you get out of those wet clothes."

"That sounds great. It's really rough out there tonight. It came down so hard that the cab driver had to pull over because he couldn't see two feet in front of us. The only other time I have been in anything this severe was last year in Abidjan, on the Ivory Coast. I thought we were going to be washed into the sea. But I'm sure I told you about that."

"Yeah sure Mike, just like you told me where you've been for the last three weeks. Go change and I'll make the tea."

The storm soon shut down all electrical power, and Monica was unable to finish boiling the water. The lightening bolts seemed to be targeting their living room and the thunder shook the walls, disrupting the meticulously hung artwork. Mike and Monica sat across from each other in the dim light offered by Monica's only candle. The air was not only fraught with the ominous atmosphere of the storm but also with their emotional tension. They found it difficult to get beyond small talk. Mike, whose facial expression was completely buried in the darkness, finally broke the impasse.

"Monica it's time we talk about us. I'm around so infrequently we should use this opportunity. I know things have been rough for you. My work has kept us apart and I guess we have grown emotionally distant as well. I now know that you are not cut out to be the wife of an active CIA agent. I'm open for any decision you want to make. Both of us are too young to get in the rut of a marriage of convenience. You deserve more than what I can give you. I didn't realize when we got married that my career was going to be so important to me and take up so much of my time. I still want the marriage to work, but I know you're involved with someone else."

"Why do you say involved? I'm working on a book with Adam, that's all." Not sure why, Monica thought it was best to deny anything other than that.

"Listen, my job, which is really my life, is to know the details about everything going on around me. You can't be married to a CIA agent without the agency knowing every move you make. Big brother keeps track of you for me and for the good of everyone that depends on me. What I want to tell you is that this shrink, is not what you think he is. Be careful! He's got a good line and can be smooth, but there's really only one person he's concerned about, and that's himself. He's not the good guy you think he is. He's been involved in some things that would shock you, but I think it's best if you don't know the details. He's left some scars on a number of people from his adolescent years. Be careful! Adam Peterson is not a good guy."

Monica was stunned by Mike's words and didn't want to believe them, yet this added to the other seeds of doubt that had already begun to grow. She was lost for words and afraid to question him. She wanted to attribute Mike's lecture to jealousy but was unsure. The lights came back on just as Mike's cell phone rang.

"Look babe, this is my life. They're sending a car for me to get me to the airport. No commercial flights yet but I have to be in Mexico by morning, or else, so they have a private jet that can get flight clearance. Think about what I said, and trust me on this one. Your boyfriend is trouble for you. Get free of it before you get in any deeper."

Mike offered another kiss on the cheek and disappeared as quickly as he had appeared.

Confused by Mike's warning and by her own feelings. Monica felt compelled to call Adam.

"Hi, Adam, did the storm hit in your area as severely as it did here? We lost power for over two hours."

"Hi, yes it's still out here. Terrific lightening and thunder, wasn't it? What are you doing? Ellen's not here, as you know, so I was all alone and wishing I was with you. Up until a few minutes ago I had no landline or cell phone service. I wanted to call you to see how you were but I couldn't."

"I'm fine. I miss you and wish you were here."

"Me too. I think about you all the time. We need to have a talk about us and the future."

"Yes we do! It's time! I think the storm has just about passed us, so I'm going to get some sleep. I'll call you early tomorrow evening."

Monica tossed and turned in bed. Mike's warning churned in her mind. Was it true or was it his jealousy?

CHAPTER FIFTY-TWO

Adam sat at his desk completing insurance papers for his patients. Amelia had arrived at the office before Adam, which seemed to be her morning pattern. Adam was thinking about her quick and intense dedication to the job when she knocked on his door.

"I thought you would want me to interrupt you for this call. There's a Doctor Taber on the line, and he's eager to speak to you. He said he has a class beginning in about an hour and hoped he would be able to talk with you now."

Adam's heart skipped a beat in anticipation of what the news might be.

"Thanks Amelia. This is a personal call so would you please close the door? Adam waited a moment to be sure Amelia complied and then picked up the phone.

"Hello Doctor Taber, I'm happy to…"

Taber didn't let him finish his sentence. "No need to be formal, I don't have time for that. I've gone further with the artifact and found some interesting facts."

"Like what? Were you able to identify it?"

Doctor Taber lapsed into German in what seemed to be a pressured voice. Then he switched to English.

"It would be best if we met in person. When can you and Monica get here?"

"We'll be sure to get there this evening, if that's okay with you. I'll book us on the five o'clock commuter flight."

"Good. I'll make a reservation for us at The East Meets West restaurant. They make some of the most interesting food. My wife, who you recall Monica knew well, loved it there. I haven't been there since…" There was a long pause and he continued, "Well you know, not for a while. The analysis of the artifact has revealed a wunderbar of information."

"I can't wait."

Adam put his finger on the cut-off button, a habit he had when ending calls. He turned white. He was sure he had heard the click of an extension being hung up. He jumped out of his chair and ran to the secretary's office. Amelia was putting a file in the cabinet.

"Were you just on the phone?"

"Yes Doctor Peterson. You had a call on line three."

Relief swept over Adam and he accepted the answer, thinking, "There goes my paranoia again."

He turned toward his room to call Monica but, just as he was just about to step out of the secretary's office, with his back to Amelia, he asked, "Who was the call from?"

Amelia didn't turn from the file cabinet and answered, "Umm, it was a wrong number."

Happy that it was not a call he needed to answer Adam closed the door and called Monica. She was also excited about Taber's call and they arranged to meet at the airport. They both laughed at Taber and his enthusiasm about going to the restaurant with them.

The packed commuter flight arrived on schedule and they quickly hailed a taxi to take them to the University. Doctor Taber, waiting for them in his office, was reading a professional journal article as they entered the room. Without looking up he motioned to them with his small fat hand to sit in the chairs across from the desk. He held the other hand against his bald head, pressing hard enough to create a red impression on his skin.

He clenched his free hand tight and tapped his fist lightly on one of the pages of the document. Adam and Monica, eager to learn about his analysis of the artifact, sat silently waiting for him to emerge from his trance-like immersion in whatever it was he was reading. After an eternity of five minutes, Doctor Taber looked up, but did not make eye contact with either of them. His voice was loud and angry.

"He's all wrong. I can't allow this to go without a response! Imagine the leading journal of theoretical physics publishing this without consulting me. It's an outrage. Jules and I have been at odds over this for years. He's wrong and too stubborn to listen to reason. I'm on the editing board of this journal. I should have reviewed this before publication, not those clowns. Neither of them is an authority in this area."

Finally Taber looked directly at Adam.

"Jules studied at the University of Wurtzburg where they insist that benzol-a-pyrene's optical properties, which are harmful to human tissue, can be converted into benzol-e-pyrene, which will not damage tissue. Jules continues to believe that this tiny alteration of molecular structure removes the harmful effects and can be used to kill cancer cells. He doesn't understand the implications of changing the compound's third ring. The only reason that he has not found it to be harmful is that his studies are biased and omit the critical variable of the electrical frequencies that a cancer cell produces. Frequency is the key!"

Adam had no response for this tirade, but that was not troubling because it was clear that Taber didn't want one. Adam looked at Monica, whose presence Taber had not acknowledged. Monica looked amused, as if she had witnessed this type of indignation before.

Doctor Taber got up from his chair and went over to give Monica a gentle hug and shake hands with Adam. It was as if the outburst had never occurred.

"I have some information for you on my latest studies of the artifact. Do you want to hear about them here or should we go to dinner and discuss it over a glass of wine? German wine of course, there really isn't any other worthwhile grape."

He answered his own question, moving toward the coat closet with his tiny steps and rotund shape.

"Good! I think talking over dinner is a better idea. We can discuss the artifact while also enjoying each other's company, and of course the excellent cuisine."

Despite his small steps he moved so rapidly down the corridor that Adam and Monica had difficulty keeping up. Doctor Taber led the way, crossing the busy street with no regard for the traffic light or the speeding cars. As they entered the restaurant the crisply tuxedoed maitre d', with a definite Mediterranean demeanor, greeted Doctor Taber as a long-standing friend.

"Thank you Alberto, it's good to see you again also. These are two of my students, Adam and Monica. May we have a quiet table? We have some research to discuss. Start us off with a bottle of my favorite Riesling. You haven't forgotten which one, have you?"

"Never Doctor, the sommelier will retrieve it from the wine cellar and bring it to your table immediately"

Alberto showed them to an appropriately secluded table in an alcove apart from the main dinning room. The sommelier arrived and poured a small amount of wine into Doctor Taber's glass. Doctor Taber held the glass up to the light to inspect its color and then buried his tiny nose, nostrils flared, in the bowl of the glass, inhaling deeply. He sipped the golden liquid, visibly swirled it around his mouth and pensively swallowed. Satisfied, he nodded his approval. The wine was served. Once alone he proceeded to the business of the artifact.

"Well, I have been diligently working to date your artifact. I'm sure you know there has to be some organic component in a substance for it to be radiocarbon dated. I have never come across any material that has been in the ground that has not accumulated some organic matter however minute the amount. But your stone is different. It is the first substance that I, and I should add my colleagues, have encountered that has not even a microscopic trace of organic matter. So, I could not radiocarbon date it. This leaves us with several hypotheses, none of which fits a conventional formulation. First, it's possible that the artifact has never been in the earth but has been in someone's possession since its birth. But keep in mind that even simple handling of an object usually leaves a trace of organic material, which under the stringent tests I ran would have shown up. Or it could be that we are dealing with something that is unfamiliar to us because it is unique or so old that we have never discovered anything else from its particular period of time."

Monica positioned herself so that she could look directly at Doctor Taber.

"And which of those hypotheses do you believe?"

"Ah! Just like all my students. I'm not finished yet! I subjected the artifact to the most advanced metallurgical tests. As best I could determine, the artifact itself is a combination of silicones of a slightly different molecular structure than regular silicon. The silicon in the artifact is the type found only in the deserts of Africa, primarily in Egypt. Once I discovered the artifact's primary molecular structure it took three days of work to identify the silicon. It's carnelian granite and arenite sandstone. Theoretically the atomic structure of these substances does not bond together in nature, but they are bonded in your artifact. It took a while, but one night I awoke with a start. I remembered that these substances are what we used in the Astro Project. I was assigned to the Astro Project while I was at the Munich Laboratory, before coming to the U.S. If you can believe it we were trying to make a geoplasmic generator. I never understood the reason, but the director of the project, Karl Hoffenman, insisted that it would not work unless we imported arenite sandstone from an obscure place in Egypt, called the Burton Dassett Hills. I'm not sure what all that means but for some reason they were unable to arrange that."

Doctor Taber chuckled. "Now, frankly I thought Hoffenman was a bit crazy. Lots of the people at the lab pulled away from him as if he had the plague when he started to talk about the Ark of the Covenant, which he claimed was a slab of arenite sandstone plated in gold. Of course the Burton Dassett Hills are thought to be the site where Moses encountered God for the delivery of the Ten Commandments. After that, his students and colleagues started to call him Indiana Jones."

With his hands on his rhythmically

shaking belly Doctor Taber emitted a loud brash Santa laugh. As the laugh wound down, he gasped, "Indiana Jones indeed!" Then he delicately picked up his glass, swallowed some wine, and continued.

"The birth of nano technology almost makes me wish I was a young man again. It's going to offer a view of the world that we can't even imagine. Sometimes I wish I could be corked and preserved in a good Riesling and then when the time was right, pop! I'd be uncorked to see that what is now unimaginable had become reality. Anyway we used this new nano-tube infra-spectrometer and we found one other substance in the artifact. It's called moldavite."

Monica and Adam spoke in unison. "What's moldavite?"

Doctor Taber dug into his crammed briefcase and pulled out a picture which he handed to Monica.

"Here's a picture of moldavite."

Monica studied the image, holding it up to the bulb in the Tiffany light above the table.

"It's a very rare substance. Moldavite first appeared on the earth about 15 million years ago when a huge meteorite hit the planet. The meteorite hit with a great deal of pressure and created intense heat at the site of impact. It exploded and sprayed a molten glassy substance onto a large surface area. That molten material was moldavite. It is the only known gem of extraterrestrial origin. It is not native to our planet. Since it is not organic, and has no carbon in its molecular structure, we cannot accurately date it in your artifact.

"Now, I want to go on to something else interesting. I subjected the artifact and its gems to the most sensitive radiation detection technology available, and absolutely nothing showed up. There wasn't even the usual background noise that everything I know of gives off. That's strange enough but here's the next mystery we're facing. Kyle, one of our research assistants, for some unknown reason left the artifact on the lab table instead of returning it to the lead lined container where we were storing it. There was a box of photographic paper on the adjoining table. The next morning Kyle was the first one into the lab. He picked up the artifact, placed it in the lead lined box, and took it back into the radiation lab. Two hours later, Sharon, Doctor Fetzer, opened the box of photographic paper and found that the top piece of paper had an oddly shaped gray image, as if the paper had been used. Sharon is the chairman of the Physics department and Kyle is directly under her supervision. She was sure that he had contaminated the box of paper by opening it without following proper procedure.

Kyle had done no such thing but he had left the artifact near the box of photographic paper. He recognized that the image on the photographic paper matched the artifact exactly. At first Sharon would not believe that the artifact was not emitting radiation. Once we proved to her that it wasn't, she became intrigued and her unquenchable scientific curiosity drove her to examine the artifact further."

Monica and Adam let their forks lie idle on their plates while they listened intently to the story. Doctor Taber was emotionally excited but this did not interfere with his savoring every bite of the meal. He signaled for the waiter to bring more rolls and asked Monica and Adam if they wanted anything else. Adam had barely opened his mouth to decline when Taber told the waiter to also bring another bottle of wine.

"Before you continue, Doctor Taber, I'm concerned about the number of people you're telling about our stone." Adam confronted Taber in a slightly stern and reprimanding manner.

"I promised you confidentiality, and you need not worry about my colleagues. Now, let me continue to explain what Sharon came up with. We are extremely fortunate to have her expertise in this situation."

Adam nodded affirmatively, his look a clear signal for Taber to continue.

"A number of years ago Sharon had the good fortune to work with a scientist named Popp, who is one of the geniuses of our time. He was interested in energy fields within the body, and, in fact, the energy fields of all living things. Popp found that when he applied ethidium bromide to DNA, the chemical squeezed into the base pairs of the double helix and caused it to unwind. Using some very sophisticated instrumentation he found that the DNA emitted light. The stronger he made the concentration of ethidium bromide, the more light the DNA emitted. From this research it was possible to establish that DNA sent out a large range of frequencies of light. Popp went so far as to speculate that some of the frequencies are linked to specific functions. Popp likened DNA to a master tuning fork. When a DNA molecule emits a particular frequency it continues to reverberate. Sharon's hypothesis about the image on the photographic paper is that the artifact was emitting photons as if it had the molecular structure of living DNA. Wild and preposterous you may say. Well maybe, maybe not. This thing is like no other. I don't know what you have but it is not within the classification of anything I know. It has some of the qualities of living matter but does not show any signs of organic material. It has the qualities usually associated with radioactivity but it doesn't emit radiation. All I can say is that I have it in the safe in the office and when we finish with dinner I will return it to you to do whatever you wish with it. Oh, by the way, one other feature is that in certain areas of the lab the artifact showed thermal activity and warmed up significantly. We have no idea what produced that or the environmental conditions that differed when it became hot."

With an expression of total contentment Taber melted into his chair. His short chubby arms fell across his belly, and he looked, as he was about to slide off the front of the seat. Monica giggled as the figure sitting in front of her suddenly turned into Winnie the Pooh. However, his voice was far from the peaceful, melodic, high pitch of Pooh Bear, as he continued to discuss the artifact. Taber reached across his empty plate and poured the last of the wine in his glass, without offering it to either of them. Fondling the glass and gazing into it as if it was a precious gem, he slowly drank.

"Very few people would appreciate the mellow taste and feel of this wine. I guess I ought to report my phone call from two o'clock this morning. It was Sharon. She seemed oblivious to the time and the fact that she would be wakening me from a deep sleep. So there I am, startled awake, and then she goes silent at the other end! Now you've got me out of bed so start talking, I said to her. Finally she explained that just before returning the artifact to me this afternoon, she had found something else. Using her lab's new micro-scopic resonator, capable of measuring the mass of a single molecule in real time, she discovered a pattern that ran intrinsically through the composition of the artifact. Because it runs through the interior of the artifact no one would have detected it without the help of the resonator. Anyway, the pattern forms a series of five linked hexagons. And each hexagon is itself a ring of hexagons. Then she says, I'm sorry I woke you, we can talk tomorrow."

Oblivious to the other patrons in the crowded restaurant, Doctor Taber leapt to a standing, lecturing position, his chair clattering along the floor.

"The hell you will just hang up! I said to her. What is it you're trying to tell me?"

Monica and Adam waited for him to continue.

"Well I don't know if you are familiar with the molecular structure of DNA, but DNA is a polymer. The monomer units of DNA are nucleotides and, of course, the polymer is termed a polynucleotide. Now, stay with me and follow carefully. Each nucleotide consists of five carbon sugar or dexoyribose atoms. Sharon claims the symbols she discovered represent these carbon molecules. The connecting symbols she believes represent a nitrogen-containing base attached to the sugar, and a phosphate group. Believe it or not this would be a representation of Adenine.

CHAPTER FIFTY-TWO

Adenine is one of the four nucleotides in the DNA polymer."

Monica looked to Adam in hope of seeing signs of comprehension in his face, but he too was clearly baffled. She motioned to Doctor Taber to sit down to avoid the public attention and whispered.

"What are you telling us? Are you saying that the stone has the formula for DNA on it?"

After a blustering string of totally incomprehensible German, Doctor Taber responded in English.

"I'm saying no such thing! Leave it to a woman to get romantic with fantasy far beyond the reality of the data. Sharon even goes to the cinema to see those outlandish fantastic distortions of reality. She believes that the patterns represent one of the pieces of the DNA helix. I prefer to believe that what she saw is a coincidental wearing of the stone, nothing more. But, I sense that you two are more in the same league with Sharon and may choose to embrace her interpretation."

Doctor Taber drained the last of the wine in his glass. Without further mention of Sharon's hypothesis, once again in an inappropriately loud voice, he vented his anger that Jules had not consulted him before publishing the journal article on benzol-a-pyrene.

Dinner finished, they headed back to

Taber's office. The artifact was wrapped in a felt cloth in its original wooden box.

"There is one other puzzle about your artifact. I didn't mention it at dinner because I wasn't quite sure how to present it. As you recall there is some form of engraving on it. No one in our archeological research group could identify it. It doesn't seem to conform to any known language. Since you want to keep the existence of this thing confidential, and rightly so, I didn't think it was my place to call in the deciphering specialists. However, I would suggest that you consider having them take a look at it."

Gently cradling the small wooden box, he placed it in Monica's hands, hugged her, and turned to Adam to shake his hand and say goodbye.

Adam asked, "What do we owe you for all your fine work?"

Taber looked toward the ceiling, his eyes flashing back and forth like a cat tracking a fly.

"Why don't we leave it? How do you say in America? It's in the house. What you owe me is to take good care of this beautiful lady. She has always been my favorite student. In all my years at the university I never came across anyone more accepting and kind to me and my wife. Maybe we could once in a while have dinner together, I've enjoyed the company."

With that, Taber turned on his heel and left

the room without a backward glance.

The noise and bustle of the airport, still crowded even though it was late, was in sharp contrast to Taber's structured world. They were walking toward the boarding gate when Adam stopped abruptly and grabbed Monica's arm.

"What, Adam?"

"That man. The one who just turned down the corridor. I've seen him before. More than once, but I don't know where. He sure looks familiar."

"I wonder where. Maybe he's from the university. Or maybe he's been on the commuter flight with us before."

"No it's more than that. I'm not sure."

CHAPTER FIFTY-THREE

Fumbling to unzip his jacket and spilling half his cup of black coffee on his trousers, the detective finally reached the screeching cell phone clipped to his belt.

"Mancini here!"

"Sir, this is Sergeant Marco De Jesus, thirteenth precinct, D.C. Detective Carol Steiner told me to call you. Two of our patrolmen answered this call at ten this morning. We have a dead young woman. A neighbor, Vincent Catton, called it in. This guy Catton says they get together every morning for coffee. He claims that this morning the door was open and when she didn't answer his knock, he walked in and found her lying dead on top of her bedcovers. Detective Steiner thought you should be contacted because we just identified her as the witness in your case of the murdered secretary in that shrink's office."

"Oh shit! You sure it's her?"

"Yeah, no doubt. Her fingerprints match exactly, and her name is on all her identifications.

"Damn! Where are you?"

"We're down in the D.C. 'hood, on Waters Street. A little different climate than you and your boys are used to over in Fairfax. Two hundred sixty four Waters. You can't miss us, cruisers all around and the site has been sealed off."

"Crap, I'll be right there."

Mancini drove to the scene, flashed his badge, bounded up the stairs and quickly found Detective Carol Steiner. Their shared look revealed more than a casual acquaintance with each other.

"Hey! Been a while, C.S. How've you been? How come you never answer any of my calls? When did I turn into chopped liver?"

"Strictly business here Mancini. Take a look around; see what you can get out of the scene. Doc is still with her. He says she's about twenty-five years old, dead for about twelve hours. Could be suicide or accidental. He's sure she died from alcohol and drug overdose."

Mancini walked around the room with Steiner following closely behind. The whole apartment was a mess, as if it hadn't been tidied or cleaned in months. There were dishes piled in the sink, clothes scattered across the furniture, and fluffs of cat hair, from the three cats padding about the kitchen, clustered in the corners of the three small rooms. Empty wine and whiskey bottles of the cheapest variety were scattered about the tables, and all the ashtrays were overflowing. Some of the butts had lipstick others did not. Two bowls of corned beef hash, a large bowl of rice, and a dish of pasta with red sauce sat in the refrigerator.

Carol Steiner stepped in front of Mancini and pointed to the food. "Looks like she cooked enough food for the week. I examined it and it's fresh. People who intend to kill themselves don't usually prepare food for days ahead. I went through the medicine cabinet in the bathroom. It's stocked with a ton of bottles of different tranquilizers and other drugs, prescribed and street bought. The smell of urine almost knocked me out but I stuck it out long enough to record what was in the cabinet. All the prescriptions are made out to different people. No two are alike."

They moved toward the bed. The dead girl was fully clothed in a flowery red and green dress and her long dirty blond hair was spread about her face. She reeked of alcohol and there was an empty whiskey glass lying on the bed beside her. Mancini lowered his head along side the medical examiner and performed his own surface examination of the body.

"What do you think Doc? Sure don't see any signs of violence. What do you think, suicide or accidental?"

"Well, there's an empty syringe on the night table and one needle mark on her arm. I can't find any other needle marks. So she wasn't a regular. I'll have to take the syringe to the lab to be positive what she used. The dusting boys are sure they're her fingerprints on the syringe. No question, Mancini, she was drunk, and I mean really drunk. She could have died just from an alcohol overdose. Look there! Next to the syringe, don't touch, just look, it's an empty prescription bottle of Phenobarb. Take note, it's a different name on the bottle, Joan Peters."

Mancini took a closer look at the night table. "Do you think this is what she was drinking Doc?"

"Mancini, I'm a medical examiner, not a liquor store owner. I'll have to do a stomach analysis."

"Doc, I'm asking, because both of these bottles are really expensive single malt scotch. Strange in this apartment. They don't fit with anything else. This brand is at least eighty bucks a bottle."

Mancini noticed another glass on the table across from the bed. He bent over it; careful not to touch it, stuck his nose into it, and with a swooshing sound inhaled deeply. "Same scotch. Did the print boys do this one also?"

Carol looked at him incredulously and with disdain. "Oh, gracious, aren't we lucky Detective Mancini is here to make sure we're doing the job right! Of course we printed and pictured it. It was clean. Not a print or even a smudge. Obviously it's been wiped."

At that moment the medical examiner motioned to his assistants to bag the body and move it to the ambulance.

Mancini turned to Carol. "This is a tough one for me, Carol. I was relying on her to identify the murderer. My gut tells me it's the shrink, himself. I had a great case with her in my hip pocket, but now, who knows. We really should get together for a drink some night to talk about old times."

"That's just what they are, old times, very old times, better forgotten. I'll have Sergeant De Jesus keep you up on everything we find. Good luck with your investigation."

CHAPTER FIFTY-FOUR

The ringing of the phone sounded shriller than usual and startled Adam, who had drifted into a twilight dream state while writing patient session notes. With a sickening premonition he picked up the receiver.

"Adam, my mother faxed this to me late last night and I must read it to you."

Adam braced himself behind his desk.

"I'll read my mother's note and then this Chapel Hill News article. 'Honey, I thought you would be interested in this piece that appeared in our local paper. Dad and I are sure we remember that he was one of your favorite professors. Needless to say our town is very disturbed by this. What is this world coming to?'"

Monica paused surprised by the complete lack of response from Adam. "Are you still there?" Adam weakly acknowledged her question.

"Okay, here's the article. 'The police are investigating the disappearance of Dr. Wolfgang Taber, a professor of twenty-eight years standing at the university. Dr. Taber was declared missing after he failed to appear for lectures on three consecutive days. School officials were unable to contact him. Police report signs of disturbance in Dr. Taber's office. Dr. Taber is recognized as the world's most prominent scholar in the field of molecular physics. He had published over fifty-five papers, is a three-time winner of the international physics medal, and has been honored by the Planck Institute in Germany as the most innovative physicist of the twentieth century.'"

"Good Lord, Monica! Do you think this had anything to do with the artifact?"

"Adam, I'm afraid to go down that path of thinking. Of course it occurred to me. But surely not. Right?"

"I don't know. I don't know. But he assured us he had not shared our information with anyone."

"Adam, how could you say that? We know that his friend Sharon worked on it, and he mentioned at least one lab assistant that was involved. As much as I care for him and think he is a wonderful man, we both know he had difficulty controlling his outbursts. Remember how he spoke so loudly in the restaurant?"

"Right! Jesus! What the hell is going on? I bet this does have something to do with the artifact. Who the hell would do this?"

"Adam, my class is arriving. I have to go. I'll talk to you tonight."

Adam had three patients scheduled in succession. He made a concerted effort but was unable to devote total attention to them and finally cancelled the rest of the day. On his way out of the building he was stopped dead in his tracks by the sight of a familiar figure standing on the steps of the front door.

"Damn it, this is the last person I need right now. "Well Detective Mancini, what brings you and your two blue coats to my building?"

"Doctor Peterson, I have an official document from the police in North Carolina, requesting me to bring you in for questioning. Although this is not an arrest I must advise you that you are entitled to a lawyer and that anything you say may be held against you. These officers will accompany you to the patrol car and drive you to the station. I'll meet you there."

"What's this about? I'm a busy man. I'm on my way to an important appointment. I can't go with you now. What's this about North Carolina, anyway?"

Doctor it's really in your best interest to just go quietly to the station and all will be explained to you."

Adam gulped as he entered the lobby of the station house and saw Monica seated on a bench in the far corner. She rose to join him, but a police officer gently grasped her arm and asked her to remain on the bench. Within a few minutes they were both escorted to the second floor and seated in a room with a large table. Two gruff looking men sat opposite.

"Mrs. Strove and Doctor Peterson, I'm detective Homer and this is captain Elroy. Don't be nervous, we just have to ask both of you a few questions. Are you familiar with a professor at North Carolina University, named Doctor Wolfgang Taber?"

Monica replied without hesitation. "Yes of course, and my mother wrote me about his disappearance. She sent me the newspaper article. So is that what this is about? Why question us?"

Mrs. Strove, I gather you were one of his students. Is that correct?"

"Yes! But realize that was at least five or six years ago. I had him for four undergraduate courses and one graduate course. He became a friend."

"And you Doctor, did you know him?"

"No, not personally, but I certainly heard

of him through Monica."

Detective Homer stared at Adam, smiling cynically, with one eyebrow raised.

"Well I'll cut right to the chase. He had both of your names written together in his appointment calendar. In fact, you were written in as his last appointment the night before he disappeared. What are we to make of that?"

Monica was set to explain, when Adam raised his hand, gesturing to her to be silent. "Monica, don't say another word until we have legal representation."

"Oh no need for that at this point Doctor. We also know that you were both on a flight back to Washington that night. You're not under arrest. We just needed to talk to you since your names were in the appointment book. I'm sure this can all be easily resolved if you will be honest and simply tell us when were there and why."

"Okay, I guess I got too defensive. We're working on a physics project that relates to my experimental treatment method of using tran-scranial magnetic stimulation to induce specific brain states. Monica knew Doctor Taber and made arrangements for a consultation regarding the physics involved in developing my equipment. I had to be sure I was correctly building an optical isolator to protect my patients."

"Look Doctor, you've already left me

behind. Remember I'm just a cop. What you need to know is that as far as we're concerned you two were the last to see him. Is there anything you can add to help us? Did he mention going away? Did you notice anything unusual about him?"

"No officers. I don't think we have anything to add to your investigation."

"Okay! You can go for now, but I'm sure we will be seeing you again."

CHAPTER FIFTY-FIVE

Monica opened the envelope from her mother.

NORTH CAROLINA DAILY

Dr. Wolfgang Taber, physics professor at North Carolina University, whose mysterious disappearance was reported four days ago, returned home safely last night. He informed police that he had suffered an episode of transient global amnesia. Dr. Taber cannot remember leaving his office last week and has no recollection of the last four days. He reported that this afternoon he suddenly "came to" and became aware that he was in a movie theater. The last thing he could recall was sitting at his desk in his office. Dr. Taber was taken to the university hospital and found to be in good physical health. Doctors confirmed that there are no residual signs to document transient global amnesia, but stated that Dr. Taber's report of his experience was entirely consistent with the diagnosis. He will be monitored by the hospital staff and will return to his regular teaching and experimental studies next Monday.

Monica breathed a sigh of relief and reached for her address book to find Doctor Taber's number. She wanted to hear his voice and be reassured that he was really all right. As she moved to dial the area code the telephone rang.

"Monica, Wolfgang Taber here."

"Oh Doctor Taber, it's so good…"

"I'm fine my dear. We can't say anything on the phone. I wanted to warn you. Be careful! The artifact you have is more important than I ever suspected. It may be dangerous for you to have it. I must go now, but I had to warn you and let you know I'm fine. I'm taking a leave from the university and will be going to Germany for awhile. Don't worry about me I will be with friends."

CHAPTER FIFTY-SIX

Despite the many distractions of recent events Adam and Monica continued to gather material for the psychobiography. On this evening they decided to forego the intimate playtime, which had become routine since Ellen's departure, and to devote their energy to writing.

"Let's start our work tonight by discussing Napoleon's early childhood. The simplest way would be for us to describe his character development within the framework of the psychoanalytic stages. This would provide a matrix for understanding the fixations and conflicts that developed between his innate impulse world and his ego and superego control mechanisms. However, that wouldn't set our writing apart or offer any new information. Other authors have already done that. It's our direct contact with Napoleon through regressions that will make our work unique. I feel as if I have formed a close relationship with him, and I think we should offer our readers the opportunity to do the same. Our writing should lead the reader to get to know Napoleon as if he were meeting a friend or even a family member. This needs to be a personal type of communication rather than an esoteric psychological psychobiography, although as we discussed earlier, we'll include information about his archetype. People will feel that they met Napoleon first hand."

"Yes! I really like that, Adam. Make it understandable and give the reader the sense of reading an autobiography. That's different from anything else written about Napoleon. If people feel as if they are learning about him from his own words we will have a real hit."

"Good! Let's go back to the opening chapter. I think it should start when I first met Napoleon in his infancy and childhood. It will be critical that the reader understand that the pictures we present about Napoleon's life are drawn not from reading but from real personal experience of him, through hypnotic regression. And of course, those regressions have only been possible because of my successful development of the formula.

It's essential for the reader to understand

the conditions into which Napoleon was born in 1769. Latizia, his mother had already lost two children, both girls, prior to Napoleons birth. There is no greater loss for a mother than that of a child. We know from psychological research that when this happens there is a high hope in the mother, even if it's unconscious, that the next child will be the same gender as the lost child. There is often an unconscious attempt to replace the lost child by identifying the next born as that child and thereby denying the loss. So we have Latizia hoping for a girl. As we know that didn't happen. Along came Napoleon, born on August 15, the day of the Feast of the Assumption of the Virgin Mary. Latizia thought it was destiny that this third child, especially since born on this day, would be a girl and naturally would be named Mary."

Monica looked up from her typing. "Adam, you should go into a regression now, while we're together so I can write while you experience Napoleon."

"What a great idea. Let's do it right now. I'll go into a trance and you record what I say."

They prepared Adam to go into a regressive trance and Monica sat ready to write.

Holding Monica's hand, Adam was vaguely aware of the pressure of her opal ring on his palm. Instinctively he took the artifact from the pouch and clutched it to his breast. Within moments he was entering another dimension, another universe of co-existence. His face blanched, his jaw clenched, and his shoulders slumped.

"Why do you want me to relieve my childhood? It was certainly not a pleasant passage. Who are you?"

"I am your son, from Eleanore! I and others of your lineage exist with you, simultaneously in another dimension. I have come to learn directly from you about your childhood so it can be made known with accuracy for history."

"Mother never loved me. I was always second to the others. My savior was Camilla. She loved me. She nursed me. I recognized as a child that Latizia couldn't nurse me but as soon as my sister Maria Anna was born, right after my second birthday, she was suddenly able to nurse her. The pangs of early abandonment coursed through my entire being. Camilla was a wonderful person but not my mother. She was the wife of a local seaman. I spent far more time in her home, during my infancy, than I did in my own."

"I must record for history your pain of early abandonment."

"I want no sympathy. It made me stronger. It created a determination to never allow anyone to make me feel that way again. I learned to never depend on anyone but myself. Men are moved by two levers only, fear and self-interest. The pain of abandonment increased my self-interest and drove me toward greatness. However, it also protected me from hurt by other women. Women

are nothing but machines for producing children and it is only in that vein that they must be regarded."

The trance was over very suddenly. Adam looked up at Monica and asked if she had been able to record the experience. She excitedly assured him, "I got every word from both of you."

"This regression verifies that he deeply loved some woman, other than his mother, and that she in turn loved him. Now, we know right from his mouth, Camilla is that woman. We have to write this to emphasize that Napoleon wanted us to know that he felt rejected. He made a point of saying that when his sister was born, when he was still very young, his mother was suddenly able to nurse her. The reader must be helped to understand what this means for a little child, to see that he had to be nursed by someone other than his mother, and yet his sister had the privilege of being fed at his mother's breast. Food for the young child is equivalent to love. So, from the very beginning our emperor grew up with resentment and the seeds for feelings of inadequacy. After all, if your mother loves your sister more than you, there must be something very wrong with you."

Monica was typing at peak speed. "Slow down Adam, I'm trying to get your words verbatim. We can edit later."

Adam peered vainly into the large mirror opposite his chair. "It looks as if history repeats itself. I certainly believe my mother rejected me and gave my sister preferential treatment. I truly believe my mother loved her more than me. If she loved me at all! But you see Monica, Napoleon and I turned it into a drive to be successful and to conquer. I think he and I are looking for the same thing and I've been chosen to find it.

"We're here to write about Napoleon, not you. Let's get back to him." Monica was faintly irritated.

"Monica, I don't think you understand. I am related to Napoleon. I am the descendent of the son of Eleonore. Our entire thesis is that we are all connected. Our DNA shares our ancestor's history. No! When we write about Napoleon, we are also writing about me and all his descendants. That was a truly amazing experience. My regression had me right along side the young Napoleon. And do you realize I was able to identify myself to him? Let's see if I can go right back into a regression to the same time period."

Again using his usual regressive formula and technique, but seemingly aided by holding the artifact and Monica's opal ringed hand, he immediately went into a regressive trance. Monica again began recording his words.

"It's awful! The poor boy! Letizia is beating him mercilessly. I don't want to stay here it's too painful for me. He is such a little boy and I can't watch the beating.

CHAPTER FIFTY-SIX

Wait! Time is shifting. Here is Napoleon the man."

"Stop! Don't leave. I know it's painful to watch. But now we are adults and can look back with the wisdom of age. I have not shared this with anyone. My mother constantly made me feel ashamed. She humiliated me by beating me in front of my siblings and other people. However, I have come to understand it and will explain to you what the situation really was. She realized my superiority and strength and knew she was powerless to control me. In her mind, it was a struggle for dominance and it lasted all her life. Don't think for one minute that she ever won. The beatings had the opposite effect of her intention. I was so strong of spirit that they only reinforced my determination to dominate not only her, but also empires. Which I did! So, don't feel bad about the beatings, she paid for it in my lack of compassion and love for her and they made me the man, the power, the leader, I am."

With that Adam came out of the trance.

"My God, Monica. This is really powerful." Adam described the images and emotions of the trance.

"I can see that Latizia had a real problem. She had no understanding of childhood behavior. We have to remember she was but a child herself when she married Carlo. She ran into a strong willed child in Napoleon and interpret his normal efforts to develop a sense of autonomy as oppositional and rebellious. However, I could also sense Letizia's own feelings of inadequacy in the face of Napoleon's dominating personality. She felt powerless to control him."

"I've recorded your contact with Napoleon and included the analysis you just provided."

"Okay! Now let's see how we can elaborate on this regression. The psychological dimension I can add to this incredible contact with Napoleon is to interpret his involvement with his mother. He was caught in the dilemma of trying to resolve two conflicting forces identifying with the aggressive side of his mother and needing, simultaneously to defend himself against her domination. Now, there's another piece. Napoleon was jealous of Maria Anna. I have never known a child in that situation who didn't have unconscious death wishes toward the sibling. In most cases the sibling lives and the death wishes soon dissipate and are incorporated into the usual sibling rivalry. However, when the unfortunate happens, and the tragedy of death really occurs, the surviving child is left with the crazy thought that perhaps his wishes caused the death and there is an enormous amount of residual guilt that could drive behavior in a compensatory way throughout life. The compensatory mechanism could be self-punishment in all sorts of forms, or it could be a number of other things, such as punishment of the world."

Monica felt increasing empathy for Napoleon. "This little boy certainly had a difficult time. Imagine growing up feeling unwanted and unloved by your mother."

Adam sat back in his chair, "I don't have to imagine it. I lived it. I still don't think you've got it. You haven't grasped the deep significance of this whole thing. It's critical that you understand what's going on, Monica. It's Napoleon, but it's also me. Do you understand the connectedness?"

"Yes Adam, I've got it. I understand." Monica was surprised that Adam questioned her.

"I don't know what you went through as you processed being adopted, but the feeling of being unwanted by my birth mother never left me. For many years I wondered why they didn't find some way to keep me if they really loved me and truly wanted me. From the time I was little I swore that if I ever had a child, there would be no situation under which I would give that child up. You must have struggled with the same thing. But you may be more repressed than I am, years of psychoanalysis left few unexplored areas for me."

"Of course, I'm more repressed. How could my self-awareness even come close to the eminent Doctor Peterson's? Especially if he's a direct descendent of the emperor himself. It's been years, but you're right, I used to think about that. I too felt that my birth parents gave me up because they really didn't want me. Just as you, I got the familiar adoption story that my birth parents were young, brilliant students, not married, who could not afford to take care of me. I think I had repressed the feeling of rejection by about nine years old and have not thought about it until you triggered it off, just now. It doesn't feel good."

"I think most adopted children go through that. Of course, Napoleon was not adopted but he certainly had a mother who made him feel even more rejected than most adopted children feel."

"Adam you take notes on this, I can tell you a story I read about Napoleon when he was a very young child. I think it supports his feelings of rejection and playing second fiddle. Napoleon related this scenario to Gorgaud when he was dictating his life history. Napoleon and his parents made a trip from Ajaccio to Bastia, to visit Marbeuf. He related that Letizia gave her entire attention to Marbeuf for the three days they were there. He and Carlo felt totally ignored and Marbeuf and Letizia spent the entire time together and in isolation, leaving them completely out."

"Good story Monica. It suggests that very early in his life he had some insight into a betrayal of Carlo by Letizia. So women not only reject, they are also unfaithful and cannot be trusted. Napoleon learns at a very early age to mistrust women. I want to go right back into another regression to see where it takes me. This is addictive. I still can't control where in history I arrive. I just had a thought. Maybe it is not my choice but the choice of the person on the other end. Let's go! Another trance!" Adam entered easily.

"Ah! Another visit. You see, I've been betrayed by many and wind up in this hellhole of an island. I don't suppose you, from my future, could tell me the historical account from this point forward. Am I correct about that?

"Yes Sir, that is correct."

"Well, there has been much speculation about my relationship with my father. It is true that as a child I felt close to him and wanted to be like him. But you must understand, we spent very little time together. As it was, I had very little contact with him in my young and later adulthood. People do not realize that in the six years prior to his death, I had seen my father but once, and that for only an hour. So, when he died I had little feeling of loss. But I remember his death quite well. I was fifteen years old and a cadet. The headmaster told me of his death and he foolishly offered me the opportunity to go to the school infirmary to cry. This was the custom for others who lost a parent. I refused, telling him that I had not come to this hour without having thought of death. I let him know that I accustomed my soul to death as to life. I told him that I was strong enough to go through the pain of this loss without the need for anyone to console me. Cry? Crying is for women. I am a man, a soldier, powerful and strong. Cry? No circumstance

will ever make me cry. Last time we spoke, you recall the beatings I took from my mother? Well, I never cried and never let her know she was capable of inflicting any pain on me. I was indifferent to my father's death. I wrote a letter of condolence to my mother, out of a sense of a son's duty, not to offer any support or comfort to her. I owed her nothing and believed that her expressed grief of his death was probably nothing more than an act for her own benefit. No one knows, but I believe dear mother was unfaithful to my father. I know from several sources, I can trust, she prostituted herself to Marbeuf. In fact, I have many times wondered if it was he, and not poor Carlo, who was my father. Enough of this visit, I must attend to many things more important than to talk to a son from another prostitute."

Napoleon having made the choice, Adam came out of the trance. "Monica, this material is richer than anything I ever thought could happen. Napoleon's response to his father's death easily leads to the assumption that he was afraid of the soft, emotional, and feminine side of himself. This can tell our readers a great deal about his character structure and his defense system. By the way, I have a speculation. You know so many pictures of Napoleon depict him holding his hand inside his jacket over his stomach. Some authorities believe this was because he was always feeling some physical distress in that area of his body. Well, it's not coincidence that Carlo died of stomach cancer.

I believe we could make a case that his arm position came from identification with his father, even though it was unconscious and he was denying the importance of the relationship. Napoleon did not die of stomach cancer, or any stomach disorder. However, he may very well have thought he was getting stomach cancer and had psychosomatic pain as a result of the identification with Carlo."

"I've recorded every regression and written pages and pages for the book. I think we should call it quits for the night. It's pretty late."

"Fine! No more tonight. I can't go through any more regressions now, anyway. This has exhausted me."

"Does that mean too tired for anything else?"

"No, I'm never too tired for that."

CHAPTER FIFTY-SEVEN

The next evening as they lay buried among the many books spread across the living room floor, their determination to focus on the psychobiography was gradually slipping away, diminished by intruding thoughts. Monica crawled over to Adam.

"Adam I can't do this. I can't focus on the book. I can't stop thinking about the artifact. What is it? Why has it come to us? I'm starting to wonder what really brought us together. It's no longer just about a book, and maybe it never was. And I can't get poor Dr. Taber's disappearance and his phone call out of my mind. I'm afraid we put him in jeopardy by having him analyze the artifact."

"I know! It's haunting me too. You're right. We're involved in something far greater than writing a book. We need to stop and figure out what's going on. What is it we have, and what are we supposed to do with it?"

"Okay! Adam let's look at what we know. I think we need to start with my lifelong fascination with Napoleon. That interest goes back to my childhood and I never understood why. I started reading about Napoleon in first grade. The other kids were reading Dick and Jane, and Dr. Seuss, and I was roaming the bookstores for books on Napoleon. That wasn't natural. I think it was the prelude to where we find ourselves today. It's not just a coincidence that I took courses with Doctor Taber and grew close to him and his wife. That obviously plays a role in all of this too. Your appearance on the scene is the next big event. I think both of us will agree that your coming to my class, totally unplanned, had some mysterious force behind it."

Adam interrupted, "Unplanned is right. In fact a highly unusual thing for me to do."

"So there must have been some force operating to get us together. Now we add to this your experience of recognizing Latizia and Carlo. Think of how puzzled you were by that Adam, but now you understand it."

"Yeah, at first I was perplexed, but then I realized how it fit with my work in regressive hypnosis."

"Yes, and then your own trances began to put you in Napoleon's presence."

"Oh yes! But we also have to include the fact that you also found yourself in the presence of Napoleon in your trances. So clearly Napoleon is the common factor."

"Okay, now what else do we know?"

"We know that, as if part of a divine plan, your father felt it was just the right time to give you Marshal Ney's material and the artifact."

"And we know that you came to the orphanage with this beautiful ring, which almost seems to take on life when we are working on Napoleon."

"Right. That ring has some connection to this whole thing."

"Adam, I keep thinking about Doctor Taber's warning. He specifically said that the artifact could prove dangerous to us. Even as we review all of this I feel that maybe we should give the artifact to the government or something. I'm scared."

"That's nonsense. Taber had an episode of global transient amnesia. Why are you making more of this than it really is? Anyway Monica, men are moved by only two levers: fear and self-interest."

"Oh you can't pull that on me. I know that's a quote from Napoleon."

"Really? I thought it was my original thought. No matter, the point is we have both. You have the fear and I have the self-interest. Power is my mistress now. I've worked too hard at her conquest to allow anyone to take her away from me. I believe the artifact is the road to that incredible amount of power Alexander and Napoleon were seeking. It's going to be mine."

"Another Napoleon quote! Adam you're the one scaring me now. You don't care anything about my feelings in this mess."

"Just stop there! We have enough to work on, without getting into our relationship, at this time. That can wait."

Monica attributed his dismissive comments to the pressure they were both feeling and let them go without a response.

"Adam let's get back to the artifact and the sequence of events that got us to this point."

"Right. I've been reading everything I could get my hands on to help us understand what's going on. If we review Doctor Taber's findings we're left with the premise that our artifact is truly a unique entity. It can't be carbon dated and seems to have no trace of any organic substance. They were able to identify that it contained arenite sandstone and specifically the type that is found in Egypt in the Burton Dassette area. They also identified that it contained moldavite, which is the only known crystal that is not indigenous to the earth and is believed to be from an extraterrestrial source. We know that the artifact emitted radiation of some sort but did not register on the radiation meter. Remember? It transmitted the type of radiation that was seen on the photographic paper. The artifact has a greenish color. Now! Are you ready for this? From my reading I've been speculating that we may possibly have a piece of what has been called the Emerald Tablet."

"That's a new one for me. What's the Emerald Tablet?"

"The Emerald Tablet is the most ancient artifact known to mankind. It's thought to contain the purest and deepest source of knowledge. Supposedly it's a green tablet that has a powerful formula encoded within it, a formula that provides the key and sequential steps for achieving personal transformation and controlling the accelerated evolution of our species. The tablet is considered one of the most revered texts in the world. It has become synonymous with the ancient wisdom and timeless science of the soul that periodically appears throughout history, despite efforts to suppress it. Some historians believe the tablet shows that there exists an eternal archetypal level of mind that determines physical reality. They say that the formula in the tablet is a code that will enable people to access that realm of mind through direct knowledge of God. Most authorities believe that the tablet's message conveys the ideas found in Taoism, Hinduism, Buddhism, and Islam, as well as Judaism and Christianity. The basic view of the universe is that "all are one," and there is a pattern of creation and decay symbolized by what is termed the Ouroboros. The Ouroboros is a representation of the snake eating its own tail."

"Adam, this is fascinating. It seems to fit with what you have been espousing and preaching, the very foundation of SELF. But it doesn't explain why we're together, you and me, or what it has to do with Napoleon."

"Don't you see Monica? Napoleon and Alexander before him were looking for the key to total power. Let me tell you what several authors have written. There's a well-known Jungian analyst, Doctor Edward Edinger, whose quote I have here. He writes that the Emerald Tablet is, 'a recipe for the second creation of the world'. Terence McKenna, a consciousness guru, called the tablet, 'a formula for a holographic matrix that is mirrored in the human mind and offers mankind its only hope for future survival'. John Matthews in his book, Western Way writes, 'there is no getting away from the fact that the Emerald Tablet is one of the most profound and important documents to have come down to us. It has been said more than once that it contains the sum of all knowledge, for those able to understand it'."""

"Where is this tablet?"

"Ah, therein lies the rub. No one seems to know where it came from, who wrote it or its whereabouts. However, everything that had been written about the Emerald Tablet refers to it as being made of some type of green crystal, in a rectangular shape, and covered with bas-relief lettering in an unidentifiable alphabet. Do you see where I'm going with this?"

"Good Lord Adam, is this possible?"

"All I know is that there appears to be a logical sequence to our meeting, our symbiotic interests, and all the events that have occurred since we met. Listen to the rest of what I found. The Freemasons were involved with the tablet. It appears that in the early 1600's the Emerald Tablet went underground and the Freemasons were responsible for hiding it, as were their predecessors the Templars. I found this in the literature, oddly enough, that Robsen gave me to read."

"Adam, this is almost more than I can comprehend. Do you really think we have a piece of the Emerald Tablet?"

"I do! I think we have a piece of the tablet that holds the codes that can explain everything that has ever happened, not only on earth, but also throughout the universe. Essentially it explains everything that is, has ever been and will be. How the universe was created, how evolution occurs, other life forms, the future, our relationship to God, in fact, God himself. No one knows where it came from, but I believe it was placed here by extraterrestrials. Earlier searchers failed to find the tablet because it was destined to be revealed only when the technology was available to decode it, and when we are able to understand it, and use it to the benefit of humanity. The artifact has energy and when we find the rest of the tablet, it will provide us with all the information I just spoke of. We'll be able to create the perfect existence for mankind. The artifact's energy mandates us to find the rest of it. This is our destiny."

CHAPTER FIFTY-EIGHT

Adam checked the caller identification sign on the phone and saw that it was from Kevin. "Monica I have to take this call, it's Kevin. Take a break from writing, I may be a few minutes."

Monica welcomed the break. She was fatigued by Adam's tenacity and work pace. "That's fine I needed a rest anyway."

"Hi Kevin, how's it going?" What's up?"

"I'm okay, but I need to know what's going on. Mom called and told me that she was filing for divorce. Is that true? I figured it must be or why would she say it. I'm scared Dad. What does it all mean for me and Will? How come you didn't tell us?"

Adam was speechless as he tried to do

something with the fury he felt toward Ellen. He was dumbfounded and never thought she would be that insensitive to tell the boys without talking to him first. Losing control of the silence he murmured, "What a Bitch! She'd use the children for her own gain."

"What? What'd you say, Dad?"

"Kevin, this is a surprise to me. I didn't know Mom was filing for divorce, I thought she was thinking things over and just living with grandma and grandpa for a while. The divorce is as much of a shock to me as to you."

"You think you could get up for a visit with me and Will. We have to talk to you about this. Mom said she would be here next weekend, but we both want to talk to you before we talk to her."

"Kevin, I understand you need to talk to me. I'll get there tomorrow afternoon. I'll pick Will up on the way. I'm in the middle of some important work and have to go now."

"Boy, same old thing. Patients, more important than us! Bye."

Adam acted as if he had ice water in his veins and totally stonewalled the nature of the call, saying nothing of the conversation and returning to the book. Monica, who was out of earshot during the call thought it strange that he didn't tell her anything, but decided to ignore it and return to work.

"Okay! We have to finish this book so we can get to what's really important. Write! I'm going to enlighten you. People fall into one of two categories, introverts or extroverts. These are core personality structures that define the person's general attitude and motivational forces that depict the direction of a person's interest and the movement of psychic energies. Now I'll define Napoleon in these terms. He is an introvert."

Monica was writing but continued to feel uncomfortable that Adam had not shared anything with her about the call from Kevin. Her sense of doubt about this man was growing. She couldn't understand his complete silence about Cathy and the possible murderer. He seemed unconcerned and uninterested in anything to do with the incident. She was disconcerted and wondered if it was an underlying lack of sensitivity in him and if the emotionality she thought he showed was all superficial and a well-learned pretense. She responded to him in a terse monotone voice. "Okay. Now, describe in common every day language the personality characteristics of an introvert."

Adam sensed the unusual tone in her voice but did not acknowledge it. "Right! The introvert is always attempting to take psychic energy away from the actual object, as though he had to prevent the object from gaining power over him. The introvert has little or no relationship with the object;

it is basically ignored or seen in a negative way. Introverted thinking is primarily driven by the subjective, or the internal character structure. As we think about Napoleon's decisions, it is important to understand that as an introvert his behavior does not derive from the actual or concrete experience he has but rather by the subjective content. The reality of external conditions and facts were not the sources of his thinking, subjective interpretations were. However, part of his mastery and success was based on his incomparable ability to present himself as if he was responding to concrete issues in the world about him. He was superb at amassing facts as evidence for his personal theories, never for their own sake or relationship to reality. We must emphasize to the reader how important this introverted personality construct is in understanding the psychology of Napoleon and his behaviors.

I think it would be helpful to describe the opposite personality organization, which Jung termed the extrovert. In comparison, the extrovert has a positive relationship to the object. The extrovert constantly affirms the importance of the object to such an extent that any subjective attitude or interest in the object is constantly related to and oriented by the object. For an extrovert, the object can never have enough value, and its importance must always be enhanced. The extrovert structures the very notion of good and evil, right and wrong, through his search for objective reality. From the perception of what is external reality the extrovert develops a construct or formula of how the world is and anything that disagrees with that construct must be wrong.

Monica, there is no question in my mind that Napoleon was, or should I say, is, an introvert. Napoleon relies excessively on the subjective factor. Too much reliance on the subjective experience of the world prevents efficient and effective reality testing. This type of introversion is often counterbalanced by a de-subjectivization which takes the form of an exaggerated extroverted attitude, which is what we see in Napoleon."

The phone ringing again interrupted the flow of work. Adam answered it in the room with Monica sitting by his side.

"Hello, Dad, this is William. Is it true? Am I going to be the child of divorced parents?"

"I have no idea what is going to happen. The one thing I can assure you of is that you will be taken care of. I am really busy right now but I just spoke to Kevin and told him I would pick you up tomorrow and we'll meet him at his school and discuss the situation together. I promise to call your mother before tomorrow and find out what she has in mind. As strange as it may seem to you I don't know anything about divorce. The first I heard of it was when Kevin called me. I should get to your school about one tomorrow afternoon. See you then. In the meantime try not to think about it. Bye!"

Adam hung up the phone and proceeded to dictate material for the book.

Monica was annoyed but held her peace. She couldn't get over the feeling that Adam was deliberately withholding details of the situation from her as a way of distancing himself from her. Her body felt an icy barrier gradually growing between them. Despite these doubts she desperately wanted to hold on to the idyllic relationship she had enjoyed for many months.

"We talked about Napoleon's thinking as an introvert. Now let's talk about his feelings or emotions, as an introvert. Napoleon was basically an anxious person and his feelings were produced by and dominated by a constant state of diffuse anxiety. He was an unsettled man in the realm of feeling. When he experienced anxiety over the possible outcome of a course of action, his response was to act anyway, thereby denying the validity of the anxiety. He would act affectionately toward the women he seduced but then berate and demean them, often to the point of verbal abuse, to be sure that they would not take advantage of him. The more I get to know Napoleon the more I see him as a mass of contradictions. I believe he was an emotional person but that he had learned from early childhood to subdue the expression of his emotions. He was stubborn and oppositional because he learned from his experience with his mother that compliance resulted in a threat to his self-esteem. Keep in mind that Napoleon identified with his father and dearly wanted the security of his father's approval. His father's frequent absence, his being sent away to a school he hated, and being sent away from the beloved Corsica of his father, created doubt about his father's approval and acceptance of him. This may be one reason he sought in his reading of philosophers and civil authorities, a more abstract father figure for identification. That brought a feeling of belonging and security."

"Adam, I am feeling distracted and having difficulty focusing on our work. I think we should call it quits for tonight. I need to get home, shower, and get to bed. If that's okay with you we can meet early tomorrow night."

"Sure, I'm going to visit the boys tomorrow afternoon but should be back by five. Let's meet at Blue Shadow for something to eat and we can come back here to work."

"Fine, I'll be there about five."

He got up, hugged her tightly, kissed her on the cheek, and walked her to the door. "I know you understand, it's a bit rough for me right now."

CHAPTER FIFTY-NINE

Three laptop computers each logged onto a different Internet address sat amid the piles of books and papers. Adam picked up from where they had left off and continued to describe Napoleon's personality type.

"Monica, do you agree with this characterization? Napoleon saw himself as more capable than anyone else. He had unbounded self-confidence, courage, and supreme leadership abilities and used these attributes to inspire others to follow him and to reach their own potentials. Ney is a good example of this. However, another aspect of his character was a need to aggressively dominate everything he encountered. His self-interest was always paramount, and if anyone opposed his goals he ran roughshod over their needs and rights. You probably will not like this, but I see him as a bully, a tyrant, and a ruthless destroyer of anyone and anything that got in his way."

"You're right. I don't totally agree with the bully and tyrant piece, but I'm starting to understand him differently. I don't want us to loose the side of him that identified with the people and genuinely tried to help France."

"Of course, no one is single sided. We'll be sure to include that aspect of his character. You have to admit he was narcissistic and this aspect of his personality dictated many of his choices. For example, he created Josephine as an idealized wife, even giving her a new name that he thought carried more dignity than her given name, Rose. He denied the reality of her lack of affection and infidelity."

Monica sat intimately next to Adam, resting her hand on his thigh.

"I've got a surprise for you Adam."

His fantasies raced from one exotic form of titillation to another. "What have you been up to?" As Monica began to talk he looked crestfallen.

"The other night we talked about why we seem to have been chosen to have this piece of antiquity and why we keep regressing to Napoleon. Our discussions about the collective unconscious and its connection with DNA heightened my life long wish to identify my parents and grandparents. I spent most of my childhood denying the need to know from whence I came and who I really am. Growing up I modeled my adoptive parents and their Irish ways and culture, pretending I loved corned beef and cabbage and Irish soda bread. Not literally, but you know what I mean. Since meeting you I've been driven to embrace my own genetic background and to finally discover and live my true identity. I imagine, being adopted, you understand what I feel. I look in the mirror and it's quite clear that I don't resemble either of my adoptive parents. Every morning I search my face, and if I allow myself to bring it to consciousness, I don't know who I am. I want to know who I look like. As a child I played the game of mirror mirror on the wall, hoping to get an answer. Now when I stare into the mirror, sometimes I see a French face, other times an Egyptian one, and still other times a Greek one. I'm convinced that we both need to know our biological ancestry to understand what brought us together. Why am I a Napoleonphile? Why did you become so interested in Napoleon? Why did that artifact travel here from Ney, through my father, to find us?"

Adam was in one of his involuted narcissistic states. He was listening to Monica but remained within himself, partially disappointed that his fantasies about a surprise were nowhere near what Monica had meant by the word. He retaliated passive-aggressively, continuing to leaf through a book and thereby dismissing what was important to Monica.

"Adam! Are you listening to me? Damn it! This is important to me and to you too. Pay attention."

Adam was annoyed by Monica's response. He looked up staring at her with angry piercing eyes. "I've heard everything you said. Don't you dare go Ellen on me. She always thought that if I wasn't looking directly into her face I wasn't paying attention to her. I can't take that, don't accuse me of that again. Just get to the point."

"Hey! Don't get so huffy. I'm not Ellen and I don't appreciate being compared to her. When I think something is important I expect you to acknowledge it by looking at me. You can't go around dismissing people with that underlying hostility of superiority. Anyway, here's the surprise. I found a number of companies that conduct DNA searches to identify a person's ancestry. Over five hundred thousand people have purchased these searches. Now, we are among the five hundred thousand and I have the results."

"What do you mean 'we'? I didn't send in a DNA sample."

"Actually you did. Three weeks ago you fell asleep on the couch while we were watching that Peter Sellers film. You were really out and your mouth fell open. I seized my moment and swabbed the inside of your cheek with the kit's cotton probe. I got a kick out of how far gone you were. You didn't feel a thing. I sent the sample off for analysis and now I'm going to impress you with how much I've learned. Maybe for the first time you'll acknowledge how bright I really am."

Adam stood up and faced Monica unaware that his hand was smoothing his stomach area. "In the words of Napoleon, I have led and won sixty eight battles and know no more about military strategy than before I fought the first."

"I don't understand what that has to do with anything. Now, listen! Pay attention. This is important to us. There are twenty major branches to the human tree. These are called haplogroups. The word haplogroup is a contraction of the term haploid genotype, which is a combination of alleles at multiple loci transmitted together on the same chromosome. This company searches specific regions of the genome for a type of mutation known as a single nucleotide polymorphism, which is called SNP and pronounced 'snip.' The SNP could go back tens of thousands of years. What happens is that the descendents of that single mutation carry it on, along with others that occur later. I guess you know all this, right?"

"I'm impressed, what did you have done, a

mitochondrial study?"

"Oh smart ass, you think you've got me, don't you? Well you don't. Yes, the SNP's of the mitochondria were studied, so they were seeing my maternal line. Actually I was hoping you could explain just what the mitochondria are."

"Well it's not so easy to explain mitochondria. They're the small organelles that lie in the cytoplasm of sucarytic cells. The really interesting thing about the mitochondria is that it is most probably vestigial remains of symbiotic bacteria."

"Too complex for me. I don't think that adds anything to what I needed to know. Wait! Look what I've got to show you."

Monica hopped over the books to find the leather briefcase her parents had given her when she got her first teaching position. Adam's focus was on her graceful body, and at that moment his sexual fantasies returned. Monica pulled out a formal looking piece of paper.

"Voila, look! Here is my certificate stating that I belong to haplogroup E or E1b1b1a1. It looks as if I go back to the Macedonians, early Greeks and Egyptians. What do you think of that? Now, when I look into the mirror I definitely see the Greek and Egyptian influence in my features. I feel like I know myself for the first time. Adam, according to the ancestral data they have on file there's a good chance that I'm related to the maternal line of Alexander the Great. That could explain some of our path of destiny."

With the mention of Alexander the Great, Adam jolted into full attention.

"This may be the connection I've been searching for. Alexander was seeking whatever the artifact represents but couldn't find it because the time was not right. Then Napoleon sought the same thing but again the time was not right. Now, if my DNA is linked to Napoleon and yours to Alexander, it makes perfect sense that we should have found each other. Monica, we have been charged to find the ancient treasure in its entirety because we have the available technology and intention to use it for the benefit of all mankind, so the time is finally right. That's what SELF is about, of course. It was divinely inspired. It's not coincidence. So what did you find out about my DNA? Am I related to Napoleon?"

"It's unbelievable Adam! Yes, the study strongly suggests that you are related to Napoleon. As you know the Y chromosome is passed on from father to son. The company has the profiles of a number of Bonapartes and can make a comparison called a haplodiagram. Your DNA is what is called a sub-profile of Napoleon and they identified it as representing a branch of his descendants. Adam! You are a Bonaparte!"

CHAPTER SIXTY

Just as Adam had predicted, they arrived at an aperture in the dark cave. An exit at last! Crawling through the jagged opening they found themselves on the narrow edge of a precipice high above the ground. For a moment both lay where they were, overcome with relief and happy to inhale the clean fresh air while they allowed their eyes to adjust to the bright sunlight. At the base of the cliff they could see a rural but paved road. Monica moved along the ledge in search of a safe path of descent.

"Adam, where are we? Look I think I see a way down. I don't see them anywhere. We made it! We got away! Let's get to the road. Someone will come along and give us a ride."

Adam was less hopeful, questioning

whether they had really escaped. "I don't know Monica. Look at us. Our clothes are torn, our arms and faces are scratched, and we have blood on us. Nobody is going to pick us up."

"Well we have to try. Let's try to get down to the road."

The descent was rocky. Adam seemed to have the agility and form of an experienced rock climber and knew exactly where to place his feet and how to guide Monica onto stable footings. It was slow going, but they made it down.

Just as they reached the bottom of the cliff Monica cried out.

"Adam look, there's a car parked over there!"

A shiny black Cadillac was stationed at the side of the road some fifty yards away. A man stepped from behind the car and beckoned urgently.

"Monica! My God, it's Leopold Robsen! What in the world is he doing here?"

Leopold Robsen opened the back door of the car and Monica and Adam jumped in. Without a word the car sped off, tires squealing, rear end fish tailing. Adam and Monica had no time to ask questions. Leopold turned sharply onto a dirt road. The canopy of oak trees brought sudden darkness and they could see nothing as they peered through the dense woods on each side. The road was rough with ruts caused by years of rain-hardened mud, and the car bounced in and out of them, jostling Monica and Adam about in their seats. They reached for the small comfort handles above the rear doors and looked at each other in bewilderment and alarm. Adam glanced at the speedometer and saw that they were moving at a dangerously high speed. With the violent pitching and lurching of the car they could think of nothing other than their immediate safety. Moments later Leopold braked so hard that Adam and Monica were thrown against the back of the front seat and dropped to the floor. The Cadillac jolted to a halt behind another large black limousine.

Adam leaped up. "What the hell is going on?"

Monica raised her head above the back seat. "Oh my God, it's Mike! Adam! We're rescued!"

Monica flung open the rear door.

"Careful Monica, I don't know what's happening. I don't think it's good. That may be Mike, but the guy next to him is my brother-in-law. And my God, the other guy is the person I told you looked familiar in the airport. Now I know who he is. It's Malvek. He was at my office with his boy. And he was the one at my lecture who pushed to get the formula. We're in trouble."

Suddenly they were looking down the

muzzle of a Beretta, held by Leopold Robsen. "Out! Both of you."

They climbed from the car. The three other men formed an impenetrable wall behind Robsen.

Mike grabbed Monica's arm and pushed her against the side of the car pinning her there.

Adam spontaneously moved to her defense.

Philip, minus his clerical collar, pulled out a Walther and waved it at Adam. "No heroics, brother-in-law. This is way beyond your puny mind. I always told Elizabeth you were nuts. You're in way over you head. Don't try anything stupid."

Leopold, while continuing to point the Beretta at Adam, barked at Phil. "Shut up Phil. That's enough, say no more."

Malvek moved close to Adam. Mike's grip on Monica's arm tightened to the point that she cried out in pain. He seemed unconcerned.

Malvek's voice was calm, but his words were threateningly measured. "Don't make this hard on yourself. The stone and the formula! Hand them over. We're going to get them one way or the other. The choice is yours. With or without pain. Which will it be?"

"Go to hell! You'll get neither. Let go of her. This is like a bad, really bad, movie. Who are you guys? Phil, what's going on? And Doctor Robsen, what is a scholar like you doing in this mess?"

Phil grabbed Adam by his collar and stared him straight in the eye. "Look, you have no idea what you have. This is way beyond you. Believe me, if you weren't Liz's brother, you and this lady would be dead by now. Hand over the stone and the formula and I promise we'll let you go."

"I don't have them with me."

Phil grunted with annoyance, released his hold on Adam's collar with a violent thrust, and moved back.

Malvek reached into his jacket, pulled his gun and put it to Adam's temple. "I've had enough of this soft touchy stuff. Leo, let me get it my way."

He whirled around and pushed the pistol against Monica's forehead, breaking the skin. "Okay Mr. Hero. How stupid can you be? She means nothing to us. Have you ever seen a bullet go through someone's head? Well you're about to. It's not a pretty sight. Just hand over the damn stone."

Monica blanched with terror and she looked at Mike in silent appeal.

"Give it to them Adam. Tell them whatever they want to know. I know Mike; I can see it in his eyes. They'll kill us if they don't get what they want. Please, it's not worth it. Give it to them."

"I don't have it with me."

Philip put his hand on Adam's shoulder. "In the name of God, man, don't be crazy. These guys mean business. Give it to us and I will make sure both of you get out of this alive. You can trust me. Where is it?"

"You'll never find it. So it won't do you any good to kill me. Monica doesn't know where it is and she has no idea of my formulas. So it looks like a stalemate, doesn't it?"

Philip dropped his arm from Adam's shoulder and stepped back. He looked at Leopold who shook his head and motioned to put them in the car.

Adam scanned the faces of all four men. "You bastards, you're the ones that wrecked my office. You thought you'd get the formula."

"Wrong Doctor, we don't kill secretaries. We didn't need to ransack your office. It's been bugged for three months and now we have Amelia there. We can tell you how many times a day you flush. We even know all about your daughter."

Monica gasped in disbelief.

"Daughter? What's he talking about? You have a daughter?"

"No Monica, it's a long story."

With a look of disgust and a decisive hand motion, Leopold said, "Just put them in the car and go to the tunnel. The chief is already there. I'll let him know we're on the way. I'll get code clearance for both cars to get past the guard gate. Put tape over their mouths, bind their hands and cover their eyes. Not that it matters; they'll never leave the tunnel anyway. But let's follow protocol."

"Mike, how could you do this? I'm your wife. We took vows. We loved each other. Mike, please do something."

Adam looked at Mike, and for one brief moment he thought Monica had touched some compassion in her husband. That hope was short-lived. Mike's face turned hard, his jaw clenched and his skin reddened. "I can't do anything. My job is also a major commitment, one that goes beyond marriage vows. You don't realize that you two found what the Agency has been pursuing for years, long before I joined. You've stumbled upon a piece of something that that could prove to be the most important treasure in human history. Something sought by Alexander the Great, Napoleon, Hitler. I tell you Monica, this is so big that the sacrifice of a few lives would be inconsequential compared to the impact this would have on humanity. Get in the car. Please don't make it any more difficult for all of us, especially me. If you care about me you'll make it easy and not put me in the position of having to hurt you and your psychologist lover."

Monica responded to Mike's words with deep disdain and hatred. Free of his grasp at that moment, she broke for the woods. Her sudden dash diverted the attention of all four men and Adam seized his chance. He charged into the woods on the opposite side of the road and screamed to Monica. "Keep going, I'm okay, these bastards need us alive."

Running at full tilt, Adam sensed that the extra sensory perception he had experienced in the cave when the stone had hung around his neck was no longer with him. Glancing back he saw that only Philip and Malvek where pursuing him. He could see that the aged Leopold had remained by the side of the car but was now on his cell phone. Adam concluded that Mike had gone after Monica. The fear of being caught increased his agility and guided his choice of direction. Adam thought, "This is one time I might have an advantage over that muscle bound hypocrite of a brother-in-law. I bet he can't move so quickly. He may be strong but he's slow. Who the hell is this other guy, Malvek? Damn these thorn bushes!"

Adam crossed a stream, stopped to catch his breath, and looking back saw neither of his pursuers. "I think I shook them. I have to circle back and find Monica."

As if dropped from the sky, Malvek stepped out from behind a tree, to stand directly in front of Adam. Adam turned, only to see Phillip coming up from behind, about ten feet away. Malvek pointed his gun straight at Adam's face. Exhausted and feeling defeated, Adam dropped to his knees. A new feeling of fear swept over him as he realized that they would kill him and take their chances of finding the stone without him. A deathly silence descended as he waited to hear the shot that would explode his brain. He wondered if he would hear the shot before the bullet hit, if there was an awareness of dying, and if he would feel pain. In the interminable seconds he also wondered what his boys would know of the situation and how they would handle it. He became aware that there was no shot. He was still alive, and both men were silent, staring at the ground beneath them. Adam realized the silence had within it an unfamiliar hissing slithering sound. He recalled hearing it in movies. Snakes! Rattlesnakes. He looked up from his kneeling position to see a tangle of snakes surrounding them. Dozens of mottled tan, writhing serpents moved toward them, clustering around Malvek who was standing directly on the rattler's nest. In a flash several struck. Adam saw their heads hit the side of Malvek's pants at calf level. Malvek screamed, and as if choreographed five or more snakes found his thighs and groin. He fell back onto the remainder of the nest. Philip, instinctively unloaded his Walther, shooting randomly and hysterically at the snakes, but Malvek was overcome by the furious serpents and succumbed to their venom. Adam was still. As if divinely directed, the snakes settled and moved about Malvek's lifeless body ignoring Adam and

Philip. With both hands steadying the Walther, Philip aimed between Adam's eyes. Adam could see straight down the barrel of the gun and closed his eyes as he again awaited the fatal shot. Hearing no sound Adam peered through a slit in his eyes. He saw Philip, no longer aiming at him but looking toward the heavens. He had dropped his arm to his side and was praying.

"God, you confront me with the serpent. Shall I like Eve eat of the forbidden fruit and kill your child for my own worldly gain? Lord you have said that we will not be tempted beyond our ability but with the temptation you will also provide the way of escape, that we may be able to endure it. You have told us, blessed is the man who remains steadfast under trial, for when he has stood the test he will resume the crown of life. I pray Oh Lord, that I resist this temptation."

With this Philip dropped his gun to the ground and walked toward Adam. "Open your eyes and fear not brother-in-law. Put on the armor of God, stand against the schemes of the devil, go and find your destiny." Philip pointed in the direction of the mountain. Adam rose quickly and ran.

When the road came in sight he saw that both cars were gone. His heart rose in his throat and he collapsed beside a tree, certain that Mike had found Monica and taken her away.

"Wait, why would both cars be gone? One

would have stayed to take me in. This could be a trap. Those guys know all the tricks. Who are they anyway? What agency were they talking about? I have to find Monica and then get the artifact."

Cautiously Adam crossed the road, wary of a trap, but there didn't seem to be anyone lurking in the woods. He tried to follow the direction he had seen Monica take when she broke loose, hoping Mike hadn't taken her hostage. Assuming the posture and attitude of a lizard, he made his way through the woods, steadily picking through the brush and vines, searching for some sign of Monica. He observed to himself that he was oblivious to the pain inflicted by the scraping branches and sharp stones. Nothing else mattered except finding her. He stopped for a moment.

"If I were Monica what would I do? Ah ha! The cave! No one could know that was a cave exit unless he knew it was there. I only knew it because of the artifact. I'm sure of that now."

Adam made his way back toward the cave opening and finally found the familiar embankment. He wondered if Monica could have made it up there without his help. He scrambled up the last few feet. There she was, sitting at the edge of the cave.

"Monica, thank God! I found you. Are you all right?"

There was no answer. Finally looking off

into the distance, she spoke in a lifeless voice. "He found me."

Adam spun around and scanned the hillside. "Is he still here?"

Monica leapt up and threw her arms around Adam. "Mike grabbed me just as I reached the cave opening. He threw me to the ground and pinned me down with his foot on my stomach. He pointed that horrible gun at me and demanded the artifact. I really didn't know what you had done with it. So I couldn't tell him anything and I guess he believed me. He just stared at me. Finally, thank heavens, he looked away and put his gun away. He said, "I can't do it. Get as far away as you can, Monica. And get rid of him. He has no idea of what he has and the agency will get it."

Relieved that Monica was unharmed and that Mike for the moment at least, had given up on the chase, Adam took Monica by the hand and guided her to a rock just to the left of the entrance to the cave. He put his shoulder to the rock, and pushing with the full force of his body inched it away from the mountain wall. He knelt and scooped up the leather pouch.

"I put it here when you were climbing down, just before I took your hand to help you balance. I figured that way you wouldn't know where it was either, so you wouldn't be lying if they asked you."

CHAPTER SIXTY-ONE

Sitting on the edge of the cliff, looking out onto the vast area of woodland, they could see the lake where the SELF-house stood off in the distance. Adam looked at Monica and then himself, appraising their appearance.

"My God, Monica, it's just now hitting me. Do you realize what we've been through? Look at us. We look like we've been put through a shredder. We're covered in blood. How did we ever get away from those guys? Think of it. My brother-in-law, your husband, a former patient, and Dr. Robsen, all involved in this intrigue."

"Adam, what is the artifact all about? What have we discovered or what has fate and destiny put in our hands?"

"I don't know, Monica, but it surely is something of the greatest importance. Did you hear him say that Alexander the Great, Napoleon, and Hitler were looking for this thing? And we could have a piece of it. I don't know what it is. But I do know that I had those powers only when I had the artifact. I believe I was accessing the collective unconscious of someone who had explored the cave before me. I was definitely being guided. I had vision in the pitch black. I had abilities beyond my human capacity. And look, when we're together with the ring and the artifact! The ring is glowing!"

Overwhelmed by the extraordinary ordeal, they stared into the forest.

"I don't know what the artifact is, Monica, but I know we have our life's mission. I know, don't' ask me how, but I know that we are destined to be off to Rene De Chateau, the ruins of Solomon's temple, and the desserts of Egypt, in the footsteps of Napoleon."

"Adam! People are dead! We were nearly killed ourselves, poor Doctor Taber's life has been destroyed, your family is shattered, and your utopian SELF group turned out to be a bloody hell, literally, and you can't see that Waterloo lies ahead. Adam, may I see the artifact?"

Adam removed the leather pouch from around his neck and handed it to her. "Monica, you still don't get it. There's always a cost to victory. Great generals see beyond the immediate effect of a few losses."

Monica removed the artifact, held it in her hand, and closed her eyes tightly. Then she raised her arm and swung. The artifact sailed in a smooth arc beyond the edge of the cliff toward the white water rapids below.

"That, Napoleon's heir, is your destiny."

Adam's eyes followed the artifact through its trajectory. All feeling drained from his face, and his voice was vengeful. You fool! You cowardly, stupid whore! You've never been able to understand, have you?"

Adam stood up, head held high, and shoulders squared. Without a backward glance or acknowledgement of Monica he spun on his heel and left. While still within earshot he barked, "There'll be no Waterloo for me."

At the foot of the hill, Adam spotted the figure of a man standing with his back against a tree and his hands covering his face. Adam dropped to his knees behind a large moss covered boulder. Was one of his pursuers still-hunting him? The man lowered his hands and Adam recognized Philip. A realization dawned on Adam. Philip had had the chance to kill or capture him earlier but hadn't. Building on this Adam quickly devised a plan to ally himself with his brother-in-law. He slowly rose up from his crouch to a full bold stance.

"Philip, it's me, Adam."

Philip riveted his CIA trained eyes on Adam but stood silent. Adam sensed his brother-in-law's indecision and for a moment his mind filled with apprehension and doubt. Finally Philip motioned for Adam to approach. Adam moved swiftly and confidently. Stopping directly in front of Philip he stepped upon a large rock so as to be above him.

"Brother-in-law, it's clear to me that we are destined to join forces. Just the two of us. You will be my bravest of the brave and together we will find the tablet. Victory will be ours. I see it plainly. Once against me, but now united by destiny, toward the same goal."

"You're right Adam, I too see it clearly. God has willed this. We shall join forces. The CIA was part of God's grand plan to get us on the same track, but I no longer need to play the agency game. The power will be ours to use for God's good."

Adam said nothing more and pointed down the narrow rural road. "If we follow this road it will take us to the SELF house where my followers are probably wondering what happened to me."

CHAPTER SIXTY-TWO

Monica had remained staring into the rushing water below. Terror infused her body as she heard the cracking of twigs, signaling the approach of someone. At first she thought it might be Adam returning, and this frightened her as much as the thought that it was one of the pursuers. Slowly she turned her head toward the sound. Mike was standing next to her. Her fear evaporated at the sight of him and her uneasiness was replaced by a sense of safety.

"Don't be afraid Monica, I've come back for you. When I looked into your eyes and said that I couldn't harm you and walked away, I suddenly grew from a boy into a man. I don't want to be James Bond, chasing spies, anymore. I know what

I want. I want you, Monica! I've been sealed off all my life but I know that with your help I can learn how to open my heart. Can we try? Can we start all over? I'm not sure what I'll do but it will no longer be with the agency. Maybe I'll teach history. I don't remember when I last said this, perhaps never with the feeling I now have. I love you. I don't ever want to be without you again. It's been lonely for me, but I didn't realize it until just a few minutes ago. I know it's been lonely for you too, so we must each forgive the other's indiscretions."

Monica felt the same rush as when they had taken their wedding vows. She realized that she had loved Mike all along, and that she too had played a part in the distance that had grown between them. She took her husband's hand and they climbed down toward the water's edge. Still holding hands, they slowly walked along the riverbank, talking about their marriage and future together.

Mike had been more emotionally open and sharing in the few minutes of this walk than he had been throughout the years of their relationship. He decided it was safe to raise the topic of Adam. "Monica, I need to tell you this because it worries me. The CIA conducted an in-depth inquiry into Adam Peterson's life. He is not the guy you think he is."

Monica interrupted, "I know that now. Do we have to talk about him? Let's focus on us."

Mike squeezed her hand affectionately. "Yes! We have to talk about him because he's been involved in much more sinister and evil doings than you suspect. But you need to understand that he has a history of violence, when he doesn't get his way, and he's ruthless. I worry that when he discovers that we're back together and he is out, he will retaliate, and you will be in danger. He's likely to convince himself that you have told me all the secrets of the artifact and his regression formula."

Monica understood what Mike was saying and intuitively picked up the danger. "Mike, I don't want to know the details, but are you sure he really did bad things?"

"Yes Monica, the agency has a dossier on him as long as your arm. It goes back to his teen years. I'm no shrink, and never wanted to be one, but I believe Doctor Peterson went into psychology and trained to be a so-called empathic psychotherapist, as a way of controlling his hedonistic anti-social tendencies. When he was sixteen he nearly killed a boy who accidentally hit him with a pitch in a baseball game, by going after him with a baseball bat. In college two girls accused him of date rape, but the families decided not to pursue it legally. There's more, lots more, but no need to go into it. You're right, let's get back to us. I'm with you now and I'll protect you."

CHAPTER SIXTY-THREE

The SELF group continued to gain followers. Adam had been spending a great deal of time in hypnotic work with the members and giving lectures. Thirty people from other states who had heard of his teachings had attended his last talk. All of them wanted to join the group. Philip was a welcome addition to the corps of troops under their leader. His theological credentials enhanced the group's ability to proselytize.

Adam had not seen Monica since that fateful day two months ago when she had thrown the artifact into the river, but he thought of her often. Unable to accept that she could just walk away from him, Adam convinced himself that she was hesitant to call because she feared his anger and disapproval over her actions on the mountain. He went to the private office in the SELF-house and phoned her.

"Hi honey, it's me. I've really missed you and couldn't wait any longer to talk to you. I know you weren't yourself right after escaping near death. Obviously that ordeal had you in such a state of anxiety that you couldn't think clearly."

Monica's, "Hello Adam," was dispassionate and unreadable.

Adam ignored the cold detached greeting. "How are you? I'd love to see you. A quiet table at Chez Benton, a strawberry daiquiri for you and a glass of scotch on the rocks for me as a start to a five-course dinner, sounds great to me. How about you?"

"Adam, I haven't recovered from that ordeal yet. I'd like to wait a bit longer before making any decisions."

"Monica, listen to me. You're making a mistake. It's important to get right back on the horse. I insist that we arrange a date. You know me well enough to know that I'm not going to take 'No' for an answer. We're destined to be together. I'm the best thing that could ever have happened to you. And you have no choice, it's written in our DNA. If it would be easier we could spend the evening at your house, send out for food, and get back to where we were. It will be even easier now;

it's definitely over with Ellen. She's filed divorce papers, claiming infidelity and irrational behavior.

She consulted a professional who declared that there is no chance of reconciliation. Frankly, I'm relieved at that advice. The boy's know about it and seem to have accepted it quite well. In fact, Kevin as much as said that he thought it was a good idea for both of us."

Monica remained silent for some time before responding. "Adam, as usual, you seem to think you call all the shots. You're not paying attention to me. I'm not ready to make a decision to pick up where we left off. We need to end this conversation. Bye."

With that Monica quickly hung up.

Adam slammed his fist into the wall hard enough to dent the sheet rock but refused to acknowledge even the slightest experience of pain. He stormed to the large bay window overlooking the lake. The weather was foul with a steady needle like rain pelting against the window and rumbles of thunder rattling the panes. With his hand posed on his stomach area, he shouted, "They're all the same. Ellen, Monica, Janette, my mother, Ellen's mother, Latizia, Josephine, none of them can hurt me! I will dominate and be victorious. It's my destiny, and no one can stop it. The point in the evolution of mankind on this planet has reached the time for all to be revealed and I am the chosen one."

CHAPTER SIXTY-FOUR

Alice Hawkins, who was working at the SELF house developing a brochure for the organization, knocked on his door.

"Come in!"

Alice stood in the doorway. Adam turned, posturing himself as if facing an enemy. She perceived his anger immediately.

"What's wrong? You look upset."

"Nothing is wrong, nothing. What do you want?"

"I was reluctant to interrupt you but there's a detective Mancini downstairs, asking for you."

Adam stomped away from the window, slamming his desk chair against the wall, knocking his pyramid shaped paperweight to the floor, and practically shoving Alice out of the way as he approached the door. Alice, taken aback, remained in the office.

"Goodness! It's almost like Adam becomes a different person sometime. It's like that time he ran after that little girl after our SELF meeting."

Without uttering a word Adam walked downstairs to stand within a foot of Mancini. Mancini instinctively created physical distance between them and addressed Adam.

"Hello Doctor Peterson, it wasn't easy to track you down. This is quite an isolated spot. The boys at the station had to do some heavy research to find this address." He turned toward the open door and pointed to two uniformed officers. "We need you to come to the station. Officer Chuffo, escort the doctor to the patrol car."

Adam turned to the bewildered SELF members who had gathered, expecting an explanation for the appearance of the police.

Adam controlled his anger and assumed a nonchalant attitude. "Don't worry, this is obviously a case of mistaken identity. It's happened before. I'll go with the officers and straighten it out. It's probably a mix-up in their files again. Be back in a few hours. Why don't you order some food from China Feast, put it on the SELF tab, and we can have dinner together when I return."

Escorted by the two officers Adam hurried

through the pelting rain and was hustled into the back of the police cruiser.

Parking at the rear of the station, the officers chose the furthest parking space from the door to the building. Adam was hurried from the car but was soaked by the time he reached the entrance. Unable to contain himself, he verbally attacked the two officers. "You guys are all the same. Animals! You don't give a shit about people, do you? This is a twenty-five hundred dollar suit, and it's soaked. You could have let me out at the front door."

Neither officer acknowledged his comments as they proceeded to hold him by the arm and roughly escort him to the interrogation room to wait for Detective Mancini. Adam was sure they were observing him through a two-way mirror, and to convey that he was unperturbed, he played several games on his cell phone. Finally, Mancini, accompanied by two plain-clothes policemen, entered, and without saying a word, paced around Adam, smirking and nodding his head. Adam made sure to read the nametags on the two other men. He decided to play a one-up-manship game.

"Detectives Olsen and Sternberg, before you get started, just know that I am a master of persuasion, an expert at interviewing, and the best at controlling situations. Your primitive infantile techniques won't work on me. Try to be mature adults and let's get on with it. What do you want to know?"

Mancini began. "Doctor Peterson, we have enough evidence to book you on two counts of murder. I wanted these two detectives to talk with you before I officially arrest you. I do the investigation and arresting. They make deals. I think you should be interested in what they have to offer."

Detective Olsen bent over the table and positioned his face within six inches of Adam's before speaking. Then he backed off and stood against the wall, hands in his pockets, left leg propped on the chair, and with piercing direct eye contact with Adam, began to speak in a persuasive tone.

"Okay Doctor, I'm here because I have the authority to make an offer to you. We've got you on two murders. The deal is, you confess to one, and although I can't promise, we won't charge you with the other. A good attorney will come up with some defense and maybe get you off with ten years instead of life. We make sure you get into a low security prison, where you won't have to bend over every day. You be a good boy, get on the right side of the warden, and maybe you're out in six or seven."

Adam stood up, assumed a commanding stance with his right hand over his abdomen, and shook his left fist defiantly. He paced back and forth in a straight line and railed.

"You guys have nothing. You can't prove anything. Get lost. Either arrest me or move out of my way and drive me back to where you picked me up. You have nothing! Did you really think you were going to get a confession from me? Mancini, you're dumber than I thought. Good-bye gentlemen and a special Adios to you Mancini. Oh by the way, Mancini, if this suit doesn't dry clean well, you can be sure you're paying for a new one."

Adam strode out and did not wait for a patrol car to drive him. Ignoring the downpour he walked to the corner and hailed a taxi.

CHAPTER SIXTY-FIVE

Several days after the police station episode, Philip and Adam, who had been blending remarkably well, met for further discussions. They had been meeting on a regular basis at Philip's church office to plan their strategy for pursuing the Emerald tablet. Their relationship had gone through a one hundred and eighty degree change. Liz had no knowledge of what had transpired between them, but she joyously accepted their new harmonious relationship as a sign that her prayers had been answered.

Adam had laid out a plan of action but Philip felt that there were many practical details omitted. He thought it was time to confront Adam with his questions.

"Adam, our plans are coming together but

I'm concerned about the dinero we will need. You know I'm used to simply submitting an expense account to the agency and having everything paid for. We'll have to travel to Egypt as well as hire special guides, who cost more than you can imagine."

Adam smiled confidently and held up his hand, palm facing Philip, signaling that he need not be concerned. "Money is not an issue, Philip. I have plenty and can easily finance everything we have to do. And there's plenty more money to come. Have no fear, the money is there."

"Adam, you haven't worked for months. Where does all this money come from?"

"Hypnosis is a great tool, brother-in-law. With my skills, posthypnotic suggestion can be used in many ways. I'm good! I have at least forty to fifty thousand deposited in my account every month, and the depositors don't even know they're doing it. Need I say more?"

Philip was speechless but seemed to get the picture. "Are you talking about brain washing? Don't answer that! Let's get back to planning. By the way, I officially resigned from the agency, giving them the reason that I wanted to devote all my energies to God's work and finishing my dissertation for the Ph.D. They'll track me for several months, but Doc assured me that he understood that my religious beliefs had heightened and that the agency was no longer tolerable to me."

Adam's suspicious nature was aroused. "Do you really buy that, Philip? Do you actually think guys like will let you off the hook that easily?"

"I understand what you're thinking, Adam, but we'll just have to wait it out and see what happens. I've always thought that Doc Robsen really liked me and that I could trust him."

Adam seemed restless. Sitting on the edge of his chair, clearly distracted by internal promptings, his eyes wandered over the room, indicating to Philip that he wanted to leave.

Philip questioned him. "Adam you seem antsy, do you have to get somewhere?"

"Yes Philip, I have some pressing business I have to take care of. I have an appointment with my lawyer. You know, Ellen is not going to make this process easy. She wants everything and is trying to get sole custody of the boys. In short, she's going for blood and of course, Daddy has provided one of the top divorce lawyers in Virginia. But my guy is good also, so I'm not really worried. I'll beat her and Daddy at their own game. And if a legal route is not successful there are many other ways I can stop her. You realize one has to be alive to get custody."

Philip moved to the edge of his chair. "Good Lord man, what are you saying? I can't believe you said that."

"Just a figure of speech, Philip. Just a figure of speech. Please say good-by to Liz and I'll call you tomorrow."

CHAPTER SIXTY-SIX

On his drive to the attorney, Adam stopped his Jaguar at a traffic light. As he looked lasciviously at the young girl in the convertible next to him, his glance traveled beyond to the doorway of the restaurant across the street. He couldn't believe his eyes. Ellen and Monica were standing together, clearly talking in a pleasant and intimate manner. The traffic light was red for a long time and Adam observed the two of them intently but the light eventually changed and he had to be on his way. Consumed with curiosity, he circled the block at a speed that assured he would arrive when the traffic light was red. They were still there talking, occasionally touching each other on the arm or hand, as if confirming agreement and understanding.

The light turned green and he circled the block once more. This time he arrived to see them shake hands and wave good-bye amicably as they went their separate ways.

In the solitude and protective silence of his car, Adam wondered aloud. "What the hell could that be about? Ellen must hate Monica and I know from the attorney that she blames Monica for our marital troubles. I'll bet anything Ellen was persuaded by Daddy to bribe Monica to admit in court that we had an affair. I'll bet that's what it is. I wouldn't put it past Monica to succumb to Ellen's type of persuasion. She needs the money and she knows that it's over with Mike. Damn, that's all I need, is for her to testify. She's liable to blow the whole thing. She might bring up the SELF group, the artifact, and my formula. Oh damn! What if Ellen has asked about my past life recovery formula and wants some dollar amount for the future income it will bring me?"

Deeply shaken, Adam went home, poured a five finger tall drink of his single malt scotch, reclined in his favorite chair, and turned his stereo to a decibel level so high that the floor vibrated. Closing his eyes, he planned several possible sinister scenarios to stop Ellen. The deafening loudness of his stereo playing *Marengo: L'Europa Scopre Napoleon*, a piece of music especially produced in 1805 for the International Napoleonic

Conference, prevented Adam from hearing the phone ring, but he noticed the flashing red light that indicated an incoming call. He had been sitting for hours, emptying several glasses of scotch, and was in a stupor. Using the remote to lower the volume with slurred speech he answered the call.

"Hello Adam, it's me, Monica"

"Hi Monica, I've been expecting you to call."

"Well, I've been doing a lot of thinking and I feel it's time for us to talk. How about tomorrow night, at my house, about seven o'clock."

"Super Monica! Why don't we go out to eat? We should celebrate our reunion."

There was a long pause. He could hear Monica breathing heavily as if the conversation was distressing to her. He broke the silence. "What do you say Monica, how about Chez Benton at seven, instead of your house?"

The answer was quick. "No Adam, I think we need to be at the house."

"Okay, I'll be there. I just figured it out. Food is not the uppermost thought in your mind for when we meet."

Adam was excited but could not erase the meeting of Ellen and Monica from his mind. His intoxication led to increased suspicion and he ran through several scenarios to prepare himself. As he fell asleep in his chair he thought that Ellen had met with Monica to tell her that she was through with him and that Monica was welcome to him. The alcohol worked and he slept without stirring.

The next day Adam was scheduled to talk at a lunch meeting at the SELF house and barely arrived on time. Despite his hangover he rose to the occasion and continued to inspire his members to recruit more members, emphasizing the need for unconditional commitment and sizable financial support. Following the meeting he made a few urgent patient phone calls and worked a bit on his transcranial magnetic coil.

Adam spent the following day at home, drinking moderately, while preparing a lecture for his class at Georgetown. That evening he left for Monica's with a sense of joy and triumph, exhilarated by the anticipation of the resumption of their affair. Using the amazing acceleration of his Jaguar he violated all speeding laws and hastened his arrival at her home. A confident and self-assured driver pulled into Monica's driveway. He bounced up the driveway, chose to knock rather than ring the doorbell, and as Monica opened the door, handed her a large bouquet of red roses.

Monica took the bouquet with a bland facial expression and did not verbally acknowledge the gift. Adam bent toward her for a kiss, but Monica turned away so that he only brushed her cheek.

"Do sit down Adam. I'll just put these in a

vase." Monica went to the kitchen and placed the bouquet on the table without unwrapping it.

Adam relaxed in his chair and Monica returned to sit directly across from him. He immediately took control of the conversation.

"God, it seems like an eternity since I've seen you. You're looking your usual exciting self. I really missed our time together. I'm not altogether sure what happened between us. But that's all water under the bridge now. Why don't you sit next to me on the couch?"

Adam began to move toward the large couch that previously had offered them moments of intimacy. Monica leaned forward in her chair and raised her hands with a halting signal. "Adam, I'm sure you know that I pride myself on honesty and being straight about with my feelings. I'm not ready to resume our relationship. There are too many things standing in the way."

Adam sat back in his chair, incredulous. He mimicked Monica's position in her chair, a learned technique to convey understanding. "What can stand in the way? We're great in bed together, we understand each other's needs, and we're genetically destined to be together. What's in the way?"

"I've had a lot of time to think and reason things out." Monica's voice was shaky and fearful, but she continued. "To get right to the point, I believe you murdered Cathy and that girl Janette. Do you know how hard it is for me to think that? I need to know if it's true. Don't lie, it's not a time for manipulation, I need to know."

Adam responded without hesitation. "What's wrong with you? You still don't get it do you? The significance of our place in the future of this earth and humanity. I am to be the supreme leader and you will share in this by being at my side. Did you really expect us to get there without bloodshed? Cathy and that girl were unimportant figures that could not be permitted to interfere with our discovering the secrets to lead the world to peace. That little bitch of a daughter. She could have ruined everything and cost me my future. How could her mother have been so certain that I was the father? There were three other guys screwing her at the same time. What did she and that betraying blackmailing bitch, Cathy, matter? And what did they matter to you? They were traitors. It was easy. Two people who stood in the way of my great cause. Damn it Monica, don't think small. I was placed on earth with a great destiny. Let's just continue with our lives together. The police will never be able to pin anything on me."

Adam jumped up with a start as the swinging door to the kitchen opened and Mancini stepped into the living room. Adam swirled around to the sound of two uniformed officers springing from behind the bedroom door. Instantly two more plain-clothes detectives emerged from the kitchen and positioned themselves behind Mancini.

Mancini, smiled, nodded affirmatively to Monica, turned to the officers and said, "Gotcha Doc, cuff him boys."

Adam showed no emotion or resistance. The officers, with significant roughness, put his hands behind his back, placed the handcuffs on, and began to move him toward the door.

"Mancini watched the process. It's all on tape Doctor, plus we have six witnesses. It's a shame, someone as intelligent as you with such a promising future to help patients. I've got you dead to rights now Doc. How much better can you get than a confession? See you at the station. Be sure to read him his rights, boys, no slip-ups. Detective Parsons please go with them to be sure the rights are read correctly and that the doctor confirms understanding."

Monica was standing off to the side, her head buried in her hands. She was sobbing. Mike emerged from the bedroom and stood next to her placing his arm around her shoulder. She looked at him with tearful eyes. "You know, Mike, I suspected it all along, but I guess until the last minute I was hoping to hear something else."

Mike gave her a supportive hug. Mancini stepped in front of them and took her hands in his.

With a gentle voice, he said, "Monica, you did the right thing. I don't think we would have been able to nail him without your help. I'm deeply appreciative of your cooperation. When you and Mrs. Peterson met with me yesterday afternoon to propose this, I wasn't sure it would work. But it did. Thank you again. I know how hard it was for you. Be assured, you did the right thing. You've brought a killer to justice."

With that he turned toward Mike. "You've got a brave young lady here, take care of her. I know your position in the CIA. Let me leave you with a word of advice. My dedication to the force ruined the best thing I ever had, my marriage to Natalie. Take care guys, I'd better get to the station."

As Mancini was exiting Monica called to him. "Detective Mancini may I have one word with Adam before you leave?"

Mancini hesitated, concerned for her safety and protocol, but acquiesced on condition that Adam remained in the car. She readily agreed and they walked to the squad car.

Monica knocked on the window and the officer sitting beside Adam rolled the window down. Monica asked Mancini if he would put something in Adam's pocket since his hands were cuffed behind his back. She handed Mancini a small velvet box. Mancini opened it to reveal the opal ring in the satin interior. Monica bent toward the car to talk to Adam. "This ring is yours. The reason for me to have it no longer exists."

"Monica, I'll be back. You have not heard the last of me. No one can defy destiny and you will see that you are part of my destiny. You may think you set a trap for me today, but they have nothing, and this will not hold up in court. There is no Waterloo for this Napoleon."

THE END

ABOUT THE AUTHORS

DR. RONALD J. RAYMOND, JR. is a Diplomate in Clinical Psychology of the American Board of Professional Psychology, a Diplomate in the EEG Neurofeedback and a Fellow of the Biofeedback Certification Institute of America. As a Certified Clinical Hypnotherapist, and a Master Level Reiki practitioner, he has perfected the use of regressive hypnosis and healing energies. Dr. Raymond has had extensive experience as a psychotherapist, a clinical hypnotherapist, a lecturer, a business and educational consultant, as the director of psychology in a psychiatric hospital and as the director of a large city mental health clinic. He is the author of the book – *Grow your roots, Anywhere, Anytime* and of numerous professional articles. Dr. Raymond's many years of experience in varied settings has contributed to his authorship of *Ring of Destiny*.

NANCY MAXWELL, BS, MSc, is a nationally certified, licensed professional counselor. She has had a lifelong fascination with 17th and 18th century French history which has been nurtured by her international background and the many years that she lived in Europe. A lecturer and teacher on the subject, she is particularly interested in the psychological profiles of historical figures